Last Year's River

Last Year's River

Allen Morris Jones

Houghton Mifflin Company
BOSTON · NEW YORK
2001

Visit our Web site: www.houghtonmifflinbooks.com.

Library of Congress Cataloging-in-Publication Data

Jones, Allen Morris.
Last year's river / Allen Morris Jones.
p. cm.
ISBN 0-618-13161-2
I. Title.
PS3610.O58 L37 2001
813'.54—dc21 2001024990

Printed in the United States of America

Book design by Melissa Lotfy
The text type is Bembo

QUM 10 9 8 7 6 5 4 3 2 1

For my mother,

and her seven sisters

Like an eye and an eyelid
United by a tear.

—*Anna Swir*

No stone so deep in Earth
as I in you
nor cloud so moved by wind
as I, by your warm hand.

— *William Pitt Root*

Last Year's River

"It's not an easy thing to tell a true story," she said.

She was a tiny, dried woman, still limping over last year's bad hip. A woman who managed to maintain a kind of self-contained elegance, even under her cornhusk skin, the swollen marbles of her joints. It was in her unvarying posture, the meticulousness with which she placed a fork over her plate. A toughness to recall certain wildflowers: how you can twist at them and the fibers in their stalks will hold them together.

She displayed her wealth in tasteful, understated flourishes: Molesworth cabinetry, an exquisite little Maynard Dixon landscape above her writing desk, a tiger skin draped over the back of her couch, its back split by a brief, hardened cut. "That first shot went high," she said.

She had taken to giving away some of her treasures — photographs, charm bracelets, well-historied watches — as if possession were a burden from which she was asking to be delivered. We walked through her emptying apartment, room to room, the woman hobbling over a man's overlarge cane.

"I'm fine from here up," she said, easing down into her chair, holding a level hand to her throat, "but this body has been giving me no end of trouble."

I asked my first question and she looked at me with eyes light and quick as bees. "I was not so naïve," she said, "as to think that stepping onto that train had not been experienced a dozen times, a hundred times before: the young lady goes west. I was not so unexposed, not so unread as to suppose that those mountains had not always existed as a potential. But how many people go west not to find hope but to put an end to it? My mother's reaction when I caught pregnant? Ship her off. The first significant betrayal of my life was not my father's death but my mother's insouciance."

She stared past the iron railing of her concrete landing, past the green, manicured skirt of lawn and into the kiln-fired reds of the desert.

"Virginia?"

"Wyoming," she said, starting. She leaned forward to touch my knee. "Let me tell you about Wyoming."

1924

1

THE WOMAN, the girl. Restless in a Pullman sleeping car. A night late in her seventeenth year, a night in the middle of the high plains. Glass rattles in its frame to a constant, quick rhythm, dust cobwebbed in its corners. The passing of the dark, leaf-dry prairie has come to match, in some oddly appropriate way, the hitching clack of the train. The tilled fields. The cottonwoods isolated in the lowest, moist pleats of the plain. Then it comes to her: the landscape has been running past her window like film through a projector.

Her aunt asleep in the next bunk, she slips out of her nightgown and into yesterday's chemise, naked under the silk and cotton. She makes her way through the sleeping car to the observation lounge, eleven cubicles empty around her, a black porter dozing in the closed vestibule between cars, chin on chest. He makes no motion, no noise. Beyond the drum of the wheels on their tracks, beyond the hollow clank of steel, it is so quiet. She steps onto the observation platform and stands with the cold railing under her hands, an inch of fabric trim flapping over her head, yellow sparks spraying away from the wheels, arcing to either side.

North Dakota. In all the world, there is no light. A war and a flu epidemic and a hard winter in 1919. A time and a place with empty chairs still set around a thousand supper tables, pieces of each family as absent as teeth from a smile.

She leans to the side, beyond the shelter of the car, and closes her eyes against the wind. The sleeping cars were so stifling. To the east, the first light of morning bruises the horizon. She reaches back into the car and pulls out a camp chair, sitting down on the platform to prop her bare feet on the rail. The infinite scroll of tracks catches the morning's new light and cuts the world with it, paring at the plains until they fall away in halves. Pages split by a binding.

The train pulses beneath her. She drops her feet off the rail and bends over her knees. Something in her would like to cry. Needs to cry. But she won't allow herself. She's already decided. Perhaps the first entirely adult decision of her life. And after a moment she sits up straight, cradling her stomach with her palms, her eyes dry and red.

No fingertip touches her cheek, no hand strokes her hair. In her breasts, in her chest, loneliness spreads like an infection. The ash-dead, baling-wire snarl of her heart. Except for the eyeless child in her womb — a pea's worth of dividing cells — she is so alone. A thumbnail with no name, no country, no language. That's all she has.

Boy or girl? she asks herself for the first time.

2

THE BOY, the man. Alone above the North Fork of the Shoshone. Digging inside a grave, head and shoulders rolling against the setting sun.

West of Cody, this hardscrabble, mosquito-bit valley. Fifty miles of clay riverbank gnawed by the teeth of the world, torn by erupting knobs of quick-cooled volcanoes. Foothills like bunched muscle, blistered to red, andesite bones. Fecundity is sparse and treasured, limited to a few acres of good hay ground in the bottoms and a hundred thousand miles of coarse wilderness back behind.

Here is a valley that displays its history, its brief succession of tiny tragedies and triumphs, as conspicuously as crumbs on a table. Human advance and retreat to be seen in each abandoned soddy, every honeysuckle windbreak blooming around a bare foundation. If this isn't home, it's as close as he's likely to get. He has always been drawn to the idea that he might be important to this country. Against the ancient cathedrals he saw in Europe, the brick-lined banks of the Seine, there is a lack of record here. His own small surface scratchings have a chance of becoming remarkable, if only for the dearth of other participants. There have been no kings here. No generals.

But three weeks back and they've already got him digging a grave, for Chrissake.

Maybe he's never left. If it weren't for the lines of tourist autos on the road — as many as a dozen to the hour, filling the recesses of the valley with dust and exhaust — he could be eighteen again, scornful still.

He digs, falling into the old rhythms. The rotation of spud, mattock, spade; a mound of fresh clay and gravel over his left shoulder. In France, the earth tossed out of a rifle pit had been nearly as important as the pit itself, and one quickly grew into the habit of *placing* each shovelful, patting it down with the back of the spade. At night, the tick of rats on the duckboards, running bay to bay, had sounded like tapping fingernails. The bodies over the crest of the parapets, the ones within sniper range of the Boche, had had to be left out in the sun until you started resenting them their stench.

He resists the idea that he could be eighteen again. His father doesn't know it yet, but things are set to change. It won't be like it was. If he took anything at all away from the war, it is this determination. It won't be like it was. *No kings here,* he thinks with satisfaction. *No generals.* He smoothes the walls of the grave with the spade reversed in his hands, chiseling at the corners, scooping out the loose scree. Six years after armistice, the magazines are still carrying ads for the most comfortable prosthetics.

He climbs out of the new hole in the earth and squats on his heels, thin enough himself, narrow enough, to rest without prominence among the crooked gravestones. *There you go,* he thinks, looking into the grave.

A sear wind blows at his back, drying his sweat. The same wind that's been blowing for weeks. An endless unspooling of air, straight out of the sun. The parched odor of woodsmoke, a yellow evening haze from the fires in the Washakie. He rolls a cigarette and lights it, unwinding his loose-hinged legs to sit half in the grave.

The boy, the man. At twenty-four, a man without qualification, although there is something in him, some hard and buried kernel, that won't allow him access to his own manhood. A mother who's half Indian and more than half crazy for religion. A father with a cast-iron eye forever set on the next scheme. Between them, the kind of quiet that comes from adjusted expectations. He thought he'd left for good in 1918, but he'd been wrong. Seems like the grooves this place had worn into him had been deeper than he thought.

There's a change coming. He can feel it. A throb in him like a second pulse. The Shoshone dam. All those tourist cars on the road. The slow consolidation of homesteads. This valley's getting ready to hold people, like it or not. He's just not sure if it's meant to hold him. He's just not sure where he should be.

It sure got ahold of old Buskin, he thinks, flicking his cigarette into the grave.

Buskin hadn't been so old as he'd looked. Fat like his mother, with his gray scrub-pad hair cut close. An index finger missing at the first knuckle. Not being much good for anything else, he'd been the one to deliver Mohr's hooch. Taking a day or two to wend his way through the mountains, approaching neighbors' farms from the most unexpected directions. Turns out he hadn't been very good at that either. His horse trailed back to the ranch three days ago, saddlebags empty, blood smeared across the pommel. If Henry's father has obvious regrets, it's only that he'll be having to deliver his booze himself. A riskier proposition than just making it.

Henry stands and gathers his tools and walks the path down from the cemetery, his shadow stretching thin-legged beside him. A dark and following absence. Up the valley, the sun edges below the horizon, rolling evening over the ground like quick oil. He'd smelled cinnamon this morning. His mother and that Chinese cook must be baking today. The thought of a good apple pie reminds him how hungry he is.

Below him, his father's Pierce-Arrow churns a tail of dust out of the valley's gravel road. Must be that girl from back east. Damn if he hadn't already forgotten.

3

SEVENTEEN YEARS OLD, with the narrow hips, the developing chest of an adolescent. The conspicuous absence of flesh between skin and ribs. A neck thin for her body.

She lies facing away from her aunt, both of them still dressed from the trip. Staring at the hand-hewn, dovetailed logs, at the loosening lengths of concrete chinking and exposed fretwork of nails and, behind the nails, twisted rolls of newspaper insulation. The single crooked window curtained in crinoline, pieced from some old petticoat. She stares at the ceiling, at the roughly milled boards with their warped edges and the roofing tin showing through the cracks, and tries to tell herself that this is an adventure. That this is a story she's within.

The old woman stirs beside her, dry flesh rustling against the blankets, and reaches up to brush her hand over the back of Virginia's head, flattening the bobbed hair against the girl's neck. Her marcelled curls still hold the shape of her Gimbel Brothers cloche.

I miss braiding your hair, the aunt says.

The girl shrugs, feeling her aunt's hands drop to her shoulders.

Short hair makes you look cheap, the aunt says. Girls with their lives ahead of them should wear their hair long.

What was it they said about a funeral tomorrow?

The aunt removes her hands. I think it's one of their help. A cowboy. They would call themselves cowboys, wouldn't they?

Mother said I might get sick. The girl rolls over to face the aunt.

Women on your mother's side always seem to get the morning sickness.

Mother said I'll need new clothes.

That town where the train dropped us off, where they picked us up? What was it called?

Cody.

There must be a place for a lady to buy clothes in Cody. We'll go shopping.

Mother said it was my fault.

The aunt exhales heavily, filling the room with the baked apples they'd had for dessert.

A bird lands on the peak of the roof, claws scratching against the tin, wings shuffling.

The aunt says, Charlie's a good boy.

The girl rolls abruptly away, tousling the smoothness out of her hair. I'll be outside, she says.

But she goes only as far as the rough steps, the half-rounds of logs nailed in an uneven tier below the door. She sits there with her elbows cupped in her hands, shivering despite the night's dry heat. It occurs to her that this is the first time she has traveled without her father. Even now, a year later, she finds his absence startling. He had been the one to decide things for her. He had been the one to take responsibility. Her entire life, the odor of cigar smoke will mean security and warmth to her. A vague sense of loss eventually disassociated from its source.

She leans back, hands crossed over her stomach. Same old stomach. Her breasts might be a little larger, though. And sore. She pushes herself off the steps, brushing at the seat of her skirt, catching her fingers on a fresh smear of sap. *A walk,* she thinks, tasting the sap. She turns north toward the river. From this distance, she can just see the undercut banks, the burgundy thumb-smears of willow, the flickering sweep of water. Water so different from the slow, wide rivers of home. Those are proper rivers, to her mind; their age measured by width and depth rather than erosion. Below the dam downstream, this water sprays through the rock walls like a thumb over a hose. Straight out of the mountains. That's what Adze had said: That water only melted yesterday, Miss.

She turns right, around the northern edge of the ranch, walking between the river and the main lodge, past the firepit toward the barn and corrals. On the north side of the barn, barely visible even from this angle, she can make out the steeply pitched roof of an attached jog, a shanty. Bunkhouse for some kind of hired man, probably. Smoke unravels from a black stovepipe and warm yellow lantern light sifts through the filthy windowglass, spreading weak and diluted on the riverbank gravel. A shadow passes in front of the light, then back.

She stands quiet, allowing herself a brief moment of envy for the figure in the shed, gifted with such warmth and light. Security. But what kind of warmth? What kind of light? Look at all the dirt on that window.

From the empty blue air above the river, she hears the deep burp of a feeding nighthawk. From the opposite bank, a deer rattles through the willows, coming down to water. But she is unable to put a name to either of these sounds and can imagine only bears, mountain lions. Red in teeth and claws. She turns and starts walking back to the guest cabin, holding herself to a measured, controlled pace, a pace that quickly uncoils into long, hurried strides, then an awkward run. Bears just behind, lions.

4

GRAY, GRAY DAWN, and already there are these soft sounds in the round corral behind the barn: the hot bellows blow of air in a horse's nostrils, the shuffle of hooves in dirt, the sizzle of a cigarette burning. The rest of the ranch quiet around them. It's an old habit. When there's something caught within him, when he's been having trouble sleeping, he goes to the corral. Working with horses distills the world down to essentials. The necessarily deliberate motions, the attempt to see yourself through an animal's eyes, the awareness of a coming conclusion.

He has always found his truest satisfactions in work, in the imposition of order on a world that erodes order at every breath, in the inevitable vanishing of time before a new irrigation ditch, fixed fence, or gentled horse. He loves the loss of himself in these jobs and, at the end, waking to find some new bulwark raised against the decay of time. Something he can trace back to himself.

He built this round corral ten years ago: thirty-five feet of packed dirt, hoof-chopped in the center where water tends to settle. Fourteen years old and struggling to set a pair of yellow pitch posts saved special for the gate. Cutting his poles up Green Creek and dragging them down behind mules, peeling them and soaking their bases in crude oil, not knowing if it would prevent them from rotting but curious to try. He bought the gate hinges from Scotty Clark in Cody, which still rankles. He thought then, and thinks now, that he should learn blacksmithing. More than just cold shoeing, anyway.

He stands with his cigarette, shirtless in the morning's early heat, and considers the horse in front of him. This filly. This little gal here. He saddled her for the first time not an hour ago, roping her to the post outside the corral and tying off one back leg, giving her no choice but to accept his old training saddle: hull cracked, stirrups worn into splintered hourglasses. Now she lifts her feet against the hobbles, shaking against the unfamiliar tack.

Horses have long been the going concern of this ranch. More than cattle anyway. Until peace dropped the bottom out of the market, horses had made his father the best money. With the spring months came their big drive from winter pasture — eighty, ninety horses trailing along shoeless and unkempt — and then a week of oats and corrals and currycombs. Green-breaking the two-year-olds. By the time Henry was fifteen, he had ridden bucking horses a thousand times. Just under it, he figured. His tongue has a ragged edge to it from the time a crow hop caught it in his teeth, and he has a wet-weather ache in one ankle from coming down off center.

He eases his way across the corral toward her. She humps

away. He chases her as slowly as he can, pursuing her without change in pace or rhythm. There are these paired shapes in the corral: the jerking, horizontal form of the horse; the man moving after, his body angled as if in a stiff wind. An aggressive purposefulness to them both. The horse rears against the hobbles and the man stands suddenly still, arms held wide. The horse looks away and he eases forward again, another few feet, until he can touch her neck, slowly smoothing a path through the sweaty hair to the shoulder. There is nothing haphazard or unplanned about the way he's moving now. He closes his eyes and drops his face into the hair and sweat of her neck, the complete envelope of her odor.

Harmless, he says under his breath. Harmless old me.

A throat clears behind him and he jerks around, the horse jumping at his movement, lunging hard against her hobbles, then lunging again, finally to settle down, trembling.

That girl from New York. Trying to look nonchalant in her dude clothes. A leather skirt too heavy for the day's coming heat. Her flat-brimmed hat and tasseled leather vest. She steps up on the bottom rail, rocking on her arches.

Nice horse, she says.

He walks toward the girl, stretching out his arm. As he comes closer, as his hand nearly touches her, she steps away from him. Frightened, then angry.

Nice horse, he agrees, pulling his shirt off the post. He turns away to work the buttons.

I should like to go riding sometime, she says.

He doesn't care for her tone. He picks the rope off the ground and takes out the slack, pulling it toward him in slow lengths until the horse stands against it, forefeet planted, the muscles in her chest enormous and unshakable.

You should take me riding sometime.

He studies the horse. Watches the mean backward tilt of her ears. Says, What about that baby a yours?

Beg your pardon?

Your aunt wants you to take it easy.

She didn't tell *me* that.

He bends to unsnap the hobbles, pulling at the rope until the filly decides to walk along with him. As they walk, he winds the rope in his hands, increasing the pace until they're jogging shoulder to shoulder. On the third circuit of the corral he sees that the girl has taken off her hat.

We haven't met, she says as they run past.

He slows to a walk. Henry Mohr, he says.

I'm Virginia Price.

He stops, his hands on either side of the horse's neck. Does she look like she likes that saddle, Miss Price?

I don't know.

I don't think she likes it too much. He gathers the rope and pulls lightly. Might be a little rodeo here, Miss Price.

He draws himself a few inches up onto the saddle, resting his elbows on the seat and dangling his legs off one side, giving the filly a chance to feel his weight. She stands puzzled. He pulls himself up higher and swings a leg over to sit full in the saddle, bracing his legs and grabbing the ridge of the pommel. She tosses her head and takes a cautious step forward. Then another. And then she is walking slowly, uncertainly around the corral. He keeps the rope slack in his open hand.

How about that, Ballo, he says to the horse, rubbing her neck. Miss Price paid all that money and there wasn't even a bucking show.

Virginia, she says. Call me Virginia.

He nods, his head moving in time with the horse's gait.

Anything but Gin.

They walk a complete circuit before he gives the first tug on the hackamore. The horse sits back on her haunches, eyes going white. He drops immediately out of the saddle and stands beside her — letting her get a good look at him — then leads her once around the corral before mounting up again, sitting a few seconds in the saddle then dismounting, then mounting again. And again. Ten times. Then he pulls off the saddle and blanket and carries them over toward Virginia, slinging them over the fencerail. He leans against a post, hands in his pockets.

It's early in the morning for horse training, she says.

He nods his head. Look there at that sunrise, he says.

I haven't seen horses trained this way before. With hobbles.

He takes off his hat and wipes at the brim with his fingers. Adze, he says.

Adze?

Adze is from California. It's how they train down south. Softest-mouthed horses in the world. Takes a lot to even buy one a them vaquero horses up here.

She's beautiful.

Army still buys a horse every now and then, but they only want dark horses. The light ones like this gal, I can take my pick, pretty much.

I didn't know the army was still buying horses.

Adze can do two things. Cook chili and train a horse.

More than most people. She closes her eyes against the new sun, tilting her head back.

He looks directly at her for the first time. You're right, he says.

She has a nice-colored hair. Brown, but gray in places. Like a field mouse. And a small nose, rounded on the end. With her cheeks wide the way they are, that nose gives her an elfish look. And that's a little makeup on there too. That must be lipstick.

She opens her eyes, sees him studying her.

A door slams in the lodge. The generator coughs, coughs again, then hums with an unvarying urgency. A light goes on inside the lodge and Frank Mohr's voice rises, faint and imperious.

Well then, Henry says, pulling the saddle and blanket off the rail. I guess that's it then.

5

THERE HAS ALWAYS been a part of her — the same part, maybe, that identifies with heroines in novels — that aches to be watched. To be seen.

Sitting with her back against the curved bricks of the fire's heat reflector, she holds up her clay mug, watching as Frank Mohr pours her a small measure of wine. His hands so clean, so soft. How does any man manage to keep his hands clean in Wyoming? Surely he has to chop firewood, for instance. Henry's hands, now. Those things have seen some work. Calloused and muscled into the half-curled postures of shovel-holding, of rope-throwing. She likes to think that she can read people by their hands. The way you judge the depth of a river by its banks. She herself wears a pair of light gray Mocha gloves, a hand-me-down from her mother.

How long has it been since she's tasted wine? A year? Since Delmonico's closed, anyway. Even after Prohibition, Del's had kept a few bottles around for favored customers. At the cabarets, she had liked to drink only gin. It had been a point of honor, living up to Charlie's nickname for her.

Across the fire, Henry sits with his mother, both of them dressed in the dark clothes they had worn to the funeral. Henry uncomfortable in his suit, loose in collar and cuff. Rose Mohr in her petticoat and gray skirts, hands bare and plump under her lace cuffs. Braided hair and coal-black eyes pressed deep into the mounds of her cheeks. Poor woman probably doesn't know that it's proper to wear gloves to a funeral. A few hours earlier, standing at the open grave, Virginia had watched as Frank Mohr bit the tip off a cigar and raised his arm, digging in his shirt for matches. Beside him, Rose had flinched at his abrupt movement. Now she lifts Henry's hand off his knee and presses it between her palms, warming it and, after a moment, setting it gently back in place. Half Indian? Virginia wonders. Her broad cheeks and the olive tint to her skin not quite so native as one would first expect. And these features are diluted even further in Henry, who, if he weren't sitting beside his mother, would look almost Italian, or maybe Greek. His dark hair and eyes.

Virginia listens to the faint mosquito whine of cars passing up on the valley road. She has heard this road variously called the Zoo Park Road, the Yellow and Black Road, and Highway 14. A lot of names for some old strip of gravel in the mountains.

Mohr steps across to show Pauline the label. Without her spectacles, and in the moving, unpredictable light, Virginia's aunt nevertheless makes a show of reading the bottle.

I would love to know where you found *that,* Pauline says.

Buffalo Bill, Mohr says loudly. He give me this bottle before he died.

Adze, cross-legged on the ground, squints up at Mohr with an unreadable expression, tossing off whatever is in his coffee mug.

Yessir, Mohr says, Bill brung a case back from the Continent and passed the bottles along to all his best friends. This one here come from the Loire. Pardon my language, ladies, but I'll be damned if any Volstead government's goin a tell me I can't drink to Bill's health.

Mohr considers the bottle's label by the light of the fire, then sets it carefully aside. First toast, he says, has to go to William Cody. To Bill!

Drama, Virginia thinks, and sips at her mug. It's not much of a wine, really. Surely nothing from the Loire. Is it possible that it's some kind of Bordeaux? She has heard that a Médoc can be bitter. She sips again. To her inexperienced palate, it tastes very young. She wishes she had seen the label. Buffalo Bill died when? Seven years ago? This wine is certainly not seven years old. Frank Mohr, it seems to her, must be one of those men who thrive on extravagant gestures. She's noticed that he wears a gold elk-tooth ring, a watch chain hung with a grizzly-claw fob. She has known people like this her whole life. Showboats. Actors.

Now to Jim Buskin, Mohr says, not unhappily.

She takes another sip. Doesn't matter. She finishes it off, and when her aunt places her own mug on the ground between them, she drinks that as well, turning away and gulping it down.

No wine since Delmonico's. And she hasn't been drunk since that last night with Charlie. It's nice to feel a little jazzed again. And off not quite two glasses of wine. Is she out of practice? She must be out of practice.

Such little fires they build here in Wyoming. In Connecticut, her father had built bonfires from entire trees. He would sit her on his lap and let her sip from his wineglass. She hasn't thought of this in years. She sees him now, cigar protruding from his walrus mustache, his features soft and blunted, and in later years ashen and mottled by drink. A belly large enough, even under his waistcoat, to use as a shelf for his brandy glass. The parties were best if the hunting had been good. After skinning the fox — slitting it hock to ass and pulling the bones from the tail, peeling it down with his fists — he would throw the diminished corpse to the dogs. The dogs, each with its mouthful of leg or tuft of unskinned foot, would pull the carcass into a cat's cradle of spreading viscera and muscle. Molly, the upstairs maid, had been the one to find him, lying quite at ease in the cold water of last night's bath. The first two fingers of his right hand seared black by the fire of his final cigar.

She looks at Mohr with disdain as he hovers over the flames of his hat-sized fire. She wonders if *anybody* out here knows how to build a proper fire. Or throw a decent party for that matter.

She leans back on her hands. All those stars up there. Closer, through the dry air, than any stars above New York. An occasional melancholic, her father had been a fine star watcher. She had once seen him quote Shakespeare up to them: "And certain stars shot madly from their spheres, To hear the sea-maid's music." If she remembers it right, her mother had been disdainful. "Fine lessons you're teaching our daughter," she had said. "Useless romantics." But then his arm went wide around her matronly waist and he tickled into her neck with his mustache — "Are you my sea maid? Are you my sea maid?" — until she laughed and pushed him away, touching his nose with her fingertip. Virginia thinks now that she can remember every single time she has ever heard her mother laugh.

Across the fire, Henry raises his eyes.

Across from him, she lowers her eyes.

"You start to remember things . . ." Virginia shifted away from her hip and stood briefly, rearranging her cushions. Wincing as she sat back. "And it isn't a line you walk. No beginnings and endings. No laws of perception to lead you away. Rather, it's water you swim through. You reach out, touching a face, a hand, a foot, trying to recreate from these pieces how it was that this particular life came to be your own. In the end, of course, you see that you've been alone in the water. Alone all this time."

She looked past me, shriveled hands rubbing at the smooth crest of her cane. "Sometime soon, I'll swim down and not come back up."

6

THIS IS her mother's house. Never her father's. A tiny castle, with its butler and underbutler, houseboy and chef and maids for each floor, its brick colonnades and walnut arch over the front door. The home of her childhood, although she's never much cared for the place. She has always felt the most treasured in Connecticut. This house, with so much in it to distract her parents, has been her competition. Four stories and twenty-eight rooms, dormers off the roof and a belvedere barely seen from the street. A widow's walk. All of it enclosed by a brick and wrought-iron fence, bulwarked with iron spikes against an imagined peasantry. The marble-tiled bathrooms with matching brass fixtures scavenged from some Tuscan villa, discovered by her father during one of their early trips together (Virginia remembers only the endless rain and her father's grin as she stared overlong at the statue of David). Every other brass and silver ornament in the house — every candelabrum and sconce, pitcher and charcoal burner, samovar and tea-kettle — has been chosen by her mother.

She steps from the bath and towels herself dry — gloriously unpregnant, virginal still — and slips into her chenille robe, settling down in front of the mirror, cracking the window at her elbow. Bath steam drifts past her, replaced by the rich odors of potted soil and wet pavement and new sunlight. She cleans her teeth and pulls out her makeup drawer, patting on a light base of vanishing cream and covering it with face powder. She traces on a careful beesting of lipstick, knowing that it will drive her mother crazy. As much as she feels herself to be in something of a panic, however, and as much as she wants to cause a stir, she stops short of using eyebrow pencil, mascara.

Wednesday morning, which means a single table of mah jongg downstairs. If it were Friday, there would be three tables and a buffet of plattered cookies, candies, and tea. Virginia dresses in her tennis flannels and hooked boots and walks down to the parlor, studying from the doorway the four old women vultured motionless over their tiles. She stands jaunty and hip-cocked: a self-assured teenage girl.

The floor-length drapes billow slightly, admitting the distant riveting of construction. Gramercy Park, that little island of greenery amid the gray cacophony of New York, has lately fallen victim to one of the shifts in fashion that constantly redefine Manhattan. Beekman Place is suddenly popular, for instance. And while their little park has remained sacrosanct, ever-higher apartment buildings have been rising girder to girder all around them. They can't open their windows without being reminded of it.

Kong, her mother says, adding a tile to her row, sliding out a discard.

Her mother's been gaining weight recently, a heaviness in her arms and thighs only partly disguised by the light jackets she's taken to wearing. Such a matronly body, all draped-over hips and folds of flesh.

Mah jongg! Alice Atkins cries, picking up the discard. Distantly related by marriage to the Pierpont Morgans, the woman has seen her heyday, and it's no surprise to find her here on this unremarkable Wednesday morning.

Oh, you lucky thing, Alice, Virginia's mother says. Now, who's East Wind?

I'm playing tennis, Mother.

Her mother glances up, then says to the women, Charles Stroud has volunteered to teach Virginia tennis.

Helen Carpenter, some sort of cousin to Juliana Cutting, peers at Virginia with bulbous, froglike eyes. The brokerage-firm Strouds? Lucky, lucky. He's quite a catch.

I think I may just kiss him today, Virginia says, suddenly refusing to care whom Helen Cutting might be related to. Virginia had her coming out in May — in the Crystal Room at the Ritz — and so it seems to her that there is little anyone can take away from her.

Virginia! Her mother's eyes widen, appalled. She glances furtively at the other women, but the women now have eyes only for one another.

Oh, I've kissed dozens of boys, Mother. Just *dozens.*

During the past six weeks, their first extended period of time together since her father's death, they have taken to stealing the smallest pleasures from each other. Virginia with these petty embarrassments. Her mother with insults disguised as advice: You're much prettier when you don't slouch. Virginia sees now how her parents had balanced each other. Her father's flippant lack of regard for consequences (he had once swum nude in Eastchester Bay on New Year's Eve, shucking off a piece of clothing for each tolling of the bell) a counterpoint to her mother's seriousness, her frowns and tea parties.

In the absence of her father, there is no moderating the woman at all.

Go play tennis then, her mother says with a patronizing weariness, turning back to her tiles. Evening meal is at seven, and I hope by then you will have rediscovered truth and civility. Your father would have been appalled.

7

IN THE EARLY SPRING of 1918, the boy travels east alone, having missed the Company K muster out of Cody. He'd had some idea that going to war should hold a larger kind of significance, should at least mean new clothes, but he had been wrong. He travels in his mud-stained canvas pants and a faded chambray shirt the color of old leaves, his feet cold in a pair of cheap brogans. In his carpetbag, inside a knotted sock, the leather medicine bundle his mother had put together for him: a piece of blue cloth for good luck, a granite stone with the profile of an eagle for good sight, the desiccated wings of a barn swallow to help him evade enemies. Probably won't work, she had said, shoving it into his shirt pocket, but you never know. Anything to help with them ironhats.

It has been a hard winter, and the cars shudder as they pound through snowdrifts on the tracks. The decision to be a marine was made lightly — the posters, "First to Fight," had a ring to them — but he nevertheless understands that this will be one of those incidental path-choosings that will sound a bell throughout his life. He's not afraid of going to war. He's not. Violence is something with which he has lived his entire life. The clenching and unclenching of his father's fist. And yet that fist — such a small thing — has always sent him packing. If he can't stand up to a single curled hand, he wonders how he'll manage in front of a machine gun.

He is enthralled by the ocean, by such an immense horizon in constant movement, but finds the humidity of South Carolina uncomfortable, even in February. He takes his oath on Parris Island and spends the next ten weeks in a new barracks with forty other men, slowly growing accustomed to the odors of drying paint and wet cement. His drill sergeant's name is Shand — a loud broomstick of a man — and at first he hates him but then he grows to love him.

Early in their training, Shand tells them that some of them will die. Look around, he says. That man, that man, that man there. You could die yourself. But you are a marine. And you can die knowing that there will always be another marine behind you, ready to shoot the sonofabitch that shot *you*.

Behind Henry, a heavy-browed man with skunk breath named Nelson leans close and whispers, in a southern accent, I ain't gonna shoot nobody that shoots no red injun.

That night, Henry throws Nelson against the tiled wall in the shower and punches him in the chest, grabbing him by the throat and staring at him nose to nose until the man looks away. Later, he hears Nelson lie to Shand about the bruises on his ribs and they become cautious friends.

Amid the daily regime of drill and laundry, potato peeling and shooting instruction, Henry finds himself, to his surprise (to his immense surprise), an accepted part of something larger. They have made him cut his hair, and with his uniform on his back he is precisely as rich, precisely as capable, precisely as valued as any man among them. He also finds, at odd moments, a communal, hushed reverence between them all, a way of glancing at one another at mess, at inspection, over the breeches of their Springfields at the rifle range — especially at the rifle range — that puts a stillness in each of them. *This is no game,* they see each other thinking. This is no motion picture. They are doing this to kill and be killed. He will never see most of these men again.

He is shipped to Quantico and crosses the ocean with five hundred other men, lying seasick in his hammock for thirteen days. As they draw near France, they are ordered not to throw garbage overboard for fear of attracting German submarines. From the harbor at Brest, he travels southeast in a cattle car, shuffling around until he can lean against a wall that doesn't have cow manure smeared on its slats. There are forty men in a car, and they sleep shoulder to shoulder, knees to their chests. He soon finds himself keeping company with a man from Chicago named David Hassler, so short as to come only up to Henry's chin, so pale as to glow in the dark of the car, but he has a constant, self-effacing wit that makes him a favorite among them. With the first belch and groan of the moving train, Hassler leans up on one hip and makes a face. Excuse me, he says. *Good*ness. Mornings, he stands at the open door pissing, waving with his free hand to villagers.

They spend a week billeted in a grammar school outside Dijon, scratching their names into the slate chalkboards with bayonets. Henry is assigned a light machine gun, an 8 mm French Chauchat (Sho Sho, they call them), which surprises him, since he has always considered himself a sharpshooter. Over the next few months, he will come to cultivate a dislike for this clumsy, ill-designed piece of weaponry, a dislike that will quickly bloom into hatred. They only give you a twenty-round, half-moon magazine, and the barrel slams back on recoil. After the first shot, you can't hit a goddamn thing with it.

The AEF are understocked, and within days they find themselves scavenging food from farmyards, chasing chickens into each other's arms and stealing the bread left cooling on windowsills: dark loaves, gritty with sand. Shortly before they leave for the front, Henry discovers a keg of wine hidden in a stack of loose hay behind a dairy barn, and he and Hassler spend the afternoon getting drunk. Their last fully enjoyable afternoon. Backs propped against the barn, the heavy keg balanced on their raised knees. Hassler has taken to calling him a variety of Indian names, and when Henry swallows wine until it spills out over his cheeks, Hassler says, Look at old Drinks Like a Fish. And later, as Henry's coming back from the outhouse, tucking in his blouse, he says, My God, son, maybe we should call you Shits for an Hour. Hassler has given himself the name Soldier with Small Prick, as in, Let Soldier with Small Prick have a bite of that monkey meat chow. After learning the Crow name for white man, however, he calls himself simply Yellow Eyes, introducing himself, more often than not, as Yellow Eyes Hassler.

They ride the trains to a station outside Paris, marching in formation under echoing vaults to a waiting line of French transport trucks. Henry had wanted to go into town and walk through the Arc de Triomphe, but what he wants has long since ceased to matter. They are driven east, and sleep that night in wet blankets beneath a colonnade of immense cypress trees. *Planted before Napoleon,* Henry thinks, alternately intimidated and delighted to find himself on the fringes of such history. The next morning, their trucks chew their way toward the front amid the growing odors of cordite and woodsmoke, the sounds of shellfire. By late morning, the sporadic barrage has become an unbroken roar. Even Hassler falls silent in the face of the frenetic motions of war. Cruciform telegraph poles erected without consideration for vertical lines. Rows and rows of tents. Excavators. Men running. Henry sees a soldier wearing a kilt, a troop of black men sitting under a demolished brick wall, eating watery eggs from a communal pot. Among the passing refugees he sees families trudging behind metal carts pieced together from abandoned Fords. Wheelbarrows piled impossibly high with chicken coops and bookcases, mounds of potatoes and turnips and cabbages. Children riding among the vegetable sacks, staring out wide-eyed at the troops. He sees a little boy marching along with the body of a mongrel dog stiff over one shoulder — the child looking businesslike, as if bringing wood to a fire — and he knows that here is an image he'll never be able to leave behind.

They pass a slow-moving line of Ford ambulances and wave at the cheers, clasping their hands together, shaking them above their heads. The marines are here, and Henry is a marine. One of them. A leatherneck.

In Lucy-le-Bocage, the shelling has taken the rooftops but left the walls, creating a game board of hewn brick and broken glass. It has begun to rain again. They stay in the village until dusk, at which time a runner comes to bring them to the front. At the edge of the village, they are marched in single file past a dead German — the first dead man Henry has ever seen outside a coffin. The corpse lies with his back against the illegible remains of a road sign, his face black and swollen, his hands pale.

They spread out with five paces between them, the final minutes of sun stretching their shadows toward the battle. *Sundials for war,* Henry thinks. *Wardials.* In front of him, Hassler dives to the ground, using the momentum of his dive to roll into the ditch. Dust pops at Henry's feet and he thinks, *Grasshoppers.* Like grasshoppers in the weeds back home. Then he's on his stomach in the ditch, and his legs are wet to his thighs. The Sho Sho is in his arms but he doesn't know where to point it. There's movement in a wheatfield ahead of them, the green expanse pocked by mortar pits, and then a matchflash of rifle fire in the trees beyond the field. Half a dozen men rise from the meadow, from the ground itself, and start running toward them, looking not unlike silhouettes on the marine rifle range. They are nothing at all like the silhouettes. Henry turns to reload, barely aware that he has been firing, and notices for the first time a dead man in the ditch beside him: belly swollen tight against his shirt, pockets turned inside out into small white flags.

Hassler lies on the other side of the corpse, wide-eyed and grinning, holding out a square tin of Sho Sho ammunition. Past Hassler, there is already a marine dead in the ditch, face down in the mud, a bullet hole punched through the crest of the helmet. There must be another wound Henry can't see: How can a man be shot in the top of the head? In later weeks, however, he will have cause to reconsider the idea of a bullet fired from the sky and will regret not turning the body over.

Branches and leaves fall on their shoulders, clipped by Maxim rounds. The air fills with the whistle of trench mortars from the woods. There are rounds that whine and explode in showers of dirt and there are rounds that are not heard at all but reverberate deep in the chest like loose drums. Worst are the hollow thumps of gas canisters, followed by shrill cries for masks. In the last weeks of the war, Henry's lips will carry festering sores, opened by a residue of mustard gas dusted on the mouth of his canteen.

This is the beginning. It is June 7. Belleau Wood. The first in a list of names that he will remember until his death, until he has forgotten most everything else. Until he has forgotten the color of the car sitting in his driveway. Saint-Mihiel. Sousson. Blanc-Mont. These foreign smears of tongue against the roof of his mouth.

8

AT TWO-THIRTY in the afternoon, following the aunt's list of instructions, Nettie backs through the kitchen door, balancing a tea tray on one hand. The heat from the kitchen, saturated with the odor of stewing tomatoes, rolls out behind her. The kitchen must be a horrid place to spend one's time. The kind of heat that makes Virginia think of Pennsylvania steel mills.

Ma'am, Nettie says, setting the metal tray on the coffee table. Her white skin flushed, crescents of moisture in the fabric under her arms. Behind her, through the swinging door, Virginia catches a glimpse of empty Mason jars arranged on the counter, an enormous kettle boiling on the stove. Even the great room, although still cool enough, is warmer than it should be: Frank Mohr has built them a small blaze in the fireplace. His misconceived notion of hospitality, maybe.

Many thanks, Nettie, Virginia says.

Miss, she says, dropping an awkward curtsy, grinning at the floor. Virginia has the sense that this is a role — maidservant — the girl enjoys. Access to a lifestyle that she has perhaps only read about. Little red-haired Nettie, limping over a leg warped by infantile paralysis. That small voice afflicted with its conspicuous Irish brogue. She was born in Laramie, and claims to have inherited the accent entirely from her mother, not having heard many other people talk as she grew up.

Pauline works herself upright off the couch and slides her feet into slippers. She touches the lid of the porcelain pot and pours the tea, rings falling loose on her fingers, rattling above swollen knuckles. Take this, child, she says. Before it gets cold.

What an old woman.

Virginia pinches lemon juice into her cup, then runs the

empty rind around its rim. She nibbles at the scalloped edges of a packaged cookie. Did you bring these biscuits with you, Auntie? she asks.

Of course. The tea as well. Good thing, too. I don't think there's a person in this state who would think to drink a cup of tea.

Just black coffee.

Just all that black coffee.

A few minutes later, Virginia pushes her cup away and stands, stretching. A nap in the cabin, Auntie.

Pauline pulls a book from the crack between the couch pillows. Good, she says. You can use your rest.

In the dust of the yard, grasshoppers flick and buzz around Virginia's feet. Not having had much else to think about these past few days, she has found herself preoccupied with grasshoppers. The large ones with black and yellow wings that fly for miles when they're jumped, whirring like rattlesnakes. The little red-winged ones that click and snap. The tiny brown ones that throw themselves over the grass with gallant disregard for life and limb, landing on their sides, on their backs. She likes these the best, finding in them any number of metaphors for her own life.

The sun bakes at the crown of her head, splitting the ends of her hair, frizzing it. No wonder everyone wears those hats. She cuts through the loop of driveway between the main lodge and guest cabins. Behind her, hammering. The hollow bounce of log on log. She had seen them up there this morning, those two adolescent cowboys. Just down the way from her cabin. They had, in fact, woken her up with their early morning laughter. Grumpy, sleep still in her eyes, she had watched them work on the bare-wall beginnings of a third guest cabin. Sliding around, trying to frame in some sort of window. Dropping nails, knocking boards off the scaffolding.

She makes her way around the south side of the firepit toward the barn, screened at this angle by a line of cottonwoods. A sound she can almost recognize . . . She cranes her head, peering through the trees. A pair of hens flush out from under her feet, cackling, startling her so that she stands gasping, a hand flat on her chest. The birds perch on the picnic table, then flap over to an old grain bin, finally lighting on the boom of a revolving shovel. The most modern piece of equipment she has so far seen in Wyoming. It sits quietly over a mound of fresh, gravel-pocked dirt. A hole that will, she supposes, one day be a swimming pool. The first pool in the valley, they had said.

She hears it again, bringing the sound to consciousness. The heartmeat sound of hooves on dirt. Another horse. A vague, systole thump as faint to her, as essential to her as the sound of her own blood. Her entire life there have been few things she has loved as much as horses.

She works her way around the barn, past the empty round corral and toward the larger corral behind with its rail chutes and arched gates and intersecting network of wire fence. Inside, a saddled buckskin mare stands backing against a riata. The rope angles tight, looped to the hind legs of a steer stretched flat in the dust. Dewey, one of the ranch's cowboys, sits on its neck, a front leg bent in his hands. Henry squats on its shoulder, one hoof caught up between his thighs and dripping over a bucket of soapy water. As Virginia watches, Henry picks up a square bottle of Fleming's actinoform and pours a measure out into his cupped hand, dousing the split of the hoof and rubbing the liquid in with an index finger. Blood trickles off the point of the hoof and into the dirt between his boots.

Hello, Virginia says. May I help? She leans against the corral rails and drops her chin on her arms.

Thank you, Miss, Dewey says, grinning up at her. Doin jus fine.

An odd, high voice, Dewey's. All the words going out

through his nose. Despite his beard and spectacles, which lend him an air of professional respectability, he sounds like a Katzenjammer Kid. A cartoon with a black felt cowboy hat and yellow Bull Durham string hanging out of his shirt pocket.

Henry sets the square bottle aside and picks up a quart jar of iodine, unscrewing the cap with his teeth and upending the bottle over the fresh wound in the hoof, dousing it and rubbing his forefinger through the cracks. Then dousing it again.

Sure I can't help, Henry?

Henry shakes his head, studying the hoof. About done, he says.

Out of sight around the barn, the revolving shovel starts up, its engine a staccato roar punctuated by the congested scrape of steel on gravel.

So this is going to be a dude ranch next year, Virginia says.

Yes ma'am. Dewey stands, wiping at his forehead with his sleeve.

Well. Are you going to have your dudes *do* anything?

Henry jumps away, grabbing at the open iodine bottle as the steer kicks free and clambers to its feet.

Dewey coils the loose rope. You don't have anythin to do, Miss?

I'm tired of just *looking* at horses.

You like horses?

I'd like them better if I was *on* one.

I guess we can understand that, can't we, Henry.

But Henry is preoccupied with the steer, watching it limp across the corral trailing a line of quarter-moon bloodstains. He ignores her, the iodine bottle cocked at his waist. The posture of a man accustomed to standing with another kind of bottle entirely.

9

HENRY HAD BEEN nine when they had first come into this country; south out of Billings, his father driving the spring wagon, his mother nursing his brother. The age of the century. Even then he had been tall enough, strong enough to saddle his own horse (if he stood on a chair), gut his own deer. He had preceded his family south around Cedar Mountain, riding his little curly-haired Galiceño pony, puffed with a small boy's self-importance. The bottom where they would be seeding alfalfa had been fallow, scalloped by the tracks of deer and elk and bighorn sheep, and the bench where they would build their cabin had been littered with the remains of a cottonwood trunk, shattered by a grizzly bear looking for ants.

He sits on the porch fifteen years later. And it does indeed seem like fifteen years. More. The aggregate weight of those years. Time slips away, like everybody's always saying, but it leaves its tracks, too. He sits on the back porch feeling tracked up one side and down the other.

He takes off his hat and lays it upside down on the rail, wiping his forehead with the flat of his hand. It's so damn hot. The kind of heat that peels paint off the walls.

Through the thick air he hears the rattle of the cellar padlock, followed by his father's bootheels clocking over the packed dirt. Late evenings, Mohr has the predictable habit of smoking one of his German cigars on the porch. Those slim, dark cheroots that burn your mouth, that fall apart in your fingers.

Henry stands up. He doesn't want to approach this man. He wants to *be* approached.

Mohr rounds the corner, a pint jelly jar of booze held close to his chest. Here is the man who raised him. A man who, by the laws of primogeniture rather than blood, must be called his father. A man prone all his life to sudden eruptions of violence: horse-beatings and bottle-breakings. An inch taller than Henry, although thinner. Hemostatic legs and wicker arms. He wears a brown leather vest in all weathers, beneath which, in a holster against the small of his back, he keeps a .32-caliber Browning automatic. A useless affectation, Henry has always thought, although what with having to deliver his own hooch, he might have a use for it after all.

Mohr steps up onto the porch and sets the jar on the railing, pulling the cigars from his shirt pocket. A fiberboard pack not much wider than the fingers of a woman's hand. He draws a cigar out with his teeth and strikes a match on the sole of his boot, tilting the cigar into the flame. He spits over the rail. Hot, he says, wiping at his mouth.

Yessir, Henry says.

I want you to look up there at that mountain. Mohr toasts it with his jar. All them heat waves. If this weather don't break soon, half this valley'll be on fire.

Jim Mountain. Healthy ground ruined is how Henry's always thought of it. The edges like cut tin. Hundreds of square miles made inhospitable by the silent crunch and tear of geology.

Heat or booze, Mohr's face looks swollen above his collarless shirt. He rubs his forehead and takes a long drink from the jelly jar. Damn me, he says. Damn me but that's good.

He offers the jelly jar to Henry, who sips at it, then sips again, nodding. I didn't think that new barrel was through working, he says.

I guess it is. Mohr takes back the jar.

How's the pool comin?

That goddamned Lester Crandall's takin his time, that's for sure. If I knew how to run that thing, I'd do it myself.

Must not have much road business lined up.

That's just it. Mohr drinks deeply from the jar.

And that new cabin?

We'd be more'n half done if those Magini kids knew how to pound a nail.

Adze told you about that steer what had the footrot.

Mohr nods. Spits over the rail. Smokes.

You might want a get the rest of them cows down early, Henry says. Where one's got the footrot, might be others.

I'll wait.

Why would you want a do that? I don't know why you'd do that.

Wait till we gather. I'm goin a sell off most of em anyway. Gettin ready for next year's dudes. Once those dudes start showin up, start payin thirty, forty dollars a week to go for a horseback ride, we'll never have to wrestle another stinkin steer again.

Finally gettin rich, are you?

The sarcasm isn't lost on his father, who turns toward him and takes a slow drink, staring over the rim of the jar. You could learn a thing or two from me, boy, he says. Thing or two about wantin somethin better for your wife, your family. Ambition.

Family, Henry says. Well. All right, then. You can take care a those dudes without me, I guess. I'll be movin on in a few weeks.

Mohr nods and smokes, staring into the hills. Henry had expected a protest. If nothing else, a polite inquiry as to where he might be going next. But then . . . he berates himself for expecting anything at all from this man. He says, I guess that girl from back east wants to go ridin.

She ain't bad lookin, Mohr says.

No she ain't.

But she's got a wide mouth, Henry. I never trusted a woman with a wide mouth. It's a indication of bullheadedness.

Mouth looks all right to me.

You know why she's out here?

Yessir, I do.

She's cookin another man's biscuit, that's why.

I heard that.

You heard that. You heard about the man?

I heard.

And you still think you should go ridin with her? You think she should go herself in the shape she's in?

I said the same thing.

His father pauses. Coughs. Thinks about it. Finally says, Sure. Go on over toward the South Fork while you're at it. Maybe take a half gallon from this new barrel. Clara Higgins is gettin dry. Gettin ready for some party. Maybe take Adze with you to keep people from talking.

Yessir.

Hell, take a gallon. It ain't like they're goin a turn it away.

All right. Henry puts on his hat, steps off the porch.

Boy, his father says, not without compassion.

Henry turns.

The man who tilled that ground still ain't filed no quitclaim on her.

What are you sayin?

Don't start somethin you ain't goin a be able to finish.

10

SLIM AS A handful of willows. *Slim and elegant,* she thinks. Made slimmer still by her Russeks silk tunic dress: a waistless, uncomplicated drape of fabric the pale brown of tobacco, of faded parchment. Made more elegant still by the opposition of the coarse hillside behind her, the sun-battered weeds clacking in the hot breeze.

Clay dust coats her slippers. She stops to catch her breath and tastes the same dust on her tongue. In her excitement at stepping outside the little circle of cabins, she wants to think that this dust has a fresher taste to it. Cleaner somehow. Below her, across the road, her aunt stands off one corner of their cabin, hand raised against the sun, anger wooden in her spine. If that old woman had her way, Virginia would do nothing but sleep and eat and read. A vessel. That's what Pauline wants to make of her. A blind, sedate instrument of reproduction.

Beside the lodge, in the middle of the trimmed lawn, Virginia sees a pair of bent backs working over a laundry tub, underwear lank on the lines around them. She watches as Nettie straightens, the sleeves of her dress rolled past her elbows, and wipes her forehead with the back of her wrist. Watches as Nettie now sees her on the hillside, and opens her hand to her.

Virginia turns and climbs higher, slowing as the hill steepens, breathing hot air deep into her lungs, chest heaving out of all proportion to the effort. It has become a temptation to continually take note of her internal climate, to judge the infinitesimal, heartbeat-to-heartbeat changes of her pregnancy — she's been imagining all kinds of things — and now she's certain that walking up a hillside has never been so hard. There's a new heaviness in her skin, an unfamiliar fatigue leaching into her muscles.

This is far enough, she decides, and picks her way around the hill until she finds a rock flat enough to make a seat. She inspects the grass for snakes, brushes off dirt with the sole of her boot, then eases down, positioning her sketchpad awkwardly across her knees.

She doesn't consider herself much of an artist. Not when the chips are down. And she's aware that even this admission is some measure of her inadequacy, her defeat. Sargent would never admit that he's not much of an artist, for instance. But she does value her ability to arrange the world, to impose on a scene her own sense of composition: edges and lines and frames. She's a better than average watcher.

Of the landscapes she's seen, she prefers the simple studies in line and light. Appreciates a good Kensett. Doesn't understand the abstractionists, all that fauvism and cubism and every other ism. She had imagined that when she sat down to draw one of these mountains, she would simplify it to its bare bones. But now she realizes that simplicity won't work at all. This is no polite Italian landscape. No Eaton's Neck, Long Island. It's too big, for one thing. It goes on forever and ever.

She uses her palm to roll the flat of the pencil across the page, creating a skipping series of smudges. She writes the word "baby." The word "cowboy." She writes her name and smears the heel of her palm across the whole mess, blurring the letters into a featureless gray. Beginning a sketch has always been easier for her if the page is marred, if the first stroke she makes is not a blemish.

Here is the ranch. Dust and heat through the soles of her shoes and a bright reflection off the river. She considers the mountain — the direction of evening sun — and draws a short, ragged line to serve for the horizon. It doesn't seem like there's an order to this mountain, no sense of culmination. Just a bunched mass of vertical rock, shadowed by pine in the creases. How do you sketch torn chunks of carpet?

She considers her line, considers the mountain, considers the line . . . and swallows against a sudden nausea, bending to the side to vomit. She hasn't vomited for months and months. Since that time Charlie persuaded her to drink straight whiskey. She swallows and spits, then vomits again, breathing hard, skin beaded with sweat. After a moment, she sits up straight. She hasn't eaten yet today, and so her vomit is nothing more than thick saliva. A viscous, yellow knot of bile. She covers it with a flat stone, patting it down.

Now. Jim Mountain. Beneath it, the roofs of the ranch buildings: the rounded sod of a shed, the high angles of the barn. The rest of the ranch is laid out haphazardly, a building here and there, but the barn looks well designed. Clean. Built in the Dutch style, it's the only structure on the ranch made entirely of milled lumber. A gambrel roof for heavy snows, pounded tin cupolas on either end, whitewashed boards weathered to a mottled gray. This has been a horse operation, she's heard, which must explain the extravagance of the barn. She hears a faint hammering, but from this angle can't see the construction. The younger of those two cowboys is kind of cute. If it weren't for his acne.

Below the mountain, the river. A quarter mile of hayfield, bisected by the dark green of an irrigation line. Breadloaf mounds of hay and an overthrow stacker at the edge of the field. An irrigated garden, empty now but for improbably green rows of tomatoes. Beside the garden, a pair of haywagons. A horse-drawn swather with rows of teeth geared into the axles. A new Farmall tractor, iron wheels shining in the sun. A furrow and seed drill, the rusted ribcage of a hay rake. All this, but she wants to sketch only the mountain in detail. The hayfields and ranch buildings should seem insignificant, to her mind. They should *hang* from the mountain.

She rubs at her moist palm and sets the pencil back to the paper, gauging the sun. You can't draw light, you can only draw light's absence. Ten miles of volcanic rock face squeezed into a mile of mountain. *It looms,* she thinks, darkening the lower slopes with the tilted flat of her charcoal. Just above the river, she draws the alkaline lines of clay deposition, raftered by cracked sandstone. Without knowing their names, she draws sage and juniper bushes, greasewood and saltbush, a desiccated bloom of rabbitbrush, knots of wild barley crowned with ghosts of seed. Then decides after all that the eye needs something to attach itself to at the bottom of the page. No longer thinking about art at all, she stretches out her arm and twists off a rubbery twig of sage, holding it to her nose.

Unfocused, through the tiny turquoise leaves, two figures cross the road toward her. Tall and skinny. Short and fat. Henry and his mother slowly working their way up the hillside. She watches them come until, five minutes later, they stand at her feet, their eyes on a level with hers. Henry with one hand flat on his thigh, not breathing hard at all, his mother half a step behind him, wheezing, thick hands crossed over her stomach. After a moment, his mother nods her heavy head at Virginia. In recognition or sympathy or complicity?

Rose? Virginia says.

If you still think you want a go ridin, Henry says, we can go tomorrow.

Tomorrow?

Tomorrow mornin. I'm deliverin mail and some a Mother's jam and things to a dude ranch over on the South Fork. You're welcome. If it would be healthy for your condition.

I do. I mean, I would like to.

If it would be healthy.

I'm sure it would be fine.

Why I brought my mother, Henry says. You might not a heard that she's a midwife. How many babies you delivered in this valley, Mother? Eleven? Twelve? Hasn't lost a one.

Rose pinches Henry's sleeve, shaking the fabric, then turns to Virginia. Sick much? she asks.

Some, Virginia says, glancing at Henry. He has pulled a cigarette from his shirt pocket and turned away to light it. Some just lately.

Blood?

Pardon?

Peein any blood?

No, she says. A match flashes in Henry's hands. No blood.

How tall was your man?

He wasn't my man.

Rose stands waiting.

About this tall. Virginia holds her hand six inches over her head.

Fat?

Not so fat.

That'll help, she says. Praise Lord. Small mare, big horse — problems. Small mare, small horse — no problems.

Anything else? Anything else I should know?

Rose pauses, seeming to consider, then says, Won't be near so much fun coming out as it was going in. She grins.

Virginia had expected anything from her but a joke. A grin from that inscrutable slab of a face. She pulls back, surprised. Then watches Rose cover the grin with the back of her hand, concerned that she may have offended. Virginia finds herself touched by Rose's discomfort, and decides to return the smile, feeling it turn immediately into a good, honest grin. Rose drops her hand. They are grinning at nothing, these two, and it's like blocks dropping into place.

11

THIS IS THE MAN she loves, she thinks. Here he is. The *one.* She is deeply satisfied during these flashes of self-awareness to see herself as a sophisticated young woman out in New York with the man she loves.

She feels comfortable with him and would like to think that

they are two peas. He's short, for one thing, and mild to talk to. He keeps a pair of spectacles in his shirt pocket, wrapped in velvet and tied with a ribbon, wearing them when it suits him to look smart. Round, thick-rimmed specs like Harold Lloyd's. Twenty-two years old, with a small, fleshy frame that contains within it the shape of his inevitable fatness: wide, nearly feminine hips, rounded shoulders. But that's all right. The men she's admired in her life have all been a little fat.

They sit facing Park Avenue, beside Calvary Church, rain drumming on the roof. The car is brand-new, a Single-Eight Packard, and Charlie's so proud of it. She watches him run his hands around the steering wheel, swivel the windshield on its hinges, play with the gearshift lever. She privately finds the car too large for such a small man. The long running boards and serpentine fenders. The square hood that is, by itself, as long as the rest of the car. Chrome and black metal and a cavernous front seat. Why is it that the smallest men always like the biggest cars?

She holds her hip flask steady while he fills it from his bottle, gin splashing on her hands. She screws the cap back on and slips the flask into her garter, allowing him the briefest glimpse of leg above the rolled top of her stocking.

Last night, she says, licking the spilled alcohol off her wrist, Mother told me I'm going to hell. Ever since I bobbed my hair she's been nothing but a wet smack.

Old Gordon and Company. Charlie holds the bottle up to the street light.

They pull away from the curb toward Broadway, accelerating past a slow-clopping hansom, its curtains drawn. The engine roars as Charlie misses a gear.

Look at that poor nigger up there in the rain, he says.

She acts like I did it for revenge or something. After Father died.

Charlie turns onto Broadway, drives through the Tenderloin and past Herald Square into a red and green splash of electric lights. They are suddenly weaving through traffic — a limousine to their right, an old Tin Lizzie to their left — and under the lighted billboards of Times Square, the advertisements for Cadillac, Victrola, Macy's.

Are you still going to work for your father this fall, Charlie?

Charlie shrugs, a shrug that turns somewhat into a shiver. I don't know, he says. I don't know. Can you see me sitting in that office? Can you see me behind one of those desks?

Virginia squints at him. Almost, she says. Thinking, *Look at me. In this big old car with Charlie Stroud. A vamp.* She delights in the idea of a world so unavailable to her mother. Theda Bara's got nothing on Virginia Price.

So where are you taking me this time? She rolls the gin bottle back and forth on the seat between them and, when she has his attention, takes a swig from it, making a face for him.

Good old Gin, he says, smiling ahead at the street.

The Black and White?

That clip joint? he says scornfully.

The Whitefoot?

Not tonight.

When are you going to take me to see *Outlook*? I just love that Alfred Lunt.

When is your mother going to Connecticut again?

Probably never. After last time? Probably never.

He turns west on Fifty-first, leaving the lights and noise of Broadway behind.

Charlie?

He parks and sets the handbrake next to an old brownstone, its three stories diminished and small between a pair of newer, cleaner buildings. The rain has dwindled, and the asphalt exhales threads of early morning fog, diffusing the yellow glow of the street lights.

Voilà la Tryst, Charlie says. He steps out and walks around to open her door, offering her his arm.

She places her fingers on his sleeve, charmed. A girl who sneaked out of her mother's house at one in the morning. French, even, she says.

She wears her favorite silk chemise and a single, long string of wooden beads. A brief eruption of pink and green on these rain-soaked streets. She loves New York at this hour. After the yawning departure of the dinner and theater crowds but before the drunken exodus from the speaks and cabarets. When each noise on the street stands so isolated and alone. Like a breath being held is how she thinks of it. Somewhere west of them, toward Hell's Kitchen, a dog barks. On the other side of the street, a cop walks his beat, heels clicking like faint applause. Glass breaks, and distant, shrill laughter drifts down from the rooftops.

At the first window, the first darkened pane of glass, Charlie turns to check his reflection. He straightens the lapels of his tux and presses at his brilliantined hair. Pleased, he takes her hands and forces her into a quick boneless turkey trot, bouncing her nearly to the curb. Charlie, she says, laughing.

At the door, he says, Your eye makeup is running, sweetie.

It's the rain, she says, touching her eyes, tasting her lipstick. The Tryst, Charlie? Now why is that familiar?

Gloria Gray.

Charlie!

Grinning, he opens the door, motioning her into a narrow, dim hallway, a thin green carpet moist with rain, smelling faintly of urine. Think what your friends at school will say.

Think what Mother would say.

Your mother won't find out, thank God. He knocks on the inside door. Last time I checked, she thought I was honorable.

The door cracks. Charlie touches Virginia's bare shoulders, then the outside of her thigh, reaching under her dress. Charlie! she says, slapping him on the shoulder. He grins and waves her flask at the opening door. He whispers into her cheek, Sorry.

Inside, he pays the doorman ten dollars for the two of them, not so much as some places but still expensive for such a late-night showing of anything. The doorman points to her hip and shakes his finger, then gestures to the bar at the end of the room. Charlie takes her by the elbow, steering her toward an empty table beside the dance floor.

Shouldn't we wait for the maitre d'?

He pulls out her chair. We'd be waiting all night, he says.

A small cabaret. Twenty or so oven-sized tables around the dance floor and a dozen stools at the bar. There are so many of these little midtown speaks now, most of them half hidden in converted brownstones in the West Forties and Fifties. Not much of a crowd, even for a Thursday night.

Since her father's death, since the removal of the only opinion in the world she had ever valued, she has come to hunger for these places. These overturned containers of smoke and laughter and jazz. Loves the sudden deflation of her stomach as she walks through the door. The involuntary smile scratched from her lips. She is starved for places with possibilities. On the best nights, anything might happen. Simply anything.

Gin Price in the Tryst.

The Tryst with garish folds of red damask draped on its walls and a dance floor made of unfinished boards set edge to edge. Not long ago, this had been someone's home. A narrow stripe of brick still shows through the plaster on the walls, floor to ceiling, where the receiving room walls were torn out.

Charlie glances around. There's Sophie Tucker, he says, jerking his head.

Where?

There.

Oh sure, she says, although there are at least ten older women on that side of the room, each with her man, each with her delicately held soda glass mixed with gin or bourbon, maybe absinthe. Absinthe has been making the rounds again.

The room smells of cigars and cigarettes, of leather soles and sweat and cheap perfume. She'll have to talk to Molly about washing her clothes right away. Before her mother can get hold of them.

Charlie pulls his flask out of his jacket and turns his back to the bar, taking a quick drink. To Izzy, he says.

To Izzy. Virginia raises her own flask. This old toast of Charlie's. Izzy Einstein, the speakeasy raider.

A cigarette girl brushes past, shrugging out of the leather straps and setting her tray on the floor. She leans against the wall and rubs her eyes, looking suddenly tired and much younger. She picks a cigarette off her ear and, after lighting it, blows smoke through her nose. Virginia makes a mental note to learn the trick.

The band members — the only blacks in the room — take their drinks to the folding chairs on either side of the stage. Costumed in a motley assembly of jackets, black and gray, with mismatched cummerbunds and bow ties, they settle into the seats, their faces lost in shadows. There is the metallic clang and rustle of instruments being raised, then a few moments of tuning, a quick glissando riff from the tenor sax, a single long pulsing note from the cornet. The alto sax player squeaks through his mouthpiece, then gives it a shake with his wrist. Virginia sees a trumpet, a trombone, a guitar. A set of drums glittering in the corner and an ancient upright piano flat against the wall. This is the first time she's seen a speak that allows the band to drink with the customers. A defiance of convention that may account for the empty tables. Even in the big Harlem clubs, the blacks drink in the back.

The lights, poor as they are, dim with an audible snap and hum. A spotlight hits the stage. The curtains rustle and the guitar player strums a high wooden chord, accompanied by a single pulsing note from the cornet. A tentative, nervous woman in frayed tassels beats a tambourine slowly against her hip. Two octoroon women, wearing only grass skirts and silver scoops over their breasts, sway onto the floor, rustling the grass at their hips. Hula dancing has been all the rage this season. A second pair of dancers follows the first, then another, until six women are swaying in a line. Charlie leans over to her and says conspiratorially, I just love these high yellows.

The dancers flank the stage, three to the left, three to the right, moving slower as the pulse of music dwindles. The band stops playing altogether, creating a tense silence, and the girls dance now only with their hands.

Into the pause, the alto sax begins playing a repeating phrase of slow, sexy blues. On the fourth beat, two thin hands pull the stage curtains apart, followed by a single bare leg. The tenor sax joins the alto and the phrase grows more complicated, faster. The drums kick once, twice, and suddenly all the pieces of the orchestra — the flashing drumsticks and swaying heads and white eyes and distended cheeks behind brass horns — blend into a single, orchestrated melody. The bare leg is followed by another, and one of the legs gives a kick. Gloria Gray steps out from behind the curtains, wearing only a flamingo-feather skirt and a mass of beads draped over her otherwise bare breasts, a carved wooden crown of snakes tilted back on her head. The band takes the threads of the earlier melody and erupts into a shredded, frantic jazz improvisation. Gloria bobs downstage, kicking, strutting, twirling on her heels. In defiance of all fashion, she has kept her black hair long and straight, draped over a pair of shoulders the color of stained pine. She steps to the edge of the floor, above Charlie and Virginia, and stands passively unwound, waiting for the music to catch up.

The band pauses, gathers, then bursts into the blues, every note as quick and hard as a heel on the floor. The woman flings her crown of snakes to the back of the stage and drops her arms, shaking her breasts in time to the music.

My God, Charlie, Virginia whispers, what is she *doing?*

The shimmy, sister.

Is she part Negro?

Polish, I think.

Virginia shakes her head, leaning back in her chair and discreetly sipping from her flask. Some part of her is appalled. Some other part of her swings her shoulders to the beat.

Charlie nudges her with his elbow and Virginia looks up to see the woman laughing down, winking hugely. She places her hands on her knees and bends down, pursing her lips at Charlie. Virginia looks at him. This man she loves. This man whose hand has found the top of her thigh. Who sits blowing kisses to Gloria Gray.

12

THEY STAND on the hillside in front of the girl, Henry and his mother. He feels her hand move from his sleeve to the small of his back. Placed there not for stability, he knows, but confirmation. Yes, he is still here. When he is away from her, she follows him with her eyes, the way a blind man will trace a wall to find its corner. She had been pretty in her youth — he has seen the photos — pretty and capable, strength in her like a raised fist. But coming home like this, seeing her fresh . . . There's damage in her. The hungry, anxious way she watches him eat his meals, the way she waits for his approval.

He flicks the ash of his cigarette.

She must like the girl, having coiled her braids into a bun. Maybe to make herself seem less Indian. The Crow he's known don't seem to care one way or the other about sleeping around.

Aware of it or not, this little white girl may have found the only woman in Wyoming not likely to see her as a whore. He steps away from them, smoking his cigarette.

She's never fit in anywhere, his mother. An orphan born into a people who value few things above family. As a girl, she had lived downstream from the tribe's slaughterhouse, and has told him how the waters of the Little Bighorn would run red on cleaning days, how the banks would bleed. Hard times, those. Typhoid, diphtheria, tuberculosis. Evenings, sitting outside their first small cabin, he would listen to her describe the rows of burial platforms blooming from the riverbottom cottonwoods of her youth: horrors painted in that soft, inflectionless voice of hers.

He has never seen his parents kiss on the lips, but, growing up, if his mother was in the mood to tell her stories, he would sometimes watch Frank touch the back of her neck, put a quick arm around her waist. Who took you away from all that? his father would ask. And she would cover his fingers with her hand. You did, Frank. You did. And he would kiss her cheek.

Those first couple of years on the North Fork. Good years. Before the sharp edge of his father's excitement had dulled into angry compromise. Evenings, his father would point and pace, gesturing at the mountains, using his hands to shape out the ranch he said he had always wanted. Telling them where the fences would run, how their first few piebald Durhams would grow into a herd. And then the looks his mother would give Frank. The admiration.

Shit, Henry thinks. And spits.

He watches his mother lift her heels in and out of her black patent leather shoes, roll a stalk of wild barley between her fingers. She's always been one to pick plants, his mother, taking walks in the hills only to bring back sprigs of foliage for the house. Not necessarily flowers, although those, too: the brief bloom of a prickly pear, small buds of phlox. More often branches of sage, handfuls of wheatgrass. A sprig of wild currant to thread through the legs of the crucifix above the fireplace.

She jabs his shoulder with her index finger and purses her lips, using them to point, in Indian fashion, toward the house. Without waiting for him, she turns and takes a series of sliding, clumsy steps down the hill, hurrying back to her laundry. He has missed something, and is left standing awkwardly before the girl. She stares at him.

You draw? he asks, gesturing at the sketchpad with his cigarette.

Well, no. Not really. Yes. Maybe.

He kneels and stubs out his cigarette in the dirt, taking the pad off her knees.

Just go right ahead and help yourself there, she says.

13

SHE WATCHES him flip through her drawings, feeling the familiar sense of nakedness, of exposure.

The first three or four pages are studies of her own ankles and shoes, the hems of the long dresses her mother had insisted she wear while traveling. Once away from the city, she had changed into a red woolen skirt from B. Altman. It had a matching jacket and gray leather belt. Here is her silk-stockinged knee, crossed over a leg. A smudged line down the flat of her shin to mark the muscle of her calf. She is proud of that particular line, that particular smear. She got it just right. She loves her own ankles. The thinness in them.

He turns the pages, impassive.

An ancient, crooked tepee that had been standing beside the

train tracks in Billings: rotten leather sagging on poles and an Indian woman beside the open flap. Virginia had drawn only a suggestion of the tepee, concentrating instead on the woman. Her dull black eyes staring intently at the train. In a landscape of utter similarity, one has no choice but to watch the one thing that will move, that will change. It had been easy to sketch the braids and the precise angle of her cheeks, but the blouse had been difficult — a man's white dress shirt buttoned to the collar, untucked over a greasy leather skirt.

He spends the same amount of time on each drawing, a few heartbeats. Without reaction.

Cat studies, sketched from memory. They had not been allowed pets at finishing school, but there had been a stray calico — a battle-scarred, accordion-ribbed old thing — which she had taken to feeding out on the ledge of her dorm room window, fattening it on smuggled chicken bones and pork ribs. She may have got the rest of the cat wrong, but that scar, that white slash running eyebrow to chin, she had got that just right.

Her aunt's sleeping face. Skin wrinkled and pale under her spectacles. The mouth loose and empty. Hair pulled tight enough to stretch the corners of the eyes. An aristocratic face, her aunt's. Kinder, somehow, in these postures of vulnerability. Looking at these drawings now, she sees aspects of her father's face in Pauline's, aspects of her own. That smallish, pug nose of hers. What is there about her that might get passed on? Odd that she hasn't thought of this before. What is there that might be worth giving to another person? She just hopes it doesn't get Charlie's ears.

Henry closes the pad and hands it to her. Lights another cigarette. Says, You should be careful.

Careful?

Rattlesnakes on these dry hillsides.

She gathers the pad under her arm.

You saw that skin stretched over the door? Down in the

lodge? Five foot three inches without the rattles. I shot it around the hill there. Not twenty feet around the hill there.

I'd like to draw a snake that big, she says, trying to elicit a reaction.

But there is no change in him at all. His black eyes. *His black eyes,* she thinks.

We'll be leaving early, he says. You might want to turn in after supper.

14

HER AUNT leans heavily on Virginia's arm, bird-boned ankles unhinging on the riverbank gravel. They step over a knot of driftwood, then around a wagon-sized boulder lodged in the sand. Her aunt says, Get your fingers out of your mouth, child. You're too old for nail-biting.

They follow a stock trail away from the river, over the rise of a small clay bank. Virginia pinches off a sprig of prairie rose and brings it to her nose, staring in at the cluster of red berries. When was the last time you saw Father?

Phillip?

Didn't you go with us on his last drag hunt?

You know what I think of those hunts. Dragging meat behind a horse. Pauline makes a face and stands breathing, resting. Is that a bluebird? No, I suppose not. It looked blue. I believe I saw him last March. Why?

What was in March? I can't remember.

Your mother changed the locks on your front door. You remember. Phillip was furious.

After he nailed the bed to the floor.

That's right.

Mother was furious herself.

Well, *she* was the one who liked to rearrange the furniture. Pauline shakes her head, touching her lower lip with a fingertip. I never knew what Phillip saw in your mother. They were so different. So different.

Virginia shrugs, suddenly uncomfortable. I was just wondering what he would have to say about all this. This ranch. I can't imagine.

I can imagine it perfectly well.

A half mile behind them, at the lodge, they hear the faint sound of the cook rattling a serving spoon across the welded chain of horseshoes hanging off the porch. They turn around at once, her aunt being part of that nineteenth-century school that still finds it proper to change costumes before each meal.

Virginia sucks her thumbnail. I'm going riding, she says, glancing at her aunt. Henry invited me.

Pauline pulls Virginia's thumb away from her mouth. You certainly are not.

His mother said it was okay. Rose.

Well. Indians. You are *not* going riding.

Adze would be going with us as chaperone.

As ugly as he is, that's one person I want you to stay away from.

He seems nice.

As ugly as he is? Gracious, child. You'll have a baby that's nothing but wrinkles.

I don't see that it could make a difference.

You remember Penny Wright? They had that flat on Forty-fifth Street? Her husband took care of their neighbor's basset hound when Penny was three months along and that baby turned out to be the saddest child you've ever seen. No. No. No. You want to be careful with things like that when you're pregnant. No, if I were you, I would be spending my time thinking about finding a husband back home, not about gallivanting around in these mountains.

I just thought while we were out here . . .

Think about finding a husband. About how you're going to explain your nice new stretch marks to him on your wedding night.

Exercise has steadied the old woman's hand inside Virginia's elbow, but the girl feels no squeeze of reassurance, no pinch of spite. Virginia walks withdrawn, silenced by the nonchalance of the old woman's unkindness.

They've been eating their evening meals at the oak dining table in the great room, under the antlers of a crudely mounted bull elk and the dusty, unlidded eyes of a mule deer buck. Between these two matched gazes, the room has been overfurnished with a leather couch and a pair of mismatched cowhide chairs, a buffalo rug and a coffee table made from the thin cross section of a Douglas fir. Above the fireplace, a buffalo's head carved from a chunk of mahogany: a rough, unintentional parody of the carving over the backbar of the Irma Hotel in Cody. Tacked here and there to the walls and folded over the back of the couch are the bright, draped blooms of Rose's Navajo rugs, Pendleton blankets.

Pauline and Virginia sit across from each other at a remove from Frank and Rose, a centerpiece of fried steaks and potatoes on the tablecloth between them. As with previous evening meals, no one else sits at the table. No ranch hands, no neighbors. Mohr's misconceived notion of class-mingling, maybe. Or perhaps, Virginia has thought, it's only a reflection of job schedules. In any case, everyone else on the ranch has to wait until they finish.

Ah Ting backs through the kitchen door, setting a single thick omelet in front of Mohr. Egg pie, he says, bowing.

Ah Ting would be a handsome man, Virginia thinks, were it not for his two big ears. She has seen the cowboys mimic them with gourds held to their temples. He retreats to the kitchen, his queue immaculate between his shoulders.

Pauline spreads a napkin on her lap. You have a jewel in that little Chinaman, she says.

He's confused, Mohr calls out toward the kitchen door. Confused about breakfast and supper. I want you to look there at all them eggs.

I don't mind them, Virginia says. Eggs are one of the few foods she can stand to eat. She's found that she can't abide steak, for instance. Every forkful tastes as if it's been dipped in coffee.

Rose folds her hands into a knuckleless ball and drops her head. Not caring much for prayer these days, Virginia keeps her eyes open, watching Rose transform herself from obedient housewife to confident deacon. The same prayer every evening: a rattle of rising and falling syllables, a chant with no single word distinguishable from the next.

Rose finishes but keeps her head bowed, hands folded. Mohr picks up his Bible from the corner of the table and thumbs through the age-inflated pages, randomly picking a passage.

This un's from Proverbs, he says. These six things doth the Lord hate: yea, seven are an abomination unto him: a proud look, a lying tongue, and hands that shed innocent blood. An heart that deviseth wicked imaginations, feet that be swift in running to mischief. A false witness that speaketh lies, and he that soweth discord among brethren.

He closes the Bible. Don't wait on us, he says.

Virginia reaches for the spatula and slides one of the smaller steaks onto her aunt's plate.

Not to mention, Mohr says to no one in particular, taking up a tin serving spoon and digging into the potatoes. Not to mention that we can't get him to stop boiling heads of lettuce. Lettuce, I said. Boils it like spaghetti.

"I'm a romantic, I suppose. As much of a romantic as you'll find these days."

She touched the pitcher of iced tea, feeling for moisture, then moved it a few inches to the side, using the cuff of her sleeve to wipe at the ring. I lifted the pitcher and set it on the knee of my jeans, drying it off.

She nodded, approving. "A romantic," she said. "A romantic who tends to believe that emotions stand apart. There are two of you, and it's true that the two of you never cease to be alone." She held up her paired index fingers, then twisted them together. "But there are thirds between you as well. Hate, envy, pride. Love."

15

THE FIRST HORSE she had ever loved was an Arabian, a high-strung (as what Arabian is not?) mare named Maiden Voyage. A lovely horse, but she had needed more riding than Virginia, at nine years old, had been able to give her. Their favorite Central Park bridle path had run beside the duck pond, and the first time she had kicked Maiden in the ribs, looking for a trot, there had suddenly been no horse under her. She had landed in the soft mud of the bank, her face twisting into a cry even as she flew through the air. She remembers the knot on her hip and her father kneeling beside her. She is in his arms and being hugged, being rocked. The smell of his cologne. The crinkling of his celluloid collar. He is hugging her and rocking her and saying, Shhhhst, shhhhst, little girl, it's all right. Nothing's hurt but a butt, little girl, little doll. She remembers the solid security of his chest, his arms. Nothing could hurt her there. He takes a folded white handkerchief from his breast pocket and pats her cheeks, cheeks that are already trying to smile. He takes a corner and dabs it around her eyes. See now.

Henry and Adze carry saddles from the tack room, a low-ceilinged, mud-mortared cabin beside the corrals. Through the open door, she catches glimpses of lariats and nickel-plated spade bits hung on hand-carved pegs; hackamores and hobbles, mecates and tightly coiled magueys. *What lovely words,* she thinks. Like marbles rolling in the mouth.

She sits on a fencerail, fidgeting, glancing toward her aunt's cabin. The morning's early light drifts slow as a minute hand down into the green shadow of the valley.

The horses stand at their grain bins, crunching oats, licking into the corners of their boxes. Adze heaves the saddle, a square-rigged Hamley, over the back of the first horse, the saddle plain but for a worn stamping of roses on each fender. Reluctantly, she has to agree with her aunt: Adze is one of the ugliest men she's ever seen. Such short legs, such a long torso. Bunches of gray hair inside his nose and ears, and wrinkles in his face deep enough to make her think of clay squeezed through fingers.

I can help with that, she says.

He grins at her, showing his few remaining front teeth. The day I let a woman saddle her own horse is the day they plant me in that cowboy garden up on the hill.

I can do it, though.

But I don't guess you will. This is old Arano here.

Virginia drops off the fence and steps up to the horse. An aging dun gelding, its tail and mane the color of tree bark. She runs her fingers along under the halter, checking the fit. Pleased to meet you, Arano.

Henry named him off a Salinas rodeo me and him went to back when Hank was just a tadpole. Remember that rodeo, Hank?

Henry nods, throwing a saddle over his own horse. A long-legged bay stallion, blazed on the nose. He cinches the saddle then waits, strap in his hands. The horse exhales, and Henry tightens the cinch, standing up in one stirrup, then back down.

This old boy here is Charleston, Adze says, patting the largest of the four horses, a big sorrel stallion. Charleston, since he likes to dance around so much. I got him from some sumbuck in Cody likes to train horses with logging chains. So just don't wave nothin around his head.

Henry stands beside the packhorse, hefting a pair of heavy rawhide panniers. Satisfied with their equal weight, he slings them over the double-rigged sawbuck, one on each side. Heya, Bear, he says, touching the horse on the back, running his fingers along an old cinch scar, then down along the tail, the hair worn to gray skin.

Do you like to dance, Adze?

Miss? Adze takes his saddle, a Visalia centerfire rig, and heaves it over the sorrel.

You named your horse Charleston.

I didn't name him. That dancin fool behind you did.

Do you like to dance, Henry?

Some.

I love to dance, she says.

Henry moves deliberately around the horses, dismissing her through the care he pays to his work.

Adze backs Arano away from the grain bins, pulling low at the bridle, one hand over the bridge of its nose. *Showing off,* Virginia thinks. He holds a stirrup open for her. Miss, he says.

She swings smoothly into the saddle, immediately feeling the most agreeable sense of . . . of . . . *slipping.* A horse under her again. But no double reins as she's used to. And she can already tell she's going to have a hard time getting used to these western saddles. Nothing like those thin, pancake saddles back home. It feels like a wad of mattress under her. But maybe it will be better for the baby.

She thinks that she should probably go pee. No outhouses in

the mountains. She decides that she certainly should go pee. Henry is already mounted, and Adze is just now grabbing his horn, lifting one short leg impossibly high into the stirrup. She dismounts and walks her horse over to Henry. You can hold these for a minute, she says, handing him the reins.

He accepts the straps, eyes lowered. Their hands touch on the common strand of leather, the pad of his forefinger on the back of her thumb. She is aware of her own skin, the heat of it. The moistness of it.

He suddenly straightens, gathering the reins. We'll be waiting, he says.

16

GODDAMNIT but he feels bad.

A tarnished-silver morning and the smell of dew. A throb behind his eyes and the ground sloshing around under him. They ride in no order or design but the one established by the horses, holding to their own idea of rank and station. He's anxious to get into the hills, away from the road. They trot through the hay meadow above the ranch. The horses, long accustomed to this field, jump the irrigation ditch with only the slightest encouragement from the heels. He leans forward and pats the horse's neck. Good ol Tony, he says. Named after the first Tom Mix movie he'd ever seen. What was that picture? Tony's six years old, so Henry would have named him just before leaving for France. *What the hell was that picture?* That's goin a bother me all day, he says to the horse.

He turns in the saddle, inspecting the panniers. Good ol Bear, he says. The horse seems settled enough, and so he threads the lead rope through a saddle ring. Not something he'd do with any other packhorse. They cross the road and turn east. At Whit Creek they startle a pair of sandhill cranes up from stilt-legged meditation. The birds take ponderous flight, calling to each other with a sound like the ratcheting of a thousand spoons down a thousand washboards. The sun cracks the horizon and the birds disappear into the morning, clapped between a pair of hands.

They turn southeast toward Britisher Creek, toward the sear brown volcanic spine of Stovepipe, the horses twitching against new flies. His mouth, already dry from last night's hooch, evaporates into a wad of cotton around the stick of his tongue. He reaches back and unbuckles his saddlebags. Empty save for that tattered copy of *Three Soldiers,* in there since the last trip. In the morning's fog of booze, he had forgotten his canteen. Goddamnit but he feels bad. Head like a goddamn church choir. The morning glows overbright and he swallows against a faint nausea. He thinks about all that moonshine in the panniers. A quick swig would sure cut this hangover.

The girl heels Arano down a sidehill and past Adze, grinning back. The Charleston horse, who doesn't understand foolishness, trots past her until he's in the lead again, kicking at Arano on the way by. Adze's dog, a filthy mongrel with the face of a blue heeler and the tail of a coyote, trails behind, eating grasshoppers. Bowing up and cocking his ears, pouncing into the grass with his forepaws and crunching broken yellow wings back in his jaws, eyes half closed with pleasure. The girl shifts around — lifting her feet in and out of her stirrups, stretching her knees — but he thinks she's just getting used to the fit of the saddle. She seems to have a good seat.

They cross Mohr's eastern fence, the wires rusted and pulled askew, twisted. In the years he's been gone, the place has sure gone to hell. Parts of it, anyway. Half a dozen cows and calves lie in the shade under the creekbank, chewing cud. Humped islands of shit-smeared flanks and catenary spines. Speckle-faced beasts, inconsistently horned and untraceable in blood or bearing. The first small herd of Durhams had been polluted and polluted again by bulls bought cheap, regardless of size, shape, or color. Beef's beef, his father always says, maintaining that the man who sits down in a restaurant shouldn't care what his steak used to look like. But then each fall he'd spend weeks moaning that his stock didn't sell for more.

His father charges forty bucks a gallon for this booze of his. That still with its big copper boiler could make ten gallons a day if it had to. Except for some competition from Jack Spicer and, rumor has it, Jimmy Tuff over on Rattlesnake, Frank Mohr's got the North and South Fork licked. Truth is, this whole county couldn't drink enough booze to run that boiler every day. Frank might be making as much as a hundred a week. New car every month.

They ride past the Finnerman homestead, the cabin stacked together from unpeeled timbers, splayed purlins, and a ridgepole sticking straight out of the hillside. Nice view of the valley, but that's pretty much all it's got. Dry, dry ground. Back behind the cabin, inside a blowdown corral, a crow-footed mule and muddy Percheron standing nose to tail.

Gussy Finnerman comes to the door, sleeves rolled high on her walnut forearms, dishpan in her hands. Here less than a year and already she's taken on the bitter, alkaline color of the soil. Henry lifts his hat to her, then sees her frown, glancing at the packhorse, at Virginia. At the split skirts and tasseled pink blouse. The woman spits off to one side and slings out a fan of dishwater before turning back into the dark hole of her cabin.

Adze puts a hand on his cantle board and twists around, smiling too broadly. How you enjoyin your stay so far, honey?

Henry settles back in his seat and pulls a cigarette from the envelope in his shirt pocket. *Temperance-lovin bitch.* She'll be gone in another year. Two at the most.

Bear stumbles behind him, his breath growing hollow and labored. Henry reins in Tony and lets the horses stand, catching their breath. By God this country's hard on a horse. He'd forgotten that part of it. Steep and hard. Mountainsides full of red gravel worse than cobblestones for bruising frogs. He digs his heel into Tony and nickers him forward.

Up ahead, Adze twists in his saddle. Be glad you're here now instead a next year, Miss, he says. It's goin a be plumb awful. I guarantee you that little yeller cook'll quit when he's got all them new people to cook for. You watch. And no way is that fancy pool goin a be finished by this winter. Hell, it'll just fill in with groundwater come spring. And some poor fool from Rhode Island's goin a pay thirty-five dollars a week for the privilege of puttin up with it all.

Henry said you were from California, Virginia says.

Yes I am, Miss. He faces forward again.

Did you grow up there?

Ohio, he says, talking over his shoulder. Pap was killed at Antietam along with everybody else's pap, so I ended up goin west with my uncle. Got me a chore boy job on the old Jobe place on the Carrizo. Talk about horse trainers. Horse-trainin fools. That's where I took up boxin. Had these fights they'd set up in the yard. Won a few bucks on the side. Nobody ever thought such a little spud would whup em. But I was fast. *Fast!*

Adze throws a few quick jabs over Charleston's head, and the horse shies under him, squatting deep and climbing off the trail: moaning, white-eyed, trembling. Adze reins him down and bends over the neck, whispering. A minute or two later, it lowers its head to feed and Adze trots back down to the trail. Anyhow, he says, riding past.

I saw Dempsey whip Firpo last year, Virginia says.

No!

I did. At the Polo Grounds.

That would a been a sight, he says. And now I'm all set to wrangle dudes. I swear. I suppose they'll want me to sing cowboy songs.

Do you know any cowboy songs?

Few, he says. Want a hear one?

Certainly.

Might as well practice up. He clears his throat into his fist, tilts his head back, and starts in on a verse from "The Mormon Wife," his voice rough and gravelly and oddly suited to the lyrics. From there he moves on to a couple lines from "Wrap Me Up in My Old Yellow Slicker," and finally sings, with great energy, "The Old Chisholm Trail": *Ohhhhh, a hoss threw me off at the creek called Mud. A horse threw me off with the Two-U herd. The last time I saw him he was runnin cross the level. Kickin up his heels and raisin of the devil.*

I like that. Virginia giggles and glances back at Henry. She makes a frown, mocking his bad mood.

That one's got about a thousand verses. Feel like another?

Absolutely.

Ohhhh, old Ben Bolt was a fine ol boss. Rode to see the girls on a sore-backed hoss. Old Ben Bolt was fond of his liquor. Had a little bottle in the pocket of his slicker.

They ride into the timber, removing their hats in deference to the new chill, to the filtered light and fecund smells of moss and pine needles, decaying logs. Flies buzz around the horses: wide as knife blades, small as gnats. Squirrels chatter through fallen limbs and trunks.

Henry wonders if she's going to put all this into her sketchbook. That tree, maybe. That gnarled, lightning-scarred tree. He likes those drawings of hers, but if asked why, he wouldn't be able to put it into any kind of words. It's more of a pleasant melancholy. She notices things, this girl. The buckles on her boots. The square shape of the buttons on that squaw's shirt.

Ohhhhhh, we hit Caldwell and we hit her on the fly. We bedded down the cattle on the hill close by. No chaps no slicker and it's pourin down rain. And I swear I'll never night herd again.

Henry is himself a watcher of things. Of trees. Of fields. Birds and squirrels. Finding in the breath-to-breath, cinematographic frenzy of these small lives a parallel to almost everything he knows about the world. When he's in the woods, he often feels as if he's on the edge of some great revelation. The border squabblings of chickadees, the blackbird harassment of a hawk. The stoppered-flute trill of a meadowlark.

Ohhhhhh, foot in the stirrup and a hand on the horn. Best damned cowboy ever was born. Foot in the stirrup and a seat in the sky. Best damned cowboy ever rode by.

They cross over out of Britisher Creek at seven thousand feet, weaving between spines of volcanic hoodoos, through railcars of tipped rock. The horses labor under them. Behind them, the valley spreads out hazy and distant. He's never ridden in an aeroplane, but it can't have much more to recommend it than this. If you look hard, you can make out the pressed thumbprints of buffalo wallers pocking the valley floor, still visible after fifty years.

She glances back at him again, smiling, trying to share the humor of Adze. A humor *at* Adze. Not knowing who he is. Not realizing how much this old man knows. Damned near *everything.* And if she so misreads Adze, how does she misread him?

Nevertheless, he smiles at her, sharing the joke. She grins wider and turns back, confident in her humor.

In the coming months, he will divide his life front to back around this ride into the mountains.

17

WE'LL BE WAITING, he had said. And what was *that* supposed to mean? She would hate to turn into one of those people who read omens and obligations into every little word. Even so. Inside the eternal push and pull of social overture and response, has he placed some hidden onus on her? Some obligation?

She wonders how he sees her with those dark eyes. Does he see her breasts first? Her growing and painful breasts? Does she favor them without being aware of it? Does he see *her* at all? Maybe he sees only a rich girl from back east. New York money.

They ride parallel to the road through a chaparral fog of juniper: turquoise folded into the hills. They weave among moss-speckled volcanic boulders and into a field of wild grass long since gone to seed, the dry stems pointing in paths toward creatures passed days before. She wonders why Adze doesn't just lead them up the road, then thinks that maybe he's trying to give her a more complete wilderness experience. At first she is offended by the patronization, then she is amused.

They cross over into the valley of the South Fork, stopping for lunch beside an abandoned trapper's cabin, its crooked aspen logs rotting into a soft humus. The man who built this cabin — who purchased these worthless logs with the skin of his hands, the muscles of his back — might still be alive, she supposes. Might be dead. No matter. Eventually to be dead with all certainty. It occurs to her that this building might be old enough to have been one of the first in Wyoming. She's probably read about it in some book. Such a young world she finds herself in.

Henry dismounts by the thin trickle of stream and takes off his hat, cupping water through his hair, drinking from his palm. The horses water at a hand-dug catchbasin below the cabin.

Above them, the pines sway in a soundless wind; below them, on the valley floor, straight, pencil-line smudges of hearthsmoke rise like steaming fumaroles. She can see for miles, all the way across the valley to the next mountain. To that ridgeline of horizon unevenly swaled, as if cut with an awkward pair of scissors. An unknown world of cliffs and canyons, creeks and coulees.

Her name is Virginia Price. She lives on Gramercy Park South. What is she doing here?

Adze loosens the horses' cinches and leads them by their bits into a rough corral tacked up beside the cabin. Henry hops one-legged around the posts, holding his boot by the arch and pounding at loose nails with the heel. The horses shake and blow and reach their noses under the poles for the longer grass just outside. Aspen saplings stand here and there inside the corral, browsed down to the thickness of a thumb.

Adze calls his dog to him, Blue Blue Blue, and pets him roughly, bouncing his head side to side in his open hands. After a moment, he glances up at Virginia. You know, he says, Henry told me just this morning about how he'd like to show you an elk or two.

The dog sits panting between his knees, tongue aloll.

Ain't that right, Hank? But they's not many down this low anymore. That six-point you killed before you left for the war? How far back in were you?

Twenty miles or so. Henry slides his foot back in his boot, stomping into the heel.

Twenty miles. There you go. Maybe after you get back from elk huntin this year you can find her a little bull closer in.

Henry looks at Virginia, then away.

He's shy, she thinks, feeling a sudden, saucy arrogance.

Henry walks over to Adze's saddlebags and pulls out a large paper sack spotted with grease. I'm glad somebody was thinkin, he says.

A few minutes later, on the bank of the creek, Virginia takes off her shoes and socks and digs her toes into the sand. What have you got in there? she asks.

Adze hands her the bag. You do the honors, he says.

She passes out buttermilk biscuits sandwiched over a paste of garlic and roast beef, refried beans and raw tomatoes. A jar of serviceberry pudding rimmed in sawdust from the icebox, a few congealed links of what Rose had called sheboreh.

Mother likes her Indian food, Henry says.

Adze slurps from a pack can of condensed milk and, when he notices Virginia's expression of distaste, smacks his lips. I've heard tell some people waste this in their coffee, he says.

They share a tin of peaches for dessert, spiking the slices out with knives then passing the can back and forth to finish off the syrup. She leans back on her hands, considering the envy of Isabel, her best friend at school. If Isabel only knew where she was right now. Drinking peach syrup out of a can with cowboys. She drops the empty can back into the bag. Inside, flat on the bottom, she sees a single white square of folded paper sealed with a dab of candle wax, Henry's name written across it in a woman's practiced, fluid hand. Rose's hand, she guesses.

Henry, she says, and tosses it across to him.

He catches it against his chest, looking embarrassed as he picks at the wax with a fingernail, shaking out a single large square of fudge into his palm. He breaks it into three equal pieces and passes one to each of them.

Adze nods his thanks, then says, You got no idea how much she's been lookin forward to havin you home.

Virginia nibbles at the edge of her piece. It's good, Henry, she says. It is.

After lunch, while Adze and Henry cinch up the saddles, Virginia walks over to inspect the cabin. There's been at least some use to it: a well-burned firepit just outside the door and, around that pile of ashes, squares of grass still pressed into the afterimages of tents. The lower limbs of the nearest trees broken off for firewood. She pushes against the warped door, wedging herself against the jamb until the boards let go with a shrill shriek. There are no windows in the cabin, and so the only details she can make out are revealed by the angle of light behind her. A packed-dirt floor and a flimsy shelf on the far wall, a few bare soup cans stacked together, their red and white labels curled loose on the floor.

An invisible animal scratches in one corner, startled by the light. There is a single, low squeak, like a nail being pulled. Then scratching again. A small puff of dust drifts into the light. She turns abruptly, standing a good three or four feet out in the yard to stare back into the gloom. Who could say what sort of odd little beasts might live in a place like that.

18

It's late afternoon when they ride into the valley of the South Fork, descending through a yellow floor of haze, the earlier, clear air having been polluted by the fires in the Washakie. There is no wind, and the smoke burns in their lungs. They cross the stream west of Castle Rock, picking east along the bank until they come in sight of Clara Higgins's Broken Arrow Ranch: the black weathervane, the gabled front porch, the doors winged by panes of red-stained glass. Mourning doves call from the strand of phone wire strung to the back of the lodge, fluttering down in waves to land beside the stream.

Inside the yard, a farrier stands bent double beside his horse, filing at a hoof, but otherwise the place is empty. This time of the day, Henry supposes most all the dudes are up in the mountains, maybe off fly-fishing somewhere. Taking naps. Adze glances at Henry, then asks Virginia if she wouldn't mind helping him brush down these ponies. Henry pulls the panniers off Bear, wrapping the rope handles around his wrists, and lets Virginia lead his two horses toward the barn. He carries the panniers across the yard. Clara is already out on the porch waiting for him, one leg caught up on the rail. Forty or fifty yards off toward the guest cabins, a dude lies stretched out under a cottonwood, propped up on one elbow, reading a dime novel.

Mail call, Henry says loudly, for the benefit of the dude.

Took your time, Clara says. She has a paper pouch in her hands, and as he steps up on the porch, he watches her pinch out a tangled wad of black tobacco and shove it deep into a corner of her jaw.

Henry drops the panniers on the porch. Not so much time, he says.

Had a rodeo this afternoon. Clara takes a sip of coffee, spits tobacco juice over the rail. Could a used you. Nobody around here can bulldog worth a damn.

Gettin old for it anyway, Clara.

You're what? she says. Twenty-four? Christ, I can't even remember twenty-four.

Got a sale goin on the hooch. Henry touches the panniers with the toe of his boot. Brought you a full gallon. Some other stuff, too. Some a Mother's good apple butter.

A *gallon?* What do I want with a gallon a that paint thinner?

Well, I guess I can haul it back.

Oh I'll take it. It ain't like it goes bad.

Figured you would.

But a full gallon? Christ. What's that pap a yours think we do over here?

I don't know. Thinkin about that party of yours. Or maybe

he's just tryin to spoil you. He's lookin to wrangle dudes next year.

Oh, I know that. She shakes her head. Bastard, she says. Give a good business a bad name. How's that little celestial they got cookin over there?

I guess he's fine. He don't say much.

Frank stole him off me, you know. I'd give my eyeteeth to get that Chinaman back.

Well, he ain't all that happy. Pap threw out a batch a rice wine he had cookin under the sink.

That rice wine, she says, shaking her head.

Stunk, Henry says. Smelled like socks boilin.

You know, people are makin bets about where he gets his booze. Where he keeps that still of his. Big mystery.

I heard that.

Even old Loomis was askin about it.

Loomis? With all that Pap pays to keep him out of it?

You ever think about goin into the business yourself? I'd rather buy this poison off somebody young and good lookin than somebody so old and sour.

Henry looks at her. Holding her coffee mug by the rim, drinking it like a man. He looks past her at the corrals and loading chute, logs so new they shine. At the slatted snowfence above her stacks of hay. Everything clean, well oiled. Way a ranch should be run.

Thought about it, he finally says.

19

THE DANCE BEGINS with the lighting of the electric bulbs strung tree to tree. Clara's biggest party of the year, and she's had the lower trunks of the cottonwoods whitewashed to resemble the pillars of a cotillion. The buffet tables, set beyond the lights and away from insects, bow under platters of sliced beef and ham, bowls of macaroni salad and baked beans, a cake that spells out, in blue icing, "Farewell Friends." Over it all, from its housing behind the barn, the persistent buzz of the Kohler electrical plant.

Virginia stands alone, feeling awkward and conspicuous. This unexpected celebration. Above her, bulbs swing to the beat of swarming moths. Her shadow trembles at her feet. She watches three men unfold chairs on a stage of overturned packing crates, two of the men carrying hard leather fiddle cases and the third walking with a long-necked banjo cradled in both arms. The banjo player pulls a harmonica from his shirt pocket and blows a tuning note; the two fiddlers twist at pegs, striking brief chords with their bows. At these first, discordant sounds, a few of the dudes emerge from their cabins to start drifting toward the buffet tables.

It turns out that the banjo player is competent, though unextravagant, sitting with all his concentration focused on his left hand, strumming more than he picks. And the second fiddle is acceptable, compensating for his simple chords by turning circles on the stage and bending at the waist, up and down, up and down. But the first fiddle player is a master, for all that he doesn't move, doesn't smile. An old man with a battered Stetson hat pulled low over his eyes and a gray pallor to his skin like cigarette ash. But he works at his fiddle as if he's fighting off bees.

A young cowboy with a fist of black hair punching out from the collar of his shirt starts to dance on the grass alone, clapping his hands. As he dances, he periodically tilts his head back and bugles like a bull elk, shrill and piercing. A couple who had been holding hands under the trees go out onto the grass, pressing chest to chest and hand to hand and moving stiffly through the steps of a cowboy waltz learned just these last few weeks. The banjo player hits the opening chords of "Backstep Cindy," and one of the older ranch hands — a man with a fleshy moon-face and a bald crown that he is already wiping dry with a handkerchief — climbs up on the stage between the fiddle players. Virginia thinks he's going to sing, but he doesn't. He curls a newspaper into his fist and holds it to his mouth and starts in on an auctioneer's banter: a wordless, nonsensical rhythm that is strangely appropriate to the tune. He's not selling anything, though; or if he is, it is only the empty dance floor. Knots of dudes stand clustered under the lights: men in boots and spurs, shirts with mother-of-pearl buttons and pockets stitched in foil. Babies asleep in slings at their mothers' stomachs. Children play tag through the trees. Eventually the dance floor fills: a green and watered island of electric light, charged with motion.

Now Clara comes to dance in the center of them all. Short and fat, her cheeks and chin flushed with the pleasure of it, the exertion. She swings with great energy one man to another, and when a man isn't to be found she stands alone, clapping and stomping on the sod with one heavy foot. Denim shirt and overalls and no distinct line between her breasts and belly and hips. Her hair braided down her back, coarse as a horse's tail. She sashays forward and back, yelling out mistimed lyrics. As she dances, small children turn to their parents, whispering. Between numbers, Clara walks to the flimsy tables flanking the stage, scooping out drinks from the cloisonné punch bowl. Fresh-pressed apple cider spiked with enough moonshine to turn it clear. (Only a few hours ago, this same woman had hugged Virginia close and called her a poor creature. Poor thing, she had said, talking in what Virginia could have sworn was a Boston accent. Staying with that Frank Mohr. He is *not* a gentleman. When you get tired of that crowd over the hill, you just come stay with me.)

Virginia walks away from the dance, carrying her own cup of cider. Sipping at it. Afraid to more than sip at it. She stops above the river and stares north into the mountains. *Wyoming,* she thinks. Above her, a black tin sky shot through with silver holes. She shivers, the bonfire gone from her clothes. The heat in the ground rises and dissipates with perceptible speed: a roll of temperature flowing foot to face. Wyoming, she says out loud.

Behind her, a throat clears. On a log just inside the fringe of willows, a dark form stretches out its legs. The tip of a cigarette glows.

You startled me, she says.

I guess I should a been talkin to myself. Henry pushes himself to his feet, twisting at his back. Dern, he says. Ain't used to all this riding.

You hadn't told me we would be spending the night here.

You got someplace you need to be?

She turns away from him. All those stars, she says.

Henry stretches out his arm, and she is very aware of the movement. Cassiopeia, he says, tracing it out with his finger. Ursa Minor. Ursa Major. The North Star. That's Orion's belt and that one there's Jupiter, I think. He drops his hand and brings it to his mouth and draws on his cigarette. I'd guess it'd be easy to forget em in the city.

A careful voice, she thinks. An enunciated voice. The rhythms of it *fit*. It makes no attempt to dominate, to carry.

We aren't going back home the same way we came over, are we? she asks.

Thought we would.

I would hate to see those same old mountains when there are all these new ones.

I suppose we could go around the other side of Table Mountain, he says, blowing smoke. Come out down on Green Creek.

That's just fine.

It'll be an awful hard day for you.

I'm not the one with the sore back.

A breeze kicks at the sand around their legs, riffles at the water. To the west, an inkblot of cloud rises to eclipse the stars: an open maw of haze.

Rain coming, maybe, he says.

The clouds flicker within themselves, like bulbs behind a shade. But before she can remark on it, tell him that she's never seen such a thing before, a single branch of lightning threads away from the first edge of the clouds and pounds into the high ridgeline above them, flashing the world into a stark negative, throwing sparks from a single, isolated tree. They blink, and adjust to the darkness again. A deeper darkness now.

Not somethin you see every day. Henry drops his cigarette in the dirt, grinding it out with his toe. A curiously delicate gesture. I guess Adze is staying here for a day or two. Got an old gal he's sweet on.

Well, I can't believe it, she says, preparing to laugh with him.

But he has already turned to leave. And rather than going back to the dance, as she had expected, he is walking farther up the riverbank. Away from her.

His absence is somehow more compelling than his presence.

20

HE HAD BEEN in school at Wapiti no more than a month before they'd started calling him dumb Indian. Nine years old and dumb as he understood animals to be dumb. Mute. Voiceless. And for all his resentment, he had been aware of where the name-calling had come from. He's just never been much good at conversation. Never seen the point in talking when there's nothing to say.

They have been riding through the blackened, checkered bones of an old burn: empty trees tilted like gravestones among weedbed thickets of aspen saplings. Four-foot pines and low clouds of serviceberry bushes. He makes a note of the serviceberries, thinking he'll have to mention them to his mother. The horses snake their way over whatever trail might be hidden in this undergrowth. Virginia rides two or three lengths behind him, trying to save her horse from getting kicked. His Tony horse has sure come to have a short fuse about Arano.

He turns in his saddle. You ride pretty good for an eastern girl, he says. But then sees his mistake even as he makes it. Eastern Girl. Her mouth pinches.

Where'd you learn it? Ridin.

Fox hunting. Mostly.

And are you likin it so far? Wyoming?

The pinch in her mouth smoothes and she seems to consider his question with undue gravity. I feel like the girl in that old Tom Mix movie, she says. Where she goes west and everybody treats her like . . . like she's from outer space or something.

What movie was that?

I don't know. *Local Color?* Wasn't it? I think *Local Color.*

Thank you, he says. For that name. Thank you for that name.

They're seven or eight miles into the mountains before they start to smell the smoke. Fresh, heavy smoke. He realizes that the horses have been smelling it for some time. In the narrow space of this ravine, under a tilted wall of hanging rocks, there's no telling where it might be coming from. He stands in his stirrups, looking ahead, looking back. Impossible to tell. The smell grows stronger as they ride, and then it is visible around them: a febrile haze that sinks rather than rises, collecting around the slightest windbreaks. The trunk of every tree unravels in acrid threads. The horses pull against their reins and break into a trot. Clattering, stumbling over stones. The light turns a jaundiced, filtered yellow. But it is only as they move into an old avalanche of tumbledown shale — the trail pressed into the rock as if with a roller — that they see the flames. The ridgeline west of them, above them, burning. The smoke unrolling from it to cloud the entire horizon. Even at this distance they can hear the roar of the fire, the feeding, bestial growl of it.

Against all impulse and instinct, Henry reins in his horse. Virginia stops behind him, Arano stepping nervously. Henry studies their narrow slice of shale. Judges it. Rejects it. Immediately behind them, the ridgeline smokes without visible flames, as if heated from below.

They sit their horses inside this bowl of burning ridges, this cupped hand of smoke.

I watched her pick cookies from a paper sleeve, arranging them around a crystal tray. "These last years of brunches and ladies' club meetings have meant so little," she said. "The days disappear as soon as they've begun. But that ride through the mountains has threaded itself through every memory I own. The day I think I might have started the long process of growing up. Growing old."

She nudged me with her elbow, as if to share a joke. "And now I am *old!"*

21

AS A GIRL, she had once upset her father's reading lamp, spilling oil and fire across the sleeve of her dress. She still has the scar, although it has diminished with age: a serpentine curl of tissue twisting wrist to elbow. She remembers the smell of her burning skin, the pain feeding up and down her arm. Molly running up the stairs, hands soapy, to smother the flames against her apron. Of all her possible deaths, Virginia has feared most a death by fire.

He turns toward her. And his face, always such a careful study in neutrality, frightens her more than the fire itself: the set of his jaw, the crescents of white showing above and below his pupils. There's a beaver dam upstream, he says, pointing.

Her eyes are fixed on him. The back of her neck dampens and dries in the heat.

Just keep goin upstream, he says. He pauses, judging the fire. We got a hurry. We can make it if we hurry.

He heels his horse off the trail and down into the draw. She follows him, feeling how Arano trembles under her, how he blows and shakes against the reins. The horse slides in the shale, losing his footing then finding it again. They cross the creek and lunge the horses up the opposite bank. Wind boils along her cheeks and hands, whipped like water stirred by an enormous hand. This is no larger version of a campfire, as she might have thought. Even before she sees the flames roll down the slope, even before she feels her horse tense on the edge of madness and then over the edge; even then, feeling the oven sear of smoke in her lungs, she can't imagine what it would be like to die in a fire like this. There would be nothing left. The heels of her shoes, maybe. The single diamond in her necklace, floating in a pool of smelted gold.

Her horse breaks and runs, tossing its head. She gathers the reins to her chest, jerking, but it's like pulling against fencewire, so tight is its head. Henry is beside her, and then he is behind her. Her horse is running, plunging into each step. She sees small flames burning at the upper edge of the slope above her: venomous winks of light churning through the dry mulch of pine needles. Grasshoppers fly out of the smoke, creating a second, darker cloud. Larger flames follow the grasshoppers, leaping treetop to treetop like a swarm of exotic animals.

Henry is not behind her. She is alone in the trees. The horse is no longer thinking of her, no longer thinking at all. They are away from the creek and she can hear the crackling of the fire even above the hurricane roar of its wind. Ahead of them, below them, through the trees, she sees a gray, flat plate of water. But then her horse is running past it. There is no Henry. She is looking back for him. She is looking back for him and then she is on the ground, gasping against a sudden crack of pain in her ribs. The branch that had knocked her out of the saddle still waves above her head and her horse is gone. Henry is gone. She takes brief, panicked breaths through her mouth, feeling herself grow dizzy with the lack of oxygen. Hunhh. Hunhh. Hunhh. She coughs, knowing that she should stand up, that she should run. But she can barely move.

She rolls over onto her stomach. Under her hands, the pine needles have taken on an orange flickering glow. She pushes herself to her knees, coughing. The smoke is worse even a few inches off the ground. How far to the water. Forty yards? Fifty? She rotates on her hands and knees until she faces the beaver dam. She won't look at the fire. So much hotter than standing too close to a campfire. She imagines the skin of her face blistering.

She jerks convulsively into a crawl, inching toward the water, taking her momentum from the slope of the hill. The fire is behind her. The fire is beside her. There is no consideration of pain, of the slow smoking in her clothes. Only the need to reach water.

She crawls faster, scrabbling over the pine needles, the cones. Her knee hits the broken tooth of a stump and knocks her away. She thinks she can feel blood inside her split skirts, but she pays no attention to it. She can pay no attention to it. She is on her feet and running, blinded by the smoke, one hand on her knee. She avoids trees only by the immediate sense of darkness in front of her, shouldering past them as through a crowded room. And then she has tripped. She has fallen again and it is a long, despairing second before she realizes that she was tripped by the water. That she is lying in the pond. That the sudden ague in her skin comes from the cool water. She slides farther in, away from the heat on her back.

Below her, she sees Henry standing on the beaver dam, balanced on the haphazard pile of branches and mud. His horse stands beside him, belly-deep in the water, his shirt tied over its eyes. She watches him stare around, his neck craning. Then he sees her and he is running, lurching through the water toward her. His horse follows, stiff-necked.

Tony threw me, he says, coming up to her. His eyes are wide but his voice is calm. We need to get you into some deeper water.

But then he is looking past her and she sees his face fall, crumple. *Like paper in a fist,* she thinks.

She follows his eyes, seeing only Arano lying in the water. How smart a horse must be to lie flat like that. But then she notices how he's struggling to rise, how his head rests on the boulder that tripped him, how ribbons of blood have fanned out from his front legs, clouding the water. The horse coughs against the water, then screams. A shrill note played through the gaping mouth. She has never heard a horse scream before and is amazed by how loud it is, how much it sounds like a person.

Low in his chest, Henry says the horse's name: Arano. Or perhaps it's only a low moan of denial. An exhalation of sorrow. The protest of an enormous rusted hinge.

Hold my horse, he says, his voice low.

My chest, she wants to say. My knee! But she takes the reins, proud of her silence.

He unsnaps a gutta-percha knife from his belt, the blade worn into a thin, milky pick, and splashes over to the horse. Arano, he says. Oh Arano. It struggles as it sees him coming, one eye red above the water, bulging like a split knuckle. Henry coming or some other. It breathes heavily between screams, splashing water with its head and shoulder. The white glint of splintered bone and tendon.

Henry kneels at its stomach, his forehead flat against the wet, blood-smeared hide. He holds the point of his knife low in its chest, just forward of the cinch, and feels with his fingers between the ribs. In a moment of sudden decision, he slides the knife in to the hilt. He leaves it there, probing until the blood around the blade bubbles, until the lips of the wound sigh deep. The horse tenses and stares at him with one eye, one single baleful question. Then it dies.

22

WHAT WILL HAUNT him later — often in floating, stereoscopic visions removed from any context — are the horses in agony. There were no friends in his childhood but horses, and he could never have imagined such a consistent, unremitting cruelty toward them. He will remember a quarter horse standing patiently, shot in the gut, a gray cheek of intestine bulging through its flank. He will remember a black gelding trying to haul a water cart after its front legs were hit by a mortar, pulling even on its knees.

There are nights when horses scream at the sound of approaching thunder, and indeed it is only thunder, and he sits in the rain tented under a poncho, playing poker on the wooden slates of a supply crate. And there are nights when the thunder isn't thunder at all and the horses scream for good reason, and he lies trying to bury himself into the face of his muddy trench.

23

HE RISES and runs his knife through the water, wiping it clean on his pants. His face is set and stern, frightening to her. He glances at the fire, then waves her over. He doesn't move to take the horse's reins. Instead, he leads them both into the deepest part of the pond. But it is neither deep enough nor shallow enough for his liking, and so he leads them back until the water stands at midthigh. A curious lack of haste about him. Now he takes the horse from her, still without speaking, and twists its ear in his fist, levering its nose against his palm. He turns its head to the furthest extent of his arms and then, after shifting his grip, turns it farther, until it is forced to follow its head and collapse onto its side, legs straight out in the water. He drops to his knees and straddles its chest, the head in his arms. The hot, living breath under his chin.

Lay down in there, he says to Virginia. If you feel yourself gettin too hot, just swim down there to where it gets deeper. I got a stay up here where the horse can lay with his head out of the water.

She decides that it will not be too hot for her.

Doves fly erratically into the pond in advance of the fire. A roughed grouse lands crumpled and broken at the water's edge. A yearling mule deer limps into the water downstream, ignoring them to stand submerged, its head and the line of its back visible. Virginia turns to study the horse but instead finds herself looking at Henry. He is looking at her. They are staring at each other, these two, the horse's head between them.

24

HER LEFT EYE is slightly larger than her right, he decides now. Slightly tilted at the corner, as if tinged with some least percentage of Asian blood. It gives her face an unbalanced look. There are bruises of fatigue under her eyes, and he thinks that her eyebrows must have been plucked at some point, although they have started to grow back. The pupils are skull deep and brown, neither perfectly round nor perfectly edged, the color bleeding away from the edges.

The sky is black with smoke. What light there is comes not

from above but from below, from the smoldering and bleeding firmament. In this ersatz darkness he sees his reflection paired in her dark eyes: the horse's head in his arms elongated by the convexity of her pupils; himself a pinpoint of skin and hat above the horse's head.

She closes her eyes and it is an abrupt sensation for him, a startling (if expected) gesture, like lights dimming in a theater. She opens her eyes and she is no longer staring at him but past him, at the fire on the shore. The reeds and floating weeds smoldering in advance of the larger flames. She shuts her eyes. She opens them.

25

SHE WATCHES him cry. A tense, uncontrolled trembling in the back of his head, in the bow of his neck. He drops his face into the water then shakes it clear, trying to smile at her. Failing.

He hasn't shaved for a couple of days, and pond water collects in drops on the stubble at the corners of his mouth. There's a smear of mud on his cheek — mud or blood — and a scar above one ear made visible by the wet press of hair. An acne dimple next to his right eyebrow and a stone-colored lightness to his short hair that she's not noticed before.

A face, she thinks, to recall certain paintings by Velázquez. *A blunt wreck ennobled*. The smear on his cheek like a heavy swipe of pigment. At these few inches, the smooth consistency of his skin fragments: not one color but all. She stares, and for a moment holds tight to his face: a hand to its pen.

26

THEY TRAIL SMOKE out of the mountains, pulling it after them like thread from a machine. Behind them, cold clouds pile up against the valley's warm air, stacking in orange, ink-blot hourglasses. Virginia rides the horse while Henry limps ahead, the reins slack in his hands. They hear thunder in the clouds, followed immediately by drops of water, heavy as loose change in the dust. The horse sees the river and trots ahead, shouldering past Henry.

Where do you think you're going, he says, pulling him back.

A plane drones overhead, lost in the roll of smoke and clouds. And that low, churning hum pulsing with distance must be the Farmall. Henry had said that they would probably be plowing firebreaks. She has seen better days. Sore in her knees and ribs, flashburned across her neck and cheeks, hair standing out in sweaty clumps. She rubs at the sweat in her eyes and sees her wrist come back smeared with charcoal. Nevertheless, she's already begun to feel a kind of startled exhilaration. *This story she's within!* Then she's appalled at the way her mind works. Does some part of her want to lose this baby? What would one of her mother's crazy psychoanalysts have to say about *that?*

He looks tired. She has seen him sweated through his shirt, cold-shoeing horses in the corral, and she has watched him spend six hours in the heat of the day splitting knot-grained firewood with a hammer and maul, but this is the first time she's seen his hand tremble as it brings a cigarette to his mouth. The first time his eyes have taken such a long moment to open after his sleeve chases the sweat from his face.

They leave the mountains at Green Creek, cutting across toward the river. Indians sit along the berm of the road, arranged knee to knee in filthy castoff trousers and patched army uniforms, nightshirts for blouses. The oldest of them, a man thin and withered through his chest, swollen in the belly, wears what she could swear is a Union cavalry jacket. There is no horse or automobile in sight. They had been watching the fire, but now they stare, expressionless, at Virginia and Henry. Henry nods, but doesn't stop.

Cree, he says after they've passed. They'll show up just about everywhere one time or another.

She thinks of the pain in her knee, her ribs. Not so bad, not so bad. *That's the way the world is, doll.* What kind of blood and sweat have already soaked into this ground? What moccasined feet have kicked out the last of their lives in this dust? What is her own tiny tragedy compared to the agonies of migration and defense still ringing through this ground?

At the river, Henry steps in past his knees, leading the horse until they both drop their heads to the water. He bends at the waist, bringing handfuls up to his mouth. Downstream, she can just see Mohr's buildings, the older roofs patched and scabbed with missing shakes. It might not be such a great loss to see the place burn. How is it that her father ever approved of it?

Virginia sits for a moment, the current brushing the soles of her boots, then dismounts, steadying herself against the saddle. While for Henry the river is only at midthigh, it boils up around her waist, nearly lifting her off her feet.

Behind her, she can feel the immensity of the wilderness, the fire within the wilderness. Such an enormous, brute potential held in this ground, in these mountains. A clenched fist of contained violence. *I almost died,* she thinks, looking at the peaks with eyes swabbed clear.

She steps around the horse, leaning on the heavy shoulder for balance. Henry has turned back toward Table Mountain, gauging the span of the fire. He needs a new shirt. The one he's wearing has started to fray at the collar and cuffs, so stained by salt-sweat wrinkles that they are set permanently into the fabric. One side of his face is redder than the other. She considers for the first time, although not the last, that she might owe him her life.

He takes off his hat and wipes at the sweat on the inside brim, then uses it to wave toward the fenceline above them, the cattle and horses standing head to tail against the wire. Should have an easy time gatherin anyway, he says.

She doesn't think about it. If she thinks about it, she won't do it. She leaves the horse, stepping away to touch him on the arm. He glances down at her, and she steps forward again, pretending to slide on the rocks. It takes him a second longer to catch her than she would like. She almost gets a soaking for her trouble.

They stand like this, the girl holding on to his arms. Then she leans into him, stretching up until she can place her hands on either side of his heavy head. Her fingertips cover the lobes of his ears. For such a large man, such small ears.

She pulls his head down to her and closes her eyes. His lips are dry and, at first, held tight together. But then his mouth is open and hers is open and the seal of their bodies is broken and she can feel his breath in her mouth. His taste — woodsmoke and tobacco and canned peaches — blends with hers, creating something entirely unexpected. A new taste that will, from this moment, reside only at the juncture of *them*.

She pulls away. He is surprised. And then he is not.

They hug, her chin barely high enough to catch his shoulder. Behind him, she sees her aunt step out onto the riverbank, walking to meet them. Even at this distance, she can see the old woman's relief. Relief, and then thin-lipped anger. At least the old woman still dresses well. Taffeta bustles and a silk overcoat in the turquoise shade they're calling sea foam and an egret-feather hat dyed to match them both.

A kiss, the girl thinks, smiling at the old woman over Henry's shoulder.

She placed a framed photo in my hand: a small black-and-white snapshot squared in gilt. "Father was quite the rounder. And so handsome."

Two men stood on either side of a bull elk, rifles propped at their hips. The shorter of the two in knickers and a corduroy shooting jacket, a gray mustache over his lips; the second man in buckskins and a cowboy hat, a goatee. Virginia touched the glass with her fingertip. "That's Buffalo Bill. This was in 1912. The only western trip I believe Father ever made. Mother told me once that Frank Mohr had taken this picture, although I never knew whether to believe her."

She placed the photo upright on the endtable. "I carried a taste of my father's death for many, many years. Only learning in my old age that death can come in any number of forms, all of them small variations on that one larger theme."

27

HIS CEILING could use a good cleaning, to be honest. Cobwebs in all four corners and a single strand waving from the bare lightbulbs to the door frame. She smells the rain on the windows and, under the rain, the stronger odors of cigarettes and decaying newspapers and fry pan grease.

She sits on his threadbare sofa, the back of her head against the wall, her palms flat on the once purple chintz. His coat, hung on the wall above her, drips rainwater onto her shoulders. This is the first time she has seen his college place, and she's surprised by the squalor. Just a single room with a small kitchen cubbyholed off to the side. Golf clubs in the corner, tennis rackets crossed on the wall. His writing desk, set in the exact center of the room, must double as a dining table, with all those chairs set around it.

Against the far wall, his bed is unmade, bare mattress showing through twisted quilts. Three of her drawings have been thumbtacked to the otherwise bare wall above it. A portrait of an uncharacteristically pensive Charlie, an incomplete sketch of the Low Library at Columbia (his graduation gift), and a self-portrait, her hands crossed in front of her. She still has a hard time with hands. His only extravagance seems to be the cabinet Victrola beside the sofa.

I thought we were going to Harlem, she calls out. To Jungle Alley.

From the kitchen she hears ice cubes rattle into a glass.

I thought we were going to Jungle Alley, she says again, her cheek dropping to her shoulder. A minute later she jerks awake, then makes herself stand, balancing against the wall. She can't fall asleep here. Her mother would kill her, just kill her.

Charlie emerges from the kitchen, waterglasses held in his fingers, an open bottle of Mumm's in the crook of his elbow. He hands her a glass, filling it until foam boils over her wrist.

Charlie, she says. Mumm's with ice?

It was warm. He bends to kiss her forehead.

That's sweet, she says. But I should go.

He brightens, and rushes over to the phonograph, filling his own glass on the way. First we need some music, he says, taking a drink. He sets a disk on the turntable and places the needle, adjusts the horn.

Charlie, she says.

What did you think of Gloria?

She was the berries. But I'm tight. And it's late.

You aren't tight. This is the Original Dixie Land Jazz Band playing here. You haven't heard the Jazz Band before, have you?

Yes. Sure.

Playing "Livery Stable Blues"?

Everyone's heard them play "Livery Stable Blues."

I met Nick LaRocca once, you know. At a party. Could he blow the cornet! The cat's pajamas.

They're so *white.* Charlie, please. I have to go.

You aren't tight. He steps up close to her, drinking deep from his glass and setting it empty on the floor. One dance?

One?

A single dance, then I'll take you home.

She sets her glass beside his and gives him her open hand.

You look like a raccoon, sweetie, he says.

She bends away to touch her eyes, her cheeks. Her fingertips come back smeared with eye shadow. Do you have a place to freshen up?

You don't need to freshen up for me. I like how you look no matter what.

His hand is on her waist. The music is bright, lively. She wants to trot across the room, Charleston up and down, but he pulls her, slows her down until they stand rocking, swaying to this fast tune. The hand on her waist moves up until his thumb is stroking the side of her breast.

Charlie! She pulls away to look at him. You couldn't have thought to bring me here for that.

Why are you here? He steps toward her again and holds her by the arms. He kisses her on the forehead.

Not for that.

They are dancing again. He says, You've always known what you were doing. He kisses her on the cheek. That's what I like about you. You always know, Virginia.

I know I don't like this.

He shuts his eyes and dances closer to her, his razor stubble like nettles on her cheek. He hums to the music, tickling her ear with his breath. She tries to pull away and he kisses her under the ear. She tries to pull away but she can't. She can barely breathe.

The hand that had been held politely at her waist drops to the small of her back, and then to her hips. He pulls her closer and she can feel his erection against her stomach. She wrenches away and stands breathing hard, staring at him.

We were having fun, she says.

Not so much fun. He reaches around her again, holding her by the waist. She feels his hands under her thighs, sliding up.

She twists in his arms, slapping him as she turns. She's never slapped anyone before, but it feels good. The bounce of his cheekbone against her palm.

He grabs her by the upper arm, his fingers like metal pincers in her skin, and she slaps him again. He avoids her open hand, drawing away to punch her temple, awkwardly with his left hand, much harder with his right. She hears his fist — like a butcher's hammer against meat — then feels it rolling down to her heels. The edges of her vision dim. With slow fascination, she watches him reach toward her through a ragged cutout in the room, through the sudden, nauseating gloom.

Light bleeds back into her eyes and she is lying on the bed, Charlie on his knees above her, unbuttoning his shirt. I'll scream, she says under her breath. She gathers herself up and says it again, louder: I'll scream, Charlie. I'll scream. He is grinning and she can't tell if he has heard her or not. Her dress is up around her waist. He is reaching up to pull down her panties. His face is so flushed, so unfamiliar. His shirt is off and he has unzipped his pants and all she can think, seeing him naked, is that Isabel had heard right: it does look like it belongs on a horse, although it's smaller.

She screams — a great gust of ancient, animal sound; a single, shrill burst of vowel — and he lunges down on her, throwing his hand across her face. His palm is in her mouth and she can taste his sweat. Her jaw hurts, pushed back at the joint. This can't be happening. This is happening. This can't be happening. She bites hard at the flesh between his thumb and forefinger, grinding her teeth until his blood spurts into her mouth.

Bitch, he says. Oh you bitch. He slaps her hard, saying, If you don't want to get hurt, if you don't want to get hurt. He lies heavily between her legs, dropping his forearm across her neck. She gags. She can't move away. He reaches down between their legs.

Across the apartment, the music finishes. For a breath there is no sound in the room at all, only the needle bouncing against the label end of the disk, a repeated, amplified scratching. A sound to match precisely the ending on the other side of the room.

28

HE LIES on his cot reading an old *Cody Enterprise,* the wavering flame of his lamp throwing shadows across the paper. He reads in Caroline Lockhart's column that "the disquieting news has reached us that unethical and dishonest bootleggers from another part of the state are preparing to turn loose a poisonous product made in tin vats which is liable to kill off a number of our leading citizens." He reads the Irma Hotel arrivals and scans the gossip lines of "Mainly About People." There are ads for a Ford Runabout, priced at $269, and for the Busy Pool Hall and Manlove Dentistry. W. R. Coe is offering a $1,000 reward for information about rustlers. He reads that duck season opens with elk season, on September 16 (almost two weeks ago now), and that there's a fifteen-bird limit. He reads the first few paragraphs of a mystery serial and, disliking what he reads, folds the paper and tosses it across the room toward the stove.

He leans back, hands behind his head. That familiar ceiling. The periodic splintering of finishing nails through two-by-fours. He hadn't been much of a carpenter in those days. He has always enjoyed the feeling of separateness that this little shack gives him, not yet old enough to recognize this impulse toward solitude as a flaw.

The tools those firefighters had. Those Pulaskis. Somebody had a good idea with those things. Sure would have made life easier back when he was working on the lines. Better than a misery whip and a bucket, anyway. Box of matches for back-burns. And then Dudley Watkins flying that old Curtis Jenny everywhere. Henry wonders idly what it would cost to get Dudley to take a guy up for an hour or two.

He lies on his cot smelling horses, listening to the muffled sounds of the river. The finger-flutter of nameless birds, the splash of ducks. He built this shed himself, tacking it onto the side of the barn after telling Frank calmly, irreparably, that he would rather die than live under the same roof. The day, he thinks now, that they really started hating each other. He used railroad ties for the foundation, tin and tar for the roof. Flagstone scavenged from Yellowstone as stove backing. A stove filled now with candy wrappers and thrice-read newspapers and dumpings from his ashtray. The place has a dirt floor, wetted down and swept out and wetted down again until it's about as hard as concrete, and probably not worth the trouble to board over. He had thought that in his absence they would be using this shed as a tack room, maybe a feed room, and he's not sure what to make of the fact that they haven't touched it. Haven't touched a thing. Did they expect him to come back after France?

Across from him, behind the hanging skeletons of his coyote traps, a shelf of mementos: a Spalding baseball signed in a New York hospital by a gassed "Cpt. Christy Mathewson," the lettering ghostly and shaky. A stacked and glued pyramid of empty Sho Sho cartridges. A framed photo of Henry and Hassler, blurry with the motion of the camera. A pair of binoculars pried from the frozen hands of a dead German. Under his bed, a crate of carnivore skulls that used to sit on the same shelf, boiled white and clean but gray in their recesses: incisors and sinuses and skull sutures.

The corners of the ceiling are hazy with gnat-filled cobwebs, and there's a heavy, elongated grain in the walls that he is still enough of a boy to shape into eyes, noses, hands. There used to be a few nights each winter when, under his layers of bedding, it was cold enough for his breath to rise to the ceiling and collect in icicles of hoarfrost. Back in those days, on quiet nights, he could lie and listen to wolves howl on the edges of the timber. Listen for hours.

That girl, he thinks. *That girl.*

A mare shifts on the other side of the wall, her late-season foal whimpering, then suckling. He reaches up to twist down the lamp.

You can't much tell what she's thinking. What she thinks of you. In contrast with his father, who always makes sure you know what he thinks of everything. A man whose prejudices structure his world. The uselessness of politicians, for instance. That's one. Then his disdain for easterners. For the girl. *The girl.*

He masturbates, then wipes a rag across his stomach and tosses it toward the stove. He rolls onto his side, arm outside the blanket. It's easier to feel ashamed at night. Of his inability to help his mother, for instance. That's one. He thinks about his father's disdain, his dismissal of the girl. His scorn for any man who would aspire to that kind of girl.

He had spent the summers of his youth breaking ground behind Mohr's draft horse and plow. Dusty, bone-jarring work unsuited to a ten-year-old boy: his shoulders threatening always to come unseated from their joints, his calves aching from the constant forward lean. He'd eat his daily dinner by the river, reading western novels, their pages held open with apple cores and half-eaten baked potatoes. He had begun resenting his stepfather —

who is the only father he has ever known and therefore his father — after learning that boys his age and younger were being paid more than a dollar a day for such work. In the mind of the boy, still somewhat the mind of the man, this unfairness had constituted an unforgivable breach of faith.

Before seeing how it is that one acquires the habit of a person, how a personality could be so strong as to capture the orbits of others, he hadn't understood how his mother could live with the man. When he was fifteen — and he'll remember this for the rest of his life; how could he ever forget? — his father had made Rose roll up her sleeves to show him the rings of bruises, running wrist to shoulder, each in the shape of Frank's powerful fingers. An exhibition of violence that was meant to be punishment for some small mistake of Henry's. He can't remember just what. Cutting hay before a rainstorm, maybe. Regardless, he had been shown the bruises not as a matter of pride so much as an observation of fact. This is what happens. Way the world works, boy.

He thinks about elk hunting, and sleeps.

29

HOW LITTLE REGARD this place must have for you now, her aunt says. Look at me, child. Look at yourself.

They face each other over the card table in their cabin, hands on their knees. Virginia taps her slippered toe nervously on the floor. Armed with her disappointment, the aunt is belligerent, strong-willed, irresistible. Product of a society in which, for a woman, reputation is everything. In her entire life, apart from her father and brother, she claims she has never been alone in a room with a man. Never.

You can't believe that he's handsome, Pauline says. With that nose?

The girl resists, shaking her head, paying the utmost attention to her hands, her forearms, the hair there singed and blackened into tiny curls. *I almost died,* she thinks. She's tempted to use this as an argument, but then thinks it might backfire. Her aunt doesn't seem to realize just how close a thing it was.

What future could you have with him? Pauline asks. Imagine him in New York. Take your fingers out of your mouth. Imagine yourself here.

He *is* handsome. And so tall.

Think about the baby.

In the end, of course, Virginia capitulates. Her aunt doesn't look well. The heat, maybe. The altitude. Pale cheeks and strained eyes and a quavering voice. The woman's almost eighty, after all.

It's only the next morning, as Virginia is walking across the driveway to the main lodge, to her bath, wrapped in a dressing gown, carrying her soap, towel, and sponge, that she considers the oddity of her aunt's final argument: Think about the baby.

It's the first time she has heard anyone consider the welfare of her baby at all.

30

HE DOESN'T SEEM to care for her drawings, but she has so little else to give him.

Not realizing that he has already ridden into the

mountains, she opens his door and drops the page beside his pillow. And only against the white paper does she notice the gray of his linens: unwashed, filthy. She backs out of the shed, wondering if she hasn't committed some horrible breach of frontier etiquette. Violating a man's room.

Within a few weeks, he will frame the drawing and hang it at the foot of his bed. It will be the last thing he sees before he sleeps, the first thing he sees each morning. But he won't see the trick of it. To his credit, it's true that the details of the fire initially draw the eye. The ridgeline of flames crossing the horizontal page, inscribing within them the negative images of trees and rock. He will think it beautiful — the first gift of this sort he's ever been given — but he'll never see that this horizon traced by flame, the shape of the ridgeline itself, is the profile of his own face. He will never see that, from this moment, he has become one of her edges.

31

THE GIRL'S BEDROOM. A cavernous, echoing space; dark hardwood austerity in striking contrast with the sense of warm security she has always found here. Her room.

As she reads her magazines, a geometry of morning sunlight draws across the floor, creeping away from the scrolled Victorian dressers, the diminutive oak tables eternally arranged with thimble-sized tea sets, piles of stuffed animals tossed aside in various postures of neglect. Between the girl's elbows, propped under her chin, the only doll she has ever cared for: a button-eyed, black-speckled dog, stitched and restitched over the course of her lifetime.

Her bare heels kick together in a private rhythm. She wears a favorite pair of silk pajamas, ragged and moist on the collar where she likes to chew. She turns a page and the sound of the cheap paper ripping against the staples echoes in the room.

Saturday morning, and she is reading *Hollywood Parade.* A new issue of *Hollywood Magazine* lies face down on the bed beside her, waiting its turn. It's been a summer of Buster Keaton and Reginald Denny, Colleen Moore and Maurice Tourneur. Betty Compson is in *The Enemy Sex,* and Jack Dempsey is canceling fights in order to act in his first film, *Winning His Way.* The *New York Times,* crumpled against the wall, is filled with news of the Democratic convention at Madison Square Garden — news that bores her to death. She had only been glancing at it for the radio schedules.

She hears the door open without a knock and primly turns a page, refusing to acknowledge anyone so rude. Her mother, of course. None of the servants would dare. Virginia aspires to perfection, to white-screen beauty, and this mother of hers is too fat, too floppy-eared, too loud. These days, Virginia has no regard for her whatsoever.

At the door, her mother says, I was in the laundry room this morning looking for my watch.

Virginia sighs and folds her magazine, glancing up at this fat, fat mother of hers, back rounded like a Russian peasant's. She stands above Virginia holding a wad of red and pink silk fabric in her fists. She spreads it apart, corner to corner, revealing a rip down the bodice. Fabric pops like a row of knuckles, and Virginia feels her cheeks go heavy.

Who was it? Her mother asks.

Charlie, Virginia says. And with the name finally (finally!) out of her mouth, she begins to cry. Charlie ripped my dress. I told him not to, but he did.

What?

Charlie raped me, Mother. Charlie ruh-ruh-raped me. She gasps with the strength of her sobs.

Stand up, her mother says.

Virginia slides off the bed, climbing toward an expected comfort. She has not hugged her mother in years, but she'll do it now. With gratitude. The relief she feels just saying the word — rape — is such that she cries from simple release.

Her mother folds the dress over her arm and slaps Virginia. Hard enough to make the girl step back.

That's for being a whore.

Virginia stares at her wide-eyed, a hand to her face. This woman whom she doesn't know at all.

Breathing hard, her mother puts the dress under her arm and slaps Virginia with the other hand. Petals of heat flare across the girl's cheeks.

That's for being a liar.

Virginia frames her face with her hands in stunned dismay, cold palms warmed by the flush of skin.

Those love bites on your neck? Were those Charlie's too?

I've never had love bites on my neck.

Her mother throws the dress at her — a stiff-armed roundhouse more appropriate to a baseball mound than this suddenly reduced bedroom. Virginia flinches, then stands still, the dress draped over her head.

I'm glad your father is dead. Can you imagine that? That was the first thing I thought. I'm glad he doesn't have to see this. See his daughter the Jezebel.

Virginia slowly pulls the dress away from her face. This mother whom she has never seen before.

You've made me glad my husband is dead.

32

HE RIDES Ballo up the western edge of the still smoldering burn, leading his packhorse through stands of lodgepole in alternating patches of living green and dead black. The fire jumped itself here and there, as big fires will do, leaving a random pox of untouched timber and brush. The world with the meat shaved off of it. A heavy mist drifts over the trees, snapping at the brim of his hat and running wet lines through the smudges of soot on his slicker. Ballo ducks her head to crop at an isolated clump of grass, but he pulls her away. She shakes the reins and stares back toward the ranch, grinding at a few blades of grass.

Get goin, he says. Nothin for us back there.

He rides twenty miles, then more. Rides until his right knee pounds, bulging as it does over his rifle scabbard. Rides until Ballo (who is still wearing her first pair of shoes) stumbles with exhaustion. Why he brought her. He has found a tractability in overworked horses that's unavailable at other times. He has always projected his own inclinations on the animals he trains, and he is himself most agreeable after a hard day's work.

They make their way through creekbottom stands of timber and then into the open, flanked by a series of bare peaks that roll and recede like slow, slow waves. He had made it a point to visit two cathedrals in France — Notre-Dame and Chartres — and had felt himself diminished in both, as was no doubt the intention. But then he'd decided that what he should be feeling is scorn. While the idea of a specific god bothers him, he has come to regard as a ridiculous arrogance any attempt to imitate that same god's creation (which is what those cathedrals must have been: if not mimicries of mountains, of forest rows, then what?).

No, give him the real thing. Not some arched and vaulted imitation. Give him these mountains, these trees.

He camps high on Elk Fork, setting up his tepee tent beside a narrow trickle of runoff. He takes off his boots and slips on camp moccasins and sits at the mouth of the tent sipping from a flask of good, bonded Canadian whiskey, saved special for this first night in the mountains. The last of the rain drifts past him: a heavy, undulating curtain that nearly extinguishes his fire and leaves pieces of cloud threaded across the slopes below. He drinks and prods at the fire, listening to the horses crop around their pickets. He is in a thoughtful mood, pleased with the little filly. *Hardheaded,* he thinks, *but goodhearted.* He stares into his fire, considering the providences of fate that put him on this particular ridge on the outside edge of this particular day. Rather than, say, tits up under a barleyfield on the Marne. When he is hunting in these mountains he feels plugged into the veins of the world and has to wonder if the girl feels the same way about New York. But then, how could anyone love New York?

In the last of the evening's light, he rummages inside the panniers for a can of pork and beans, ratcheting it open and setting it into the coals at the edge of the fire. The label peels away and the metal turns black. When the beans start to boil, he ducks his hands into the cuffs of his jacket and mittens the can out, lodging it between the soles of his boots. He scrapes away the top layer of ash and slurps at the scalding, thin gruel. One of the few things he knows for certain: food tastes better the higher up you go.

An elk bugles somewhere in the clouds below him. In the creekbottom, maybe. A small bull by the sound of it. A shrill whistle that neither rises nor falls. He'll be lucky if he finds a bull big enough to shoot. Elk, like everything else in recent years, have dwindled under the frenzy of possession afflicting the West. Possession of everything. Antelope, moose, and mountain grouse are species rare enough to have attained the status of rumor.

The night clears and he goes to sleep watching the long-legged shadows of his horses feed up and down the walls of his tent.

33

HE HAS COME to think that Hassler must be drawn to his stillness, to his attempts at self-containment, perhaps in the same way that he is drawn to Hassler's constant nervous chatter. Having these spaces filled is more comfortable for them both. At night in the trenches — because marines, like doughboys, are issued only a single army blanket — they lie side by side over the duckboards, Henry's blanket under them, Hassler's over them. Just one of the many tricks of war they've picked up. Henry has learned to remove himself from violence, for instance. He will be thinking about Christmas oranges, and later, in the midst of a bombardment, some part of him will continue to think about oranges. He has learned to shoot slightly low in covering fire: if you miss, the bullets nevertheless create a visible impact. And he has learned to distinguish Allied from Boche bullets, the rubber-band stretch and whine of each distinct caliber. He has come to see the piled mounds of dirt horizoning the trenches as either coils of intestine or the turnings of some enormous plow, depending on his mood. But the haphazard stretches of wire will always look snakelike to him — serpentine coils of metal caught in apoplexy, in the constricted throes of dying. He has learned the broken-bone itch that comes from looking in the face of a man as he dies, and the contentment in knowing that most men are unaware of their own deaths. They are simply alive, and then they are not. He has come to live with the knowledge that he could die at any moment. It could be this moment. Or that one. Or this one here.

And he has come to think of Hassler as his best friend, despite being witness to the man's slow unraveling. There is an afternoon when Henry sits and watches him flick at the back of his own hand with the point of his knife, holding it low on the blade and popping the skin until blood wells up in a single heavy drop, finally to break and spill down his wrist.

Hassler, he says. David. Hey, David.

Hassler glances up empty-eyed, focusing on Henry with a visible effort. I've been so good at dodging these bullets, he says, I wasn't sure I could bleed anymore.

It's the very next day, or perhaps the day after that, that Hassler is shot. A neat, gray hole through the muscle of his upper arm, the same size as the Maxim bullet that made it. But he's back a week later, sporting a wrap of bandage and a new army uniform restitched with his own marine buttons, carrying a paper sack filled with union suits. As always in his nervousness, he overexplains himself. The first thing they did, he says, is throw that old uniform away and give me new clothes — they don't have any more marine uniforms — and it was such a goddamned relief getting rid of these cooties — almost worth being shot — that I figured all you other guys would appreciate a change of drawers. Course, I had to sneak these out. The army's not all that cheery about outfitting us marines. And you wouldn't believe how pissed off some of those doughboys are about seeing us get all the glory for Belleau Wood. Hell, I almost got in a fistfight a couple of days ago.

This same night, Hassler, nervous to be back sleeping on the boards, tells him that he's going to sneak into town for a drink.

He's heard about a place on the other side of town. Get a drink. Get a little ass. He slaps Henry on the back.

They walk through a village with the life gone out of it: muddy ruts deep as their knees, streets trimmed in a fretwork of shattered brick and hanging rafters. Henry looks through a ruined stone wall and sees a young man and his wife at supper, their faces lit by a plate of half-melted candles. The woman eats with a baby at her breast, the maroon blotch of a severe burn on her arm spreading past its bandage to crawl up her elbow.

It turns out that the café is only a converted farmhouse, sparsely furnished with three crooked tables. A pair of sawhorses and some warped boards for a bar. They order watery bowls of beans from the pot on the stove and are served by a limping, thick-legged farm wife whose only English seems to be the words "one dollars, one dollars." They eat picking strands of her gray hair out of their bowls.

They finish eating and have begun to drink a dark, yeasty beer from ill-fired mugs when a young woman comes in the back door. Younger than Henry but nearly as tall, she has tied her hair back with a fraying strip of cotton ribbon. Curls have broken loose to corkscrew out over her ears. He sees in her the kind of beauty found only in vulnerability. He has been fighting for two months, and when he looks at her it is like a stiletto in his side. Every breath a conscious effort.

By the time their mugs are empty, the clay has softened and the dregs of beer at the bottom swirl in soft, muddy veronicas. They start drinking wine, passing the bottle between them, wincing at the faint vinegary taste. Henry drinks staring at the woman. Waitress, he finally calls.

Whore, Hassler says.

He cannot look at Hassler. He is looking at the woman. She walks over to him, her eyebrows raised, pointing to the wine bottle.

He shakes his head. Can I see you?

Comment?

Can I see you?

She shrugs and glances at the farmer behind the bar. The smell of pigshit in the room comes from this man. Henry leans around the girl. Do you speak English? he asks.

The farmer considers the question. Okay, he says to Henry. Okeydokey.

There is a shed behind the farmhouse, a shack set up with a cot and a wall calendar turned to February 1911 and a bedcover pieced together from seed bags. She undresses and stands naked in front of him. You're just the prettiest thing I've ever seen, he says. Every detail of her subsumed by a larger, collective beauty: a nearly hairless body and narrow mouth, tiny nipples and a ragged scar across her ribs. He thinks the scar must have come from an appendix surgery, but then he realizes that it's on the wrong side. The faint rings of ash and dirt around her neck and wrists mark the edges of her dress. She is sixteen, and the comforts she has so far found in life have arisen from an awareness that suffering borne well excuses most other flaws. She tells him in French that he must pay her forty francs.

He shakes his head. I don't understand all that bird talk.

She holds up all the fingers of her hands and opens and closes them four times. Cheap fare even by the standards of the time.

He nods. And afterward, when he has given her fifty francs and she has tried to return ten, thinking he has misunderstood, he refuses it and she blushes deeply, as if the extra money were some comment on the quality of service he had just received. Her name is Solène, and he will see her five nights in a row until his regiment moves on, following the war.

34

IN THESE FIRST DAYS of October, she finds herself inhabiting a peculiar moment of pause. A state of suspension. Counting out the hours, studying each morning storm as it builds over the peaks. The residues of snow that creep down the slopes, closer every day. In all her life she never thought she would be able to watch a season descend. She wakes before her aunt, and after spending time in the outhouse — the odor pleasantly diminished in the morning chill — eats her breakfast alone. Oatmeal with a dollop of honey. An apple. After complaining to Rose about constipation, she's been eating nothing but oats and apples for breakfast. Surprising how easy she has found it to talk about her body with Rose, as if that implacable face — all possible reactions buried under the slab of fat — frees her.

She takes her morning tea out on the porch. Adze's dog, Blue, rises up to nose into her palm, and she runs her hands absently around his ears. Some mornings, she'll bring a scrap of ham or sausage out to him. Her favorite time of day, just a few minutes after sunrise: the ranch rolling over and stretching, coming awake with the hollow crack of chopping wood, the slap of trout feeding off the riverbank. Sipping at her tea, she walks over to the barn, knowing that Rose will have started milking. She lets herself in through the large double doors and walks the dark length of the barn, stall to stall, coming out from under the low ceiling of the hayloft and night calver bunkhouse to the larger, open-ended milking stalls. Pigeons flutter and coo unseen above the rafters. She takes up her accustomed position on a milk can behind Rose, one ankle crossed over her knee, tying aimless knots in her shoelaces. Rose squats on her stool, hands working under the cow, round cheek flattened against its flank. As she works, she hums under her breath, occasionally mumbling brief phrases: Oh, washed in the waters of Zion, she'll whisper. Wash, wash my sins away.

The moist odors in the barn — hay and manure and milk — lend a calmness to Virginia's morning. A serenity. Rose spends fifteen minutes on each cow, squirts of milk resonating in the lard bucket between her knees. And when it's Custer's turn — an especially gentle cow, Custer, and one unlikely to kick — Rose sets the bucket on the floor and milks with both hands, stripping at the teats with enough strength to raise foam. Barn cats gather in a loose ring at her knees, hoping for an overturned bucket. The oldest cat, split-eared and warp-pawed, sits directly under the cow's udder, waiting until Rose is inclined to send a squirt of milk straight into its mouth.

Did you find those oats I put out for you then? Rose asks, talking into the cow's hip.

Yes I did. Thank you. They were very good.

Always liked oats myself, but hardly ever have em anymore. Nobody else'll eat em, so they're not hardly worth the trouble to fix. My Frank calls it horse food.

Well, I like them.

Even with honey, Frank won't eat em.

Where do you find your honey? Do you have bees?

Them Barnetts, down toward town. We'll trade cakes a butter for a quart or two every now and then. Traded some just the other day, gettin ready for Henry. He's always had an awful sweet tooth. Now *he'd* eat oats, I guess, if you put enough honey on em.

Henry has a sweet tooth?

Oh, awful sweet tooth. Rose grins into the side of her cow. I remember I'd leave a pie out on the counter — you know, just kind a leave it out on accident like — and it'd be plumb gone the next morning. He'd get up in the middle a the night and come lookin. There now. Rose wipes her hands on her denim overalls and struggles to her feet, setting the full bucket aside. She picks up her stool by one leg and carries it over to the third cow.

I'm surprised he's been in the mountains so long. Henry, I mean.

Well, that's elk huntin. The trick is . . . Rose holds her breath as she lowers her bulk down to the stool. Trick is to keep him here once he gets back. That's the trick. Frank and him don't get along too good. I guess you've probably figured that out by now.

Why is that, do you suppose?

Rose rests her forehead against the cow's flank, feeling for the udder. After a moment, she says, Just one a them things, I guess.

Rose has a taste for hot, fresh milk, a taste that Virginia, in one of the more surprising cravings of her pregnancy, has come to share. They strain the milk through cheesecloth and carry it sloshing to the kitchen, passing the teacup back and forth between them, sipping at a liquid warm and thick as blood.

In the kitchen, Virginia sits on the corner stool watching Rose pour milk into her DeLaval cream separator. The chore boy, Gus, carries in an armful of split wood, then leaves with a bucket of stove ash, a dishpan of vegetable peelings. At nine-thirty, Pauline enters from the great room, pulling on her rabbit-fur gloves and motioning Virginia outside for their walk.

Her aunt prefers the south side of the river, and so these morning constitutionals are most often spent cycling up and down the road, stepping aside to make way for passing vehicles. A delivery truck slows as it goes by, growling in low gear, its bed piled with stove-sized chunks of coal. A young man's face stares out at them from above the steering wheel, at these two incongruent splashes of civility in the wilderness. The older woman with a parasol and bustle, the younger with her thickening waist and tasseled silk skirt and a sports sweater from Vantine's. Since their fire (she thinks of the fire now as *theirs*), she has ignored her cowboy clothes altogether — those ridiculous cloth chaps, the cowboy hat dented by her luggage, the boots so large she'd been stumbling over them — in favor of her New York casuals. If she rides again she will wear jodhpurs, at least until her pregnancy outgrows them, and then she'll wear canvas drawers, stitched from the same cloth as Henry's work shirts.

I don't like to see you working with the help, her aunt says, gathering her skirts and stepping back up on the road. Working like some Negro. You have ancient blood in your veins, child. Plymouth blood.

I don't mind it.

Do you remember? Do you remember what a precocious child you were? What an innocent child?

Not so innocent.

Oh, but you were. Remember playing charades with your father?

Virginia nods. She supposes that such a thing might have happened.

We all loved you so. The only child on those evenings of adults. Men with their brandies and cigars, women with their tea and gossip, all in the same room. You made such a lovely charade of a flower growing. Do you remember? Stretching up straight while your fingers opened beside your cheeks? Do you remember how we applauded, how your father swung you around the room?

Were you ever in love, Auntie? Virginia asks. In her most generous moods, she will often ask after her aunt's youth. A polite, harmless pandering that is the only thing in the world capable, so far as she can tell, of putting even the slightest expression of pleasure on the old woman's face. A pink blush to color the chalk-white cheeks.

Virginia! What a question.

But she can see how it pleases her aunt. How the woman

holds a hooked finger to her lips before taking Virginia's hand, swinging it as they walk. I was younger than you are now, she says. And his name was Adam Mills. He had the loveliest red hair.

What happened?

It was rumored that his grandfather had emigrated from Ireland. Can you imagine? Irish!

Irish are good people.

Pauline releases her hand. Anyway, his hair wasn't all that lovely.

Virginia prefers her evening walks on the north side of the river, through the shattered foothills of Jim Mountain, when her aunt is too tired to leave the cabin. She uses the altitude to place herself according to the rest of the world. North, south. The river, there. Like a child — perhaps the child the rest of the ranch perceives her to be — she finds herself creating an internal dialogue. Telling her baby, swollen into a knot at the base of her stomach, coiled below her navel, what names it might come to carry, boy or girl. Describing to it the world in which it's going to shortly find itself. Once she has this child, she knows that she will no longer be able to conceive of a time when she *didn't* have it, so completely will it come to fill her life. Or, given her mother's plans for the child (and she corrects herself with a sudden, predictable deflation of her lungs), the *idea* of it will come to fill her life. Only the idea.

She places her hands on her stomach. These are the days when I didn't have you, she says.

35

Just after lunch, he pickets his horses in the snow and dead grass half a mile below the treeline, tying each of them off by a hind foot. To let her know she's roped, he steps Ballo forward until her leg pulls out behind her. Young and flighty as she is, it might save a broken bone.

He climbs using both gloved hands, a pack empty on his back and a rifle slung over his shoulder, binoculars bouncing against his chest. By the time he's out of the trees, he's breathing hard enough to feel the old cigarette smoke in his lungs. Just below the crest of the ridge, he props his rifle against a boulder and eases himself down into a comfortable seat. He leans back on his elbows. Up this high, he could probably see into Yellowstone if he cared to look. But he turns his binoculars north, down the creek. Scans a series of open ridgelines, naming the landmarks as he goes: Battlement Mountain. Pinnacle Mountain. Sheep Mesa in the distance. The peaks of his youth. Like seeing his own face in the mirror.

He loves these binoculars. About the only good thing he took away from that war. Lenses scratched and the housing dented, heavy enough to anchor a small boat, they are still a rare luxury. They'll save him some walking, that's for sure.

The slight breeze dies away and the sun filters through thin air, warming the surface of the rocks. No elk out in the open, but it's early yet. He rolls a cigarette and smokes staring out over the prettiest country in the whole goddamned world. Maybe that's something else he got from the war. A sense of perspective. A new way of looking at the place where he grew up. Seems like he never realized just how . . . pretty these mountains are. He guesses that's the right word. He tosses the cigarette into the rocks and leans back, hat tilted over his eyes.

Half an hour, maybe an hour later, he wakes to the sound of fingers snapping. *Hell,* he thinks, struggling to sit up, *place is getting more crowded than town.* He lifts his hat and runs his fingers through his hair, glancing around, shaking off sleep. Then he looks downhill.

A hundred yards away, at the base of the shale slide below him, a grizzly bear is picking its lazy way along the flat rocks, clicking stone against stone. A big blond boar. Seven, maybe eight feet. What little wind there is seems to be blowing up the hill, and as Henry watches he sees the bear pause, lifting its nose. All the nonchalant carelessness of a warm afternoon falls away. It tenses its enormous shoulders and rises on hind legs to get a better look down into the timber. Down toward the horses.

Henry levers a cartridge into his rifle. Hey there, mister bear, he says.

The bear drops to his feet and shuffles around to face him, its black little coal-chip eyes squinting up.

Nothin for you down there, mister bear, he says, louder now.

The bear takes a step up the hill, then another. It gives out a low *whuff* of frightened curiosity and chomps its teeth.

Hey! Henry says, climbing to his feet. That's enough now. Hey! Get goin! He waves his arms, rifle in his hand. Get goin, you! Hey! Get!

It's finally too much, and the bear pivots on its hind legs, sprinting back the way it had come. Running hard until all that's left of its passing is a thin trickle of stones bouncing into the trees.

Henry stands with his arms still raised, slowly lowering his rifle. He balances it in the crook of his arm, grinning at nothing, no one. I'll be damned, he says out loud. He glances around, shoulder to shoulder. Wanting to share the experience. I'll be damned, he says again.

36

The swimming pool has been making no progress at all. That great metal contraption of a revolving shovel sitting silent in the middle of the yard, the stick-and-mud beginnings of some sort of nest piled in one corner of its bucket. More than once, she has seen Frank Mohr standing on the edge of the half-finished hole, smoking a cigar. Once she saw him climb up into the machine's cab, then back down, not having touched anything. His frustration has given a tense, stale-air atmosphere to the place. Everybody's walking around on pins.

Chickens gather at her feet as she scoops a coffee can of cracked corn out of the feed barrel. One of the few jobs that the cowboys have allowed her to work at by herself. Chicken feeding. It seems that a ranch woman may do anything in the kitchen or garden, but feeding real livestock isn't allowed, not even tossing out a few flakes of hay. They'll watch her carry firewood across the yard, often awkwardly, but the idea of her splitting that same wood would have appalled them. And so Virginia has been rising each day from her afternoon nap to feed the ranch's twenty-three chickens. Twenty-six if you count the three broody hens that need lured out of the coop.

Nice chickens, she thinks. *Nice chicky chicky.* White-and-black-speckled Dominiques, their breeding already starting to be diluted by the blood of the dark Cornish cock Mohr has thrown in with them. Unaccountably, there's one ancient, clown-faced hen pecking always off to one side. This is Virginia's principal job of the afternoon, and she works at it slowly, scientifically, paying close attention to those chickens that don't get their fair share of feed, then standing over them, dribbling corn from her fingers. Often, if she is in the mood for conversation, she'll trail corn in a line across the yard to the corrals, the entire flock following at her heels. Our little chicken herder, Adze has called her.

Adze stands by the corral gate, wrists loose over the poles, watching Gus practice calf roping. She stands beside him, pinching down corn. The boy avoids her eyes. Twelve, perhaps thirteen years old, on the brink of adolescence, it seems to her that Gus must be the hardest worker on the ranch. As chore boy, he is constantly subject to anyone's beck and call. It's nice to see him with some time of his own. He ties his little scrub calf to the snubbing post and leads it away until the rope swings taut. He backs up and sprints down the rope's length, catching the calf under its belly. The calf is too large for him, however, and he ends up having to lever it against his thighs, hairless cheeks reddening with the effort. Once the calf is on the ground, he drops a knee across its chest and throws a piggin string around one front hoof, roping the hind legs as well and throwing up his hands in frustrated self-mockery. At the fence, Adze looks down at the pocket watch in his hand. Twelve seconds, he says. Five minutes and twelve seconds.

When she had first imagined Wyoming, she had thought of cattle drives. She had expected herds of horses and swinging ropes and campfire smoke over hot branding irons. She had expected anything but idleness. Not laziness so much as lassitude. She wonders where Mohr gets his money. Inheritance, maybe. There's no sense of urgency about the place. No sense that money *needs* to be made.

The Magini brothers, Perry and Pete, are still working on their cabin, climbing around up on new log rafters. Dewey and Adze have finally brought the last of Mohr's horses down from their summer pasture. Thirty-one long-legged, scruffy animals, the remnants of a herd long since culled by the army. All of them skittish and dangerous, some so wild as to need to be tied off to take a saddle. Adze has been riding them up and down the road, around ranch buildings, putting them through figure eights when he knows Virginia is watching. Dewey spends his time inside the corral, pulling shoes and trimming manes and currying out burrs. Getting them ready to trail down to the leased winter pasture by the lake.

There are two ranches here, Virginia has decided. When Frank Mohr is away on one of his errands — if the Pierce-Arrow is gone from its stall — laughter floats out over the river. A campfire after supper and moonshine in coffee mugs, the liquor diluted with apple cider or homemade root beer or, on at least one occasion, a poorly gelled kitchen dessert. The cowboys drink and play poker on the picnic table, holding their cards down against the breeze with red volcanic stones. She sits by the fire, thinking that she would make a pretty good poker player herself. But she can just imagine what they would say at the prospect of a woman playing poker, the expressions they would give her, and so she contents herself with sitting and listening. And if she is quiet enough, they soon forget she's there at all.

Adze pulls up a pants leg to scratch his shin, the skin of his calf so white and hairless as to be translucent, his hand and fingers the color of stained oak. Like two species of creature in the same body.

Old Nez Perce gal I took up with over in Fort Benton, he says, dropping his pants leg. Hell, that was a cold, hard winter. Had plenty to eat, more'n enough to eat, but I guess I must a lost twenty pounds caught up in that little shack. Good Christ but that woman had energy. Had a thing about bear grease. Jars of it from her brother. I woke up near every morning stuck to the sheets.

Virginia snorts and Adze glances over, either ashamed or making a good act of it. Sorry, Miss, he says. Got carried away with my storytellin.

Think nothing of it, she says.

The lodge door slams, and they all look up to see Pauline walking toward the fire, skirts bunched in her fists. A puzzled expression on her face, as if she has suddenly found herself stepping off a train in an unexpected station. Adze finds her a piece of unsplit firewood large enough to make a seat, moving it close to the fire then a bit farther away until she nods her approval. Thank you, Adze, she says, managing to squat regally over the chunk of log.

Virginia feels a pang of disappointment. They never forget themselves when Pauline's around.

And they never forget themselves when Frank Mohr is *anywhere* on the ranch. It becomes a different place entirely. No poker after supper. No campfire. He is a man, she has found, whose strengths and weaknesses are mirrored in the ground he owns. Meticulous when it suits him, he trims his nails at every opportunity but goes without shaving for three or four days at a time. Similarly, even though the lodge was plumbed this past summer, a ceramic toilet sits crated in the barn, waiting for sewer pipe, a drain field. A rubber hose running from the kitchen sink to the riverbank regurgitates fans of soapy dishwater three times a day. And while the ranch seems to be prospering, there is a past poverty to be read in the baling-wire haphazardness of the place. Ax handles held together with screws. Saddle blankets pieced from throw rugs. Half a copper boiler for a bathtub, split along its rivets and set up inside a two-by-four frame.

To her credit, she has considered that her dislike for Mohr may be nothing more than a return of the dislike he obviously feels for her. He has never made the slightest gesture toward her, the slightest overture, reserving every civility for her aunt. Out of consideration for who's paying the bills or disdain for her condition, she has yet to decide. Henry has been gone for almost two weeks before she has her first real conversation with him.

She is sitting with Adze at the dining room table, a checkerboard between them, tin cups of cider at their elbows. Adze leans back in his chair and pulls a Hamilton watch from his pants pocket. He glances at the grandfather clock in the corner. That there clock's always about five minutes fast, he says, putting the watch back in his pocket. He lights their oil lamp with a match struck off the sole of his boot. A few minutes later, the lightbulb over the table flickers and dims, dies away.

King me, Virginia says, jumping a piece.

Oh my. Look at that. Adze sits back to study the board. Just gettin warmed up, Miss. Just gettin warmed up.

Frank Mohr comes in from the kitchen, a lamp swinging in his hand. He stands watching, then says, You wouldn't hardly think an old man could hide checkers up his sleeves.

Evenin, Frank, Adze says, not looking up from the board.

Frank pulls out a chair beside Adze and drops a sheaf of papers on the table. Kitchen kindling box is empty, Adze. Mind takin a break and seein to it?

Adze stands, scratching his stomach. I'm about wore out anyway. Finish this tomorrow, Miss?

She nods, pushing her own chair back. I'm tired too.

Frank glances up, then makes a downward motion with his fingers. Want you to take a look at this before you go up. If you would.

What is it?

Brochure. He smoothes the topmost paper and turns it around for her to read. His fingers long and delicate, scarred white along the knuckles. Advertisement for a dude ranch over on the South Fork, he says. Northern Pacific helps work these things up. Tryin to get people out here.

Oh. I've seen these before.

Well, we're goin a have to have us one for next year, and I was just wonderin what you might do different from this one here.

She takes the pamphlet and holds it under the lamp. A newsprint cover, illustrated with a charcoal sketch of a Rocking T brand, then pages of columned text, photographs of calf branding, horse herding. Scenic shots of the lake and mountains, each captioned "Our Back Yard," "Our Front Yard," "Home on the Range."

I'd really have no idea, she says, pushing the paper back to him. It looks fine to me.

I was thinkin maybe more pictures.

That might be good.

He nods and slides the papers back in their folder, straightening them against the tabletop. Somethin you should know, he says, and I been tryin to figure out how to tell you. So I guess I'll just tell you. I don't know what you think about Henry. You and him . . . that kissin in the river. I guess that's between you and him. But one thing you should know. He come back out here after spendin a couple years in an asylum back east.

Pardon?

Nuthouse. He was in one a them nuthouses. Two years. Mohr shakes his head.

Well.

Told you some things, but he didn't tell you that, did he?

I'm sorry, she says. Why do you think I should know this?

Just in case you were waitin for him to come back. Just in case you were wonderin about him.

Well, I'm not. I wasn't.

Well. That's good. Mohr stands up, tucking the folder under his arm. You have a good night, Miss. You sleep well.

Instead of going to bed, however, she decides to take one of her walks over by the river, following the curve of willows to a gravel bank she has come to call her own. She sits with her legs dangling over the edge, heels kicking runnels of gravel off into the water. She drops her hand to her stomach. You know, she says, rubbing at the swelling of it, I almost died out there. Those forest fires can kill you just like that! She snaps her fingers. But I was faster. I'm so fast. One of these days you'll have to tell your children how your mother outran a forest fire.

She kicks at the bank and bites her thumbnail, glancing west. To the blue and silver mass of land, unlit by the moon.

Hunting, she says.

No. She is certainly not waiting. She is not wondering. She is doing nothing at all. And she is doing it all for Henry.

37

HER MOTHER SITS in the foyer with her morning coffee, dried magnolia blooms crumpled in a dish at her elbow. The coffee has cooled but the woman sips at it nonetheless, occupying herself while Virginia stands waiting by the window. Oddly, considering all the empty space in the house behind her, this foyer has become her mother's favorite room. It's where she displays her husband's travel mementos: splay-nosed clay masks from East Africa stacked like bowls, suicide knives from Japan in an umbrella vase by the door. A way of presenting her husband's death even to the casual visitor. It is also, Virginia knows, a way of cleaning him out of her house.

In her insolence, in her displeasure at having to leave New York, Virginia hums a series of jazz tunes. Mumbles around the words to "Washington Square." She says, Do you like Cole Porter, Mother?

Her mother balances the cup of coffee on her knees and reaches into the lightstand drawer, picking out a Chesterfield from its brass case. Deliberate in her movements, she rolls it between her fingers, taps it against her leg, strikes a match and holds it to the wick of a lighter, then the lighter to the cigarette. The room fills with the odors of lamp oil and cigarette smoke. A priestess among her clouds. That dress she's wearing, however — a red and white silk skirt to her ankles — is months out of style.

Through the smoke, her mother clears her throat, breaking a ten-minute silence. She tells Virginia that she must make a good impression. Your father knew them, she says. He went hunting out there. He always said it was very nice. Nice people, he said.

And after Wyoming? Virginia leans heavily against the door, staring obliquely through its etched glass, presenting her mother with a profile.

I've told you. It's been decided.

Will I be able to visit it? After?

You won't even know the parents. It's best this way. It's been decided.

The girl draws back the curtain. Here comes Auntie.

If you weren't so stubborn, of course, none of this would be necessary.

Virginia nods: slow, mature. That's true, she says.

We won't fool anyone, you know. We only need to provide them with an alternative to disgrace.

Virginia opens the door and steps back, making room for Theo to walk the first of her trunks to the street. Unshakable Theo. Spine bent with age, doubly bent now with the leather-handled weight of her trunk. The top of his head a monkish tonsure, gray bushy hair curling around his ears. She holds the door open for him.

Thank you, Miss, he says.

Molly follows behind Theo, Virginia's portmanteau in her two small fists. Molly sets the case on the floor and turns her back on Virginia's mother (*What a brave gesture,* Virginia thinks) to take the girl in her arms. Virginia is surprised at the strength of the hug, the thin band of Molly's ring pressing hard into her back.

I'll miss you, Molly says fiercely.

Virginia soothes her, placing her hand on the laced shoulders of Molly's apron, patting the narrow back. The only one who has believed her. The only one. Molly, who has been a maid in this house for nearly twenty years, head housekeeper for five, and just as much a parent to her as her mother. After hearing Virginia's story, she had asked quite seriously if they shouldn't find somebody to castrate that sonofabitch. Money can buy a lot of things, she had said. They've not always seen eye to eye — Virginia has often been frustrated by Molly's obsessive rage for order, by the moral condemnation of an unswept floor or an unwashed slip — but these past few weeks Molly's support has meant the world to her. What a relief to be believed.

Her mother says Molly's name. Then says it again, sharply.

Molly steps away, grinding at her eyes with her palm. I'll get this out to your old aunt, she says, picking up the case.

Her mother stares at the retreating back, then says, I may come visit you in Wyoming.

Virginia steps across the floor, heels clacking on the marble, and pulls the cigarette from her mother's mouth. She leans forward to kiss her cheek. The lightest brush of lips on the skin.

Liar, she says.

38

THE CROW WORD for elk is *iichíili* . . . something. Like horse, he knows that it starts with *iichíi*.

In the bottom of the ravine, puddles of water reflect shards of blue sky and tumbled boulders and his own horizoned form, rifle over one shoulder. He thinks that it's late in the year for an elk to be bugling, but then he hears it again. Closer now. Really more of a chirp than a bugle. He drops to his stomach, shrugging out of his rifle. Antlers emerge from the undergrowth, six points on a side, and heavy. Then the elk itself: flanks smeared with mud, the thick hair of its belly clotted with urine. It tilts its head back and bugles, the sound so shrill, so *large* in this confinement of rock and pine. It stops to dig at the water, scalloping into the mud with its antlers.

Henry shoots while the head is lowered. At this distance, he feels justified in aiming for the neck, not willing to risk losing the shoulder meat. But rather than dropping where it stands, as should have happened with a good neck shot, the bull leaps away. Then stops, puzzled. A rope of blood, thick as a finger, pulses in a stream from the base of its neck. It takes a single small step, then another, the blood dwindling to a slow seep. The strength drains from its front legs and it collapses, knees to neck. The wires of intention suddenly gone from every joint. The antlers stay upright for a distended moment before they too sink slowly, bonelessly to the ground. Henry sits up, nervous. Shaky. Hands fumbling over his face, over his legs, coming to rest finally under his thighs.

Within the next hour, he will clean the elk surrounded by the odors of urine and mud and the heavier, sexual smell of musk. He will peel the skin away from its haunches and shoulders, sharpening and resharpening his knife. He will carve the cooling meat from the bones and saw the antlers from the skull and leave the mountainside afflicted with that most insidious of humors: melancholy. Time is passing, even now. Granite turns to clay and every tree has to fall. Here's one day less that he'll be living. One hour less, one minute less. He loves hunting, but could do without the killing.

39

MOST OF THESE marines have spent their entire lives passing October 4 unaware that this was the day they were going to die. They had spent the night listening to the Allied bombardment, watching mist roll into the valleys toward Sommepy, and now they move forward through the same mist, through the early morning dark, each man following the hunched shadow of the man ahead of him. A barrage precedes them in the long hours before dawn, but sunrise finds them exposed on a slope empty of cover. Some of the men are carrying the soiled, sodden blankets in which they'd spent the night draped around their shoulders like towels. They sit on the slope waiting for orders to attack. But there are no orders, and the German shelling begins as soon as it's light enough to make out targets: round after round whistling down from Blanc Mont Ridge. Henry and Hassler crawl away from the main force to huddle together in a shelter pit rimed by yellow lyddite, bullets whining, ricocheting over their heads.

There is a shouted order for gas masks, although Henry doesn't see the gas itself until, beside him, Hassler starts to cough. Heavy, ophidian threads of it settling into their pit. Through the scratched lenses of his mask, he is horrified to see Hassler barefaced, scrabbling around the outside of his pack. Greenish-yellow blisters already rising on his ears, his mouth. Henry can only watch, helpless as Hassler kicks his pack away to lie face down on the bank, forehead digging into the dirt, spine convulsing. He lies there for a long moment, motionless, before sitting up, eyes closed, lids burned. He pulls himself to his feet, having come to a decision, and takes a step up toward the rim of the pit, then another. And then he is shot. Henry hears the single, isolated report, kicking Hassler back into the pit and onto his face, legs twisted. Blood gathering at the bottom of the pit.

Henry doesn't want to roll him over, doesn't want to see. They are all familiar with the way mustard gas blisters the skin, but he somehow imagines that Hassler's blisters have gone deeper, have accommodated the agonizing enormity of this event to peel the skin back, to flay his face, to leave only a caul of flesh and fluid, the mouth lipless and grinning.

Henry is not adequate to the terror of this event. He cannot rise to it. Who ever thought he should do this? Who picked him out? He's from Wyoming, for Chrissake. A clot sticks in his throat, past which he's unable to swallow. This must be the final destination. The end of the war. He has provided the germ, the seed around which this violence has coalesced. It will end him and then the war will be finished. He is suddenly not up to the grave responsibility of his own life.

Men are moving slowly past him — in a charge, it is seldom that men run — and Henry joins them, leaving Hassler behind. They drop into the first trenches just behind the German retreat. The Boche have held this position for four years. There are men running through the trenches ahead of them, and Henry fires at their backs, running, shooting as he runs. He has never been more of a soldier than he is at this moment. If death is nothing, then nothing will be a relief. There is a stubble field past the first trenches, and the initial round of return fire catches him precisely in the middle of the field. Machine guns on either flank, and he is suddenly running exposed through a tunnel of flying shrapnel. He dives into a shallow rifle pit, hugging his machine gun close. The barrel is hot enough to blister his skin. There's a dead man in the pit with him. A French soldier, by the shreds of uniform. A face blackened by the cycles of swelling and drying, hands still clutching at a missing rifle. A good Crow warrior would see black as the color of victory, but for Henry it has become the color of death, the color of profound defeat.

He lies on his back. To sit up, to roll over, is to invite a bullet. His life is limited to the six inches above his nose. Over the next ten hours, he dozes and starts awake, dozes and starts awake. The sun rolls across the sky. He keeps expecting reinforcements to knock out those German flanks, but the reinforcements don't come. Somebody should have given this attack some thought.

As the day wears on, he finds himself talking to the corpse. A captive audience. The rapt, wide-eyed attention. He whispers that he's in love with a French whore. Maybe you know her, buddy. *Mon frère.* Psst, buddy. He says that he just needs somebody to take care of. He sees now that this is what's been missing in his life. Responsibility. He says that he wants to buy her clothes in America. He wants to learn French and translate every word for her.

Toward evening, the Germans begin to shell the stubble field, pounding at it, knocking his heart into a new rhythm. Amid this cacophony of shellfire, the corpse begins to answer him. Henry covers his ears. Words that he would be able to make out if he let himself listen. But rather than listening, he starts talking to himself. He's got no interest in what a dead guy's got to say. Second Division, he yells. Second. Duh. Vee. Shon. The corpse says something about honor. Or is it *on her?* Sixth Reg. Uh. Munt. Henry has never fully understood this scaffolding of command and responsibility. The assholes back behind. Assholes! he screams. The corpse grins and says the word "mother." He fails to say the word "father" and there is a conspicuous pause. Henry finds himself repeating a single name to the rhythm of mortar fire, screaming it until it loses all meaning, until it exists only as pure sound: a steady timpani beat within the larger, drowning orchestra. So-lène. So-lène. So-lène.

40

SHE SITS with her feet curled under her, a novel open on her lap. The front cover and first few chapters have long since dropped out of the spine, and so she has been making a game of trying to decide just what it is she's reading. The narrator, Victor, is in terrible straits. She reads that he has been shunning the face of man, and that joy and complacency were tortures to him. Solitude was his only consolation.

She turns a page, shifting position, the cold leather of the couch cracking under her like ice. She wonders if it might be bad for the baby to read such a morbid novel. Somewhere outside, a sheet of tin bangs in the breeze. It's cold in the room, even with a fire, and she wraps herself tighter in her aunt's gray cardigan, smelling the lingering powdery odors of the old woman's perfume. She hadn't thought to bring much in the way of warm clothes herself. Nothing, in any case, large enough to stretch and drape around her stomach.

The kitchen door bangs open, making her jump. Nettie rushes in and collapses onto the couch beside her, crossing her feet on the coffee table, sighing and studying a fingernail. What a day, she says.

Busy? Virginia marks her page and sets the book aside. So much for her quiet evening by the fire.

Jaysus, she says. I can't even begin.

A faint odor of brine about her, and Virginia suspects cabbage. Sauerkraut. Dear Nettie. It's how Virginia has come to think of her. A constant and glowing good humor from the girl. *Dearest* Nettie, she thinks occasionally, and not without cynicism. Nettie with her windblown red hair and ceaseless, breathless busyness, her exaggerated rushing from one job to the next.

Nettie leans her head back and blows at a single strand of hair over her eyes, then stretches an arm across the couch, touching Virginia on the shoulder. I've got me a secret, she says.

Oh?

Bet you don't know where Mr. Mohr went in that big motorcar of his.

I can't imagine.

He's bringing something back for you. Something from Cody.

I don't suppose you're going to tell me what it is.

Oh, I can't. I *can't.* But you'll just *love* it.

Virginia imagines a list of tourist knickknacks — Indian headdresses and figurines of Buffalo Bill, dinner plates with Old Faithful painted on them — any one of which would appall her and about which she will be forced to act pleased. Nevertheless, she finds herself touched. A gesture, perhaps, to make up for his earlier rudeness.

I might be able to give you a hint though, Nettie says, surprised by Virginia's lack of interest.

I don't know. Perhaps you shouldn't.

It's something from New York.

It *is?*

Nettie grins, finally having elicited the reaction she was hoping for. Something your mother sent along, she says.

Well, I can't imagine.

I'm not going to tell you any more.

But she doesn't have to. Virginia knows just how her mother thinks. A trunk of winter clothes. Blouses and wool skirts and her alpaca driving coat. The woman had been conspicuously absent as Virginia had packed, but she would have noticed what was left behind. No wonder Nettie is excited. A trunk of new clothes would be unimaginable to this girl. Virginia has never seen her in anything other than these baggy denim jeans with the rolled-up cuffs.

Virginia feels a sudden, unreasonable flush of excitement. A direction to the day! That's what's been missing. Only this. She hasn't anticipated anything for weeks and weeks.

Lord, is that the time? Nettie stares at the grandfather clock, feigning dismay. She jumps to her feet. I don't think I told Ah Ting how long to boil that cabbage.

After she is gone, Virginia opens her book but soon closes it again, distracted. Tired and hungry. Pleasantly, the nausea lingering always behind her eyes, waiting for the slightest whiff of frying lard to send her rushing from the room, seems to have left her. But she finds the sensation of hunger itself more pleasurable than the eating would be. And so, rather than going to the kitchen for a snack, she decides to walk to her cabin and read herself to sleep. Reading in a cold room under warm blankets. One of the central comforts of her life. She decides that she will wake to the ringing of the supper bell and walk down to giggle with Nettie over her new clothes.

She steps out on the porch, shivering. It's dropped at least ten degrees since morning. At the end of the lodge, Henry's packhorse and filly are tied to the fence, his panniers set off to the side, saddle blankets steaming on the rail. Of all the days. This old cardigan and her hair ratty from her habit of twisting it in her fingers as she reads. Why couldn't he have waited one more day? Until she had her clothes?

It's forty or fifty yards across to her cabin, and she almost makes it. She has her hand on the door before he calls her name. She turns, brushing the hair away from her face. He stands beside his horses, a curry comb looped over his hand. He waves at her with the comb, then makes a nonspecific gesture toward the horses. Does he want her to help brush them out? Is he inviting her opinion? Is he — God! — is he making some sort of joke about her hair?

She points to the cabin and, using what she hopes is just the right mix of nonchalance and courtesy, calls out, Getting cleaned up for dinner.

He shrugs, then squints up toward the road. Listening. A moment later, she hears it too. A car's motor. The Pierce-Arrow with her clothes from town. Is it her imagination or has the engine, usually so whining and insistent, taken on a tone of benevolence? She steps into the cabin, just out of Henry's sight, and turns back to the open door, her aunt asleep on the bed behind her. The car pulls up to the lodge, its top down despite the cold. Except for a leather mailbag, the back seat is empty. But the passenger seat's filled. It certainly is.

Charlie has grown a mustache. That's her first thought. A mustache. He steps out of the car and stretches, staring around at the mountains, at the cabin. He smoothes the wrinkles from the lap of his trousers and pulls spectacles from his jacket pocket. Despite herself, she thinks that the mustache suits him. Ages him.

The bed squeaks behind her and Pauline comes to stand at her elbow. Well, she says, that looks like Charlie Stroud. Charlie! She pushes past Virginia even as Charlie swivels toward them. Their eyes meet over the hood of the car. He is staring at her. He is staring at her.

Despite the chill, she feels sweat beading on her skin. He's here. He's *here.* She starts to float over the driveway and then, with a sharp breath, pulls back into herself. She steps aside and closes the door against her aunt, against Charlie, against Mohr and his damn Pierce-Arrow, against Henry. She stands in the darkness a long time, studying the grain of the door and the pattern of diseased sun streaming through the cracks.

41

I THINK we should get married, he says, smoking his cigarette. Blood from the bite on his hand has run down the length of his arm, drying at his elbow. He has put his other hand inside his trouser pocket to stand cocked shoulder and hip against the window, the glass pale with the morning's first light. He turns toward her. The worst is out of the way, he says.

She lies on the bed, naked below the waist, her dress bunched up at her breasts, torn at the neck. She pulls at the bloodstained sheets twisted around her legs and tastes the corner of her mouth. She traces at a tooth cut inside her cheek. She had forgotten how dark blood became after it dried. How the losing of it could turn one so suddenly mortal.

What do you say, sweet? Charlie takes the cigarette from his mouth and studies the end of it, wetting his fingertip to adjust the fire. She hears the sizzle of moisture. You should marry me, don't you think? The worst is out of the way.

I'd rather . . . She sits up, trying to consider what she should say. There is something expected of her here, some social form or decorum. But it's so difficult to think. A fog in the room, in the corners. She stares down the length of the bed to focus on her toenails, painted red the night before. Painted by such an innocent girl. And then she thinks that she's been staring at her feet for a long time. The light from the window is so bright. She swings her legs over the edge of the bed and reaches down, blindly searching the bare floor for her underwear. They are under the bed, and she brings them out in a wad, laying them crumpled on her lap.

Rather what, sweet?

I'd rather not say. She stands and steps into her panties. She twists at her dress. The collar has ripped and the top buttons on the back have popped loose, but if she can find her coat none of this will be noticed. If she can find her coat she'll be ready to leave. But it's summer. She doesn't have a coat.

Between your money and mine, we could own this town. And you'd rather not say? He moves toward her, shaking his head, smiling down.

He reaches out his hand. She jerks away, trembling. He frowns at her and reaches out again. She moans, and he opens both his hands to her, palms out, moving his lips. Hush, he says. Somehow, she manages to hold still. He reaches and cups her cheek in his hand and bends to kiss her forehead. I'll take you home, he says.

42

THEY LIE TOGETHER, her back to him, her breasts in his hands, his thighs positioned to match the tilt and angle of her hips. She flinches as he brings his cold feet up to touch her smooth calves. He wonders if home might not be a place at all but a person. Earlier, he had experienced this idea as a revelation. Leaving her each evening has been like coming away from a good moving picture. For several hours, he has been left blinking away her particular reality.

In the time he has been gone, she has decorated the shack, replacing the calendar with a series of family photos, ancient likenesses framed in tin or paper or not framed at all: ambrotype, ferrotype, calotype. Photos of ancestors all facing the camera with the set, unchanging expressions of antiquity. Old age and approaching death. For their day, the oldest photos are the most lavish. After a certain generation, the splendor of the clothing begins to decline, her family's misfortunes dating from the time of the Paris Commune. The indication of her aristocracy, the single dull syllable *de* between her names, is no longer any reflection of circumstances.

His hands on her breasts, his mouth next to her ear, he whispers in French that he loves her. But there is no reaction from her. A deeper breath, maybe. He has had this speech crudely translated for him, has memorized it syllable by syllable, and he thinks that maybe he is mispronouncing the words. He says it again, *Je t'aime.*

She turns to face him with slow effort. She has a slight, nearly invisible mustache, moistened now, the hair thickened by his own lips. She stares at him and he's still not sure that she has understood. He takes a breath and she shakes her head. Very lightly kisses his mouth. She has understood after all. And he thinks, like a child, *No. No. No.*

Yes? she says. So? She smiles at his pronunciation. He hopes it is at his pronunciation.

So you do speak English?

She shakes her head. Yes?

He tells her in a rush, a string of words he doesn't understand, that he loves her and that he cannot imagine life without her and that he wants to marry her: *Je veux t'épouser.*

And then he sees her understand. Her mouth makes a little O. Something about him has been explained. She touches his hair, uncut these long months in France, and runs the back of her finger along his smooth cheek. She kisses him on the forehead and repeats the word: *épouser.*

Je t'aime.

Then there is a reaction from her indeed. A broad smile that reveals even her lower teeth, her only imperfection, crowded and stained in their recesses. A smile that he misinterprets and leans forward to kiss. But then the smile becomes laughter and she swings her legs off the bed to stand naked before him. He sees her searching for a word, looking toward the ceiling. She wets her lips and tries the shape of the word in her mouth. Then grins down at him. Boy, she says. Child. Then she says, *Mon petit.*

He is older than she is by a year or more, but he nevertheless understands her reaction. A boy who falls in love with a prostitute. He sits on the edge of the bed to say it again, *Je t'aime.* Querulous now.

She leans forward, and he tilts his face up to kiss her, but she moves only to smooth a strand of hair away from his brow, to bend and kiss him on the crest of the head, beside her open hand. Through his hair, he feels her lips forming the word again — Boy — and then the shape of her teeth behind a smile.

The thought has occurred to him that, if nothing else, he will bring away from this war experience enough to bear anything. Hassler's death, the voice of a corpse. Anything. But now, already, here is something that is beyond him. This . . . humiliation. He could take anything from her but condescension. A man's only got his self-respect.

He stands, and as he stands he swings around with the back of his hand, his open knuckles rapping against the bones of her wrist, knocking her hand away from his head. She steps back, rubbing her wrist, still smiling. Then the smile turns mean, her eyes narrowing. Staring, she pulls her dress off the back of the chair and, with one hand on the doorknob, turns and spits at him. Leaves him standing mute, defenseless. A white line of spittle running slowly down his face, eyelid to chin.

43

IT IS WITH REGRET, but no real surprise, that she sees Charlie welcomed extravagantly, received on the ranch like a breath into a body.

She has been sitting in her habitual place at the firepit, her back to the heat reflector. Here she feels protected. Safe. Vacillating between grief and the awareness of her grief. Between a dull, formless hurt and the observation of that hurt. And through it all, like stitching in a hem . . . fear. He's here. He's *here.* The skin of her face hangs heavy from her skull and there are no thoughts she could think that would not be violent.

He has changed into what she is sure he is calling his country clothes: a pair of brown corduroy trousers and suspenders, a white cotton shirt with the sleeves rolled to his elbows. His spectacles and brilliantined hair. He waves his fedora at Mohr, emphasizing a point. She cannot think of this man in terms of anything but crude verbs: hit, kill, slap. And maybe it's the low, oblique firelight on his face, maybe it's the way he tilts his coffee mug to stare at Mohr over the rim, but she suddenly finds something birdlike in his face. His narrow nose and chin made smaller by his four-day smudge of beard; eyes that, while not particularly large, seem to bulge. *A vulture,* she thinks, and touches her stomach.

Only this morning, Mohr had set up benches on two sides of the fire: split logs spiked over old chopping blocks. Across the fire, sitting on the ground, Adze winks at her. Some sort of joke between them. Beside him, Dewey lies on an elbow, tracing out patterns of smoke with a smoldering branch.

The men with their coffee mugs, the women with their glasses of lemonade or orangeade or tea, the chipped slivers of ice still holding the indentations of a pick. The rise and fall of conversation.

Pauline leans over to her and whispers, It must cost Frank a fortune to maintain this kind of staff.

A point they've made to each other several times over the past weeks. But Virginia is in no mood for polite conversation. What are *we* paying? she says loudly. No one looks around, but she has certainly been heard. *That's right,* she thinks. *I'm a paying customer.*

Pauline sits back. I'm afraid I'm not liking you much these days. You're turning into the oddest child.

A breeze blows through the cottonwoods. After a moment, Pauline says, They're bringing out the piano.

Virginia pulls herself to her feet. I'm going over to say hello to Adze.

Pauline grabs her by the elbow. You'd do better to say hello to Charlie.

Virginia wrenches her arm away. I'll say hello to whomever I want, Auntie. She turns to walk around the fire, at the periphery of several conversations.

A pair of cowboys, two of Mohr's part-timers — Victor and . . . is it Bill? Will? — push the ancient pianoforte out of the car shed, its panels loosened by the dry Wyoming air, its legs wobbling. An instrument with a carved signature and a traceable lineage — spring wagon, train, and boat — to Leipzig. A piano that might have been played by one of the masters. And now it sits nailed to a crude dolly, carted back and forth on wooden wheels. The only place for a party, Mohr has said, is around the campfire. And the only time for music is at a party. The piano must therefore stay outside.

Nettie steps onto the dolly, scooting the stool to the keyboard and pounding out a few quick chords, a tricky A-minor blues phrase in a high register. Somehow the instrument is still true, has retained some measure of its original sound. Nettie starts into a halting, awkward version of "Hard-Hearted Hannah," then a clumsy take on "Baby Face." She plays with great energetic nervousness, poised and tense, tracing melodies with her right hand and pounding out whole-note chords with her left. A missing B-flat in the middle register, a broken wire, perhaps, creates tunes filled with abrupt starts and stops, like a clutch slipping. Adze climbs to his feet for a brief clog, then sits back down, laughing, shaking his head.

Virginia walks unseen past the Magini brothers, with their rough haircuts and Stetsons, their half-washed faces, the sponge having stopped at the ears and throat. Perry bends at the knees to reach for the coffee pot and fill their mugs.

Them Mexico weaners, Perry is saying, are a couple a cents cheaper than them California ones. And better stock, too. I got that letter from that El Paso buyer who says he can get em for five, five and a half cents. Then maybe fifty-cent commission he says.

Lot a good a bunch of Mexican cows'd do us up here, Pete says.

Just tellin you the market.

Them Idaho steers, them two-year-olds, were seven and a half cents. And that's weighed off the train here in Cody?

That's right.

That means about six cents, after shrink.

I suppose.

Virginia thinks, very much against her will, how vulnerable she is here. She is not so much the woman who rode through the fire as the girl who doesn't know what "shrink" is. She can hunt foxes. She can play that piano. She can draw. But she can do nothing useful. Nothing at all. Beyond this baby in her belly, what good is she?

Nettie makes a chord transition from "Baby Face" and begins a halting, repeating melody. A slow ramble up and down the keyboard. And because it avoids B-flat, Virginia suspects it might be Nettie's own composition. A strangely poignant, hollow dirge.

She walks past two women, strangers, standing together away from the fire. Ranch wives, she supposes; young and wide-hipped, flat-chested, all vestiges of their girlhood hidden by sunburn and frazzled hair and thick hands. They hold their heads close. But only, Virginia realizes, to try to conceal the machine-rolled cigarette they're passing back and forth.

I don't guess he has use for two sopranos, the first one says, sipping at the cigarette.

He ought to use you anyway, says the second, after sayin he would.

I don't guess he has a use.

He ought a be obliged. The second woman takes the cigarette, pinching it between her fingers.

Where'd you find that hat? I love that hat.

You like it? Fifty cents is all.

Where'd you find it?

Elsa Lundgren had that sale she's always been talkin about.

And I missed it!

They glance at Virginia. An apologetic smile. A frown.

Past them, she sees Henry sitting on the ground beside his mother. She wants to tell him something. What does she want to tell him? On the way around, she walks behind Adze and Dewey.

Give it ten years, Dewey is saying, and every one of us'll be glad Coolidge got reelected. Man knows how business should be conducted. And who is it runnin against him? Nobody, that's who. That Davis guy.

Adze, Virginia says, touching him on the shoulder.

Miss? He glances up.

I think my aunt might need a bit more lemonade.

Oh? He stubs out his cigarette and climbs to his feet, walking over to the pitchers on the picnic table.

Henry sits with his arms on his knees, a cigarette forgotten in his fingers. Beside him, Rose is using a hunting knife to carve shavings off what looks like an enormous pinewood earring, six or seven inches wide.

Virginia kneels beside her. That's nice, she says. Very pretty.

Thank you, Rose says, nudging at Henry's leg with her finger.

It's a blab, Henry says. You put it on the nose of a weaner calf still trying to nurse. He looks up, glancing suddenly past her.

And a hand grabs her arm just below the shoulder, fingers digging into the space between the muscles. Your boyfriend has something to tell you, Frank Mohr says, pulling at her, forcing her to follow him around the fire.

Charlie avoids her eyes. I have an announcement, he says. He raises his arm, nearly touching her shoulder. His proprietorial arm. I have an announcement! he says louder, waving a hand. The talk around the fire dwindles away, and now all faces are turned toward them.

He says, As much as I appreciate everyone's hospitality — thank you especially for that cobbler, Mrs. Mohr — I didn't come west to be a dude. I came west to ask Virginia . . . He swallows. Grins. I came west to ask Virginia to marry me. To persuade her to be my wife.

Virginia closes her eyes against the clapping. Someone whistles. She feels Charlie's hand move to her back. His proprietorial hand. She steps away from it, listening as Mohr tells Charlie that this here bottle of wine came from Buffalo Bill. She opens her eyes. Her aunt is stepping around the fire, holding out her hands. She takes Virginia's wrists and leans forward, smiling tenderly before hissing violently in her ear, You smile at him, child. Smile!

To engagements! Mohr yells, brandishing the bottle. And

then she hears him say to Charlie, You should be married in Wyoming. At the Irma, maybe. Or here on the ranch.

Virginia untangles her hands, smiling so directly into her aunt's eyes that the contact hurts them both, takes something out of them both. Then she is walking away through the crowd, hearing the conversation fall quiet behind her. She steps out of the light and there is no sound behind her at all. The cracking of the fire.

Wyoming, she thinks.

She hopes that she had walked through them in a regal manner. She would hate to have been seen retreating. She did not retreat.

44

FOR LACK OF any other direction, he walks back toward his old barracks. It's turned cold again, and he breathes through his hands, smelling Solène. *Whore,* he thinks, wanting to cry. *Bitch*. He hasn't been spat on since grade school. Dumb Indian, they had said. On the northern edge of the village, a bonfire has been lit, and from this distance it seems that the entire town must be dancing around the flames. Yet another celebration of armistice. Foul wine and a goat, maybe a pig. They eat horses here too. He is not in the mood for wine, or horse either. Nevertheless, he's drawn to the fire.

As he gets closer, he sees that it's not a celebration but a cottage burning. A clapboard shack with a thatched roof and attached barn, twenty or thirty sheep milling frantically in a pen off to the side. Shadowy figures in a line, passing buckets hand to hand, pump to flames. To no good end. As he watches, their motions slow, like a clock at the end of its wind, until one by one they come to stand limp, exhausted. Underfed. Beaten by four years of war. All of them watching the flames. He realizes, with an internal stillness, that everything he has ever thought about himself, every conclusion he has made, he has been wrong.

He turns and, within his sorrow, follows the reach of the flames with his eyes. Follows it well above the cyclone of fire and heat, above the floating detritus of leaf and glowing filament snarl of hay, follows it until the sparks of the fire hang alone and unwavering, bright even against the adamant stars. He blinks and touches his eyes and descends through the pillar of smoke to stare, staggered, at this newest image of himself.

45

THERE IS NO MOON, but she doesn't care to risk a light. She walks blindly across the yard to the riverbank, then follows the bank toward the barn, stumbling on ruts, pieces of gravel. Frightened by her own audacity. Her aunt lies asleep in their cabin behind her, Charlie in the next cabin over. If anyone sees her, she's sleepwalking, she's looking for the outhouse. She can just see his shed — the narrow wall attached to the barn, the smoke-tinted window. But there's no light inside. No light anywhere.

Past the cottonwoods, she puts her hand on the corner of the barn, the rough, poorly nailed section of boards. Inside, she hears a horse shift in its stall. The heavy splatter of urine.

She hasn't yet left behind the evening's sense of *watching.* And among the things she can see clearly is herself. For now, she knows just what it is that she needs.

The jog of his shack sticks out from the far corner of the barn, dark inside. She studies the door, the vertical row of thick boards hinged in ponderous iron. She taps on the door with the flat of her fingers. And after a moment, when there is no response, she knocks with her knuckles, wincing at the noise.

An inarticulate, startled assent behind the door. A rustle of bedclothes. She'll say that there was a bear. If he turns away from her, she'll say that there was a bear scratching outside her door. That she was frightened. She's from New York. He'll believe that.

A flare of light in his room, then a muted glow flashing between the boards.

He eases the door open, hinges creaking. His lamp, half hooded, lights only his legs. Denim jeans with no belt and a bare chest. Narrow feet, heavily veined. Behind him, she can just make out the hovering white shelf of his cot. That's where he sleeps. He looks at her. He is not saying anything.

She straightens. I was molested, she says.

He raises the lamp higher and she sees the question in him, then a self-conscious shock. He becomes aware that he should show his surprise. His head drops forward slightly, and for a moment he looks helpless, as in the seconds before a sneeze.

Raped, she says. In case you were wondering.

He doesn't answer. He is looking at her. He is not saying anything and she can feel herself hardening, turning away. But then he is reaching out his hand, his arm stretching on forever. He cups her cheek, and there is only the slightest, unfelt, unimagined pressure on her skin, around the line of her jaw. His fingertips. He backs away, drawing her inside.

46

AT FIRST he thinks only, *If this is what you want.*

But then he finds himself surprised by the strength of his own response. The need to touch her skin with his skin. He wants to touch it all. Wants her to touch him. It's not something with which he is unfamiliar, this kind of need. But nothing exactly like this. Nothing before.

They stand together above his cot, his fingertips on the bone of her cheek. A hand on the soft flesh under her thigh, bringing her hip around him. She is so thin under his hands, each rib a curved wire, the baseball knot of her pregnancy rising with a firm flaccidity between them, away from the adolescent profile of her torso.

He lays her on his cot, and with each motion he comes to give her, the slight rise of her stomach interrupts their mutual fluidity, their connected horizon. He cannot lie entirely close to her. Within minutes, a few moments only, he's pushing at her urgently, delving, staring past her into the fabric of his cot. And within this motion, he finds an involuntary ebb and pull of words matching the rhythms of their sex. He thinks, with the beat of an engine, *Whore. Whore. Whore.*

He groans then, and falls into her neck, appalled. Where did that come from? *She's a pretty good old girl,* he thinks. She *is.* Later, however, her head heavy across his chest, he thinks, despite himself, *How many times has she done this?*

In this way, another uncomfortable potential has been added to the person he had thought he was.

47

And now a period of respite. A night in the lee of the world.

They lie together afterward. After words. His elk blanket heavy over them. For the first time in her life, the warmth in her bed cannot be traced back to her own body. They listen for unusual sounds outside the shed, for the footstep in the yard, the slamming of a door, the rattle of kitchen pans. For Virginia, perhaps more than Henry, the act of making love will soon come to be associated with a kind of constant watchfulness, a necessary awareness.

She lies within his arm, fingering the ragged, greasy edge of the hand-cured skin. He has bathed since coming out of the mountains, but there is still an odor about him that she thinks can only be from the elk he killed. Strong enough to linger after even several washings. A musty, rutting smell.

This was not pleasure as she would have normally interpreted it. It's true that she did enjoy the surrender of intention, the way her body responded to him so immediately. There is a whole sphere of herself about which she has been ignorant. In earlier years, she had worried that when the time came, she wouldn't know what to do. A ridiculous fear in retrospect. Still, there wasn't much pleasure in it. Some pain, in fact. And it had been over so quickly.

He pulls away from her to step over to the stove. A pale form lifting the stovelid, face briefly illumined by the weak glow of coals. He drops in a scrap of board and a handful of bark slivers, replacing the lid with a clang, twisting at the flue. He climbs back in beside her and sits up under the elk hide, his back against the wall. The fire revives. He fingers tobacco across a trimmed square of newspaper, tightening it with delicate motions of his thumb and forefinger and then lighting it with a match struck on the wall. She lies on her side, crowded against the wall and making no attempt to cover her breasts. A brave gesture that he seems not to notice. She asks him for a puff and then decides to keep the cigarette, idly curious as to his reaction. He waits a moment, then moves to roll another one. This eternal tide of social aggression and surrender.

Where did you kill your elk? she asks.

Elk Fork, he says, the flare of a second match shadowing his nose, his cheekbones.

She puffs at her cigarette, liking the taste: stronger, more pungent than the machine-rolled cigarettes she had occasionally smoked at home. There's a sudden clattering on the roof, like a handful of dropped marbles, and she jumps, inhaling too deeply. By the time her coughs have subsided, the first heavy wash of hail and rain has dissipated into a steady soft drizzle. She smells the moisture. Cold rain with a metallic tinge to it. Like water on the cheek of a bell.

She settles back again, the cigarette pinched between the tips of her fingers. She is someone's lover now. A new identity to pluck off the rack.

The stove hisses, flares, burns bright. She adjusts the elk hide, contriving to get a better look at what makes men tick. He sees her at it and folds the skin back for them both. He is looking at her as well, and she resists the impulse to cover herself.

So that's what all the fuss is about, she thinks. She can't take her eyes off it. This thing men keep hidden. And not just this man, all men. He is watching her. He kisses her lightly, then more strongly, sliding down, pulling her down after him. She hadn't been aware you could do it more than once in a single night.

There is less frenzy in him now, more consideration. Later, she lies surprised, lip-bruised, perspiring. She thinks, *So. Now.* Reordering all the convictions she had created not fifteen minutes before.

She is determined to take some new understanding away from this night. She wants to think that she has become a different person. That certain rooms have been opened to her. She thinks about it, and decides that now she understands why men take the lead on the dance floor. Why it's their right to call the tempo and mood and motion of a dance. She understands now why Baptists don't like jazz.

No wonder, she thinks.

The sound of rain patters away. His arm is empty around her and his breathing deepens, grows hoarse. Later, as the room lightens, she realizes that she hasn't slept at all. In a few minutes, she will dress without waking him and open the door to a landscape dulled by three inches of new snow. Heavy nailheads of snow still falling, the sharp edges of the yard blunted into bent elbows and knees. For now, however, inside his arm, studying the rhythms of his sleep, she thinks that this night, this hour, will remain with her, will stand within this particular month, this particular year, like a pivot.

48

MOTIONLESS, eyes half closed, he watches the girl dress. An hour ago, she had slept with one arm over his elk hide, one white breast exposed, marred by a small mole, by a faint blue web of veins. She is smaller than any woman he's ever slept with, and it seems very like a crime, a shameful act, to top a woman of such a size. But some part of him relishes it. Holds it close like a good hand of cards.

After she leaves, he dresses and walks around to the barn, past the calving and milking sheds and into the horse stalls, grabbing up a double handful of oats and opening the stall door, standing quiet while the grulla mare, her late season colt beside her, licks his palms clean.

Lucky, he says, running his hand across her withers.

His mother's favorite horse. Thirteen, fourteen years old and bred nearly every year, despite her light color.

Just cause you're gentle, he says to her. Just cause you're gentle.

His mother grew up with such violent, mean-tempered reservation beasts. Flogging roosters and a single mongrel stallion tethered in the yard, zebra-striped on its hocks, culled from the Pryor mountain herd. That's what she says she remembers from those early days.

He leads the two horses outside, shutting the mare inside the corral then dropping a loop over the colt's neck, leading it out to the snubbing post. In the corral, the mare paces and turns, bucks against nothing. He slides a halter, cut down to size, over the colt's nose, buckling it against the animal's nervous jerking. He ties it off to the snubbing post with a short length of rope. The colt rears a little, jerks against the rope, then jerks again, hard enough to knock itself off its feet. It hangs half throttled by the halter until it manages to squirm upright, jerking again, more tentatively now.

Henry stands close by, ready to jump in if need be. He's seen colts die being halter broke, for no good reason at all. Spirit broke, maybe.

The back edges of the storm blow past down the valley. The snow dwindles away and the first glints of sun pierce the clouds. Might turn into a nice day. Through the cottonwoods, he watches his father pull out the Pierce-Arrow and leave it running in front of the house. With that back seat hollowed out and that engine big enough to outrun most anything on the road, he's got himself a booze runner's car if there ever was one. But wherever he's going this morning, it's going to be cold. That car top is still broke. One of the metal guides needs soldered. He looks at the colt, looks at the car. He smokes his cigarette and spits, pinching tobacco off his tongue.

After the sun is well up, he unties the colt (standing quiet and still now) and leads it into the corral with the mare. The foal first moves to suckle, but then pauses. Turns back to stare at Henry with the distant, puzzled gaze of an animal suddenly set upon by the world.

She swept the crumbs off the table and into her hand. "There should be a word for that moment of pause after sudden violence," she said. "The first deep breath after a car crash. The hollow seconds after a pistol shot. In the same way, there should be a word for the quiet after love. For the kind of pleasure that comes only in the absence of pain."

49

LET ME SHOW YOU the valley, Frank Mohr had said to Charlie. Welcome you to Wyoming proper like. And now she rides slewed side to side, willingly loose-boned, bounced by Mohr's inexact management of the clutch. Smug with her secret. She has shown *them*. They don't know it, of course, but she has shown *them*.

She has taken enough slow, brooding walks on this road for the new speed of the car to strike her as something remarkable. Despite the fact that Mohr has never seen fit to show *her* the valley, she rides exhilarated by the passing landscape. Mohr has put the top down — for the view, he had said — and so they ride fully exposed to a valley painted in broad strokes of white by bristle-twists of gray. As the day warms, wheelbarrow-sized clumps of snow fall from yellow, fall-leafed cottonwoods until they are preceded, and followed, by muted whumps, by bursts of bright color within this monochromatic stillness. They spin and bounce rut to rut, peeling up moist, tire-wide strips of snow behind them. Rocky mud ticks under their tires. Magpies, clustered around a deer carcass, unroll off the road in a sheet. Virginia stares at the back of Charlie's neck, his big ears; her aunt shivers beside her, huddled down in a mound of scarves and skirts. They drive east, accompanied by Mohr's nonstop narration.

Cattle prices are down, he is saying, sheep prices dropping through the floor. People got money but nobody's spendin it. These rich people, hell, all they want is to be entertained. I don't have to tell you that.

Greed knows greed, she thinks. The way dogs recognize each other.

Pauline gives her an unreadable look, then leans forward to interrupt Mohr. How is your family, Charlie? she asks, touching him on the shoulder.

Father never changes, he says. Buying and selling money.

But what a good name he's built for himself.

That Howard Eaton, Mohr says to Charlie, he's the guy who figured it all out first. Dude ranchin.

Virginia takes her aunt's hand, imbued with a generosity of spirit that she is, for the moment, inclined to share.

They're goin a be comin by trainloads, Mohr says, gesturing out past the windshield. That Howard Eaton? He got the railroad to add four Pullman cars just for this year's Fourth of July. Just for all them folks stayin at his ranch. Hell, him and the governor are best friends.

They drive past a snowman slumped in the Wapiti schoolhouse yard, then over a steel truss bridge, and finally down into a car camp above Shoshone Lake. They park amid the litter of empty tin cans, tent stakes, and magazines riffling in the wind. The two men walk away from the car, Mohr's hand on Charlie's elbow. Virginia sits listening to pieces of conversation brought close by the breeze. Something about oil, coal, and space. Most valuable things in Wyoming, Mohr says. And what this valley's got is space.

She loves it. Loves sitting in the car with her aunt beside her, the old woman returning the firmness of her grip, albeit in commiseration rather than camaraderie. Loves it that she has left her lover sleeping. That he is awake now and thinking about her. Shaving. Combing his hair. The morning rituals as private as his own clothes. She wonders which side of his face he shaves first, and tells herself that she must remember to notice. Most of all, she loves it that she has joined the company of women.

Charlie turns, his hands in his pockets, his elbows overextended against the cold. He winks at her.

Hollywood's goin a shoot a movie here, Mohr says. Somethin bout a horse. *Devil Horse* or *Satan Horse* or somethin.

She eases back in the seat, leaning her head against her aunt's shoulder, warming the old woman's hand between her two palms. A hand narrow and long as a spatula, the bones brittle, the skin spotted with a hundred freckles. She sure hopes that the baby doesn't get Charlie's ears.

50

THE BEAM of his father's flashlight runs floor to ceiling, trembling in the dirt corners still moist from last year's flooding, past floor joists stuffed haphazardly with strips of asbestos. Tomato plants hung by their roots from wire hooks, dirt walls reinforced with fenceposts, boards moldering at their corners, shelves stacked with rows of candled eggs, jars of jelly preserves, canned meats, and apple butter; sacks of flour and sugar set off the floor with lumber scraps turned on edge. An unheard-of extravagance in this country: a log cabin with a basement.

He walks to the wall of preserves — to the conspicuous,

shoulder-wide space between the shelves — and pulls a nail jutting out at the level of his head, then another at his waist. A pair of wide boards swing inward on concealed hinges, revealing the entrance to the hidden section of the cellar. He hooks his fingers through the handles of his two tin jugs and steps into the space, closing the door behind him, wedging it tight with a sack of sugar.

In the wavering beam of his flashlight, Mohr's booze distillery seems like some ill-assembled monster, some cave creature caught sleeping, curled nose to tail. A fifteen-horsepower boiler with an eight-inch chimney pipe disappearing into the ceiling. A single half-inch copper pipe feeding an empty mash barrel and another one running from the mash to the doubler. The rim of the room's ceiling ventilated with sewage pipes open to the outside. The boiler's stovepipe has been incorporated into the great room's chimney, which — give the old man credit — is a bright idea. Keep a fire burning in the room up above, Mohr has said, and nobody ever need know this thing's down here. Half the law in the state'll be lookin for smoke lines and horse trails but nobody'll ever think of looking under a man's own house.

The walls are lined with paper sacks of sugar and larger, deflated sacks of cracked corn, a gray metal cashbox of caked yeast set off in a corner. There are half a dozen fifty-five-gallon barrels of working mash and, along the base of one wall, two rows of stone jugs trucked up from Mexico, large jugs behind, smaller jugs in front. The bragging rights of this particular operation. In the absence of bottled hooch, every bootlegger worth the name has a trademark, a signature to set him apart from his competitors. There are men who cut fresh peaches into the jugs. Who dribble real booze (Canadian Club usually) into each gallon. Mohr's claim is that these stone jugs impart an essential cleanliness to the alcohol. Clean as mountain snow, he says.

Henry sits cross-legged on one of the mash barrels, smoking a cigarette, tapping the ash into his shirt pocket. The dry, unfired boiler. The copper pipe gleaming in the light of the upturned flashlight. They had dug this cellar together, boy and man shoulder to shoulder, and at the end of that first day Frank had given him his first sip of whiskey. He'd been twelve years old, and he can still remember that burnt-rope taste on his tongue, the immediate association of having done something well. The closeness he'd felt to his father. But then a few days later Frank had given him one of the worst beatings of his life. A shaving strop across his back until the edges had cut blood from his skin. Henry had left a corral gate unlocked, and that big jenny mule of theirs, smart enough to lift a gate latch with her nose, had let herself loose. The scars are on his back yet.

Henry wets his fingers and pinches out his smoke, puts it in his pocket. If he's going to do this thing, he'd best get to it.

He kneels over one of the large stone jugs, uncorking it with his teeth and lifting it to his knee, tilting it until a thread of clear booze trickles into his own tin jug. He pours a cup or so, then nudges the stone container back into its ring of dust. Before replacing the cork, he tops it off with a cup of water from the second of his two containers.

It's only when he's halfway down the line, when his first jug is nearly full, chilled by the evaporation of alcohol, that he stops to consider the row of stone jugs. There should be a couple of them missing. *Buskin,* he thinks. Those empty saddlebags and jugs that had disappeared off Buskin's horse. Disappeared when he died. But there are not, in fact, a couple missing, and Henry stares at the row of containers for a long time.

He finally decides that it doesn't matter. He's making a stake and heading out. That cloud of dust on the horizon is Henry Mohr.

When he leaves the cellar, he has been underground for no more than fifteen minutes, although it feels like longer. Time spent in the dark is a different kind of time altogether. He leaves carrying two jugs and three jars of canned tomatoes. Everyone knows he loves canned tomatoes, and they'll serve as a reason for his trip should anyone see him.

The storm has passed quickly, as these late fall storms do. A few last threads of cloud linger over Rattlesnake. His tracks in the snow (he hadn't thought about leaving tracks, and now he berates himself for his stupidity) have melted into snowshoe-shaped absences, the grass already springing back into place.

It's not guilt that he feels walking away from his father's still, carrying twenty dollars' worth of booze. Not guilt, but the sense of a return to childhood. The innocent, nervous expectation of getting away with something. He finds himself invigorated.

51

SLEET SPLASHES against the windows. The candles on the table flicker, and an oil lamp moans through the mouth of its chimney. The dining table, previously unadorned, sits expanded now with two leaves, decorated with silver candlesticks and wool placemats, crockery from the pie safe wiped clean of dust accumulated since Christmas. Virginia thinks that Frank must have found a book of etiquette somewhere. She had earlier watched him tentatively supervise the table arrangements. The placement of forks and knives. The filling of new finger bowls with warm water and floating slices of lemon. While Ah Ting and Rose had folded napkins and brought out fresh candles, he had stood at one end of the table, pointing chair to chair and saying, Charlie, Virginia, Adze, Pauline, Henry, Rose . . . Boy girl, boy girl.

They sit around the table as they have sat every night since

Charlie's arrival, passing bowls and murmuring notes of acceptance and decline. Sweet potatoes sauced in molasses (which Rose had managed to position, with a grin at Virginia, in front of Henry's plate) and sourdough biscuits mounded in an iron tureen. Knuckles of ham and a chicken fried in corn batter. A bowl of string beans topped with strips of bacon. At Virginia's elbow, Charlie piles his plate nearly as full as her own. Across from her, Pauline sits behind a small chunk of sweet potato, a single chicken wing.

Even Henry has taken to dressing up for dinner, wearing a clean white dress shirt buttoned to the neck. Beside him, Rose fidgets in a navy blue petticoat, tight around her shoulders and upper arms. Virginia wears the clothes she's worn for three days. Since Charlie's been living in the cabin next to theirs, every stitch she owns has sat at the foot of his bed, and she has sworn to herself that she's not going to be reduced to asking Charlie for her own clothes. She sops up the last of her potatoes with a biscuit then finishes her buttermilk. She is in a fine mood, and decides to have another biscuit.

Mohr glances at her, his face unreadable. He leans back, pushing his plate away with his thumb. He lights a cigar and waves it at Charlie. Did you ever join up with any of them college societies you hear about? he asks. Them fraternity societies?

Charlie nods and swallows a bite of food, starting to speak, but Virginia clears her throat first, and says with great seriousness, He joined the society for men with tiny little tallywhackers. Isn't that right, Charlie?

He stares at her, closing his mouth with a toothclick heard up and down the table.

She leans back and pats her stomach. A comment either on the meal or on her authority to make such a pronouncement. We were all real proud, she says.

She grins down the table at Henry. At her lover. But he's

looking only at Charlie, then at Pauline, finally at Adze. Ticking them off one by one. She follows his eyes and finds herself, like him, fascinated by the varied reactions around the table. Her aunt, gray head bowed and the claw of one finger to her mouth, as if to scratch away a sob. Adze with the wrinkled corners of his mouth containing a grin. And Rose, wide-eyed, puzzled. Frank Mohr has half stood from his chair and is just now sinking back. A vulgarity at his table, in his house. Committed by a woman. And a woman here under the aegis of another man.

He sits farther back, studying her. And still there is no sound at the table.

Charlie stands up, raising his waterglass. To my fiancée, he says.

What? Virginia says. *What?*

To my fiancée. Whose tongue is sharper than her judgment of size.

Frank guffaws, lifting his glass to Charlie. Hear, hear, he says, leveling his eyes at Virginia. No one else lifts a glass. No one moves.

After a moment, Virginia stands with her empty mug of milk. In a snapshot of this room they do indeed seem a pair. These two young people at a table of gray-skinned, gray-haired patrons. Frozen statues of celebration. Charlie in his suitcoat and weskit, Virginia in her aunt's cardigan, her corduroy skirt three inches too long and soiled at the hem. An old story, this snapshot. An ancient tale of affluent patron and ragged wastrel.

To the man who raped me, she says. Whose understanding of women is . . .

Enough! Mohr jumps to his feet, chair clattering back behind him. Enough out of you, young missy. I've had *enough*. Paradin around here with your books . . . Look at me when I'm talkin to you goddamnit! Your books and your drawins and actin like we was all here to be walked on. Well that's fine, but when this good man here follows you two thousand miles to do the honorable thing and then you treat him like *that,* well, that's just *enough.* You'll be quiet . . . Look at me goddamnit! You'll be quiet and you'll know your place and you'll! Stay! In! It! He pounds out these last words with his fist.

Virginia stands frozen. Frozen for true. She has never been cursed at before. *No,* she thinks. *One other time. Just the one other time.*

Well, Pauline says, her hands fidgeting up to her plate, then back down to her lap. Virginia looks at her, lowering her glass.

Well, Pauline says again softly. An old woman defeated.

52

DON'T MAKE *too much of this,* he thinks. This little girl who's come up out of the blue and is likely to leave in just the same way. When a storm blows in quick, it's going out quick. Nevertheless, he feels uncomfortable. That sonofabitch doing everything he can to embarrass her, to belittle her, just to make points with that other sonofabitch.

She looks like she's going to say something, those narrow eyebrows going narrower still, but then she keeps quiet, leaving a conspicuous absence at the table. She's watching him, and he can feel how she wants him to say something. How suddenly she has been set against everyone in the room.

He drops his eyes to his plate. Peels a thread of chicken meat from its bone, chews at it. Works out a piece of gristle. Picks up that little bowl of lemon water and takes a sip.

53

THEY SIT on the edge of his bed, staring at the wall. Her hands folded in her lap, his hands caught under his thighs. Six inches of thick, unyielding space between them. She had stayed away the night before, finally managing to sleep despite the lingering salt-tang taste of his skin, the remembered feel of his thumbnail against her tongue. This sear of anger like air frozen in her nostrils.

I'm sorry, he says. He picks the envelope of cigarettes off the nightstand, leaving it unopened in his hand.

You said that. She bunches her skirt into her fists. I can't believe . . . I mean, you just *sat* there.

Sorry.

Your mother even came to me and apologized. I didn't come to her.

She's always apologizin for somethin. Henry opens the envelope, picking through the loose tobacco and flat papers until he finds a rolled cigarette. He pulls it out and tightens it idly between his thumbs and forefingers.

I don't know how she can stand to live with that man.

Henry shrugs.

I almost didn't come here. She smoothes her skirt flat.

Why did you?

She stares at her hands, at the trembling she can feel but can't see. For the first time in weeks, she wants to cry. And she's so tired. Two o'clock in the morning and her name is Virginia Price. What is she doing here?

This was a mistake, she says, standing up.

Virginia.

All a mistake. She lays the palm of her hand flat on the door.

Despite herself, she pauses. The cot creaks behind her, and she feels her hand taken. She leaves it limp. You could have said something, she says.

He leans heavily against the door beside her, holding her hand by its fingers. Only way to deal with Pap is ignore him.

How can you possibly ignore what that man said to me?

You can ignore most anything if you put your mind to it. He traces her arm from wrist to shoulder to neck. Where'd you get this scar? he asks.

She pulls her arm back. I think I hate him, she says.

He touches her hair, brushes a fingertip down her face to the edge of her eyes, to the curve of her cheek. He's nothin to you.

If I were a man, I would have punched him.

I ain't punchin nobody. He touches her lips. Rests his fingers there lightly, the way a flame rests on its candle. Then he kisses her.

Afterward, lying inside his arm, she says, I don't know how your mother can stand that man.

Have her tell you about her first husband sometime. My real pap.

Why?

Ask her.

The stove ticks. A cold night breeze rattles the latch on the door. Virginia says, No one seemed surprised when I said rape. Last night.

Oh?

He twists away from her, pulling his cigarette makings off the nightstand. She stares at the immutable, knotted rope of his spine, the close-cropped back of his head, then punches him hard on the shoulder, her elbow bouncing first against the wall, taking the strength from the blow. He glances back, licking his cigarette. What was that for?

Tell me, she says, shaking his shoulder. Tell me. Tell me.

Your mother.

What about her?

Wrote us a letter. Said you had you a good imagination.

A good imagination. But you didn't believe it?

Never believed it.

Later still, she listens to him sleep. Watches him. Finding a perverse satisfaction in his contradictions: the contained strength in his arms, the open vulnerability of his bare chest. She draws back to watch his eyes roll under their lids.

What is he seeing?

What could he be seeing?

54

A CLEAR DAY, but cold. Engines of heart, blood, and bone pounding through the horse under him, clouds of steam out through her nostrils. He works Ballo in the hayfield above the house, neck-reining her side to side until he can feel her growing tired, frustrated. He tries to back her up a step or two, then trots down to the house. Leaning beside the porch steps, Adze smokes a cigarette. Henry drops the reins around a rail and walks up to him.

How's she doin? Adze asks. He flicks ash off to the side.

Good, Henry says. Hardheaded, but good.

Best horses I've ever had all been hardheaded. Stubborn enough to stay loyal.

Thinkin about startin her in on a bridle.

Already?

She's plumb got the hang a that hackamore. Henry studies the horse, standing hipshot at the rail, dozing.

I wouldn't hurry it.

Henry nods, then glances at the coffee cup on the rail. Don't you ever work?

I work. Sure I work. Hell, I worked some last week.

Adze flicks his ash, and Henry notices his right thumb, red and swollen.

Gettin rusty on the dally in your old age? he asks.

Hell, that Charleston horse. Can't throw a loop off him without there bein some kind a wreck. Jugheaded sonofabitch.

About give up on him?

About.

Henry grins at Adze and, after a moment, Adze grins back. The smooth sheath of gums broken here and there by a crooked, brown-rimmed tooth. As far as Henry knows, Adze has never given up on a horse in his life.

Henry picks up the empty coffee cup. Sniffs at it. Says, Not much to do, I guess. Just that dude ranch comin up is all.

Just like to keep up with the news.

Henry nods, then says, I guess I don't know what that means.

They are standing on either side of the porch stairs. Behind them to the left, the open window of the great room. To their right, the blowing curtains of the master bedroom. Regardless of the temperature, Rose believes in airing out her house. Adze cups a hand behind his hairy ear and tilts it first to one window, then the other. Just keepin up with the news, he says.

Henry steps around Adze to the first window. Behind the curtains, he hears the rustle of paper. Then, quite clearly, his father's voice: . . . here, see? Here's how that ground comes down to the road. And now here . . . Henry hears papers rustling again. Now here's that creek I was tellin you about.

Henry draws on his cigarette and walks along the wall, sliding his feet against the boards. Outside the master bedroom, he hears the flap of a linen sheet unfolding, then his mother's voice. Pregnant women should drink lots of water, she's saying. You been drinkin lots of water? Makes your blood thin. And you don't want no men around when it comes time. Gives you a long labor. And don't eat no cooked meat right after. Maybe some jerky, if you want. Oh, almost forgot. You'd better sleep with your feet to the door. Makes the baby want to come.

He hears a pleasant contentment in her voice. A note that he hasn't heard for a long, long time. Virginia asks a question, her voice low and removed, and there is a pause before his mother says, in a voice nearly as low as the girl's, He ain't a bad man. He's just got his bad days. I don't know. The Lord giveth, that's all I know. And sometimes he don't take away again for a good long while. Grab that corner there, would you please?

Henry pulls abruptly away from the window, stepping back toward Adze.

They still talkin about you?

Henry shakes his head.

Know it or not, you got you a fan club buildin there, son.

Is that a fact?

Adze nods, winks.

Well, Henry says. You know. New York.

What's that?

Nothin.

Adze takes up his empty coffee cup and tilts it back, trying for one last sip. He sets the cup on the rail and lays a hand on Henry's shoulder. They're good folks, son. Good folks. That old aunt of hers? I told her I used to drink a little tea now and then back in California and she went and give me a whole tin of it.

How's it taste?

Awful. Adze shakes his head and starts to chuckle, then coughs. Never said I liked it. But still. Good folks.

55

SHE WOULD DESPAIR at the thought that love is nothing but an excuse for sex. A justification of pleasure. And yet it occurs to her.

She has been trying to isolate the odors in his shack. Gun oil and a dry, fetid meat smell from the box of skulls under his bed. Urine. Leather from the elk skin. She worries about her own odors, about the odors of their sex. In the past, in her girlhood, she had tried to imagine every facet of love. The sweat. She had thought about that. The pain. But the odors she had never considered. She worries about them now, through the fog of their illicitness. The vaguely disagreeable, athletic, confined odor of their sex. How is it that everyone, simply everyone, doesn't smell them? Henry doesn't keep a clock, but she supposes it's probably one-thirty, maybe two in the morning. She'll need to be back in her own bed by three at the latest. Afflicted with the problems of the aged, her aunt sleeps lighter as the night progresses.

She plays with the slight ring of hair around his nipple. The trail of tiny hairs below the navel. It's the same pattern, the same line, as the trail of brown skin that has appeared with the stretching of her stomach.

Who do you envy? she asks, her fingertips pressureless on his skin. A game she used to play with Isabel at school. Rapid-fire question and answer. No pauses allowed.

What?

Who do you envy?

Never thought about it. He raises an arm over his face and turns slightly away from her.

What do you love?

He shrugs.

What are you ashamed of?

Don't know.

What do you regret?

Isn't that the same thing?

She sighs, blowing against the back of his neck, ruffling the short hair. Rose wouldn't tell me anything about your real father.

Oh?

She said she'd never been married before.

Well. That's her story to tell, I guess.

I guess, she says. I guess.

She has begun to think of him as a place. A point. A point within a triangulation. The way her father used to describe how lobstermen find their traps. A place where she dives to find herself. Again. And again. She thinks that she needs him much more than he needs her.

56

HE RIDES Ballo up the old Cannonball Trail, crossing what used to be H Bar pasture, stepping her over a curl of tangled fencewire before turning north, following a set of faded wagon tracks. Two thousand feet above the valley floor, he leads his horse down the face of a clay hillside to Galileo Donahugh's homestead cabin. Nice little two-room outfit, cedar shakes, a thread of smoke curling from the lava-stone chimney.

Gal stands hitching up his suspenders in the doorway as Henry dismounts. A man unremarkable in appearance save for the slab of scar tissue up one side of his face. An old carbide burn running temple to cheek to collar, tightening the corner of his mouth into an unvarying smile and putting a lisp into every word. He carries a handkerchief knotted up in his hand, always ready to blot at the spittle trickling from the corner of his mouth.

Dammey if it ain't Henry Mohr, he says, taking Henry's reins.

Henry nods. Hello, Gal.

How'd the war treat ye then?

Treated me fine, Gal.

Well then. I suppose ye'd best come in and have ye a cup of tea then. Tell me some'n about it.

They sit before a kettle of oolong tea at Gal's kitchen table, the pinewood top beveled and mitered, and the tools that did the work wrapped in greasecloth in the corner. The kettle rests on a potholder stitched from scraps of leather. Henry drinks from a bone china cup warmed before the tea was poured, deciding after the first sip that he doesn't like tea too much, either. But he does admire Gal's meticulousness. Always has. The considered care with which he approaches every job. An attention that arises, maybe, in compensation for the haphazard wreck of the man himself. Gal cuts his own hair, and while everything in sight of the mirror has been neatly combed and trimmed, the hair around the back of his head stands out in clumps.

Henry says something about the war, about where he had been billeted, then politely asks after the farming.

Gal leans forward and drops his heavy forearms on the table. The aggressive concentration of a man too much alone. He tells Henry that he's still proving up on this 640 acres. And that little reservoir above the house with its gravity-fed irrigation lines? Not nearly enough for what he's got planted. Good crop at the head of the field but just a few leaves at the bottom. Long way from here to Nebraska. Longer way from Nebraska to Scotland.

A ninety-two-year-old mother in Kirkwall. A dead wife and daughter. A burned-out smithy in Kearney. A hundred private names for the stands of rock behind his house: spires named for dead children, dead aunts, near-forgotten uncles. Favorite dogs.

After the third cup of tea, Henry walks out to his horse and returns with one of his tin jugs, setting it on the table beside the kettle. Gal carries it back into his bedroom, emerging with a small wad of folded bills. Henry sticks the wad in his shirt pocket without counting it.

Ten minutes later, Gal stands elbow-propped in the door, watching him leave. He is still watching as Henry tops the hill, a quarter mile away.

Henry thinks that maybe his mother's got it right. It could be that fear of the Lord is the beginning of all wisdom. And if not of the Lord, then just plain fear. But he thinks that fear should figure in there somewhere.

57

HER PREGNANCY has begun, at times, to offer her an unexpected clarity of perception. A sharpening of the senses that mirrors the effect of alcohol. The way booze dulls her, this baby brightens her. She sees, for instance, that Nettie is the real master of this house. If she defers occasionally to Rose, it's only for the sake of appearances. Arriving at seven each morning, she rushes into the kitchen red-cheeked, breathless from having ridden her horse up from Post Creek. Glancing around the kitchen, appraising the stack of dishes in the sink, the water boiling on the stove. To make sure it's been set to work, she peeks under the cheesecloth laid over Ah Ting's sourdough behind the stove. Finally, as she starts in on the dishes, she lays out the day for them all, often under the pretense of asking Rose for advice.

Don't ye think, she says — her Irish coming through strongest in the mornings, after having spent the night with her mother and father — don't ye think we should beat out those bedroom rugs this week? Maybe this mornin? And it'd be good if little Gus could bring up some fresh blocks from the icehouse. And if those cakes of butter haven't gone over, maybe we could trade for a few oranges from the Durrels? That daughter of theirs just got back from San Diego.

Rose nods, accepting Nettie's suggestions as the way the day should certainly go.

When she can, Virginia prefers to follow Rose as she does the day's chores. Standing at her elbow, ready to help her grease a bread pan, carry rugs to the line for beating. There's something inexplicably calming about the woman. The deliberate way she walks through her house. Once a day, they polish the cherry-wood jewelry box Rose keeps by her bed. And if they are alone in the room, Rose opens the box to show her again the old photos of Frank and Henry, the blue-and-red-beaded rag doll she'd had as a baby, the tiny moccasins shiny with grease and wood-smoke.

Virginia enjoys the work (at least she finds it not unpleasant) — the uniting with Rose in a common end — but she also enjoys the way it irritates Charlie. When he is not with Mohr, he follows her around the house. Asking politely after her health, her mother. When do you feel like going back to New York? he'll ask. And it's much easier to ignore him when her hands are busy, when she can devote all her attention to peeling carrots, to scooping ashes out of the fireplace. Eventually he'll turn away, pretending to take an interest in a blanket tacked to the wall, an antelope skull hung with fishing line. He'll pick up one of Mohr's shotguns racked by the front door, swinging it around, dry-firing it at the ragged pheasant mounted above the fireplace.

The two women strike a curious balance. Nettie and Rose. Young and old. Thin and portly. Rose works silently, competently, implacable as machinery. Nettie talks constantly, avoiding those jobs that would keep her on her feet. Even when she chooses her work with care, the limp that's barely noticeable in the morning becomes a thrusting stagger by late afternoon.

On Monday mornings, regardless of the weather, Virginia and Nettie set the washboiler over the firepit and fill it with buckets of well water, cakes of homemade lye soap arranged beside it. Virginia watches Nettie boil the clothes, pushing them back and forth before slinging each piece over into the washtub to be scrubbed up and down. Everything goes through two rinses and then the handwringer before being passed back to Virginia to hang. Nettie takes pains even with how the clothes are dried, insisting that each shirt be attached to its neighbor by a common clothespin, that the colored pieces be turned inside out, that the clothes in need of ironing be brought inside, still damp from the line, to be pressed with one of Rose's flatirons heating on the stove. If the day is cold, their routine doesn't change, except that the clothes are brought in frozen and stiff to finish drying by the kitchen stove.

Even this job, with its way of wrinkling Virginia's hands and turning her temper short, has its pleasant compensations. A sense of camaraderie. She enjoys watching Nettie push at the clothes. Her infectious good humor.

Kate she is a bonnie wife, Nettie sings, pointing to Virginia and bouncing out the rhythm with her forefinger. *There's none so free from evil. Unless upon a washing day. And then she is the devil. For 'tis thump thump scrub scrub. Scold scold away. The de'il a bit of comfort here. Upon a washing day.*

Hanging up a pair of Frank Mohr's spotted, threadbare underwear, Virginia says, If I'd known what you can find out about a person from his drawers, I doubt I'd have gone to all those petting parties.

Jaysus. Petting parties! Nettie grabs Virginia's forearm with her soapy hands. You've *been* to those? Do you read *True Story*? All that talk about petting parties. Is that all a bunch of horseshite?

No. It's real.

No!

On a whim, encouraged by the conspiracy in Nettie's little face, Virginia says, I have a boyfriend, you know.

I know you do, Nettie says, holding up one of Henry's shirts, looking for stains.

It's Henry.

Eh? Nettie wrings out the shirt, then lets it splash back into the tub. What's that? *What?*

Henry, Virginia says.

But that's perfect! Nettie hugs her, leaving two damp, soapy smudges on her back. Perfect! Two nicest people I know!

Well thank you, Nettie.

Oh God, she says, grinning wide, then holding her hands over the grin. Old man Mohr'd just snatch himself bald. Him and that Charlie? Best friends.

So I understand.

Nettie sits on the edge of the washtub, facing her. Now, she says. Tell me all about it.

58

HE MUST BE COLD. She watches him shiver and blow into his hands. Watches him squat to buckle into his angora chaps and shrug into a sheepskin vest that she knows still stinks of lanolin. He steps off the porch, the loose bottoms of his chaps flapping, and takes the reins from Adze, mounting up just as Frank and Dewey ride around from the barn. The four of them trot across the road then break into pairs and disappear into the foothills. She takes a breath and turns away from the window.

She thinks that anyone would be able to see Charlie for what he is. Or what he isn't. His heavy-soled work boots up on the breakfast table, as innocent of dirt as the day they were pulled off the shelf. He leans back in his chair, affecting an interest in the ceiling beams. Blowing smoke rings.

She takes up the dishes from the table, drawing forks and knives into her fist and scraping off the remains of egg and toast and apple butter onto one plate. She'll get the coffee mugs on her next trip.

Charlie says, I don't like to see you doing housework.

I like it, she says.

Housework like some nigger. He drops his feet on the floor and taps ashes into a saucer.

I don't think there's a black man in this whole valley.

There's yellow niggers, he says. And red ones. He winks at her.

She sets his coffee mug off on the table and picks up his saucer, adding it to her stack.

As soon as the road melts, he says, I'll take you into town and buy you some decent clothes.

A ring of moisture leaks off the dishes and onto her shirt. I don't want you to buy me anything, she says, backing into the kitchen.

Well, it might be spring, anyway. The way it looks out there now.

Ah Ting is sitting in the corner on his low stool in his socks and thongs, cubing potatoes, tossing the chunks into the iron kettle between his feet. He glances up and wipes his nose with the back of his sleeve. He tosses his head so that the queue lies more easily down his back. Nettie stands with her back to the door, scooping jam back into a jar. Virginia sets the plates on the counter and touches the back of Nettie's head. A single twisted braid, nappy and unwashed, the color of rusted pipe. Nettie turns and smiles at her. That quick, instinctive grin.

You have the loveliest hair, Virginia says.

59

WIND SKITTERS through the grass at their feet, blowing the last few tendrils of old snow into drifts.

Henry looks to the west. It's goin a rain, he says.

His father shakes his head. Snow if anything.

Frank Mohr is not a lazy man. Not lazy like you think of lazy. No afternoon naps, no cut hay left rotting in the field. But he has a lazy man's habit of putting off what he doesn't care to do. Jobs that don't make him the money he thinks he should make. As if his time was so valuable. Early November and they're just now getting around to fall gathering.

They ride up the western edge of the lease toward the timber, on the rim of a runoff coulee. I thought you was headin out, Mohr says.

Not for a while now.

I suppose you think you can live here without a care in the world. Come and go as you want. Eat my food. His father glances at him, his hat down tight against the wind.

I'm ridin here beside you, ain't I? I'm helpin you now, ain't I?

You goin a make it a habit?

Henry slow-closes his eyes. Opens them. Yessir, he says.

His father nods. I've got a whole list of things after we get these cows down.

What can you pay me?

Can't afford to pay you.

What about all that money you're makin off a the hooch?

Hell, half that goes to Loomis, keep him and that deputy out of our hair. The other half goes to the makins, sugar and yeast. Not hardly worth the trouble by the time you get done with it.

Yeah, you've always been real good about doin things out a the kindness of your heart.

You watch that mouth, boy.

After a moment, Henry says again, It's goin a rain. There's a moist warmth in the wind that they can both feel. Henry unbuttons his vest, thinking how heavy the chaps are going to be when they get wet. Found any more a that footrot? he asks.

Mohr shakes his head, glancing up at the wind in the trees. Of all the shittin days to gather, he says.

Henry crosses the draw and rides into the foothills parallel to his father, in and out of scrub juniper, then heavy timber. The rain comes while he's in the timber, and at first he's not sure if it's rain at all or maybe just the wind, but then the heaviest drops make their way down through the branches to fall like cap shots on his slicker. He rides at a pace measured to stay even with his father, and when he comes to the border fence he cuts back across the draw, riding up just as Mohr is trying to light a cigar, shielding the fire with his hand.

Maybe up by that Black Toe rock.

Maybe.

His father tosses the cigar to the ground, disgusted, and they ride farther up the mountain, parallel to the fence. Henry drops down into the timber, but the timber is empty save for a single deer clattering out ahead of him. He's always thought that if there were any good bucks left in this low country they'd be in the timber. Why they're good bucks. He pats his horse, realizing that he doesn't even know the animal's name. Gettin a little headache, he tells the horse.

He circles back up to his father on the edge of the Black Toe clearing, the rock formation rising tall as a barn, narrow, and just now ready to fall, as it has been ready to fall for a thousand years. Half a dozen steers lay ringed in the lee of the rock, chewing cud. Two of them climb to their feet, nervous and wild after a summer in the mountains.

He and his father sit their horses, studying the steers. Mohr spits. Says, So why are you stickin around?

What?

Why are you stickin around?

Henry shrugs, then snorts up into his nose and spits. Wipes at his mouth. Mother's lonesome, he says. She gets lonesome in the winter.

His father's shaking his head. Never stopped you before, he says.

I'll run a trap or two this winter. Come spring I'll look for work.

Let me tell you what, boy. I know why you're stayin.

And why would that be?

Saw the way you were lookin at that girl at supper the other night. You didn't like it one bit what I had to say. Did you?

Henry shrugs.

You need to stay away from her, he says. Then heels his horse toward the steers.

Henry follows behind. You got some kind a deal goin with that Charlie?

His father is thoughtful. Choosing his words. We got this dude ranch thing licked, he says. Everythin but the dudes. Got the ground. Got the horses. Got a place to stay. But I've always figured if it was going to work we'd need somebody back east tellin folks what a good place this is. Hell, if those folks are goin a come and stay six, eight weeks, they got a know what they're gettin into.

There you go, Henry says.

That's right. His father nods, pleased. And just when I was about to go back east myself, along comes this Charlie.

That's between you and him, I guess. Doesn't have nothin to do with me.

Their horses roll under them, heaving up a cut in the hillside.

Let me tell you about women, Mohr says.

I know all about women.

Damn me. Anybody'd say those words don't know a thing at all. Not at *all*.

It don't seem like you had that much luck. Way you are with Mother.

Your mother and me got things figured out. But that girl down at the house. Well. Now.

They circle around above the steers, watching the rest of the animals struggle to their feet one by one. The snow is heavier this high, and the animals have worn a trail around the base of the rock. At fifty yards, the cattle startle and break and run out ahead of them.

His father says, Give it a year or two and that girl down there'd be just like a wolf in a trap.

I don't got the faintest idea what that means.

You know what it means. Fox. Coyote. They'll get in that trap and they'll do anything to get away. They'll chew their leg off. But a wolf. If he can't drag it or pull loose, he figures he's enough of a rooster to hunker down and wait it out. He figures he can take care of anything that comes along. They're in it for themselves is all I'm sayin. Mohr holds up his hand as if against protest, although Henry has said nothing. Now, now, now. I know what you're goin a say. *Everybody's* in it for themselves, and you're right. You ain't wrong. But men are weak. You got your friendships. You got your work. You got what that bartender on Saturday night's goin a think of you. Women, now. That girl. That girl big with another man's git. She's goin a look up after a year or two with you and she's got that baby at her hip and she's poor as a church mouse out here in the boondocks and things ain't quite as romantic as they used to be and she's goin a hightail it back to New York. Don't think she won't.

She's got some money a her own.

Mohr snorts. Sixteen-year-old girls don't have money a their own.

Seventeen.

They don't either.

She'll have it.

Not if her mother has somethin to say about it. You saw that letter.

I saw it.

That letter. Mohr shakes his head.

I saw it. God*damn*it.

You watch that mouth.

They ride unspeaking, pushing the steers down toward an open wire gate. Henry shivers, and pinches the water from the raised collar of his vest. He sneezes, then sneezes again. As the steers follow the slope of the hill past the opening, he says, That gate is at just the wrong angle.

Mohr spurs out ahead, cutting at the cattle and pushing them back. Henry cuts at them from the uphill side. The lead steer twists and kicks then bolts through the opening, the others just behind him. Henry sits in the open gate. His horse blows, shaking against the reins.

Mohr rides up to him, pulling a cigar from his shirt pocket, ducking his head to the match. You can't trust her, son, he says, puffing until the fire's well lit. That's it more'n anything. Can't trust a woman carryin another man's git. She'd never be loyal to you. Not entire. Look at the way your mother is with me. Has she ever been mine? Have you? Hell no. You've seen it. We've all seen it. I was just her best bet.

It ain't like that.

Frank ignores him. With that bun in the oven that girl's just like his wife. And you know what the Good Book has to say about that? He tilts his head back, pursing his lips. Proverbs, ain't it? But whoso committeth adultery with a woman lacketh understanding. He that doeth it destroyeth his own soul. Now. I want you to stay away. And that's all I'm goin a say.

They sit in the open gate, the horses shoulder to shoulder. Each man watching the steers trot down toward the river. Half a mile away, on the other side of the pasture, Dewey and Adze ride back into the timber, having pushed down two pairs.

What're you goin a do if I don't?

Mohr shrugs, spits.

Maybe you're goin a kill me like you killed Buskin?

Mohr studies the end of his cigar. Why? You been stealin hooch off a me too?

Buskin was stealin booze off a you? A little booze?

Little, hell! He was stealin me blind.

Jesus, Pap. You killed him?

Couldn't take him to the sheriff, could I? Couldn't put him in jail. Mohr reaches over and touches Henry's shoulder, squeezing the muscle between his thumb and forefinger: endearment or warning. You're a good boy, he says, but you do have some learnin to do. Or maybe it's unlearnin.

Mohr turns his horse. Best thing about bein married to your mother. Ever now and then I can have these heart-to-hearts with you and there ain't much you can do about it. I tell you, son, it does feel good to open up now and then.

60

DESPITE WHAT Rose had predicted, the birth down the valley takes place in the early afternoon rather than the morning. A wagon rolls into the yard just after lunch, driven by a stilt-limbed young man, lip and chin dusted with a velvet growth of blond hair. His name is Clive, and his coat sleeves fall short of his wrists by a good inch or two. His pants ride high above his boots. Only his floppy, sunken hat seems to fit. He stays on the wagon, calling into the house for Rose.

Rose and Virginia come to the door together, Virginia drying her hands on her apron.

Crissie's havin pains, he says, his face a study in conflicting emotions: concern and poorly contained delight.

They ride back down the valley, Rose sitting in the middle, her black medicine bag lodged firmly on her lap. Hinges rusted, leather cracked along the seams, it holds, as she's told Virginia, rolls of antiseptic gauze, balls of cotton, tweezers, a clinical thermometer, a well-sharpened trocar. A jar of olive oil to wipe off the baby in the manner of the Crow, bottles of carbolic and boric acids, horehound drops for the older children.

Clive's cabin sits above the river, surrounded by a low windbreak of clematis. They ride through the windbreak and into the yard, cottontail rabbits scattering to cower in the weeds and grass. A red-tailed hawk circles low overhead. A woman sits waiting on the porch, rocking. Clive whoas his team to a stop and throws the reins over a seat stanchion, jumping off to reach back for Rose's hand, then running around to offer a hand to Virginia. On the porch, the woman stands up, shapeless knitting like a swatch of brown fur in her hands. She is wide-shouldered and squat, pale and gaunt through her cheeks. Virginia's first impression is one of hidden disease. Clive shoulders past into the house, carrying Rose's bag. The woman hacks once into a handkerchief, then again. Wet, rattling coughs. Consumptive, Virginia would bet anything. There are no children, and Virginia feels disappointed for Rose that she won't have an opportunity to give away her candy.

Tentatively, Virginia and Rose follow Clive into the house. The walls are covered in a house lining of coarse muslin, strips sewn together and stiffened with a light green, kalsomined flour paste. Through a crack in the bedroom door, Virginia can just make out the curled steel post of a bedstead, one corner of a brightly colored quilt stitched in a wedding-ring pattern. Rose has a quilt of the same design. The bed rocks slightly, and Virginia hears a low moan.

Rose takes her bag from Clive and sets it on the floor, rolling up her sleeves. Hot water, she says. Clive raises his bony hands helplessly, then glances toward the doorway, toward the woman still standing there quietly, eyes fixed on Virginia. After a moment, she moves to the stove, lifting a teakettle off the rack overhead.

More'n that, Rose says, and the woman reaches under the stove for a metal canning crock, coughing as she extends her arm.

Rose? Clive says, bending to unlace his boots. You know Crissie's sister, Minnie?

Rose nods, squatting to open her bag. From the bedroom, they hear another moan, then the woman calling Rose's name.

Hurry with that water, Rose says, straightening and turning into the bedroom.

Minnie? Clive says. This is . . .

I'm Virginia. Pleased to meet you, Minnie.

The woman stands at the stove cupping water into the crock from the cistern at her knees. You're that girl up from New York, she says. That pregnant girl.

I suppose that's what I am.

Minnie feels the heat of the stove with her open palm, then lifts one of the plates to drop in a piece of kindling. You the one who got followed out here by her man?

Virginia shrugs, not caring for the woman's tone. Not caring for it at all.

Minnie turns to face her, and Virginia shrugs again, standing with her forearms crossed over her stomach. Minnie crosses the room toward her, coughing into her handkerchief. Close enough for Virginia to smell her breath. An odor of beef lozenge and blood. Spoiled buttermilk in her clothes. Consumptive without doubt.

This here's a Christian house, missy, Minnie says.

Beg pardon?

Rose? Minnie calls into the bedroom, keeping her eyes on Virginia. This here's a Christian house. This is going to be a Christian child.

I *beg* your pardon, Virginia says.

There is no sound from the bedroom. Even the squeaking of the bedsprings has stilled.

The woman coughs, then reaches out with her free hand to snatch at Virginia's elbow, pulling her toward the front door with enough strength for Virginia to stumble.

You just wait out there on the porch, missy, she says, keeping hold of the elbow. I don't want you in this house.

Virginia takes her arm back, prying at the dwarfish fingers. The pan on the stove hisses. They stand facing each other, Virginia the slightly smaller of the two women. The water begins to boil.

After a long moment, Virginia decides that there is nothing to be done. This is indeed someone else's home. No matter how deplorable a person, it is her home. Virginia takes the three or four steps outside, then turns back to lock eyes with the woman. Glaring through the cabin corner to corner, she makes a face. As if this were all she could have expected from such a primitive place. How Christian is it, she finally asks, to raise a child in the same house with a lunger? I wonder. She reaches inside for the door, slamming it behind her.

On the porch, she drops into the woman's rocking chair. A piece of furniture that must have been brought out from the East, carved in a maple-leaf pattern on its back. Every joint loosened by the dry air, rocking nearly as well side to side as forward and back. She sits for an hour, then two. Chilled and hungry. At one point, she walks over to the wagon, the team standing patiently hitched, to retrieve a blanket from under the seat. Just as she has decided to demand something to eat from that ridiculous woman, she hears muffled screams from the closed bedroom window. Piercing, insistent cries that soon roll out of the house in an unbroken stream, stabbing even through the hands that Virginia holds flat to her ears.

She leaned her cane against the wall and reached up to smooth at the hair of a mounted bighorn sheep, picking the remnants of a cobweb away from the curl of one horn.

"Don't you think that most of us are drawn to what we're not? We spend our days trying to fill absences. Why, after all, would anyone ever desire *what you already possess?"*

She steadied herself on my arm. "What we love the most are those things that are missing in our own lives. Those things without which we are incomplete. Lack is felt as want.

"There is so much to say and so few words that say it."

61

SHE IS FAMISHED FOR HIM. A hunger renewed each night. Each morning.

He lies against her back, his hand on her stomach, her hand over his. The tired smear of his lips on her shoulder. She feels his lips pull back in a grin, and then he says, Did you see that Charlie this morning?

No. Why?

Pap put him up on that Smoke horse a his.

The pacer?

No. Pacer? Hell, no. That Smoke horse ain't no pacer. You should a seen that Charlie up there. Looked like popcorn bouncing.

Together, their hands trace her skin from the base of the sternum to the slight declination of her navel.

He takes up a rag from under his cot and wipes at his nose, at the palm of his hand. She herself feels a little tickle at the back of her throat. A little congestion.

Something inside her, child or anger or contentment, turns over, rotates like a leaf in the breeze.

There! She says, sitting up.

What was it?

A kick. I think I felt the baby kick.

Oh?

A kick. Or maybe gas. But I think a kick. Here. Put your hand here. There! Did you feel that?

No.

I'm not sure if it's something you would feel outside. It kicked inside.

Virginia lifts his arm and drapes it around her shoulder. He carries within him something unastonishable, unsurprisable. It frustrates her that this shouldn't astound him.

What did you do after the war? she asks.

Why?

There's what, four or five years there.

Worked some. Traveled around. Stayed broke most of the time. Rode a few rails. What? What is it?

Nothing.

Tell me.

Nothing.

Pap probably told you I was in a nuthouse.

Were you?

You ain't the first one he's told that to. His way a lettin on that I ain't welcome on this ranch.

Were you?

He shakes his head. In denial or dismissal? Says, Callin somebody crazy in a war? That's like puttin em in a boxin ring then callin em a bully.

62

THE BULBS over her head, hooded in flowered porcelain, pulse faintly with the give-and-take of the generator. The fire in the fireplace flares and falls back. The room is thick with the kind of warmth that can only come from having a storm outside. She sits at the dining room table guarding a small pile of matches, her stomach belled out over her thighs. Foot-swollen and skin-flushed, she has never felt so assuredly pregnant as she has these last few days.

She stares with exaggerated consideration at Adze and Dewey, each with his handful of spread cards and pile of matches. Dewey studies his cards, touches his mustache, arranges his matches into smaller piles. Adze lays his cards face down on the table and pulls a fifty-cent piece out of his pocket, dancing it across his knuckles then back again. She had suggested they play for pennies, but Adze had shaken his head, saying, Ain't seen a friendship ruint yet wasn't ruint over a monied poker game.

They've been playing simple games: five-card stud and draw and wild-card variations on the two. Dewey handles the cards with a greater adeptness than Adze, the deal gliding through his hands so quickly that there is no noise of individual cards, just a single unbroken slide. But under his tangled eyebrows, Adze keeps a sharp eye on the movement of cards. Dewey puts the deck in his right hand and Adze makes a hissing noise. Dewey grins, switching back.

Why? Virginia asks, looking one to the other.

Why what, Miss? Dewey asks.

Show her there, slick, Adze says.

Dewey gathers up the cards he'd just dealt, then shows them the top card on the deck. A ten of clubs. He deals another round and shows her the top card again. A ten of clubs. Then he deals again, the deck buried in the umbrella of his left hand, and shows her the top card again. Ten of clubs.

If you can't see your cards go out of a man's hand, Dewey says, might as well give him your money right then.

They are the only ones playing, but there are four chairs at this end of the table, and she has been moving back and forth between the two empty spots, closer to or farther away from the fire, according to the dictates of her internal climate, sweating or shivering.

From the other end of the room, she hears Mohr say to Charlie, Maybe your boy'll be a politician, sittin in all them chairs.

Rose and Nettie sit on the couch, a basket of Nettie's yarn between them. Rose has been working on her casting row, yarn threaded off and on her forefinger and thumb. With yarn jumbled on her lap, she digs a spoon into the jar of apple butter wedged into the corner of the basket. Beside her, Nettie prattles endlessly on about how much fun that Halloween dance in Cody had been and how she had tried to dress up like George Washington, with a tricorne and her hair in one long braid and a bunch of flour in her hair and how the flour streaked with sweat once she'd started dancing and how it stuck together in clumps and how she was a whole Saturday getting it out. But then there is the Nettie with the knitting hands, the calm, wordless concentration that drives the quick-circling staccato needles. She's been working on a sweater for her father, something in a brioche pattern. Virginia looks up and sees a collar, then again half an hour later to note the beginnings of a sleeve.

Virginia finds herself well suited to poker, as she knew she would be. Any girl of her society, her time, is necessarily a student of faces. Consider the twist of an eyebrow that invites conversation. The single word that ruins reputations. Dewey touches his mustache at the corners, clears his throat. Selects his discards and keeps what Virginia thinks must be a mediocre pair: he's no longer *acting* so nonchalant. Adze stares with exaggerated despair at his cards, rubbing a fingertip into the corner of his eye. Good Lord, he says. Pardon my cussin, Miss.

Dewey snorts. The only time I ever seen Adze smile at cards was when he bluffed me into foldin three natural kings.

Adze discards two, keeps three. *A pair and a high card for a bluff,* she thinks. She herself is within a card of a jack-high outside straight, and asks for a single card. She draws an ace and immediately tosses down her cards. With the next bad hand, she'll play it out for a round or two, just to keep them guessing. There had been a huckleberry pie for dessert — that thick and sticky crust — and she wonders how she might sneak into the kitchen to have another slice of it.

Where's your aunt tonight, Miss? Adze takes his new cards and shakes his head. Slides three matches into the pot. Considers, then slides in two more.

A little fever. She'll be all right. It's going around.

Can I do anything for her? Adze watches Dewey match his bet, then add a pair of matches to it. He shakes his head, dropping his cards face down on the table.

Excuse me?

Can we do anything for her?

She'll be all right.

Henry sits cross-legged on the floor, taking noncommittal sips from the coffee cup by his knee. He cradles an old Kodak pack camera on his lap, bellows extended, and holds the disassembled aperture up to the light, using his shirt cuff to rub at a residue of solvent. He blows into the bellows. Stretches his legs. He's so at ease in any position. She's never seen anyone inhabit his body quite so well.

Charlie and Mohr have been pacing circuits around the room, the tall man leaning into the shorter man's conversation. She can see why Mohr is drawn to Charlie. Indeed she does.

The corona of confidence that Charlie carries with him. The satisfactions of judgment-passing that surround someone who has never known a world without money. The two men have been toasting each other, toasting the future that they have apparently come to share. They pause in front of a pair of framed sketches on the wall. Two drawings by Olive Fell: an elk and a sheepwagon. Mohr mentions how her postcards are going all over the world. How they may not be Rembrandts or nothin, but people are seeing em. Thousands of people, Frenchmen and Eyetalians and what all.

They leave the drawings, continuing their somewhat drunken march up and down, past the table. Virginia sits hunched into one of her shivers, hands buried in the sleeves of her sweater. Before she can pull away, Charlie bends to kiss her cheek, leaving his warm skin next to hers for a moment. Mohr asks him if he has decided on any names for that baby. Virginia's eyes go to Henry. He is staring at her, a dry rag in his hands, rubbing at the camera's lens with a tight fury.

Adze tilts his chair back, clearing his throat. He squints across at the window. The night is dark and anything to be seen would stop at his own reflection. Nevertheless, he says, Looks like the weather's set to break. You watch. We'll be fifty degrees and sweatin before the week's out.

63

SHE HAS COME to insist on small excursions, despite her aunt's arguments against straining herself. She needs to be outside at least a few hours each day. Needs to shrug off the strangling sense of stale, tepid air lingering in the cabins.

In one of the few extravagances of his ranch, and perhaps in a reflection of his own disregard for certain kinds of labor, Mohr buys much of his firewood from his neighbors. A load or two of coal from Cody. But as the weather has turned colder, it's been difficult for the deliveries to keep up with the need, and so Henry and Adze have been spending the past few mornings in the timber above the ranch, returning in the afternoons with a cord of wood. Sometimes more.

At breakfast, Charlie had asked to come along, to take Adze's place. Part of his stated determination to see how things work around here. It's better, she supposes, that there be no fuss, that she be able to keep an eye on him. If there is a hornet in the room, she wants to know where it is.

And now she sits on a fallen log scraped clean of snow, watching the two men saw at a thirty-foot fir tree, the piston motion of elbows and shoulders matched and mirrored on either side of the crosscut saw. These aren't large trees, but she's surprised nevertheless by how quickly they've been falling. Half a dozen or so good hard runs of the blade and the tree starts to sway; another lick or two eases it off its trunk. It's hard work, and Charlie's face reddens as the day progresses, collecting a sheen of sweat even in the chill. His light, self-satisfied chatter gives way to a sullen silence, to quick, resentful glances at the man strong enough to dictate the speed of their work. The rhythm slows as Charlie starts to pause, wiping at his forehead and breathing deeply before pulling at the blade. But then Henry draws the saw back without hesitation, and with such strength that Charlie is occasionally yanked into the body of the tree.

They rest with the blade between them, passing a jug of water back and forth. Charlie considers his palms — the blisters rowed under his fingers — and then the waiting wreck of splintered branches and shining butt ends of logs. He stands up, telling them that he'll only be gone a minute. He walks into the timber and Virginia thinks he has gone to pee, but when he is gone for fifteen minutes, she knows that he won't be coming back. Henry runs his hand along the slick metal of the blade, fingering the curved teeth. He knocks the flat of the blade with his knuckles and seems pleased at the resulting gong.

He finishes off the water and pulls a double-bitted ax from the sledge, moving with it among the fallen trees, clearing away their smaller branches with short, precise swings. As more trees lay stripped of limbs, bare as fenceposts, he drags them to the sledge and props them up against its bed. He judges the length, then cuts into each pole with a handsaw, stacking the lengths in the bed. He stops to sharpen his saw, running a round file down each tooth. She watches him work, studying him the way she once studied her textbooks. But no, this isn't right. There is no memorization. No dry rote. She is finding a *feeling* for him.

Only for something to do, she starts clearing away the branches, tossing them into the brush. Wood chips work their way into her cuffs, her collar. He leaves the saw and picks up the ax, moving around to trim branches again. She wipes her hands on her pants and steps in front of him, struggling to roll a log into a position where he might more easily reach it with his ax. He nods his thanks.

Most of his face is hidden under his hat, bent to the ax, so that she can see only the high points: the foreignness of his broad cheeks. He looks more Indian from this angle. That flat ridge of his nose. Has it ever been broken? She squats to the next log, using the opportunity to glance up at him. She can just see his eyes, intent on his ax, the blade of it just now pinched by the settling of the log. He jerks it loose and bends to the log again, swinging and chopping into a branch caught against the ground, bowed with the weight of the log. It flips back, hitting him on the cheek beside his eye. He jerks away as from a striking snake.

He moves to pull off his gloves, then sees her watching him.

64

When she is deeply moved, he can see her retreat into herself. He's noticed this before. A smile that collapses, folds like a tight wing. She steps toward him across the ankle-twist scattering of limbs and twigs, straddling the middle part of the largest tree and swinging her legs over. Her shoulders, narrow as clamped knees, only emphasize her breasts. When he's talking to her, or watching her walk toward him, it's difficult for him to keep his eyes away from her chest.

Raped, she had said. And he believes her. He does. But violence, real violence, is so rare. So unexpected. And he certainly wouldn't expect it from that nervous little man with the spectacles. He can't imagine why she ever liked him in the first place. He's short, and maybe that's it. She can look him in the eye.

The blood from his cut wells and trickles down his cheek. As he moves to wipe it away, she catches his gloved hand in both of hers. The blood inches down the line of his jaw. She stands on her toes beside him and stretches up to kiss his lips, lightly, dryly. Then she dips her head to his cheek, touching the blood with the tip of her tongue. She pulls away, tasting, then rises toward him again, her neck stretching up, the flat of her tongue following the line of blood along the length of his face. When she withdraws, his blood is creviced in the corner of her mouth.

65

AN ACHE in her that, until now, had always indicated the absence of something essential. Of water. Of air. Is this love? What else if not this? This toothache in her chest. The Greeks believed that the veins were hollow, were filled with aether, bleeding only when the skin was violated. Her veins are hollow now. He has hollowed her.

This feeling can't last, she thinks. Nothing like this ever lasts. For now, she hoards it like a child with candy: *All mine.*

She tells him everything, often as it pops into her head. He lies and listens. She's sure he's listening. That concentrated look on his face. He responds only to direct questions. Most often smoking, staring at the end of the cigarette as if pondering the weight of her words. She thinks him profound, and would believe anything he tells her. She does believe everything he tells her.

He reaches under the cot for his rag and blows his nose. Rubs at his eyes. He is not staring at the ceiling. Rather, he is staring at her drawing. Her drawing of the fire.

How do you decide what you want to draw? he asks.

Whatever excites me, I guess, she says. Whatever makes me feel, I don't know, romantic, I guess.

Would you ever want to draw me?

Would you want me to?

You don't think this is romantic?

Why is it that men are always confusing sex and romance?

But she's only teasing him, charmed that he does, in fact, like her drawings. She turns his hand in hers, studying his palm as if it is an apple. As if she is ready to eat her way around the bruises.

I thought you'd never done this before. His voice is muffled against her neck, his words a vibration in her skin.

After a long moment, she deliberately rolls away from him, pushing his heavy head off her shoulder with the blunt muscles of her palms. As if she has suddenly been made aware of some contamination on him.

She often thinks that she carries awareness within her like an illness.

66

HE CARRIES his plate of sourdough pancakes into the dining room, a pewter creamer of molasses hooked over one finger, coffee in his fist. He finds his father sitting alone, hunched forward, reading an old *National Geographic* flat on the table. Tracing the lines of text with a fingernail.

Henry sits at the other end of the table, tucking a napkin into his shirt collar. He covers the pancakes with a soup of molasses, then takes a pleased sip at his coffee. A clear morning outside. New snow on the ground, skiffed like heavy frost.

Frank turns a page, then says, Look here. If that Great Wall in China was brought over? It'd stretch all the way from Philadelphia to Topeka.

Henry sips at his coffee.

Frank wets his fingers and flips a page, then says, Adze ever tell you about all them dry-stack stone corrals they keep down around Mexico? When he was down around Chihuahua? Claims they run about as straight and square as a wire fence.

Indians built em, Henry says. Back when they was still stealin horses.

That a fact? Frank closes the magazine and stands up. Come out back when you're done eatin.

Yessir.

Got a job for us.

All right.

Frank picks his hat off the rack and steps outside, blowing into his hands.

Ten minutes later, Henry finds him behind the barn, using a spade to cut flat shovelfuls of snow and sod from a marked-out square. Beside him, a stack of log trim, cut to size.

Frank nods toward the cottonwoods, toward another spade stuck upright in the soil. That look like fifty feet to you?

Yessir.

You can tell just by lookin, can you?

Henry shrugs.

You goin a dig or just stand there lookin pretty?

Figured I'd do both. What am I diggin?

Horseshoe pit.

Henry walks over to the other spade and uses the point to scrape away snow, then to lever a few inches into the sod. Marking out his square and scooping soil off to one side. A few minutes later, he walks back for the log trim, setting the pieces around inside the hole and kicking them into place. By the time he's finished, his father has produced a length of lead pipe and is screwing it down into the dirt, tapping it with the flat of his shovel.

Henry walks up to him, looking for another piece of pipe, and his father says, Had Adze collect us some sawdust. Should be in the barn there somewhere. Why don't you make yourself useful and bring it on over.

Just inside the door, he finds a seed bag tied off with twine. He brings it out and sets it down beside Frank and stands smoking.

Frank sits back on his heels, then reaches into his shirt pocket for a wad of fabric tape measure. He stretches out fourteen inches and holds it up against the pipe, taking a piece of red stone and marking it out. He picks up a hammer and bangs the top of the pipe with an echoing, metallic clang. Then he says, People are startin to talk about you and that girl.

He bangs the pipe again. Henry, who since the war hasn't appreciated loud noises, flinches.

I heard that Nettie sayin somethin. *Bang!* Tellin your mother about it. *Bang!* Just a gigglin about it. *Bang!*

Frank stands, grabs the top of the pipe, and pulls it back and forth, judging its strength. Now, he says. Enough's enough.

You got no right to tell me what I can do. I'll tell you that right now.

Frank throws the hammer hard into the dirt. I ain't goin a let you louse this up, boy. Tell you one last time. If that Charlie goes home pissed off . . . well, I just don't want a say. Hell, I've already sold off most a my cows! Half of em.

Henry squats on his heels and tests the pipe himself. That don't have nothin to do with me.

If this deal don't work out, your mother's goin a be just as broke as me. You thought a that one?

Broke? Hell, you got more money than Butte.

Frank raises a forefinger, as if to make a point, then uses it to jab Henry hard in the shoulder. Enough's enough, boy. That's all I'm sayin. Enough's enough.

67

SHE SITS on the edge of his bed, waiting, smoking one of his cigarettes. Playing with the bone buttons of his shirt. She has been stealing his clothes in the same way that she had once taken his cigarettes, hoping for a reaction. Any reaction at all. The heavy wool rough on her skin: tight across her stomach, loose around her thin shoulders. A faint greasiness in the fabric and a collar tented up around her neck. She studies her swollen ankles, the leather of her shoes cutting into her skin.

When the last, moist inch of the cigarette heats her fingers, she steps outside, grinding it under her toe. This has never happened before. That he hasn't been here waiting for her. She tilts her head back against the door, dizzy from the cigarette, her eyes closed.

She would love to be able to talk about this. This place. To present it to Isabel as some kind of adventure. *A colonial life,* she thinks. The conspicuous, self-conscious politeness of the cowboys. The crack of splitting wood and the haze of smoke on breezeless mornings.

She opens her eyes to the moonless night sky and thinks immediately that she must be passing out, that she must be very dizzy indeed. The streaks of stars. But then the streaks take on form and pattern and she stands hammerstruck.

She hurries across the yard, banging through the cabin door to shake her aunt awake. The shoulder like hot kindling under her hand.

Her aunt's breathing pauses, then she says with clarity, What do you want, child?

Come outside.

And why?

Just come outside. Please.

Pauline sighs and gathers her quilt around her, laboring to her feet. Outside, Virginia positions her just beyond the eaves of the roof, unwinding the quilt from her fists to stand next to her.

Look, Virginia says, touching her aunt's chin, tilting it back.

Oh my.

Falling stars. Dozens of them. Hundreds. Glowing threads slicing into the black sky. During the course of any single held breath, five or six swing into sight and immediately fade, to be replaced by six more. A silent and cold Leonid shower of splintered light. An emptying of the heavens. They stand together for twenty minutes or so, unspeaking, until each star holds again to its right and solid place in the firmament.

Virginia feels how her aunt is shivering. The heat baking off her. The fevered, hard, brittle pod of her. How the hand on Virginia's shoulder presses down with such weight. Concern runs through her, the memories of the flu still vivid. The wet rattle of congested lungs.

Are you all right, Auntie?

I've picked up a little cold is all.

You should see a doctor.

I made it through the flu without seeing one of those snake-oil salesmen. I believe I can make it through a little chest cold. She hugs Virginia briefly. Coughs.

Maybe you should, though.

Some cowboy in Cody? He'll probably give me an antler to chew on.

Go east, then.

Come with me? You and Charlie?

Virginia knows what her aunt is asking, and she shakes her head.

Child, her aunt says, coughing. Brushing Virginia's hair back. Did you know that Charlie has been paying for our stay here?

I did *not* know that.

Sixty dollars a week for the two of us.

Why didn't you tell me?

He didn't think you would accept it.

Well. He was right.

What's wrong with young people today? Is it the age? This sinful age?

It's not the age, Auntie.

Am I too old, then? Am I too old?

You're young at heart, Auntie.

The old woman shakes her head, coughing. At heart, she finally says.

Virginia hugs her, and it's like hugging a hot bundle of pot-handles. She pulls away. You're burning up, she says.

Hogwash. You have this blanket around us so tight.

They hear footsteps in gravel, and turn to see Henry stepping around the corner of the house, a pair of tin jugs hooked over his fingers. Ladies, he says, tucking one of the jugs under his arm to touch the brim of his hat.

Quite the show, Pauline says to him.

Pardon?

The meteor shower.

Was there a meteor shower tonight? He stares at Virginia. A flat, emotionless gaze, like something detached inside him.

You missed it? Pauline is saying.

A meteor shower? He is staring at Virginia.

Much later, they lie together again. Every flinch and shudder, every unconscious bridging of the back, matched by the other. Her mouth, his tongue. This is Virginia. This is Henry. She has been slipping into this bed an uncut book, unsure how each night will go. A gift that he has given her. These nights that previously had been unimaginable to her. If nothing else, this.

Her hands are on his chest. He has taken her by the waist and rolled her over, his two big hands rounded over her stomach. Her stomach no longer between them, her breasts no longer pressed by his weight. A new perspective entirely, and it's true that he is better looking from some angles than others. She has to admit this. The way his shoulders are nearly the same width as his stomach, the way they give his torso a perpendicular bluntness.

She sees an unexpected aggression in him. His eyes are open but he is looking past her. He rubs at her breasts, her nipples between his thumbs and forefingers. Stretching at them, pulling at them.

You're hurting me, she whispers.

68

A SATURDAY AFTERNOON. And for its size, the town seems very loud. After the weeks of distended silence at the ranch, civilization has become nothing so much as noise. They turn east on Sheridan Avenue, wheels spinning in frozen muck, then drive under a giant, whitewashed letter C on the hillside. Henry turns to Nettie in the seat beside him. Didn't your pap help paint that?

Nettie nods, stiff and uncomfortable in one of Virginia's silk dresses, her hands clasped around a patent leather purse. Mama too, she says.

They park at an angle in front of Dave Jones Clothiers. The car sputters, then quits. Virginia's ears register the varied, distillate sounds of town. The churning of a ditching machine outside of town. The screaming laughter of children running up the street. A faint train whistle north of the river.

Charlie steps out into the mud and reaches back in. Virginia? he says.

She grasps his open hand, using it for balance as she takes one enormous step through the mud. When both her feet are solidly on the concrete sidewalk, she twists her hand away and steps back, adjusting her dress, untying the scarf from under her chin and wrapping it around the crown of her hat.

Gin Price, he says, looking at her splattered boots. Dressed for a trip into town.

Her name that he manages to corrupt so completely: Vir — Gin — Eee. He has always said it mockingly, teasingly: a northerner imitating a southern accent. VirGinEee.

He has a right to make fun, she thinks. This outfit of hers that looks as if it's been pieced together from a dozen different scarecrows. A pleated cotton skirt gathered above her stomach. A chemise from the trunk in Charlie's cabin, hanging loose over the skirt. A sweater vest over the chemise. All in a failed attempt to hide her pregnancy.

A bell jangles, and the door to the Cody Trading Company opens ahead of them, releasing a pale, paunchy man in a cowboy hat and, on his arm, a gangly woman twirling a yellow parasol. The woman's eyes travel from Virginia to Charlie, then to Henry and Nettie behind them, then to the bulge of Virginia's pregnancy, and finally back to Charlie. She smiles, revealing a pair of white teeth jutting out like knuckles under her lips, obviously pleased to see two such clean, happy young people on the way to starting their life together.

Nettie has told her about the Trading Company (its motto: "We Sell Everything"), but Virginia is still taken aback by the size of the place, by the long, narrow aisles and square white pillars. The pressed-tin ceiling and hanging, tulip-shaped chandeliers. Some part of her that has been dormant for a long time blinks awake, and she finds herself wandering aimlessly among glass cases filled with men's cowboy hats and fedoras and dress shirts; riffling her fingers over rotating hangers of scarves, open cedar shelves stocked with folded sweaters and heavy shoes and women's hats in round boxes. One entire corner, which she avoids, is devoted to sporting goods: vertical rows of rifles and hanging steel traps and cases of ammunition. She browses up and down the aisles, heels echoing on the pine floor.

At the edge of her vision, Charlie flips through a display of new Kruppenheimer suits, then moves tentatively into the women's department. He pulls a maternity dress off the rack and holds it up, sizing it against Virginia on the other side of the store. One of those Lane Bryant dresses, she notices. Checked gingham with lace collar and cuffs. She turns away, resolving that she'll never wear anything he buys for her. *Not ever.* Henry is standing at the front counter, and she waves at him, although he doesn't see her. When they leave the store, Charlie is carrying half a dozen flimsy boxes crimped under his arm, all bought without her permission.

At the Temple Theater, an Indian boy in a black worsted suit and string tie takes their money for the matinee. Ten cents each. He calls Henry by name, and Henry gives him a dollar tip, telling him to give them good seats. The same boy starts the newsreel and runs into the orchestra pit to switch on the automatic piano. They sit through the screen notices — No Smoking and Ladies Please Remove Your Hats — then the titles for a Buster Keaton two-reeler, a movie she saw a couple of years ago. A parody of every western she has ever seen. Buster is a cowardly villain who robs a saloon by holding a cutout from a wanted poster over his face. He is a jilted lover who walks into his cabin to find his wife with another man. He tilts his face toward the camera, crying like William S. Hart, then shoots them both, turning them over only to find that it's not his wife, not his cabin.

Charlie drops his hand over hers. She tries to pull away, but he pinches her fingers against the wooden armrest. Rather than make a scene, she satisfies herself with reaching her other hand across to Henry's knee, tracing his leg up to his thigh, then to the fingers resting over his hip. She covers them with her own.

69

IT'S A MEASURE of Charlie's importance to Frank Mohr that they've been given the use of the Arrow for the day.

Henry drives them along the North Fork improvement — a terrace carved into the cliffs above the dam (the older road below them already littered with gravel slides) — and through the limestone canyon, past George Beck's brick power plant. On the west side of town, they coast slowly between frame houses and empty weed lots, past a junkyard of abandoned automobiles scavenged for parts and a filthy, emaciated dog limping through stacks of tires. Since he's been gone, the town's changed hardly at all. No buildings newer than five or six years. Despite Buffalo Bill's early and profligate efforts at establishing a tourist trade, at presenting Cody to the world — the Irma Hotel, built in 1913 and named after his daughter; irrigation lines on Irma Flat; hunting lodges at Pahaska and Wapiti — the city has succumbed to the state's larger depression. Cattle prices down. Horse market flat. Oil money hasn't taken hold. A town filled with little more than a thousand people: two whorehouses and half a dozen churches and two newspapers on either side of Prohibition. A town of homesteaders who, after failing to prove up on their anemic chunks of ground, have ended up frying potatoes at the Irma. Cutting wagonloads of firewood and hawking it on the street. Selling ice cream from carts. It's not a place where he enjoys spending time.

Since leaving the ranch, for the past hour or so, he has been feeling his old vertigo. A familiar, light nausea of displacement. But rather than shaking it off, as he usually does, it grows. Grows until the street tilts, until he stumbles as he steps out of the Arrow. By God, he just can't shake off these drunks like he used to.

Nettie bounces beside him, limping and humming, unreasonably pleased to be walking down a sidewalk in Cody, Wyoming. Ahead of them, Charlie in his tailored serge suit, his straw boater, carrying himself like every wealthy tourist in the world. They stop in front of the Trading Company, studying the display of camping gear. A canvas tent and a pair of folding chairs behind a gas camp stove and a hand-lettered sign that declares, "Never Before Seen in Wyoming!" Next to Charlie, Virginia carries herself in a slow, considered manner, every movement deliberate, as if she's walking under water. Henry's been noticing a new heaviness to the skin around her face and mouth. She's so goddamned pregnant. On this day at least, Charlie is husband to her.

Inside the Trading Company, Nettie draws a crumpled dollar bill from her purse and buys a pack of Beeman's gum, offering a stick to Virginia. Henry buys two boxes of Ansco film and, on a whim, decides on a bottle of perfume for his mother. A tiny fluted bottle from Paris. Shotgun Ellis at the back counter picks up the bottle and reads the Houbigant label through his bifocals. How Big Ant, he says, and shakes his head. That's five dollars. *Five dollars,* Henry thinks.

There's Virginia browsing like she owns the place (and it occurs to him that maybe she *could* own it, if she wanted it), and five dollars for him is like bleeding out of the wrists. In a place like this, with so much to buy, so much to spend, she's not the same girl that she was on the ranch. She sure isn't.

He gives Shotgun his mother's list, telling him to box it up if he would, to put it on the family account, and he'll be back to pick it up before closing. Charlie comes up behind Henry with a round tin of Luckies in his hand. He glances at the perfume, then back at the two girls. At Nettie trying to blow a bubble and giggling over her failure. Bet you could go a long way with a little country girl like that, he says.

Henry sticks the perfume in his shirt pocket and stares at Charlie in the makeup mirror on the counter. Say that again and I'll kick your ass for you.

Behind him, Charlie grins, holding out his palms. Whoa, cowboy, he says.

Here's the kind of man, Henry sees now, who hides his cowardice behind a façade of good humor. How do you punch a guy who's trying to share a joke? When they're standing in line at the movie theater, Charlie nods at the dollar bill in Henry's hand. Put it away, he says with exaggerated generosity. Spend it on boot polish or something. Henry immediately hands it to little Micah Walking Bear, knowing that his pap will end up drinking it away, probably smacking the boy around for having gone to the trouble of making a buck. But Charlie can take his New York money and shove it up his ass.

Henry slides into his seat with a sense of profound relief, of release. He has always enjoyed theaters. The magic of a piano playing alone and a photograph that moves. The dark rustle of clothes. Muted coughs into fists. The odors of cigarette smoke (despite the rules) and unwashed bodies. He crosses his legs and puts his hat on his knee, bending down below the horizon of chairs to hide the flash of his match. He hoods the end of the cigarette with his last three fingers and taps the ash onto the floor

He settles back, grinning as Buster Keaton's name flashes on the screen. How could a guy who never cracks a smile be so funny?

There is the touch of a hand on his wrist, and it's like water on his neck. Virginia takes his hand and raises it to the armrest. He is not so much willing as will-less, caught between Buster Keaton and Virginia. She drops his arm and slides her hand under his. Her flesh cool. Boneless. The dimples of her knuckles. He finds himself surprised, over and over again, by the size of her hands.

After a moment of consideration, he brings this tiny hand to his mouth.

70

SHE LIES on her side, running her hands over her belly, listening to the stertorous, labored breathing of her aunt. *I will be kind,* she thinks. In the face of her aunt's illness, she has made the decision of kindness. She has intentionally overfed the stove, but even so the old woman shivers on the bed beside her, curled under the quilts.

Her aunt mumbles into her pillow.

What's that, Auntie?

The old woman clears her throat and spits into a basin by the bed. Go to sleep, child.

Yes, Auntie.

Surprisingly, she does fall asleep, albeit a thin gruel of sleep. The only kind she's lately been able to manage. If she dozes off on her back, the muscles above her hips cramp and jolt her awake. And then she's never been much of a side sleeper. But lately she's found a new position, half on her side, hands tucked between her legs.

Rose seems to place an inordinate value on dreams, and so

Virginia has been making an effort to remember hers. Is a dream that's aware of itself still a dream? She's floating over a valley. This valley or some other. Staring at a ground painted in colors that glow as from the wet squeezings of jewels: burnt red stone, green growing things, blue water. But she feels herself to be the color of drab sand, of one of her own drawings. She opens her mouth and feels the space between her eyes and chin take on the colors of the sky behind. She reaches a hand down, thinking to dig up a finger of color and spread it across her cheeks, but the colors are beyond her. When the gods want to punish you, they put your most urgent desire just out of reach.

She starts awake, drops of color still dangling off her nose. There is another knock, hard enough to make the cabin door swing inward and catch against its loop of leather.

Virginia? A voice says.

Virginia feels Pauline's hand fumbling around her back, reaching for her shoulder. It's Charlie, the old woman says. Charlie.

Virginia sits on the edge of the bed, pulling on a pair of denim trousers that she likes for their enormous waist (she has no idea where they came from), then standing to crack the door. Charlie leans against the frame, still in his suit, hat in his crossed hands. Despite herself, she feels the faintest pull of sympathy. *Go home,* she thinks.

I thought we might go for a walk, he says, replacing his hat. He takes a quick, balancing step to the side.

You're drunk. She glances back at her aunt then slips outside, closing the door behind her.

What did I ever do to you, Gin? You used to love me. You told me that. Do you remember that? I bet you don't even remember that. He reaches a hand out toward her, to touch her cheek.

She jerks her head away from his fingers. Back to the cabin, hands on her stomach. What did you ever do to me? she asks. That's swell, Charlie. That's rich.

Even now, you don't see, he says.

I see that you're a son of a bee.

You don't see this.

What don't I see?

That's part of me in there, he says, reaching across to touch her stomach. She stares at the shadowed hollows where his eyes should be. For the rest of our lives.

By no will of my own.

Virginia, he says. Virginia. I want to do what's right here. I want to do what's right. He leans forward. I want to do the honorable thing. To fulfill my obligations.

They have been speaking softly out of courtesy to her aunt, just a wall's thickness away, but now she says, quite loudly, If you try to kiss me I'll scream. I'll scream so much, Charlie.

He shakes his head. Oh my, he says. And then he says it again, to himself. He takes off his hat and drops his eyes. There is moisture on his cheeks.

Is that why he took off his hat? she wonders. So that she could see that he is crying? But he has already turned his face away.

He says, Don't you think that if I could have that night back — that one night, that one small mistake — don't you think that if I could take that night back I would? In a heartbeat.

A heartbeat?

He turns toward her, imploring. But then I think, No, I'm grateful for it, it ties her to me.

What do you want, Charlie? She's tired now. Hungry. And she needs to pee.

I want to buy you earrings and necklaces. I want to show you Paris. I want to . . . I want to watch you raise our child. His voice is low now, subdued. Reasonable. The kind of voice Henry uses to train horses.

I've seen Paris.

He steps toward her again, and she can tell that he's going to try to kiss her. Charlie, whom she did, after all, say that she loved. He is bending toward her, her back against the cabin, her hands flat on the rough, half-skinned logs.

And then he is gone. And she draws a slow, shaky breath.

He is leaning heavy and off balance against the cabin beside hers, his upper arm held in Henry's fist. Oh, hey, he says. Hello.

71

IT IS NOT a question of throwing punches so much as recognizing the opportunity for punches. You can't think about it, just like you can't think about how you're going to hit a baseball.

I'll scream, he had heard her say.

He must have four or five inches on this guy. An advantage that would make him ashamed if he thought about it. But he's not thinking about it.

That scrawny little arm in his fist, that pasty white face turned up toward him, limp as a flower on its stalk. And are those tears? Henry releases the arm in disgust — like dropping a snake — and uses the same motion to slap him across the face. It's hardly enough to draw blood. Yet there it is. A thin trickle from the nostrils.

Oh, hey there, Charlie says, surprised. He touches his nose with the back of his hand.

Henry watches as the realization of violence hits him. This little man who has never had a lesson taught to him in his life. Then he watches him come to a decision, right hand clenching, his left hand flat on the cabin wall. He comes off the wall swinging, lunging forward, so it's an easy thing for Henry to step back, to let the swing slide past him. It throws Charlie off balance, sending him heavily to the ground.

After a moment's consideration, Charlie climbs to his feet, slapping the dust off his pants. Going to fight dirty, huh? He glances at Virginia. Says to her, Something you want to tell me? Or him?

He has never fought before. Henry can tell that before anything else. Never had to. Rich boy. Probably had bodyguards. Rich boy.

What's that? Charlie says, stepping toward him, elbow already cocked behind his head.

Again Henry lets Charlie swing past him, but this time he catches the wrist in his hand, trapping it across Charlie's body. Twisting it until Charlie is forced to bend down, to stare at his own feet.

Henry looks at Virginia, who is nervously gripping the tails of her overlarge shirt (*his* shirt, he notices), and wants to think there's a hunger in her face: her eyes wide. He nods, and without releasing the wrist, turns to punch Charlie on the cheek. Then again on his ear. And again, a glancing blow, on the bridge of the nose. You never try to punch a guy in the nose, you try to punch *through* the nose. He wrenches his wrist until Charlie drops to his knees, whimpering, then he swats him on the back of the head with his hat.

Henry, Virginia says. Henry.

Let's hear about honor, Henry says, swatting him. Tell it to me. Let's hear about obligations. Tell it.

He releases the arm, pushing Charlie back against the wall. The little man cowers there, hiding behind the open palms of his hands. Stop, he says, chest heaving. Stuh-stuh-stop.

72

HE RUNS HIS HAND above her body, not quite touching it. Across her breasts, the bulge of a nipple, down over the mound of her stomach to linger at the navel — his index finger lingering on and circling her navel — then quickly down to her thighs, to her knees. Emphasizing her sex by its exclusion. *No one else,* she thinks, blind waves of motion rolling down her body. No one else could understand this kind of . . . of . . . absence.

Later, he lights the lamp above their heads. They sit in a room of translucent darkness. Her favorite time. Her most private time. When only the peaks of his flesh are visible, when her imagination can recreate the rest of him. The time when he is most entirely her own.

They lie together in the partial dark, these two lovers in a book. Lovers in a book, maybe, that she will write. She considers how she might describe him. And then, more interestingly, how he would describe her. She puts her hand on his chest and asks him.

Quiet, he says without hesitation. You think a lot.

She doesn't disagree, although she's surprised. More, she says.

Do you want it crude or polite?

Polite, I think.

Faraway, he says. Is that a word? Faraway? He drops back into his pillow and holds her hand. He brings it to his mouth, kissing it. You go away sometimes.

I'm not sure I care for that version. Give me the crude one.

He brings one of her fingers to his mouth and bites at her nail, making a parody of consideration. Nipples, he says with authority. Nipples like door handles.

Henry! She smacks him on the shoulder.

You could black an eye with one a them things.

Well. Mister. Let me tell you something about what you get here.

Where?

Here . . .

He kisses her, then drops back, saying, Pap won't like it that I whupped up on your boyfriend like that.

Why not?

No more Someday Mountain.

What's that?

Somethin Mother and I used to talk about. Way Pap thinks, there's always another river that's got more gold in it. Another mountain with better graze. He's spent his whole life lookin for Someday Mountain. Never wanted the cards in his hands.

He licks his lips and turns away from her. Anyway, he says. Jesus, where'd all that come from?

I like it, Virginia says. Someday Mountain. It's poetic.

Oh hell.

Not very gentlemanly, though. Cussing around a lady.

She can feel a sudden tenseness in him. The immediate, unmistakable sense that she has said something wrong.

He sits up. Who ever told you I was a gentleman? he says.

73

HE THINKS of winter in Wyoming as he once thought of war. For the most part, France had been one long waiting in line. Weeks of boredom periodically broken by eruptions of terror and violence. And it's the same here. On this ranch.

His father stands in the shadow of the porch, the fire of his cigar brightening, dimming. Henry's first thought is of the tin jugs buckled into Ballo's saddlebags, their threaded tops just visible in the corners of the flaps. But his father ignores the horse, gesturing with his cigar back into the house. Let me show you a thing, he says.

Henry tosses the reins over the railing and follows his father through the great room into the kitchen, the house quiet around them. Rose, alone at the sink, is draining a pot of boiled potatoes, shaking them into a colander. Without preamble, without permission, his father lifts the back of her blouse.

Bruises on her ribs. The soft, fleshy rolls of skin below her arms marred by knots of green and blue. Day-old evidence of violence, armpit to belt. Like fingers in his eyes.

Henry can't breathe. He can't look away.

His father says, Next time you're thinkin about beatin up that man who's goin a make us all rich, you think about this first.

His mother has paused over her potatoes, head lowered. After her husband drops the tail of her blouse, she starts punching lightly into the bowl with a metal serving fork, never having turned around.

You have nothin more to do with that gal, his father says.

Henry exhales heavily through his nose.

Maybe you should go trapping, his father says.

Not enough snow.

Maybe you should go anyway.

Not yet. Henry turns away, every muscle clenched. If his father touches him now he will explode. If his father speaks to him he will splinter and crack. But his father does not touch him, does not speak. Rather, Henry hears him kiss his mother's cheek. A light fingersnap of lips and skin. Henry walks back out to his horse alone.

It is one of the mysteries of his mother's religion that to think an evil act is to commit that act. It has always seemed to him that an earnest subscription to this view would fill the world with adulteries and murders. If a guy is going to hell for thinking it, he might as well go to hell for doing it and have some fun on the way. But this is the kind of good sense that most preachers don't like to hear.

He trots Ballo across the road and up through the hayfields into the foothills of Table Mountain, considering all the possible ways Frank Mohr might die. Slow, painful deaths, with and without skin. Quick deaths with the surprise still in his face. Deaths where he is made to watch the slick unwinding of his own innards. Deaths by suffocation that leave no mark on the body. There are a thousand roads to stop that twisted, beating muscle Mohr calls a heart, the only requirement being that Henry watch it happen. He remembers the muffled smack of Mohr's fists on his own childhood ribs. At night, sometimes, he jerks awake hearing it still.

But it's a fine day, and his horse is a good horse, and the world refuses to blink at atrocity, even at a hundred thousand deaths of men like Hassler. Why expect sympathy or justice for his mother? He walks Ballo through the trees and down into Green Creek, then over a bare hillside to the sawmill. A shroud of humidity hangs always in the arms of these hills, even when the old steam-powered tractor they use for power sits idle, as it does now.

He rides through the mill yard, smelling sap and fresh wood, a tinge of the gasoline they use to clean the blades. Ballo's hooves crunch over pieces of curled bark, broken slats. That summer he'd worked the edger here, back in 1916, there had been forty, maybe fifty thousand board feet in this yard waiting to be milled. But now, with the summer milling past and not enough snow to sled trees down from their lease, the yard is empty.

Billy Bell had bought the steam tractor from Wallop-

Montcriefe and geared it into the mill himself, running the sawblades for nearly ten years. He'd died while Henry had been in France. Gangrene of the knee, Henry has heard, cut trying to catch a Case knife between his legs. Henry's seen some tough men in his day, but never anybody like old Mr. Bell. His whole life, he'd had problems with his wisdom teeth. But rather than taking the time for a dentist, he would work with golfballs of infection swelling up in his lower jaw. Work until his teeth opened up their old scars, draining blood and pus down his neck. That old man never quit. Never quit.

Henry rides past the cookhouse, then the storage shed, dismounting in front of the bunkhouse. These buildings, faded to the color of dried clay, were fresh and white when he worked here. Each plank cut in the first days of the mill. Some wide as a dining room table. Some narrow as Bibles. Now all weathered and splintering, eyed with empty knotholes and the red teardrop stains of rusting nails.

He knocks on the door, then knocks again, wondering what he'll do with all this booze if nobody's around. *Pour it out,* he thinks, seeing his mother's bruise. *Piss in it and put it back.*

But the door opens, and Henry says, Well, Ed Simpers. Didn't know you was workin out here.

Simpers stands bare-chested, a chunk of lye soap in his hand and a steaming tub of water on the table behind him. Two stringy arms and a bullet scar on the round slope of one shoulder. A squint-eyed man, always looking at you like the sun's behind your shoulder. Henry remembers how he likes to chew balls of lodgepole sap, claiming it helps the digestion.

Simpers steps back from the door. Expected you tomorrow, he says.

Figured you boys'd be itchin for somethin to do, what with there not bein snow for so long.

Right about that.

Later, as Henry walks back in the door with his jugs, Simpers says, Two gallons? Christamighty boy, what kind of booze-hounds do you think we are over here?

Which is more than Henry's ever heard him say at one time in his life.

74

THE DAYS PASS. The earth turns, forever east to east to east. Mornings bright and chilled, the nights frozen blue. A wind comes and, for fourteen hours, blows with such direct force that she comes to see it as a separate event, a cleaving apart of something to which she hasn't yet put a name. The riverbank cottonwoods are, but for a last few petrified husks, blown bare of leaves.

The days pass without Henry, off always on Mohr's endless errands. It is perhaps this daily absence (along with the continuing presence of Charlie — a moth to light around her, closer every day) that lends the sense of contained energy to the ranch. A coiled spring pressed flat is how she thinks of it. A subdued silence, even when they meet for meals. The muffled clink of silverware. Of chairs scraping. Rose's quiet, quiet face. And, on the days when her aunt feels well enough to join them, the muted, constant coughs.

Despite the cold, Nettie has been sneaking out in her scarf and fingerless gloves to play the piano. Pounding out a quick-time version of her own private melody then rushing back into the house. In the yard, the smell of woodsmoke. A motor running rough up on the road, its sound brought close by dry air.

Then this floating, intangible melody. When played fast, it has a bit of jazz to it. Stitching in front of the fire, Nettie will be humming her tune and Virginia, if she is close, will improvise a lyric or two. Always to brilliant grins, no matter how horrible the poetry. Henry and me, she'll sing. Fingers in a glove and the teeth of gears. Let me grab his bum, let me kiss his ears. Nettie bounces out the rhythm with her finger, then grabs Virginia's arm and hides her face in Virginia's sleeve. If Charlie happens to come into the room, they make surreptitious, mocking faces at each other until he leaves. She has thought that maybe shyness, politeness, is what comes with humility. Or the reabsorption of a certain kind of brutality. There had been a time — a few days, nearly a week — when she had been sure that he would be leaving. How could he stay? And yet here he is. His confidence gradually returning, inflating in accord with the shrinking of his swollen cheeks, the fading of a bruise on his temple. Despite her objections, he buys her gifts, returning from a trip into town with chocolates under an arm, flowers in his fist. She feeds the chocolates to Adze's dog. Lights her stove with roses.

The days pass, forever and all without distinction from days previous, days to come. And Virginia has come to see herself as existing in this same stasis. Time clocked only by the growth of the child in her stomach. The watery kick and swim. The fist of a head, the swing of an elbow (or perhaps a knee) briefly mounded above her navel. In the early mornings, her aunt wheezing beside her, Virginia lies on her back until the false contractions come, indulging her growing concern, her developing fear. Yet the contractions are unsatisfying. Just a vague reminder of her monthlies. The most painful thing in a woman's life, her mother had said. Not so bad, Rose has said. Once or twice, in the outhouse, she has made an effort to inspect herself. Pushing, pulling, probing, vaguely embarrassed by her own curiosity. *How in the world,* she thinks.

And just when she wants to sit down and have a good chat with Rose, Frank Mohr appropriates her. What an odd man. Doesn't give his wife the time of day for months, then all at once he's doting on her. Pouring milk for her at the dinner table. As he works around the ranch — shingling the roof of the new guest cabin, swinging a mattock at the bottom of the swimming pool — he asks her to stand above him, below him. Not to work, so far as Virginia can tell, but simply to observe. To act as audience for his plans: the sweep of an arm up the valley, finger lines drawn in the dirt. A man inconstant in his poses, in his awareness of an audience, he'll work frantically for ten, fifteen minutes, caught up in his own propaganda, then, realizing the futility of the job, he'll stand back and hook a thumb in his pocket and light a cigar.

In the afternoons, Virginia sits on Ah Ting's stool in a corner of the kitchen, eating chunks of raw carrot dipped in freshly whipped mayonnaise, watching him bake his pies, cakes, bread. He had been a cook in San Francisco. Seven dollars a day in a fan-tan house, he says, stirring a cup of potato water into bread dough. Served up lots of small, many-course meals like the Chinese like, he says. Not like here. Made good money before the tongs ran me out.

When he mentions the tongs, he stops talking altogether.

Evenings, she naps next to her aunt, often for three or four hours. She finds herself tired all the time. Exhausted by work, by not working. Exhausted by the way this scattered collection of buildings has become her world. By her unexpected inadequacies. (Drying Nettie's dishes, her hands will go suddenly numb.) Exhausted by the growing separation of muscles in her stomach, the tiniest split in which her baby pooches out. She is exhausted by the way people have begun to feel sorry for her, the uncomfortable way they watch her struggle out of a chair.

Her first daily sight of Henry comes when he sits alone in the kitchen, eating his supper. The half-lit horizon of him, elbows and chin perched over his plate.

The days roll quickly away, but the nights, *their* nights, go on forever. Inside his shack, time refuses to pass. It accumulates.

75

HE WATCHES HER STUDY the hand muff, turning it over and over on her lap. He's been thinking that he should buy her a gift, some piece of clothing or jewelry, and this is the most extravagant gesture he's been able to imagine. It would be so easy to wrap up a square of coyote fur into a tube and line it with his mother's silk pillow cloth. Instead, here is this leopard-skinned thing, expensive enough to account for more than five gallons of booze. But she seems to like it, rubbing it against her cheek, holding it to her nose.

She smiles, and kisses him on the cheek. I love it, she says.

Look at that short fur, he says. It's got that pattern, but look how short that fur is. Hardly any hair to it at all.

He wishes he had known her as a child. There are so many years he'll never be able to touch. A regret at lost time. If he had known her as a child, he would know what she has become.

What are you looking at me like that for? she asks.

Like what?

Like *that*. She makes a face, using her index fingers to pull her mouth down at the corners.

He likes her least of all like this. Mimicking him. A man's only got his self-respect. But he does like her humor. Her unexpected eruptions of laughter. How she laughs at magpies squabbling face to face, bouncing on limbs like neighbors arguing over a fence, at Ballo's twirling, trying to reach the tail she has just braided for her. He occasionally lets himself think that this laughter is traceable, in some way, back to himself.

She sets the muff aside. What do you love?

I guess I can't say.

Well, what do you hate?

I guess I don't like New York much.

New York, she says.

Although I wouldn't mind seeing a game in that new Yankee Stadium. I've never seen Babe Ruth.

Oh, you have to see him. You just have to. That big man with such little feet.

Maybe. Maybe watch him go up against Walter Johnson.

Johnson's over the hill.

Maybe.

Have you ever been in love?

Not really.

Who was she? Her voice takes on a light, bantering tone.

French girl. In the war. Waitress.

What happened to her?

Got in an argument.

And?

I paid for my food and left.

What was her name.

Can't remember.

What's your biggest secret?

Secret?

Everybody has secrets.

He considers it, wetting his lips. A cave, he says. Old Indian place.

A cave? A cave is your biggest secret.

Well.

Don't knock yourself out. She slides down into the blankets, beating at the elk hide.

He touches her shoulder, then cups it in his palm. Indian place, he says. Old chief buried in there all dried up. Anybody else ever found out about him, I guess it'd make newspapers all over the country.

So why tell me? She turns back to him.

Nobody's ever asked me if I got any secrets.

An Indian place.

Not that I'm all that much of an Indian. Pap took us off the reservation when I wasn't more'n three or four years old, I guess. Hardly know anything at all about it.

What do you know?

What?

What do you know about being an Indian?

Mountain Crow.

What?

Mother's half Mountain Crow. Big Lodge clan.

So what do you know about being a Mountain Crow?

He turns slightly away from her, raising one arm and dropping it over his face. Crows don't like to say goodbye, I guess. They'll say come again, but they won't say goodbye.

Well. That's interesting enough.

Tobacco's kind a holy, I guess. The smoke. They got tobacco societies.

You're kidding. Societies?

You don't want to hear about this. He turns his back to her, reaching for his cigarettes.

I want to hear about everything, she says.

He lights a cigarette and blows out the match.

And with the extinguishing of this light, a knock on the door. They had heard no footsteps. They both remain still, the cigarette smoldering in Henry's lips.

Yeah? he says to the closed door.

Virginia, they hear Rose whisper, her voice carrying.

Yes? Virginia touches Henry's leg.

Your aunt's lookin for you.

Pauline? Virginia moves to stand, but Henry motions her back, shaking his head.

The door stays closed. A squeak of boards as Rose leans against the jamb. I told her you was in the jakes, the voice says. Your aunt was in the house lookin for you and I told her you must be in the jakes.

In the jakes?

When you see her, you tell her you was in the jakes.

The boards squeak again, and Rose is gone.

Virginia looks at Henry.

Outhouses, Henry says. She means outhouses.

76

SHE WALKS to the fire with her hair still wet from the bath. Behind her in their cabin, Pauline lies feverish, trying to sleep. Recovering, she claims, from the fright Virginia had given her the night before. The girl walks with her hair tied back with a piece of string, freezing in loose curls around her cheeks. She enjoys wearing it long again. Better than having to worry about marcelling it with that iron.

She's hoping that they'll be playing poker by the fire. It's cold, but no wind. This late in the year — the final days of November — she had expected the weather to be more ferocious. Had been steeling herself for blizzards and hurricane winds. But other than a few inches of snow here and there, it's been clear.

She finds Adze by the fire, talking, leaning toward a dwarfish form hunched on the bench next to him. From this angle, little more than a hairy brown coat with ears. As she approaches, Henry steps into the light of the fire, carrying a soda bottle stoppered with cork. He touches the coat on its shoulder and slides the bottle into one of the cavernous pockets. A gaunt and bearded face tilts up from the coat's collar, staring at Henry with an absurd expression of gratitude.

She eases down next to the heat reflector, wondering what she has just seen.

Virginia? Adze says, glancing up. This here's Victrola Foley. Vic, this here's Miss Virginia Price from the city of New York.

Your name's Victrola? Virginia says.

The man looks at her, eyes warped behind a pair of thick spectacles, nose a swollen, blue-veined mound. He shrugs bashfully, glancing sidelong at Adze.

Had the first phonograph in the state of Wyoming, Adze says. Ain't that right, Vic? Only had one record and he played it . . . you played it what, two years, Vic? Over and over. Why your wife ran off with that Bible salesman. What was the name of that record, Vic?

Don't remember, he says, wiping his nose against his sleeve. His voice surprisingly deep for such a small man.

Two years and a Bible salesman, Adze says, shaking his head, rubbing his hands along the seams of his britches. I do love that story.

77

THE PENCIL gives her license to stare at the most intimate details of him.

She sits naked on his only chair, the pad on one thigh, elbows cocked around her stomach, sketching him entire: toe, penis, knee. The ivory of his skin, the polished muscles, in relaxation, devoid of vein or tendon. *A sculpture,* she thinks. But nothing of stone or marble. Nothing here that might hold detail. His skin more like a finely grained wood.

She tears the drawings from her pad recklessly, spinning them across the room. An act more binding than any ring. Here is me, here is you. She has never found drawing so easy. She draws him supine, feet first, legs slightly open, feeling an extraordinary sense of . . . entitlement, of privilege, being allowed access to the hairy folded skin between his legs. He has never looked at himself from these angles, she's sure of it. And so her pleasure is accentuated by a sense of gift-giving, of providing him admittance to his own body.

The attraction she feels during these sessions isn't sexual. It's after sex. After the night's bruising, frantic, tooth-and-tongue coming together, after the desire has left them both: yolks from eggs. The attraction she feels is more objective, more analytical. He lights the lamp, stretching out his arm to adjust the flame, then faces her on his side: a beached sea creature peeled from its shell. She wonders if it's not the oil lamp that makes it easier. This single source of light. This harsh, abrupt shadowing. She loves the way it illuminates the crest of his hip, the coffee-ground splattering of shaved hair down the back of his neck.

For the first time in her life, her hand produces lines more deliberate than she had intended. Heavier. More self-assured. She intentionally breaks the tips off her sharpened pencils. *If nothing else,* she thinks. *This.* If nothing else.

78

HE TAKES A NIPPLE in his mouth, grimacing at the taste of sudden fluid. I guess I won't be doing that anymore, he says, wiping his mouth.

These are the moments, she thinks, unaccountably depressed. *These are the moments we will spend our lives wringing dry.*

Later, she walks nude around the edges of his room, perspiring, studying the walls, luxuriating in the awareness of her own immodesty. She says, offhandedly, Most of what I know about you comes from this room.

I don't know what that means. He lies outside the quilts, smoking a cigarette. When he is most content, he consumes himself with cigarettes.

Look at how well oiled those reins are, she says. But then look at that ratty cot. And those dusty old paperback books in that beautiful little case. What wood is that? Apple?

Crabapple.

Crabapple, she says, touching a pair of skins hanging by the door. Rubbing her thumb over the dried, greasy knobs of their noses. And this? What kind of fur is this?

Coyote.

I don't think I could ever shoot a coyote, she says. Too much like a dog. And what's this? She bends down to the stove, peering back behind at the white Masonite boards tacked onto the wall as heat reflectors. Handwriting?

Writing, he says.

"May 12, 1914," she reads out loud, "five thousand one hundred and forty-five steps to the Wapiti schoolhouse. June 15, 1914, dug twenty-three postholes and caught four trout for dinner, one 18 inches." What's this?

Diary, he says.

A diary, she says. On the wall?

He shrugs, drops his head back into his pillow. I was a kid.

"September 3, 1914," she reads, "yearling black bear on the roof of the bunkhouse for no good reason. September 22, 1914, saw about a million geese flying south. October 1, 1914, first snow. Wolf tracks on the road. October 15, 1914, shot three-point mulie in the head at two hundred yards. Argued with Pap that I meant to do it."

She squeezes in behind the stove to read the entries lower to the floor, wincing as her thigh touches hot metal. "August 17, 1916," she reads, "cleared rocks on North Fork Road. Spent day working beside Mary Cunningham." Who was Mary Cunningham?

He blows a smoke ring with rounded lips. Prettiest girl in the valley is all. Had this yellow hair.

Virginia makes a sound with her tongue and bends again to read. "August 20, 1916, Patches kicked in the head by sorrel stallion. August 22, 1916, Patches died before breakfast." Who was Patches?

Little brother.

She stands up slowly, her hands flat against a light pain in her lower back. He is not looking at her. He is not smoking. The cigarette above his chest bleeds smoke to the ceiling.

Your brother? she asks.

Half, he says. He does not turn toward her. Does not meet her eyes. He gives her no opportunity to commiserate, to express her sorrow.

So Frank . . .

What?

Well. I mean. You aren't your brother.

Got nothin to do with it.

What was he like? Your brother.

Can we talk about something else?

She lies down beside him, sliding in under his arm. I keep a diary too, she says.

Oh?

You can read it if you want.

I guess I don't read much anymore.

What do you regret? she asks.

He brings his cigarette to his mouth, then wets his lips. I guess I'd like it if there were more places left to discover.

An explorer?

I'd like to put my name on a creek or two.

I know at least one country that's left.

They put a flag on the South Pole ten years ago. Not to say I haven't thought about it. They ain't finished there yet. Not much left in the Arctic, though. Maybe a few places. Maybe Russia. I don't know about that. He smokes. Anyway, Russia. He dismisses the question. Guess I'll probably stay here until I'm rich enough to move east and start payin to come back.

I'm cold, she says, hiding her face in his side, molding her disappointment into his ribs. He doesn't understand her at all.

Do you want this blanket?

What did you do after the war?

After the war?

Yes. After the war.

Oh, I don't know.

Tell me. *Tell* me. She shakes the loose muscles of his chest with her palm.

Fought fires for a while.

Where?

Great Falls.

And?

He shrugs. What did *you* do?

Did you like it? Great Falls?

It was all right, he says. He stubs out his cigarette and leans back into his pillow, throwing his arm over his face. It'us all right.

What then?

Logged.

Where?

Oregon. Astoria. And he closes his eyes and falls asleep. Or perhaps he only closes his eyes.

She was growing tired. She rubbed at her eyes. I suggested that we continue another time, but she waved me away, concerned only that I was interested. "Are you sure?" she asked. "Are you sure? Just an old lady's ramblings. Seventy-five-year-old conversations. But they were so important then. I can still smell the odors of mice and cut wood and that skunk that was always under the floor of his shack. Isn't it odd how an ordinary place can take on the sanctity of a church? The bed where love was made, the room where a death occurred, a desk where a great book was written. But who is it that makes these decisions? Who sanctifies the bed, the desk, the house?

"We do, I think. We're the decision makers. We decide."

79

How sensitive the skin becomes when attention is paid to it. When it is cherished. He runs the palm of his hand down the small of her back, her moisture still drying on his skin, rubbing at the paired muscles on either side of her spine. *Strong for a woman,* he thinks. Maybe because of her pregnancy.

She rolls out from under him, preferring to lie inside his arm, her elbow a lever into the machinery of his chest.

Under her eyes, he is distilled. A pot boiled to its grit. In certain moods, he can feel her staring at him, the way a tongue works at a sore tooth: constantly, gingerly. He thinks of it like an excavation, a plundering. Every question, every curious glance a lifting of bandages. And her growing frustration at his reticence.

He takes great pleasure, at these moments, in these early

morning hours, in thinking about Charlie alone in his cabin. Asleep or awake. But he likes to imagine him awake. And wondering about Virginia. About him. And what does *she* think about him alone in his cabin? She never mentions him at all.

She kisses his cheek, and his arms descend to cover her neck, her back. The growing rise of stomach pressing into his side. Like an inadvertent smudge of knuckles across wet paint.

80

THEY HAVE BEEN having an argument about his socks. Heavy, black woolen things, raveling at the heel. Draped over the collapsed skin of his boots. She says that she can smell them from here.

No you can't, he says.

Well. I can. You should have Nettie darn them at least.

Nettie doesn't have to do anything for me.

No. No. No one needs to do anything for you, do they? You can do everything, can't you? She is aware of the resentment in her own voice but doesn't care to contain it.

Henry stays silent.

Name one thing you can't do.

Oh hell.

One thing. Just one thing.

Can't help my mother, can I? There's one. Can't tell Pap what I think of him, can I? There's another. Oh hell. Shit. He kicks at the covers. Shit.

It is her turn to stay silent, taken aback by his reaction.

She has never seen him more than impassive — even during

their fire. She watches the lines of his face stretch, twist. His lips go thin. His cheeks flush and he turns away.

Shit, he says again, under his breath. She reaches beneath the covers to find his hand and brings it awkwardly to her breast. And he, at least, leaves it there.

81

TELL ME, he hears her say.

Tell you what?

Why? Her hand runs up the length of his arm, then back down.

Why what? He refuses to look at her. Okay. Listen . . . all right? I don't want . . . there's some things I just don't want to talk about.

Henry, she says. Henry. And kisses his neck.

He takes back his hand and rolls over, starting to speak. But then he sees the way she's looking at him. Concern in her widened eyes, narrowed eyebrows. The kind of concern that he has never seen anyone point in his direction. It twists kinks in his heart.

82

THE DARK of the moon and a plum-red glow from the stove. They lie quiet, gradually turning drowsy, content. His hand absently strokes her skin. *This is fine,* she thinks.

This is fine. Give her a lifetime of squabbling over dirty socks if, at the end of it, there are heavy quilts and the sea-salt odor of love and a calloused hand gentle on her breast. If asked to make a wish at this precise moment, she would wish for nothing so much as a longer night.

She whispers, You don't have to wash your socks.

They are nearly asleep when they hear feet crunching through dry leaves and snow. A soft knock on the door, and her aunt calls Virginia's name. Henry sits up. Under his chin, Virginia fumbles at blankets, pillows.

The door opens slowly, tentatively, lantern light bleeding into the room.

Virginia? her aunt says.

Virginia glances up at the light, a corner of the elk skin bunched in her fist. She has learned a trick of quiet from Henry. Of obstinate quiet. And so she stares at a point above the lamp where her aunt's eyes should be, trying to see what the old woman must be seeing. Her inflated drum of a belly, the distended navel. A brush of pubic hair. Henry's flaccid sex.

Below the light of the lantern, behind the flakes of snow swirling through the light, her aunt's feet are bare, toes rimed with frost. Pauline's shoes sit beside Henry's boots. Virginia had worn them to cross the yard. Her feet have been so swollen lately.

A sudden palsy in her aunt's shoulders, in her arms, and for an instant Virginia thinks the old woman is fainting. Instead, she holds the back of her hand to her mouth and chokes out a wet, rattling cough. Behind the open palm, she manages to say, Think what people are going to say.

How dare you, Virginia says. How *dare* you.

Henry stands off the bed, uncovered. Solid. Hostile in his nakedness. No, he says. No.

Her aunt's mouth widens around her strangled coughs. She is trying very hard to keep her eyes fixed on his face.

You can't tell nobody about this, Henry says.

What? Pauline says. Virginia? What?

Pap'll hit my mother, ma'am. He'll beat her up.

Please, the aunt mutters, glancing at the floor. Cover yourself.

The air thickens, hardens between them. A room filled with poured wax. Virginia has never been so aware of her pregnancy as she is now. Aware of it as a violation. Snow blows through the door, contracting her skin. She rubs at her thigh and watches her aunt wrap a length of her own hair up in her fist, pulling at it, jerking her head away from the sight of Henry's nakedness.

He slowly reaches toward the bed, pulling the elk skin away from Virginia, wrapping it around himself like a towel.

Please, he says.

83

HER AUNT is not asleep, not awake. Virginia slips into bed feeling a tremble in the bedclothes. The sandpaper rasp of breath and, outside the cabin, the kind of insulated silence that comes from falling snow.

Virginia shifts, rearranges her quilts.

Don't talk to me, her aunt says.

All right.

But within a few minutes, her aunt coughs, twisting her head over the edge of the bed to spit into her basin. You'll need to find a real doctor, she says. Your mother . . . we never thought you would be out here this long.

I like Rose, Auntie. She's a midwife. A good one.

I would go to Chicago. They have a twilight-sleep clinic there.

I'm sorry, Auntie.

Pauline does not answer. Then, her voice slurred, she says, Don't ever think you can change a man, Virginia.

I am sorry, Auntie. Sorry that things . . . are the way they are.

In the darkness, she sees the white cotton back of her aunt's nightgown sigh deeply. Then nothing.

84

LOOK AT HIM. Just look at him. Christ.

At the age of fifteen, in the mountains alone for the first time, his horses had run off and left him. Two days' ride back in the Beartooths and he'd done everything the way you're supposed to: hobbles and cowbells, good water and feed close by. But both animals — Bear and a three-year-old idgit of a bay named Gene Debs — had spent the night hopping their way back down toward the Clark's Fork. In France, he'd had a boat motor quit him. One of those tour boats out in the middle of some graywater lake in the Alps. Three dollars for the pleasure of bobbing out there six hours waiting for a tow. A lesson he should have learned by now. Just when you start to depend on something, it quits you. It just doesn't make sense relying on anything other than two hands, two feet.

This first night in which she hasn't come to him.

He's angry, yes, but only at himself. How could he have let himself get this worked up? Where's the future in it? Where's the percentage? Where could they ever have gone with this thing?

He has been lying awake waiting for her, dozing in and out.

Stoking the fire then lying down again. Starting awake at three or four in the morning to realize that she isn't beside him. That this fist in his gut comes from her absence. That these shards of glass in his throat are loss. He feels the fist, the glass, then becomes aware that he feels them.

He paces around the room. Just goddamn look at him. Under his bed, a tin jug of booze. He pours an inch of hazy liquid into his coffee cup and tosses it back. Pours himself another. This late at night, he'll still be drunk when he goes to breakfast, but that's fine by him. That's just dandy.

He takes his third drink and steps outside. The firepit, the lodge; past the lodge, her cabin. All of it lit blue by the moon and the moon's reflection in the new snow. More snow on the way.

85

SHE TWISTS her hands together. Says, I never would have thought you'd just stand there like that.

He sits on the floor unthreading a horsehair pack rope, his back against the cushions of the couch. She had thought that he was waiting for her to speak, but now that she has broken the silence he moves only to toss another stick of wood into the fire.

How did you spend your day? she asks. Want to know how I spent my day?

He doubles the loose threads into a loop and starts to splice them back into the rope. The back of his head unreadable to her.

I cooked the broth out of a chicken and tried to get her to sip a cup of it.

She wants nothing so much as to be consoled. For him to

whisper that things are okay and then smooth the hair away from her face.

He scratches the side of his nose.

Then I went and told your father that she's getting better.

Why'd you do that? He sets the first length of rope aside and picks up another.

Henry, you didn't even have the decency to cover yourself.

I didn't see you makin no run for the blankets.

She deserves respect. Maybe you don't understand that.

I'm not the one sleeping with a red Indian.

What?

All them questions. Isn't that it? He tests the loop in the rope with his fists, then sets it aside. Red Indian?

How dare you.

Curious, I guess.

You can't say . . . You don't believe that.

He shrugs and yawns, stretching out his arms until the joints pop.

You're just a country bumpkin. That's all. You don't know *any*thing.

He gathers up his ropes, coiling them under his arm, and pulls himself to his feet. He turns to face her.

A *crazy* country bumpkin.

He levels his eyes at her.

A crazy bumpkin. And a . . . a liar.

But not a whore, he says, his voice flat.

She hears the word, feels it stretching, bulging like fabric in water. She is not imagining this. In the half-darkness of the room, the word takes on substance, spreading solid between them, lingering even as pans drop and clatter in the kitchen. Unaccountably, the child's rhyme goes through her head: *Sticks and stones. Sticks and stones but only words can really hurt you.* Her life balancing on the blade of a single syllable.

The kitchen door bangs open and Adze steps into the room, finishing off a last bite of pie, wiping his fingers on his shirt front. What are you two doin in here in the dark? he says, flicking on the light.

They stand blinking, the couch between them.

Behind Adze, Nettie carries a bowl of popcorn. She glances at Virginia, then at Henry, aware of some interruption. Dewey pulls up a chair and tosses a pack of cards down on the table, nodding at Adze. Check the seal and break em open, he says.

Virginia? Henry? Adze pulls out the deck and does a quick one-handed shuffle. Poker school's open.

I'd keep an eye on Henry, Virginia says, her voice wanting to catch. Make sure you cut the cards well.

She goes out on the porch, cupping her elbows and listening to the muted, puzzled conversation in the room behind her. Then laughter. She touches her stomach, feeling the retained heat of it. Wishing she could just step away from it. Step away and leave it as he has left it.

86

MOST OF THE WEATHER here seems to come from the north and the west. She had made this comment to him not long ago, proud of her observation, but he had reacted to it not at all, taking it as a given. And so she had thought, *Of course. Of course.* But now this storm seems to be rolling in from the east, and she wishes she could talk to him about it.

She'll never entirely adjust to the idea of watching a storm arrive. The clouds catching on the ground, unthreading in charcoal washes of moisture. A curtain of snow sweeping up the valley, consuming river, road, trees. She stands outside her cabin shivering, wet snow stitching into her hair. Through the cracked door behind her, she hears her aunt cough, then draw a wheezing, painful breath. A moan. Then a second cough, weaker than the last.

This must be only an inkling of the worry she'll feel as a mother. If the responsibility for her aunt's life — this desiccated husk that is, in fact, a life already lived — worries her so much, she can't imagine what a child will do to her.

The cold becomes too much and she steps back inside, pulling up a chair to sit beside her aunt's bed, a book in her hands. As she starts to doze off, she hears the doctor arrive, stamping his feet outside. She opens the door, taking the hat he hands her, then his heavy wool coat.

Miss, he says, his eyes going briefly, politely to her stomach.

A serious man, she sees, approving. The chain of a pocket watch spanning his rounded waistcoat and a gray anvil of goatee jutting from his thick double chin. She hadn't been sure what to expect. Like her aunt, she had half expected a snake oil salesman, garters on the sleeves.

Pauline lies with her arms thrown back, her forehead white and wrinkled, cheeks flushed with fever. The page-turning rattle of her breath. He sets his case on the floor beside the bed, reaching inside to untangle a stethoscope.

Your aunt? he asks, touching Pauline's wrist.

Great-aunt, yes. Pauline.

Well, now, he says. Let's see now. Pauline.

He sits on the side of the bed and pulls her aunt's arms down to her sides, sliding the bedding away from her chest. The old woman's eyes roll open to stare at him blankly, feverishly.

He undoes the top two buttons of her gown and slides the

stethoscope against her chest. There now, he says, there now. He probes lightly at her side with his fingers, into her ribs, nodding at her pained whistle of breath. He places a thermometer under her tongue and closes her mouth on it, holding it for a count of thirty. He looks at the thermometer in the light then turns to Virginia. How long has she been unaware?

Just this morning. Only this morning.

He shakes out the thermometer and pulls the stethoscope from his ears. Your aunt has pneumonia, he says.

I thought so. I thought she did. I thought so.

He looks at Virginia's stomach, then glances at the pillow on the bed beside Pauline. Have you been sleeping here with her?

Virginia nods.

Dear child. If you were to catch sick at this stage . . .

My aunt. What can we do for her?

Nothing. Almost nothing.

The doctor stands with difficulty. She will win this fight or not, he says, wrapping up his stethoscope and bending to his bag. I'll give you a packet of Dover's Powder. Morphia. To help her sleep if need be.

Nothing . . .

If she were younger, I would dose her with strychnine for her heart. Pneumonia weakens the heart. But strychnine is strong for a woman her age. I have seen it take patients younger than your aunt.

Virginia touches her aunt's foot under the blankets, pressing the toes with her fingers.

Keep her bowels loose. Cold drinks will reduce the fever. Soda water is good. And if she begins to recover, if she can take food, her diet should be light. Broth. Milk. Eggs. No beans. Nothing to cause flatulence.

No beans, Virginia says.

Now. About you.

About me?

You haven't seen a doctor, I understand.

Yes. Early on. In New York. But there's no —

Ah, he says, pulling his stethoscope back out of his bag. I still need this. You're how far along? Six months?

About that, yes. But really —

And you've felt the baby kicking? Kicking and rolling around in there? Strong baby?

Yes, she says, touching her stomach, feeling an absurd twinge of pride.

Let me listen.

He drops to his knees in front of her — this fat, stern doctor with a wedge of coarse hair four inches out from his chin — and helps her roll up the front of her shirt. For the first time in her life, she exposes her belly to a man other than Henry. Other than, she supposes, Charlie. He holds the stethoscope's hollow bell to the skin above her navel. The metal freezes a circle in her skin. He places his hand on the flat of her back and presses the bell hard into her stomach.

There it is, he says. There is his little heartbeat. Breathe, please. And hold it. And again? Fine. Fine. He struggles to his feet, using the bedpost for leverage.

Have you been bleeding? He covers her stomach with his big hands, his thumbs probing. His palms hot, dry.

No.

Cramping?

No.

Gaining weight?

Yes.

How much?

I'm not sure.

Ten pounds? Twenty?

Maybe ten.

Good. You can gain another ten or so, but no more.

Why? Why no more?

Eclampsia. Convulsions.

Can I hear?

Sorry?

Can I hear the heartbeat?

The skin around his eyes wrinkles, and she thinks he must be smiling under all that hair. You can try, he says.

He pulls the stethoscope plugs from his ears and wipes them with a lace-trimmed handkerchief, raising them to her ears. She touches the plugs with her fingertips. The doctor blows into the bell, raising his eyebrows at her. She nods, surprised at the amplification. He places the cold, hollow circle again on her stomach. It will be very fast, he says.

She hears her own heart first. The rhythmed meter of her own time-passing. And nothing else. She shakes her head and the doctor presses harder, denting the flesh. And then . . . there. A faint pulse. A machine-gun *chunk-chunk-chunk*. Like a finger drumming on wood.

So fast, she thinks. *So fast.*

87

IT HAS BEEN SNOWING for three days. And hell, it could snow until April.

When he is profoundly unhappy he talks to himself. A habit from the war, and one recognized only by his mother, who treats it with respect. An Indian's respect for inner demons. Half-bursts of phrases, oddly stressed profanity. One thought leads to another to another until he finds one he's ashamed of.

. . . can't believe it, he mumbles.

He does not know what he wants. Does not know what he expects. Unmoored, flapping sails inside his head. He's not worth much. He doesn't know what that girl expected of him. He's not worth anything.

. . . *any*thing, he mutters.

He slings his panniers over Bear's double-rigged sawbuck and ropes them down. Bear, he says, slapping the horse on the shoulder as he walks around. Good ol Bear. Scarred on the flanks from that leather-cinched hull Pap had given him when he'd started riding Bear to school. He thinks of those horse stalls, built before they'd even had a building, when the classes were held in a canvas wall tent. Those stalls had faced into the wind, and more often than not you were better off picketing your horse behind them rather than inside. He had been twelve years old and riding an energetic, unpredictable two-year-old Bear to school. A kid named Mel Stone, two years older and a few inches bigger (although not *that* much bigger), liked to spit into his fingers and flick the spit into Henry's hair. And Henry never did a thing about it. Never punched him in that lopsided nose. Never shoved the twisted pair of black eyebrows into the dirt. Never did a thing.

. . . . goddamned *thing.*

He leads out Sally, a ten- or eleven-year-old buckskin mare with more good looks than sense. But she should be okay behind Bear, who's old enough, calm enough to settle most other horses. He saddles her and brings out another pair of panniers, hefting them, slinging them up.

Two pounds of ground coffee. Ten pounds of flour and a tin of yeast. Sugar. A ten-pound bag of beans. Five pounds of bacon. No tinned meat. No canned hams or chickens. Unlike every other trapper he knows, he eats the animals he traps. Likes a bobcat cubed up in flour and fried in bacon grease. Coyote's not bad if you boil it most of a day. But he won't eat a weasel. Fishers, martens, or wolverines. That musk taste coats your tongue like black thirty-weight.

Twenty-five cans of sliced peaches in heavy syrup. When he's trapping hard, he craves peaches. Back in the woods, surrounded by snow, this little taste of civilization.

An hour later, he rides up the road on Tony, leading Bear with Sally tail-tied behind, diamond-hitched bales of traps and chains on each packhorse. The snow falls heavier as he rides, and before he's past the mouth of Elk Fork he's wondering if it's not already too late. There is no traffic on the road this time of year, not up this high, and so the grade has become little more than a beveled ridge of snow inverted against the mountains: unblemished, transected by the tracks of crossing deer, by the light, erratic scuffs of rabbits, by the heavy bound and brush of a mountain lion. The lion tracks are only just now beginning to fill in, and the horses shy as they ride past. Sally rears, jerking and trotting away from Bear, finally settling down, rope trailing between her front legs. Bear stands with his head down, panniers knocked crooked, calm even with ropes swinging loose under his belly. Good ol Bear, Henry says, straightening the panniers. Later, after he has chased down Sally and retied her to Bear's tail, rubbing his hand over her withers, he says in a soft, calming voice, You're lucky I'm no horse beater.

He doesn't stop for lunch, instead eating a can of mixed fruit as he rides. Holding Bear's lead rope in one hand, reins in the other, tilting his head back under the jerk of the can.

It's nearly dark when he turns north out of Pahaska, clouds stacked and boiling on either side of a clear slice of sky. *Just the beginning,* he thinks. The horses lunge through stunted creekbed saplings, slip on unseen rocks. But after he finds his old trail, the first heavy hatchet scar blazed in the bark of a pine, they walk easily, long after it's too dark for him to see much. He pats Tony on the shoulder. Almost there, he says.

His cabin sits back in the trees, hunched into the hillside like a frightened animal, half sheltered by the hanging face of a cliff. A building remarkable for its absences. No bed. No table. No cabinets. A single uncomfortable chair and rough-hewn shelves at chest level. Nails for hanging clothes. A fifty-five-gallon-barrel stove, its door cut out with tin snips and hinged with baling wire, the chimney pipe elbowed from the back rather than the top, sacrificing draw strength for a flat surface where he can boil his traps. Empty stretching boards stacked against the back wall: solid boards for cats and martens, and larger, wedge stretchers for coyotes and wolves. He drops the traps on the floor and goes back outside to unsaddle the horses and turn them into the corral, giving them each a half gallon of grain dumped on a stamped circle of snow. He builds a fire and unrolls his sleeping bag and hangs his saddle blankets by the fire. In a few days, when he's up here for good, he'll trim some pine boughs for his bedding. He likes the smell of them. The smell more than the feel, the way they break up the odors of fleshed skins and urine lures.

It snows another eighteen inches that night, and he wakes with the blankets to his chin, sensing the mounded weight on the cabin. He dresses and builds a fire and boils his coffee, finally standing in the doorway with a steaming mug, blinking against the flashfire whiteness of the world. The three horses huddle together nose to tail, taking shelter under the branches of that big fir tree he'd left uncut inside the corral for just this reason.

He feels his nose running — a line of moisture guttering along his lip — and brushes at it with the back of his hand.

What astounds him most is the way he has come to occupy the same stretch of time he had wondered about so many years ago. And how little things have changed. In France, he had thought that if he could only live to see this particular place, this particular time — his old trapping cabin in the mountains, snow on the ground, and horses shaking in the corral — he would be fulfilled. He would find some measure of satisfaction. But it hasn't worked out that way. He's looking back now from a high place and discovering that it's not high at all.

He brushes at his nose again and glances down at the back of his hand. The blood stops him, a red slash a quarter inch wide, already wrinkling and dry. He dabs two fingers to his nostrils and both come back with dimes of red on their tips. Shit, he says out loud. Goddamn nosebleeds. Goddamn dry air.

He hasn't had a winter nosebleed in years, although as a boy he would get one or two a week.

He squints against the faint itch under the bridge of his nose, the gathering of moisture in his nostrils. Twin bulbs of blood grow and break and run out onto his lips. *Christ,* he thinks. He stands with his head over his knees. The bleeding is high in his nose, above where it might be pinched off, so he knows from experience that it's best just to let it run its course. He watches in dull anger as his blood augers a steaming hole in the snow. Three or four minutes later, he wipes off the last large drop and spits. Washes his hands in snow.

He feels so old. So stretched and thin: each muscle in his arms, his back, like wool threaded across a loom. He tosses the dregs of his coffee into the snow. He should unpack and get back down to the house before another storm rolls in.

Time and tide, he says, turning to get the saddles.

88

SHE WOULD LIKE to believe that her aunt has forgiven her. All the little sins. A trip to Wyoming and shoes sitting by the door. In her old age, she will want to believe it so fervently that she will nearly convince herself. It should have happened this way, and so it must have happened this way. But it did not. Her aunt never rolled over to her, never touched her face. Never said that she had been wrong. That she should love this cowboy. It never happened that Virginia was freed of guilt. She was never, never astounded by the lifting absence of her guilt.

Instead, she wakes to find her aunt dead beside her. This first morning of not being forgiven. The old woman warm still, her skin improbably flushed, but dead nonetheless. She should still be alive. Even those shoes sitting by the door. Such a small thing until it becomes so important.

Pneumonia or heart failure. *But no,* Virginia thinks. *Failure of heart.*

The girl supine beside the body of her aunt. Sharing the same position with which they began: face to face on the bed, a new stomach between them. The girl still young but growing old so quickly. She sees it all now, how the remainder of her life will go. The details, of course, are beyond her, but she sees the timbre of it. Oscillations of desire and regret broken only by rare grace notes of contentment: one here, one there.

She does something very adult now.

She takes her aunt's hand — stiffening, so that spreading the fingers is like bending curled wire — and brings it to her chest, cradling it between her breasts. Her aunt's head shifts slightly on the pillow: eyes half closed and collapsed under the lids, a line of yellow fluid pooled under the corner of her mouth. She bends forward to kiss the old woman's forehead. Her lips are colder than the skin of her hand. She says, When you were sixteen you fell in love with a boy named Adam Mills. He lived on East Thirty-second Street. He had curly red hair that coarsened and turned gray in his old age, but when you loved him it was soft and long. You kissed him once, you said, and remembered what his hair felt like in your hands. She pauses, and kisses her aunt again. Your entire life you regretted not marrying him.

The flaccid tip of her aunt's nose. The eyelids paper thin, translucent with age. This absence of Pauline.

89

SHE HEARS SAWING. A faint, pulsing buzz and a clanking of boards, a hammering. In the first confusion of waking, she thinks, *Adze is building a casket.* But then she remembers the one waiting in town. Mahogany, with brass handles.

The baby wakes inside her, kicking as she rolls over to her side, dropping the back of her hand onto the cold, cold sheets on the other side of the bed. She steps into her pants and the baby kicks harder: a rhythm of hard little bubbles. Sometimes she'll think it's only indigestion, but that's when it kicks hardest of all. She digs her hot-water bottle out from under the quilts and carries it sloshing across the yard, stepping high through the snowdrifts at the edge of the driveway. The sounds of building have stilled, and now there's only the wind. A whistle in the eaves of the house. Behind her, she hears Charlie's cabin door open and close, but she doesn't glance back.

She finds Rose and Nettie in the kitchen, Rose leaning

heavily against the sink, a drying rag dangling from one hand. Nettie is reaching up to place the last of the morning dishes in the cabinet. Something is missing here, and it takes her a moment to place it.

Rose? she asks. Where's Ah Ting?

Rose dries her hands. Tosses the dishtowel into the empty sink.

Where's Ah Ting, Nettie?

Quit.

Quit?

Went to work for that Buffalohead Café in town. I guess he can cook all the eggs he wants at a mornin café.

He didn't say goodbye?

Nettie avoids Virginia's eyes. He might be back, she says.

Place is emptyin out, Rose says, shaking her head at the sink. Emptyin out. Your old aunt, Henry . . .

Virginia pours a cup of coffee and steps out onto the porch. In the few minutes she's been inside, the draft horses and sleigh have been led out from the barn: mouse-colored, elephant-sized beasts, shaggy and restless in the traces. Leaning against their collars, then relenting. The sleigh with strips of crimped tin nailed under the runners and muddy chaff piled in the corners. On these days of heavy snow, Adze and Dewey have been feeding morning and evening, forking hay from the sleigh to the thirty-five or forty remaining mother cows recently separated from their calves. And a week ago, she had watched the two of them saw blocks from the heavy ice at the river's edge and use these same horses to draw the blocks up a log ramp into the icehouse.

Now, Adze and Mohr emerge from the barn carrying her aunt. What she assumes is her aunt. The two men shuffling and grunting on either end of a long wooden box. Not a casket but a polite covering for the trip into town. A box thrown together from the scraps and ends of boards: an unpainted house door, a piece of roofing tin, sections of fencepost at the corners. *A need-*

less effort, she thinks. And one that Adze must have performed only for her sake. Perhaps for what he regards as her delicate countenance. Through the cracks in the sides of the box she glimpses her aunt's cerement: the last yards of Rose's blue and white gingham. The body (frozen now, surely) will have to be thawed out. She has heard that undertakers embalm in arsenic, and she wonders how the freezing and thawing will affect the embalming.

She must be sure to thank Rose for using the last of that gingham.

Adze heaves the forward corner of the box onto the sleigh and hurries back to help Mohr, the two of them pushing the box until only a foot or so is left hanging off the back. Adze sees Virginia on the porch and touches the brim of his hat. Miss, he says.

Thank you, Adze, she says, stepping off the porch and walking across to him. She hugs him. The first time, maybe, that she has ever touched him. A hard and withered rope in her arms. *Kindness,* she thinks, moisture collecting in her eyes. She turns away and tilts her head back, an instinct from the days when she wore eye makeup.

Charlie is walking up from the outhouses, his boots crunching in the snow. She stands and lets him come, and when he puts his hand on her shoulder, she lets its rest there. Although it's not really comfortable, it is, at least, a touch. That night in his apartment. That had been a kind of death too, she supposes. Yes. But not death in the sense of ending a life. It was an absence of life, and therefore, she supposes, an absence of death. It was nothing.

They're taking her into town, she says.

I know. I'm going too.

You are?

Care to go with us?

She shakes her head.

Charlie takes a cigarette from his shirt pocket and lights it, holding it with his lips while he shoves his hands in his pockets. The past few weeks he's been growing a beard, and has taken to wearing a series of heavy shirts and pants passed along by Mohr. A red woolen coat that Henry must have worn as a teenager. Adze's old galoshes. It's not the Charlie she knew back east. A new creation entirely. He belongs here somehow. More than herself, anyway. He hasn't worn his spectacles for days.

Can I have one of those? she asks. A cigarette?

He gives her the one in his mouth, then lights another for himself.

Good for the digestion, he says.

Adze walks to the blindered horses, stroking their noses, patting their necks. He pulls a carrot from his pocket and breaks it in half, feeding a few bites to each. After it's gone, the horses nose at him, knocking him side to side. He grabs their collars for balance, and since he's already there, he walks them half a step to the left and right, cracking them out of the ice that has already collected on the runners.

She breathes the smoke, feeling pleasantly dizzy. Warmed. A cleaner taste than Henry's cigarettes. No bits of tobacco on her tongue. Charlie's hand is on her shoulder again.

You're not missing New York, are you? he asks.

I miss my radio, she says.

Your radio?

I miss *The Eveready Hour* of all things.

I've wired your mother. Did I tell you?

No. About Pauline?

Of course.

Virginia wonders how her mother will take the news. This close to Christmas, Virginia supposes that she'll be spending her days doing charity work: walking door to door in Little Italy carrying wicker baskets of sliced ham and candied apples, sitting with other society women wrapping boxes of inappropriately expensive socks for that orphanage in the Bronx. She will be twisting pine boughs along the banisters of the house and stacking poinsettias in the shape of Christmas trees. Virginia knows how her mother will be spending her days, but as much as she tries, she can't see the woman's face.

Mohr, who had disappeared into the house, is out in the yard carrying a pair of heated flatirons in towels and a leather belt of sleigh bells, a pie wrapped in cloth and a stone jug hooked over one finger. He sets down the flatirons and pie, and piles the bells in a foul-noted jangle ahead of her aunt's box, wedging the jug into the box itself (glancing briefly at Virginia).

Charlie draws deeply on his cigarette and tosses it hissing into the snow. Sure you don't want to come along? It might do you good.

She shakes her head, shivering.

Well, then. All right.

After they're gone, the drum-clopping of the horses lingers, disembodied.

She has not been aware of snow falling. The sky is so gray, so depthless that there has been no detail within it. But when she tilts her head back, indulging in a long moment of self-pity (her small, dark figure standing so alone in this big yard, yesterday's snow unraveling from the roofline, blending into the smoke from the chimneys), flakes touch her face, dropping onto her skin like muted piano keys.

90

HENRY TOLD HER once that if you cut out the heart of a deer in the few minutes after it dies, it will continue to beat in your hand.

She is feeding chickens away from the wind, in the alley between the barn and the tackroom, a space as tight and narrow as a train car. Snow has drifted across the openings. Two portals of light, north and south, and between them the oblivious scratchings of randomly insane chickens. The eternally rutting rooster treading his hens with a great flap and fuss, then returning to his bit of seed. She has long since named him Fatty Arbuckle, and has made it a habit to count the number of hens mounted during their feeding sessions. Today she has counted six hens in the last ten minutes. A record. Perhaps having something to do with the weather.

Midafternoon and very cold, the world the color of dirty ice. And he is suddenly standing horizoned at one end of her train car. She hadn't even known that he was back from his trip into the mountains. The wind throws his collar up against his ears. His form recalls a crucifix: his fingers brushing the corners of each building, his legs blurred in the tendrils of old snow. He is walking toward her, and there is no misreading his intentions. The purposefulness of his walk. She thinks back to her first sight of him, months ago, as he was training his horse. Centuries ago.

She tilts the open jar loosely in her hand and sprays corn out in one long motion against the side of the barn. The chickens erupt in a frenzy of scrabbling. He walks through the pool of birds, his eyes on her. Only her. *It's too cold for this,* she thinks. *It's never too cold for this.*

She waits until he's an arm's length away and then slaps him, surprised that he would let her hand reach him. But it feels so good. This contact of palm and cheek. She slaps him again, and still he does nothing to avoid it. A twitch of his face. He is looking at her. He moves toward her and now he is too close for slapping.

He backs her against the wall, his hands on her hips, his gloveless hands inside her coat, reaching under her shirt. His hands on her stomach, on her breasts. Her back is against the wall. And then he is turning her, bending at her.

91

HE TOUCHES his own torso, tracing the curve of his ribs: the floating rib and the paired abdominal muscles and, beneath the muscles, the intestines, the kidneys, the liver that he can feel if he probes deep. And here's an organ that's had its work cut out for it lately.

What is there about him that she could possibly care for?

He has lived his life familiar with the interior geography of animals. With the grain of muscle as it cools and becomes meat. With the wet suction slide of intestines spilling onto the ground. The wash of blood over viscera. He knows precisely the way skin pulls away from fascia to become leather, the webbed spread of fat and the torn-newspaper sound as it's cut. But he doesn't know anything about that girl. About what she might be thinking.

He pours himself another drink and sets the jug under the bed, his hand coming back with a second jug, a container so light as to at first seem empty. He shakes it next to his ear, listening to the paper wash of bills inside. He's had his eye on a used Ford Runabout for sale in Cody, and thinks he would like to drive to San Francisco. But then, he's also been thinking about a house in Missoula. A house like the one Sid Burton, his old section chief, had built. A plank house with hanging trees and a fence and the river just behind. But chances are he won't be buying either one. He enjoys money for its possibilities, not its particulars. Nevertheless, after this year's trapping, he'll take a pair of tin snips to the jug and see just what kind of future he's created here.

Good and drunk, he's been staring at the wall, at his childhood map recently resurrected from the attic. Lacking any cardboard or canvas, he had glued sheets of newspaper to a half-square of tin and painted the sheets white. A record of his trapping successes and, by extension, his failures. Inked lines of creekbeds and triangular cones of mountaintops, a paper bulge of unevenly spread glue. The abrupt line of Yellowstone Park where his trapping area formally ended (although he sometimes went over that line, as who did not?) and the more gradual white space on the north and east, the squiggled lines of creeks and ridges reaching into the blankness like fingers. Scattered among the marks, dozens of small red letters: W for wolf, C for coyote, B for bobcat, M for marten. The map never really helped him much — he could always remember where and how he caught most every one of his pelts — but the drawing of it had given him such a feeling of satisfaction. Something about seeing himself as a mapmaker. The thought that he might be making a contribution. It's been nearly ten years, but he still remembers that satisfaction.

Avoid the white, he says, toasting the map.

If his year is good, he might make as much as $1,000. Buster Howell claims to have made $1,500 last year. But that's Buster Howell.

Where does it all go? Not time, of course — everybody knows where time goes — but ambition. You just wake up one morning touching a space where *want* had been. He wonders if he's grown up. If complacency is evidence of manhood.

He falls into a light sleep, waking a few minutes later to the sound of footsteps outside his door. He recognizes her quick, determined pace, and he sits up, spilling the remainder of his booze across his chest. The room spins and he lies back down.

The door opens. And that quickly, Virginia is kneeling beside him, her forearms stretched across his chest.

Will you marry me? she says.

He is astonished. A question he never in his whole life expected to hear. A woman asking a man. But then, he has always been astonished by her.

Do you love me? she asks.

Virginia . . .

A simple question. Do you love me?

He hears it like an accusation. Please, he says, touching her arm.

She stands, stretching herself tall. As tall as possible. The faint bars of moisture from her arms burn into his chest. She says, Your whole life . . .

She turns away from him. He has begun to get an erection. She clears her throat and says, Regret this.

92

SHE LEANS BACK, drawing up her knees as far as her stomach will allow, the sketchpad on her knees. She takes up her pencil, the square cut of wood finding its familiar place in her hand. The smell of cedar. As is her habit, she pages through previous drawings, lingering over favorites.

The chin-wattled aunt. The clean-muscled Henry. On the last page, a study of the soles of his feet. *How odd this would seem to someone else,* she thinks. The fibrous, chapped skin of his heels, the two big toes jutting out at angles, the smaller toes curled like the legs of a dead insect. The nails warped and buried.

Nothing less than map after map of her own perceptions. A portfolio of what she finds lovely. Here are these bodies. Portraits. A small one of Dewey, hidden in a corner of the page, tilting back the brim of his hat with his thumbnail. A larger one, on the same page, of Adze, lariat coiled on his shoulder. It is, she realizes with some discomfort, an appropriation. She's been capturing these people. Sketching them with an academic's curiosity.

There is a jangle of bells outside. Through the window, she sees the sleigh pull into the yard. Despite herself, she feels a thrill. For the past few days, she has not been anticipating the return of these men so much as dreading their absence. She's been living on a ranch with the life gone out of it. A patch of skin without blood. Rose waking late and cooking breakfast still in her pale blue cotton nightgown: watery eggs over a stove only half warm. Nettie riding her little horse in at ten-thirty, eleven, only to stare distractedly out the kitchen's westerly window, into the mountains. Even little Gus, splitting his kindling, cleaning September's potatoes, seems to harbor a puzzled, tight-lipped resentment.

These webs of debt and duty that never fail to catch her.

After Frank Mohr wraps up the reins, after Adze drops down off the bed of the sleigh to attend to the horses, Charlie sits a little longer. He's bought himself a new two-button worsted suit and matching fedora, a calf-length chesterfield driving coat. He's had his beard trimmed. He leans forward, and she sees for the first time the form seated beside him. A rolled cowl of blankets. A large woman made larger by the thick splash of quilts.

Virginia watches as her mother sheds the first of her blankets and passes it down to Mohr. A woman accustomed to servants. She wraps a second quilt around her shoulders like a shawl, glancing at the lodge, at the guest cabins, at the barn through the bare cottonwoods. The disdain is visible in the tight set of her lips, in the heavy, permanent wreck of her face.

One chance, Virginia thinks. One last chance. These final moments of her womanhood. The few last minutes before, once again, she'll be the spoiled girl who lies.

She backs away from the window and goes out the back door, across the yard and around the mounds of snow and dirt above the empty hole of the swimming pool. Below her, the river is nearly frozen, cracked in its center by a motionless snake of black water. There is no smoke coming from Henry's chimney, and she wonders if he has already left. Gone into the mountains. A sense of resignation washes over her. *So be it,* she thinks. If it's fate, she will resign herself to it.

But he is indeed in his cabin, naked on his blankets, feet crossed. He is less sensitive to cold than anyone she's ever met. His eyes are open and staring at the door. He has been waiting for her.

Her sense of desperation dissipates in shreds. This is Henry here. This familiar, comfortable body.

She kneels in front of him (isn't kneeling appropriate for what she has in mind?), covering his bare skin with as much of herself as she can manage. But then, she doesn't want to beg. Doesn't want to prostrate herself. She pulls back. Will you marry me? she asks.

He stares at her dull-eyed, hair clumped on his head like pinched clay, the empty cup of booze resting on his chest.

She draws up, feeling steel in her back. There is nothing left of her now but this resolve. Do you love me?

Virginia . . .

Do you love me?

Virginia . . . His voice has notes of placation in it. Of patronization. He's scolding a child.

Her mouth dries and she sees how it will be for the rest of her life.

She wants to hurt him. To flail him. This condescension! All these weeks, months of being used. She has had that *thing* in her mouth.

Above all, she wants to show him what he'll be missing. Unfold his life for him then grind it under her heel. She wants to give it all to him and take it all away.

She stands, trying to call to mind the strongest words she

knows. She can think of only one, but she gives it to him like a witch's curse. Spits it. If language could taste, if words held a flavor, this word would be blackened toast and stove ash and withered bones. The taste of teeth broken in the mouth.

Regret this, she says.

93

SO THIS IS THE WOMAN. The woman whose judgment the girl hears when she hears a judgment.

He leans against the open barn door, pack frame at his feet, ribbons of leather shoelaces that had hung it from the rafters trailing off to the side. He'd played hell finding the thing.

Steam rises behind him, drifting through the open door. A barn cat drops lightly from the fence and minces along the wall, twisting rubber-backed against his leg. He's never trusted a tame barn cat. Comes from not earning their keep. Comes from that goddamned cook setting out scraps. He kicks it, catching it under the ribs with his boot. It jumps with the kick, using the momentum to carry itself on a run out the barn door. Goddamn cats. Can't kick em even when you want to.

He's in a foul, foul mood. So anxious to get up in the mountains. Away from people.

More than anxious. Desperate.

He wonders if the mother knows. Sitting there on the porch, so implacable, so self-assured. The kind of prim, self-righteous command that comes only to women of a certain age, a certain wealth. A sanctimoniousness shared only by the very religious. As if wealth or belief were entitlement to arrogance. He wonders if she knows how much she is despised by her daughter. How much she is revered.

He watches Charlie step out of the lodge, yawning, stretching. Watches him sit heavily on the bench beside the mother, union suit flashing bright red under the tail of his jacket. He takes the mother's hand and brushes it against his lips.

Jesus Christ.

Henry grabs his pack frame and walks around the outside of the barn, retracing the cat's path.

94

KNOWING WHAT SHE KNOWS NOW, it's hard for Virginia to imagine this woman as a mother — generically a mother. Receiving the burst of semen, tending a union of sperm and egg, placing a suckling infant to her breast. Or had there been a wet nurse? Virginia realizes now that she may have been wet-nursed. Probably was. She's never thought about it.

They have lodged her mother in Ah Ting's old room behind the kitchen. Virginia opens the door, smelling apples and the faint tang of Ah Ting's cheap toilet water. Her mother's coat hangs on a nail above the lighter squares of wallpaper where the ancestral photographs had hung. The woman herself sits on the edge of the narrow bed, her back to the door, brushing her hair over her shoulders. Virginia does have to admit that her mother has lovely hair, at least when she lets it down. Thick and wild, silvering in streaks. She turns as Virginia enters, and stops her brushing.

Sit down, Virginia, she says, pinching an invisible snarl from her brush. A favorite elephant-hair brush with an ivory handle, the sight of which takes Virginia briefly back to New York.

Virginia steps around a brass-barred clothing trunk to sit at her mother's hip. You've not packed much, Mother. A dozen changes?

A dozen or so. Her mother takes her hand, a polite formality in her voice. We won't be staying long.

We? Virginia asks.

Have they been treating you well, Virginia?

Very well, Mother, she says, then thinks, *So it's going to go like this.*

The food has been good?

Good enough.

You wouldn't believe what I had to go through to get even this little private room. That man Mr. Mohr wanted to put me in that little cabin with you.

I can't imagine.

But your health, Virginia? Your pregnancy?

No problems, Mother.

None? None at all?

No.

I thought you would be sick early on.

Rose has been very good with her advice.

That Indian woman.

And how are things in New York?

Her mother sighs and drops Virginia's hand to pick again at her brush. Not well, Virginia. Not well.

No?

They're talking about you.

Well, I've been gone what? Four months?

People know, Virginia. My game table knows. About the baby. About Charlie.

So you had to tell, Virginia says, feeling her face flush with anger. Do you really hate me so much?

Her mother studies her briefly. That friend. That little school friend of yours. What's her name?

It wasn't Isabel, Mother.

Isabel. I told you to keep this secret. I told you people would talk.

I did. I did.

You didn't tell Isabel?

Virginia shakes her head, pulling a twist of her hair. I don't . . . think so.

New York's dead to you now.

The entire city? Please, Mother. Virginia is appalled to hear the plaintive whine in her own voice.

Tell me how you'll ever be able to look my friends in the eye again. You can't imagine what it's been like for me. It's all *I* can do to look my friends in the eye. You realize, of course, that you only have two choices.

You planned this, didn't you, Mother? Charlie following me out here.

Two choices, Virginia.

And what's the second choice, Mother?

You could stay in Wyoming, I suppose.

I can't stay in Wyoming.

Well then.

Well.

What was that? Virginia! Did you hear that?

An owl, Mother.

There it is again. That little scream.

An owl, Mother. That's why you came out here, isn't it? No other reason. You don't care about Auntie. You never have.

But you're my daughter and I love you.

Please, Virginia says. Please, Mother. You can be such a liar.

I have never liked this about you, child.

What's that?

This melodrama. These tiny little speeches on a stage. Her mother touches Virginia's leg, picking at the loose seam of her trousers. Where on earth did you find these clothes, child?

I have to go to bed, Mother.

Well. See if you can find me a spare blanket before you go. I could catch Pauline's death in here.

95

SHE PULLS A STRETCH of yarn from Rose's basket and lets it fall to her lap. It's such a hard thing to do: knit every row on the right side, purl every row on the wrong side. She would never have imagined that it could be so hard. Making a simple stockinette scarf. Dexterity plus attention still equals, more often than not, a loose cast. But maybe that's what she likes about it. She thinks if she ever becomes so adept at knitting that it no longer distracts her, then she will certainly quit. She knits, and does not think about Henry, who never cared for her, who did not love her, who was only — should she even think the word? — only *fucking* her. She realizes now that she could never have loved a man with such a bare chest. Can't imagine why she even tried.

Later, after her scarf is finished, she will see in it an accusation similar to that which she has come to see in her drawings: a knot-by-knot record of her preoccupations. For everyone to see.

Nettie sits beside her, a square lace pillow on her lap, its round bolster bristling with clusters of stickpins. Virginia has never seen lace made before, and she has been pausing often to watch Nettie braid the threads, bobbins clanking like muted chimes. The stumble of Virginia's needles provides striking counterpoint to the fluidity of Nettie's hands, their stained darkness in opposition to the delicate white artwork scrolling off her bolster.

Virginia's hands begin to tremble, and she puts down her yarn and needles. One of the hundred daily reminders of her pregnancy.

Feet stamp on the porch, and the door blows open, sending a brush of snow across the floor. The breeze rolls at the yarn piled in her lap.

I spoke to your mother, Charlie says, stamping his feet again.

Yes.

He walks across the room to sit on the armrest of the couch. He takes her hand, ignoring Nettie. He says Virginia's name. Then he says it again, tenderly: Virginia. He clears his throat, and while she's expecting him to propose again, he says only, I would like to stay here another few weeks or so. A few loose ends. After that we can go to Boston. You've heard about those twilight-sleep clinics? They give you a little ether and bingo, you wake up with a baby.

Bingo.

If you like, I can wire them to reserve a room. Next trip into town.

Whatever you like.

There is the same ritual formality between them as between her and her mother. Charlie seems to be waiting for something else from her, but she only picks up her knitting.

Good, he finally says. I'll do that. Is there anything else I can do for you.

Not unless you know how to knit.

Charlie laughs out of all proportion to the joke. I'll find you someone who knows how to knit, he says, stroking her shoulder. He stands and rests his palm on the crown of her head. Oh, Gin, he says, tracing the line of her part with his fingertip. But when there is no reaction from her, he takes his hand back, rubbing at his palm with his thumb. Good, he says. Then leaves by the kitchen door. From inside the kitchen, she hears the sound of the icebox opening.

Nettie has laid her bobbins on the pillow and set her hands flat on the couch. She leans her head back, closing her eyes.

It's beautiful, Virginia says.

Eyes still closed, Nettie shakes her head.

Oh, but it is. I don't know how you can make something so beautiful out of a bunch of old string.

Nettie shakes her head again, and at first Virginia thinks that she is denying the compliment. You don't know *anything,* Nettie says, opening her eyes. You don't know *shite.*

With her eyes fixed on Virginia, she grasps the top of the pillow, yanking her ribbon of lace off its bolster and spraying stickpins across the floor. Bobbins unspool, clanking together. She goes to the fireplace and, to Virginia's surprise, to her gape-mouthed astonishment, tosses her lace into the fire, bobbins and all.

96

THEY RIDE up the valley into the bulging white of his map. A desert of lack. He has always thought this valley, should it suddenly be found in Europe, hidden in the south of France, would be listed among the wonders of the world. Pilgrimages would be made to it. These phallic thrusts of stone. Blood-red ridgelines and rounded eruptions of boulders. But here the best they can do is name them all after cathedrals, steeples, gods. Holy City. *Bad words,* he thinks. *These rocks aren't holy.* Rather, they're a perversion. A twisting of the natural order.

Ahead of him, Adze coughs into his fist, hunched on his saddle like a flagellant. Blue, his dog, drops off the road to piss on a pine sapling, half burying himself in snow. When they reach the trailhead, Adze will ride back to the ranch with the horses, leaving Henry to snowshoe to his cabin alone. Adze has lately been so quiet, living around the corner of some nameless insult, some grief.

Henry thinks now how little that girl knew. He corrects himself: how little she *knows.* She'll be gone when he comes out of the mountains, and he has already started to think about her in the past tense. She once asked him how much they paid to have ice delivered way out here. And during a generator failure in the early weeks of her stay, she had asked them all (the dinner table in sudden darkness) how long it would take for the electrician to arrive.

Henry heels his horse up close to Adze, saying to his back, No way would it have worked out between me and that girl.

His voice breaks an hour's silence, and Blue stares at him.

What would be the best thing for that baby? Let me ask you that. Its real daddy and Fifth Avenue or bein a bastard and runnin traplines. Dodgin grizzly bears. And how about that mother of hers. Jesus H. Christ, can you imagine bein obligated to that woman for the rest of your life?

Adze says into his collar, I don't give a shit one way or the other. He shrugs deeper into his coat, holding the reins to his chest. He glances at the sky. When it decides to snow, it sure decides to snow, don't it?

97

SHE HAS DECIDED to believe in the final ends of things. She'll find virtue in facing forward. Spilled milk and all that.

The ranch burns its garbage once a week, storing it, in the meantime, in a wooden handcart outside the kitchen door. Adze pulls this handcart with difficulty, its wagon wheels punching crookedly through the crusts of snow. She follows a few paces behind. This is her first visit to the dump, and as they approach she sees that it's not really a dump but rather an empty stone foundation squared inside the burnt remains of a log building. The rotten fang of a stone chimney and a fifty-five-gallon drum scorched black, overflowing with charred apple cores and crimped canning lids, newspaper scraps and chicken innards, potato peelings and empty cans of condensed milk. When they arrive, magpies flush off the rim of the barrel.

Adze takes a can of coal oil from the cart and sets it aside, then bends to grab the spokes of one wheel, upsetting the cart around the base of the barrel. He pours oil over the stack, lights a match, and holds it to a dripping wad of paper. Flames spread slowly under a growing mound of foul black smoke.

Virginia steps toward the blaze, ripping a sheet from the sketchpad under her arm: a detailed study of tree bark, intricately shaded. She flashes the page at Adze. Pretty, she says, and tosses it onto the burning pile. One corner lightens, the tree bark curling, turning translucent before disappearing in bottlecaps of floating ash.

What are you doin, Miss?

I don't think I'll be needing these anymore, she says, ripping out another sheet. A study of a bobcat skull from under Henry's bed: blunt-nosed, sharp-toothed.

She wonders if maybe her mother was right. Maybe there's some part of her that likes being on a stage.

Lettin go, are you?

She rips out half the pages at once and steps forward to drop them flat into the flames, tilting her head away from the smoke. This is not a tragic gesture she's making. She is doing herself a favor. Her older self. What she will become. She's sure that she'll be a hard-tempered woman, cold-eyed with opinion. She will be her mother, and her most acute satisfactions will be found in the passing of judgment. Having made her sacrifices, she will expect everyone else to sacrifice as well. She does not want to be an old woman afflicted with these drawings.

She drops in the remainder of the pad, finally her pencils, watching the unpainted cedar sticks catch in a series of bright green flames.

Not a bad idea you got there, Miss. Adze draws a plain white envelope from inside his coat. Despite herself, despite how much she wants to be involved in her own moment, she finds herself staring. At the envelope, at his knotted, cigarette-stained hands. She thinks, *I should draw those.* But then she berates herself. *No, no, no.*

He tears open the envelope and shakes the contents into his open palm, catching and closing his fingers over a short piece of rope. What she at first thinks is rope. A knotted piece of twine, weathered and gray.

He rolls it between his palms then holds it to his nose. She was a real lady, he says. A real lady.

Not rope, Virginia realizes. Not rope but hair. Gray hair. A box lidded with doors not for her or her delicate sensibilities but for her aunt.

Adze? she says.

At first I thought she'd want me to have this, but now I ain't so sure.

It seems that this self-treasured faculty of Virginia's — her ability to observe — isn't worth a hill of beans. How could she have missed this? While her aunt had been sick, Adze had been, more often than not, the one to bring them an afternoon bowl of soup, a measure of Rose's cedar-berry fever cure — but Virginia had dismissed his attention as politeness. Courtesy. She remembers now how he had *watched* Pauline, studying how she held her fork, how she cut her steak. The way he had jumped to pull out a chair for her. Virginia had taken it for curiosity. But now he stands with the lock of hair trembling in his palm, under the split discolored nail of his curled thumb.

The heart hath its reasons, she thinks. Who was it said that? Aquinas. Or Pascal. Not Shakespeare. *Of which reason knoweth not*. Even a heart as old as Adze's. *A muscle that beats in fits and starts,* she thinks, experiencing the idea as a revelation. Fits and starts. Moments of profound surprise, days of endless resignation.

But then, what does she know?

Kindness, she thinks.

She touches his elbow, pressing his fingers with her own until they close over the lock of hair.

She says, You keep that hair.

98

THE MIRROR in the front foyer, between the gun rack and the mounted antelope skull, is the only reflection on the ranch large enough to contain her girth: her profile this way, that way. Her chin with its extra little lap. She drops her chin, raises it. Her stomach is so big. Bigger than she thought it ever would be. And she's only in what? Her seventh month.

When she is sure no one is coming, she lifts her shirt over her belly and breasts, rolling the fabric under her arms. If the baby's head is pointed up, or mostly up, then that bulge there, that slight lopsidedness just above and to the right of her navel, must be what? Its shoulder? Elbow? That must be its back pushing out below her navel. That hard knuckle.

Little Molly. *She'll be so smart,* Virginia thinks. And every bit as kind as the old Molly. And the boys will just love her. She'll be a fat baby — Virginia herself was a bit chubby — but the chubbiness will be cute, and will fall away later in life. Staring at herself now, she wonders if she has lost weight. The doctor had said that gaining a little weight was good. But now she wonders if she has gained anything at all. Her belly protrudes dramatically from her, like something attached — she hasn't been able to see her feet for weeks — and her hands are so bony, her eyes so dark, so large in the sallow face. From the neck up, from the breasts up, she has achieved a comeliness she never would have thought possible in herself. She sees a kind of removed grace in the mirror. A detachment.

Little Molly. She's sure it's a girl. A boy would be too odd. She knows nothing about boys. Less now than ever. It must be a girl. She will have someone to grow old around. To bind the pages of her life to. Her nights will be desolate, but her days . . . her days will be spent with her child. *Her* child. The idea of it thrills her. She hopes it will be a girl. She would love to buy it clothes. To shop uptown for miniature versions of her own dresses. A girl who will have no choice but to wear what she buys. Virginia will have something, for a while, that is entirely her own. This future of hopes and fears and ambitions and failures distilled into a rolling, kicking fetus. This little *person* who will always trace itself back to her. Someone to grow beyond her. To complete her. A child who will like math, for instance. Who will have a good second serve.

She has, once or twice, attempted to broach certain practical details with Charlie. Where will we live? she has asked, dreading the thought of his squalid college apartment. Where will you work? We need to buy clothes. A cradle. But he has been so strangely reticent. Visibly squirming at the questions. And she hasn't pressed him, deciding that they will, inevitably, get to there from here.

99

ALL THESE YEARS of trapping and he still doesn't understand the first thing about it. Not really. Not about what's important. This clockwork of claws and popping teeth. He has preyed upon it like some enormous parasite, but he doesn't understand it.

His ancestors *thanked* the animal. They had their rituals to appease the spirits. Which only makes sense. Bobcats. Coyotes. As soon as you think you know what makes them tick, you get knocked back on your ass. They're so goddamned smart, you end up thinking that they *are* giving themselves to you. No other explanation for it. Sacrificing themselves for some larger order about which you are unaware.

He works wearing his buffalo coat, the collar buttoned to his ears, a knitted cap deflated on his head. A coat that weighs damn near as much as his pack, but it's worth it. A guy could sleep in it if he had to.

He thinks about her at awkward times. Her expression just before he kisses her — the eyes closed as if against a spray of water — and her slight, inadvertent smile. An expression she wears at no other time. He would like to think that this is the natural set of her face, the moment without control. The way the fingers of a resting hand will curl slightly, the way a horse will stand asleep with a hoof cocked at a certain, precise angle.

He lays a number 4 Newhouse wolf and coyote trap on the ground and steps on the springs, holding it steady with leather gloves. Crow word for wolf is *chéeta,* which he has always loved. Word for coyote is . . . something. He sets the pan into its catch and reaches under the jaws with his thumb, tapping at it until there is less than an eighth of an inch of metal holding the jaws. *Esakuateh.* That's the word. Old man coyote. He eases the open trap down into a hole spaded between the elbow roots of a Douglas fir, snaking the twisted, two-pronged drag out into a narrow trench beside the hole then covering both drag and chain with dirt. He places a square of homemade wax paper over the trap's jaws: half a sheet of newsprint run through a cakepan of wax heated on his mother's stove. The old-timers, he's heard, liked to use wool. They would set a ball of wool under the pan. He takes up his siftbox and shakes it slowly, layering fine dust over the paper and trap until they are covered, flush with the surrounding earth. He tosses leaves and pieces of leaves over the trap like cards, finally stepping back to consider his work. She had really been getting the hang of poker.

This square foot of soil is a square foot no longer, but only one part of the entire impotent hillside. If she were here, she'd probably say something about it. How could she ever set her foot down on the mountain again, she would say, without thinking about this whole mountainside of unremarkable soil. He takes one of his small medicine bottles and shakes a urine scent around the base of the tree, stoppering the bottle and dropping it back into the box at his feet. With any luck, the urine will still be good even after all these years. Taken from the eviscerated bladders of trapped coyotes, it might work for wolves too. But he's never been sure. He reviews the steps to building a good set and knows that he has done them all, but he also knows that he hasn't done everything. He gives this particular trap about an even chance.

He removes his gloves without touching them with his bare skin and drops them into the box. Far above him, a gust of wind blows curling ribbons of snow off the corniced edge of Cathedral Peak. Down here in the ravine there is no wind to speak of.

This is his twelfth set. He intends to run fifty traps on a circuit that will cover thirty-five or forty miles. More traps than anyone he knows. He'd planned on running thirty, at the most forty, bringing along the extra traps for spares. But once in the woods, alone with his work, regret bouncing around inside his skull, he finds no reason not to throw himself into the labor. What does he have to lose? Nothing. And what does he have to gain? Bobcat pelts are going for damn near forty bucks each.

He wants to take this country filled with blood and money and wring it dry. Red cliffs like knife slashes in a white dress. High mountain cirques of marble. Trees of frosted cake. The horizon-to-horizon sheet of crumpled paper.

There is little regulation of trapping. Little oversight. Predators are competition, and there is no reason not to take as many animals as possible. The only requirement is a certain courtesy to other trappers. No overlapping of lines. No stepping on toes. But this trapline is so high that competition won't be a problem. He will work for weeks without using his voice. He will carry his backpack filled with dried meat, cooked beans, and canned fruit, and over the course of a four- or five-day circuit will replace the food with skinned pelts, frozen raw until he's able to work on them in his cabin. He will use his .22-caliber pistol to shoot no fewer than forty-two martens, twelve bobcats, three coyotes. A wolf caught in a coyote set will drag its trap nearly twenty miles before the chain catches in a deadfall. He will shoot the animal from a distance of five feet, both of them wet and exhausted. He will walk his line, inspecting each trap with his binoculars. And if a set is undisturbed after three or four circuits, he will pull it and use the trap elsewhere. He will take off his snowshoes only to sleep, most nights wrapped in his sleeping bag and tarp under the umbrella limbs of a fir tree, burrowed in mounds of dry needles. Once every couple of weeks he will unfreeze the rolled pelts, scrape the flesh from them, turn the ears, stretch them out to dry.

At the end of this most productive period, before the stillness and the whiteness and the loneliness begin, in turn, to wring their allotted measures of blood from him, he will trap a lynx in a deadfall set less than a mile from his cabin. A cat that might go fifty-five, sixty pounds. The largest he's ever seen. He finds it crouched at the farthest length of the chain, paw tucked under its chest.

He squats and steadies himself against the deadfall, digging into his jacket for the pistol. He flips open the gate to check his loads. A week of trapping and he has only three bullets left. Three's plenty.

Their eyes meet and neither looks away. As his breathing settles, he hears a low growl deep within the animal, like the starting and stopping of a propeller.

He stands and, in one abrupt movement — a reaching out of his hand, the motion of blessing — he shoots the cat in the head. It scrabbles away, staring up at him, astonished. Blinking deeply a yellow eye now a shade darker. Blood runs from its open mouth. The next shot, overhurried, cuts a slice into the flesh between its front legs. Shit, shit. One of the finest pelts he's seen and he's set to shoot it all to pieces. The cat hunches into itself, blood burning darkly through the snow. He steps closer. A brooding visitation on this life. Has the cat imagined him? Having lived its life through the squeal of dying rabbits and the crunch of bones, the squabbling of magpies, has it ever envisioned its own death? All these years arrowed toward this final instant, and is his the face that the cat has been trying to see? The shape of this pistol in his hand? From less than three feet away, he squeezes the trigger again, flinching as the hammer falls on a dry round. A loud click in the stillness and the heavy panting of the cat at his feet.

Christ, what a mess. Trembling, he reaches into the deadfall and breaks off a dry limb. All because of him. Because of *him.* He steps toward the cat and, without thought or consideration, beats down with the heavy end of the limb. The cat's head rolls away from the blow, twisting hard over the frozen ground. A marble under a boot. It stares up at him, dirt smeared across one open eye. No longer astonished so much as deeply puzzled.

Gasping, he steps forward again, beating down.

"After Henry left the ranch, all the bustle went out of Rose. You could see it happening. The wind out of a sail. At the same time, Frank Mohr found new energy. He smiled more often, and called me Missus. He held doors open for me.

"The only thing I disliked more than that man was my own response to his attentions. It's been a failing of mine. I've never been able to not *return a smile."*

100

THE WAPITI SCHOOL PARKING LOT is full when they arrive, although it's early. They park on the shoulder of the road and walk across a sludge of mud and manure, the two women holding their skirts high. The weather lately has been coming in pulses: islands of cold air displaced by tidal rolls of warmth. Since yesterday morning, these chinook winds have made a swamp of the entire valley.

Frank Mohr opens the door for them, his hand flat over a Christmas wreath, the cowbell on the doorknob sounding with a dull clang.

Back in twenty, maybe thirty minutes, Mohr says, then shuts the door behind him. Arm in arm they go over to the edge of the dance floor, staring at the laughter, the fiddle music. Shuffling and fidgeting until they've worked their way around to the pie table. Baked crusts shiny with butter and lard, split by swells of huckleberries and raspberries and apples. A dozen or so cakes towering over plates of cookies and brownies, square cuts of fruited gelatin. All wrapped in muslin and tagged with white squares of paper. They stand together, Virginia and Charlie, her hand in his arm. Virginia's mother's hands are crossed over a brass-beaded Dorothy bag, tasseled with silver chains.

They watch the floor fill with dancers, each couple stepping forward and back to a slow fiddle waltz: middle-aged men in gaudy print shirts and white cowboy hats, women in print dresses and hats topped with shiny clumps of wax fruit. Hand in hand, heads tilted back, open-mouthed, wide-toothed, heels shuffle and scrape over the dented pinewood floor.

It occurs to her that she'd never had the opportunity to dance with Henry. A dancing fool, Adze had called him. But she doesn't even know what kind of music he had liked.

Likes, she thinks, correcting herself.

At the far end of the room, a fiddler stands stiff and pale before a blackboard. To one side, just beyond his palsied, pumping elbow, an American flag wrapped in gold tassel. It's the same fiddle player she had seen at Clara's. No doubt about it. Not only the same man but the same posture, the same clothes. The only difference is that his trousers (mud-caked past the knees) now are tucked into his boots, revealing a pair of crooked aces punched into the leather. The music from his fiddle could tap the toe of a corpse, yet the old man stares only at the ground, oblivious to his own rhythms. Beside him, Nettie sits struggling with a heavy piano accordion, leaning back in her chair until she can hoist the bellows clear of her lap. Virginia hadn't known that she could play the accordion. Didn't know there was one in the valley. She watches Nettie squeeze out a quick phrase then rest the instrument on her lap, fingers moving over nickel-plated headboards. She wipes at her forehead and blows an exaggerated burst of air out of her cheeks. Their eyes meet, these two girls', and they both look quickly away. A moment later, Nettie pumps the accordion with particular force.

Virginia holds tight to Charlie's arm. Under the swinging beam of Nettie's gaze, she feels an itch of internal discomfort. Despite her earlier, unspoken hopes, she's not so sure that she could have lived out here. Just look at these people. Not to mention how much she misses Times Square. The electric baseball board and traffic cops. How she misses her tea dances. Her stuffed animals and riding trophies, a bathroom wall hand-painted in the designs of her childhood: purple teddy bears and carousel horses.

Across from her, an old woman with cropped gray hair and liver spots, a granddaughter at her hip pocket, is telling a neighbor that this little girl here is just getting over the bloody flux. With all this new snow, she says, I'm having to do some feedin. And then I'm runnin in the house every ten minutes to make sure she ain't expired on me.

Expired, Virginia thinks, amused.

Nettie and the fiddler start in on the first bars of a schottische called "Flop-eared Mule." The dancers take up some semblance of a pattern, a circle, but then let it fall apart. The air in the room warms, amplifying the smells of hay and manure and unwashed bodies. Virginia asks for a handkerchief from Charlie and holds the scented fabric to her nose. Above the handkerchief, she sees Clara shoving her way through the dancers, ignoring the annoyed expressions she leaves in her wake. The same overalls. The same rounded cheeks and nose, the same horsehair braid down her back.

I thought I was the only one who put on winter weight, Clara says, hugging Virginia with one big arm. She pulls back, and Virginia sees her registering the lipstick, the dab of rouge on her cheeks. The maternity dress and choker string of her aunt's pearls.

Good to see you, Clara.

Pressin down pretty hard on them shoes, I see. Pregnancy suits you, girl.

It's good to see you.

This is the feller that put you in this spot, I reckon.

Nonplused, Charlie looks away. Studies the pie table.

Virginia pinches the inside of his elbow. Charlie, this is Clara. Whom I told you about. Clara, this is my . . . my husband, Charles Stroud.

Husband, is it? She offers him her hand.

Soon, he says, studying the hand before he shakes it. Soon.

Clara turns to Virginia. I'm still waitin for you to come see me, she says.

Oh, well. That's sweet. But I'm afraid we're leaving in just a few weeks.

When?

I don't know. Charlie? A few weeks?

He shrugs and pulls Virginia's hand away from his elbow.

Clara steps around until she has presented her back to Charlie. She crosses her arms and glances sideways at Virginia, lines of distaste wrinkling around her mouth. Henry's up trappin, I suppose?

Virginia nods.

He's going to make somethin of himself, that boy. You watch.

Is he.

Is that Ah Ting over there?

It must be. Yes.

Watch and see whose pies go for the big money. I got a go see if I can hire him away from that greasy spoon in town. Excuse me, Virginia.

Charlie reaches for her hand and places it back inside his elbow. Crude woman, he says.

She did go to Harvard.

No she didn't. Did she? No.

Virginia nods, knowing nothing of the sort but still liking the idea of penetrating Charlie's arrogance. And then a thought strikes her. Is this how the rest of her life will be spent? In the push and pull of petty revenges against the father of her child? Her children?

I hear you're leavin us, young missy.

Dewey stands at her shoulder, leaning close with the momentum of booze.

Dewey! Yes, yes. I'm afraid so. In a few weeks.

Well, I'll give you this now, I guess. Give you somethin to do on the train. He pulls a small package from his vest pocket, clumsily wrapped in brown paper and twine.

Dewey, she says. Really. You didn't have to. Should I open it here?

You want to, he says, embarrassed. Just a deck a cards. He grins and leans into her. Since you're leavin us and all . . . Aces have one star in the left corner. Face cards and tens have two. Everythin else has three.

Dewey!

Tell Adze and I'll never forgive you.

No.

Don't say I never did nothin for you.

I'd *never* say that. She puts her hand on his shoulder and kisses him on the cheek. Whispers to him, If only you were a few years younger . . .

She pulls back, thrilled to see him blush.

I should get on, he says, turning abruptly.

The music pauses and stills and the fiddler lays his instrument down on his chair, giving the strings a last wooden strum. The crowd thins toward the punch table, and there is a general, disordered milling out the back door to the outhouses. Nettie has disappeared. A young couple, wedding rings flashing new on their hands, dance alone on the floor, swaying to a private rhythm.

In this pause, Rose, a pair of pies in her hands, steps through the front door wearing a blue cotton print dress with a Pendleton blanket for a shawl and a beaded leather belt pinching into the rolls at her waist. Behind her, Mohr carries an applestack cake under his arm. He has found a black frock coat somewhere, which he wears over his habitual leather vest. A red string tie is knotted in a loose tangle at his throat. Rose sets her pies on the table and takes the cake from her husband, setting it beside the pies. She fills out her tags and stands against the wall a few steps away from Virginia, staring wide-eyed at the floor, deaf to conversation, laughter.

The old woman who had been complaining about her granddaughter's flux glances sharply at Rose, up and down — this rounded eruption of blue cloth and brown skin against the white wall — and takes her companion's arm. They hear her first, fiercely whispered sentence: . . . Indian woman I was tellin you about.

Rose doesn't move, doesn't react. She shifts her feet, picks at her sleeve.

Mohr winks at Charlie, patting at the pocket of his vest where he keeps his flask. They leave together through the side room. Virginia is left standing between her mother and Rose. Her back is starting to hurt, and her feet are throbbing in the arches.

Those two are just thick as thieves, her mother says.

Rose? Virginia says, turning away. Are you going to be bidding on any of these pies tonight?

Rose shakes her head. Leave that to Frank, she says.

Thick as thieves, her mother says.

Yes, yes, Virginia says. It seems so.

I don't understand men at all.

Rose? Virginia asks. Are any of these good-looking cowboys going to be asking you to dance tonight?

Henry was here, he'd ask me to dance.

Henry?

He'd ask me to dance. And Rose looks up at her.

Virginia's never been able to read Rose's expressions. Is this reproach? Not self-pity, certainly; not from Rose. It must be reproach. But nothing that's happened is her fault. It's *not.* It's not her fault that he's off in the mountains. It wasn't even her decision to be here in the first place, in Wyoming.

Rose glances away from her, then walks over to the punch bowl, where she stands in just the same posture: hands crossed, head lowered.

I've never understood men, her mother says.

Virginia takes her mother's arm, suddenly inclined to be generous. Then we have at least one thing in common, she says.

Her mother pulls away. He's buying you a car for Christmas.

Who? Charlie?

We're buying you a car, I should say.

She can see her mother's peevishness. In an attempt to placate her, Virginia says, He couldn't afford it himself?

Said he was putting his money somewhere else. Some sort of investment.

I don't know how to drive.

I guess you'll learn, won't you. And act surprised.

That won't be hard.

Isn't there a punch bowl here somewhere? Isn't there someone who might find a lady a drink?

I'll get it.

I'll get it.

The night passes. Her lower back throbs, her feet pound. Adze and Dewey find a soft chair for her and carry it across the dance floor to her, the stuffing leaking from its arms. She goes to the bathroom three times and tells herself that she has to stop drinking so much punch. The bake sale begins two hours later, the auctioneer having given the men ample time to get drunk. He tells them that this money's going straight up to Lodge Grass, helpin to put shoes on feet and hams in ovens. He tells them that he's not makin a dime off this, not leavin here with any money in his pocket, and he sees no reason why anybody else should either. He starts the bidding on the first pie at two dollars.

As the night finishes, Rose dozes sitting on the floor, chin on her chest. Virginia folds her coat over her arm and makes her way to the back of the room, where Nettie sits alone with her accordion, experimentally pressing the studs to produce low-toned half wheezes. Humming to herself. Tapping to an unheard rhythm.

Nettie, she says. I just wanted to tell you how beautifully you played.

Nettie stares at her fingers. Squeezes out a discordant note.

And to say I'm sorry.

Nothin to be sorry about. Nettie closes the bellows and moves to flip shut the latch, then thinks better of it.

I've disappointed you.

Got that right.

Well. I'm sorry.

I just wish . . . Nettie turns away, the flesh of her chin wrinkling.

Yes?

She shakes her head, then shrugs. Nothing, she says. Not a thing. She bends back to her accordion and inflates the bellows, closes her eyes. Squeezes out the first few bars of her little song. But on this instrument, the sad, repetitive notes take on a higher, plaintive tone. Every phrase ends in a question.

101

NOT LONG BEFORE he springs his traps, leaving them to rust half buried around the eastern rim of Yellowstone, he starts singing to himself. He thinks that the absence he's been feeling must be noise. For the past six weeks, he has been hearing only the hiss of snow building into drifts, the squeak of swaying branches, the croak of flying ravens.

How many days, he mutters, squatting in his cabin, slicing fascia from a marten hide. *How many days. How many days till I see Santa Fe again.*

And later, measuring a cup of beans into boiling water, he sings, louder, *We came to save the froggies, came to save the Brits. Aim to shame the kaiser, mean to kill a fritz.*

Snowshoeing, he shouts, *Don't bury me under the mulberry tree, where once I kissed your lips. Throw my bones on the river stones, where you let me grab your tits.*

As his nose bleeds, he moves his head in circles, in squares, drawing patterns in the snow with the dripping blood.

He has been struggling through a conflation of space, two dimensions of black and white. And music. A tune that begins and ends with the turning of his head into the wind. He tries to find words for it. A melody. But hears only that endless song of Nettie's.

He spends most of a day trying to find a deer to shoot for food, but instead spots a coyote running through the pines, spooked by the vague imaginings, real and unreal, that always seem to spook coyotes. Once it's out of the shallow snow under the trees and running hard in the open, porpoising in an ocean roll of drifts, he levers a shell into the chamber and takes a rest off his knee, following the animal with his sight. A gray snake in the snow a hundred yards away. It stops and stares at him, only its head visible, its ears alert. Then it starts running again, angling back into the trees. He lowers his rifle and watches it go.

Never in his entire life has he passed up a coyote.

102

SHE WAKES with false contractions. The baby shifting, pushing down. A sharp lightsocket of pain running groin to stomach. She rocks back and forth on the bed until she gains enough momentum to switch sides, moving like a boulder pried from its seating. She tries to sleep but sleep is gone, so she dresses and makes her way across the yard to the kitchen, to her mother's bedroom. Inside, she stumbles against the slight slope of the floor and catches herself on the wall. With her next step she bangs her shin against the trunk at the foot of the bed.

In the darkness, she hears her mother gasp and sit up. What? she whispers hoarsely. Who is it?

Me, Mother.

Virginia?

I couldn't sleep.

What time is it?

I don't know. I couldn't sleep.

The blankets rustle, and she hears her mother's head drop back to her pillow. Go to bed, Virginia.

Mother? She sits on the edge of the bed, touching the hip mounded under the blankets.

Her mother sighs, fumbling on the nightstand for a match. It's cold in here, she says. The match flares, touching the wick of the lamp. After adjusting the flame, her mother tilts up the face of her brass-belled alarm clock. Three o'clock? Good Lord, child.

I don't want you to leave me here, Mother.

What?

I'm scared.

Her mother touches an eyelid, wiping away the sleep. Of course you are, she says, studying her fingertip.

I've been having pains. Virginia is whispering now.

Her mother looks at her sharply. What kind of pains? Like monthlies?

Like monthlies, only worse.

You haven't been bleeding, have you?

Virginia shakes her head, pinching a strand of hair and bringing it around to her mouth.

You'll be all right. Her mother's voice is soft, and she hugs the girl. I'm sure you'll be fine.

The relief of this touch. This enfolding. She returns the hug with strength. But the arm stiffens around her, and her mother pulls away to rub at the skin under Virginia's eyes, wiping at tears that aren't there. I miss your father, she says.

I miss him too.

He would know just what to say to you.

He would, Virginia agrees, her voice soft. He'd say that this isn't my fault.

A long moment of stillness between them. The alarm clock ticks. Her mother breathes heavily through her nostrils, then lies back, curling her legs under the quilts. Stretching until her toes rest under Virginia's thigh. Charlie told you, I suppose. I'll be meeting you in Boston. In a month or so. Six weeks.

He didn't say you would be there.

I'm your mother, aren't I?

Virginia places her hand on her mother's calf. I don't want to get married, she whispers.

We all do things we don't want to do. Her mother raises up and twists down the lamp wick. You should make your peace with that right now.

I miss Henry, Mother.

That Indian? That cowboy?

Yes.

Why would you miss someone like that?

We were . . . friends.

Maybe you can invite him east sometime.

I don't think so. I don't think he would come.

Well, you never know. You never know what anyone is likely to do.

103

VIRGINIA'S CAR arrives four days after her mother leaves the ranch, in mid-January. This is a time when most automobiles are a safe, nondescript black or beige, but Charlie has given her a car painted bright red. Santa Claus red, he calls it. A Chandler Roadster, square in all its corners, the bulbous headlights set above rolling front fenders and spoked wooden wheels; curtains on the windows and an oak steering wheel and black leather seat cushions pleated and gathered with brass buttons. It arrives in the final days of this last, lingering thaw, having been shipped west on the train from New York at what must have been exorbitant cost.

She is hesitant to drive it at first, and so it sits on one side of Mohr's car shed (the man's generosity toward Charlie apparently not extending to displacing his Pierce-Arrow). From a distance, looking at the car, she is reminded of blood blotted on white paper. It is understandable, she supposes, in these latter days of her pregnancy, to have blood on her mind.

By the end of the month, under the pale blue of a coming storm, she abruptly decides that she must learn to drive. Now or never. And so she stands at the front grille, watching Charlie pump the gas pedal, press hard on the self-starter. The cold battery turns the starter sluggishly, grinding before it catches. Charlie revs the engine. He steps out, rubbing warmth into his hands. His arm goes wide around her waist and he gives her a peck on the cheek.

Did you pick this out yourself, Charlie?

Who else?

My mother?

Charlie purses his lips. She didn't have anything to do with it.

Later, as they're settling into the seat, he adds, Maybe this will keep you from missing that cowboy bastard of yours.

At least that cowboy was gentleman enough not to curse in front of a lady.

Don't play games, Virginia. Gentleman!

She drives with Charlie's hand over hers, pressing her palm into the gearshift knob, squeezing her through the progression of gears. He tells her how to work the clutch, how to ease it out. The roads are dry, frozen, and she comes close to getting the hang of it in a single one-hour session. She had not expected to enjoy it quite so much, and wakes the next morning eager to try again, despite four or five inches of new snow on the ground.

She drives in an overcoat, two sweaters, a pair of Mohr's old riding gloves, and, in a moment of her old bombast, her mother's leather jodhpurs unbuttoned over her belly. After the first hour, Charlie steps out to follow her up and down the road, Adze joining him, the two men running at her bumper, ready to push her out when she spins. What should be a scene of absurd self-effacement, of slipping and rolling and snowball fights, has instead an air of condescension on the part of the two men, grim determination on the part of the girl. She thinks that this might be her only way out. That in the coming years, when she wishes to get away from Charlie for an afternoon, a week, she will drive herself.

It's later that same night, or perhaps the next, when she lets herself into the lodge, squatting and poking at the fire, laying sticks across the coals. The wood flares and catches, and she drops heavily onto the couch, legs spread by her belly, watching the faint glow of cloud-shifting moonlight pattern the floor. Over the course of an hour, the glow dims and darkens until the fire at her knee is the only light in the room. From the spatter of wind against the windows, she supposes it's snowing again.

The door opens and fresh wind moans through the eaves, stirring a chill at her ankles. Charlie stamps his feet on the rug. Virginia?

She says his name.

What are you doing up?

Couldn't sleep, she says.

May I sit with you?

She nods in the darkness, then says, Yes.

He takes off his boots and pads across the floor toward her. Quite a storm all of a sudden, he says.

She stares at the fire. The cushions bend, and his arm drops over her neck. She leans her cheek against his wrist, her face warmed by the fire. His lips are on her neck. On her cheek. She thinks of all this being somehow behind her, and kisses the knob of his thumb.

She is being turned in his hands. He is turning her onto her back and his hands are on her breasts. Her sore breasts. He unbuttons the chamois shirt she likes to wear over her dresses and, like a parent with a child, slips her arms from the sleeves. His hands are rolling around inside her dress, on her thighs, shoving the fabric up to her waist, above her waist. She lies on her back, staring at the log rafters of the ceiling. This man she's going to marry. She lies on her back and waits for him. She waits, then looks over the bulge of her stomach. Do you want me on my side? she asks.

He has sat back on his heels. I didn't think you'd look like this.

What did you expect?

I don't know. He wipes at his mouth, then buttons his pants. I don't know.

104

It's not that he's in love with her. It's only her *lack* that's driving him mad. The itch of a missing limb. He thinks of all the words that mean whore, dully surprised by their number. Prostitute, cocotte, harlot. Tart, trollop, tramp. Jezebel, bawd, strumpet. He could make a poem. A song. There's that much rhythm to them.

He's been imagining life without her. Seeing himself a lonely old man, draped in a blanket, hunched next to his stove. *The stove and I will grow old,* he thinks.

It's not that he loves her, it's just that he despairs of life without her. He is still looking. Still searching. Where is the one for him? The thousands birthed each day, and where is his? He wants his, goddamnit.

There remains a constant silence behind his back, just *there.* And there.

God he could sure use a drink.

He is tired. Exhausted.

It's not that he loves her, it's just that she could never have loved him. Never. Just look at him.

His last days in the mountains will go largely unremembered, although pieces will recur throughout his life: flashbulb detonations of memory. He will remember chasing coyotes off a deer carcass, then the bland, frozen marbles of its blood in his mouth. The way they melted and how his stomach fought against them. He will recall a young mountain lion, about the size of his trapped lynx, jumping up on one end of the log where he's sitting. The shine of its fur and the fat loose on its hips in mocking opposition to his own tattered thinness. The cat regards him with feline detachment, as if judging the amount of meat versus the amount of trouble, but when he waves his knife at it, it jumps away, trotting loose-pawed and lazy into the trees. Most of all, he'll remember crawling on his elbows through the tilted fumarole entrance to his cave, the cave of his childhood.

He has not visited the place for seven, eight years, and in that time the entrance has become a tight fit. His jacket catches, and for a horrible instant he's certain that he'll be unable to move at all, forward or back. In a hundred years they'll discover two skeletons in the cave. But then his pocket tears at the corner and he is loose, sliding elbows first onto the floor.

He stands slowly in the utter darkness, one hand cocked above his head. His fingers touch the shallow slope of the ceiling. In the sudden absence of even the slightest breeze, the cave feels warm, a sensation accentuated by the moist smell of dirt.

His eyes adjust to the darkness until, when he strikes his first match, it lights the entire cavern. Behind the shield of his hand, he carries the flame to an anchoritic row of candles glued by their wax to a stone shelf. Still here. Everything still here. Colored birthday wicks, thin and elegant dinner candles, and squat, square-bodied camp lights bought for a penny each at the Trading Company. A cheap string of black rosary beads and a desiccated apple core. He crumbles the core between his palms and shoves the dry pieces into his mouth, working at them until they're soft enough to chew.

When the candles are well lit, he turns to face the other side of the cave, his shadow stretching monstrously over the wall. The corpse lies undisturbed in the corner. A chief of some now nameless, voiceless people, curled like a macabre fetus inside its swaddling of brittle sheepskin. It lies half buried, one empty eye staring out level with the dirt, one hand tucked under the fleshless, jutting chin. In years past, Henry has sat here for hours, regarding the chief. Trying to recreate the man's life. What hopes? What fears? But he has never disturbed the body, vaguely dreading the thought of an ancient spirit turned restless. He is not a superstitious man — not outside the flickering light of this tiny cavern — but he nevertheless doesn't care for the idea of a ghost wandering around with his name on its lips.

He lowers himself to the ground, candles guttering in the slight breeze of his movement, and stares into the corpse's face. The way he used to stare when he was a child: eyes wide, startled. This was his place. No one else's. His.

After a long time of doing nothing, he begins to hum. Then to sing. Tunelessly, wordlessly. The frail lack of sound in the cavern shatters around him. He tells the corpse about Virginia. That rich white girl from New York. He talks about the money waiting for him under his bed at home. He says that one day he'll come back and buy this whole damn valley. He says that his father doesn't know shit. The way Pap is with his mother.

You don't know shit, he says, his voice bouncing back from the walls. That girl's nothin at all like a wolf in a trap.

And then he answers himself, his voice changing, modulating into some basso mimicry of his father. Teenage girls don't have money a their own.

You don't know shit, he says, his voice changing, his words bouncing off the walls. I could trust her. She'd be loyal.

His voice goes deep. She's like his wife, son.

Nothin like his wife, he says, his voice like fabric tearing.

You're crazy, son.

I ain't crazy.

You're ignorant.

I ain't ignorant.

You're a coward, son.

And here it is, finally. The crux of this matter. The worm inside.

So how does he answer, this boy, this man? Scarred to the wick by war and women. Crouched inside this volcanic bubble, this serrated, incidental crack in the heart of a mountain. He won't recall a reply. He'll only remember standing hours later in the middle of the cavern, hugging the corpse to his chest, dancing, shuffling in time to music creviced in his head. His laughter fills the chamber, echoing in tones various as a played instrument. He is dancing inside a crowd of laughter and the chief is dancing with him, odorless, held together only by stiff skin and pale, translucent tendon. The bones empty of muscle. The skull topped by a knot of wild black hair, the lips pulled back in a grin to mirror Henry's own. They are laughing and dancing together, these two. A gay revelry within the mountain. Then they stop suddenly, as if at the beat of a drum, and Henry is left staring into the empty eyes of the skull. Like lovers in a doorway, these two. Henry reaches down for a bony hand and raises it to his eye. With some effort, he separates the index finger from the fused bones of the hand and points it toward the ceiling. He follows the finger with his eyes but sees nothing. Darkness. An eyelid reflection of light. He takes the finger and puts it to his own mouth in a parody of consideration.

Nipples like doorknobs, he says, and laughs.

He is laughing and the corpse is laughing and they are dancing.

He could sure use a drink.

105

IF SHE WERE a bird flying, if by some grace she were given a larger perspective, she thinks that her little red car spinning, lurching over these inches of moist snow would resemble the fox in that painting of Winslow Homer's. And if she is indeed a part of that painting, then those magpies rising off the road must be the crows. Or maybe Frank Mohr is the crow. Hunched over the steering wheel, the unlit stub of a cigar mangled in his jaws. He flips it around in his mouth, front to back, then maneuvers it inside his lower lip like a dip of snuff.

The car stalls in the narrow drift between fences, and he grinds the gears, forward and reverse, punching them out onto the road. Sitting in the back, her legs stretched out along the seat, she wills Charlie to object, to say that this is their car and that he can drive on these roads as well as anybody. Instead, he sits looking blankly out his side window. The road has been recently driven on, and so long as Mohr keeps the tires in the previous tracks they travel at a good pace.

She sits with her hands buried in the leopardskin muff, its gaudy yellows and blacks incongruent with the austere grays and ribboned whites of her maternity dress.

Car has some punch, Mohr says to Charlie.

Charlie turns his head obliquely toward Virginia. Doing all right back there?

She nods. Fine.

After a moment, he says, I like your muff.

Thank you, she says. Henry bought it for me.

Charlie does not react, but Mohr jumps as if punched with a fork. He turns in the seat, driving with one hand. Henry bought that for you?

She nods.

Where'd he get the money for somethin fancy like that?

I don't know. Ranch work?

Not on this ranch.

You didn't pay him enough to buy something like this?

You didn't bring that thing with you?

She didn't bring it with her, Charlie says.

Virginia pulls her hands out of the muff and studies it, rolling it in her hands. What was he doing here if you didn't pay him?

Mohr rolls down his window to spit, wiping his chin with the heel of his hand. I was just askin myself the same thing.

They drive west up the valley, angling into a roof of clouds. Wet fingers of snow snap against the windshield. They drive past the Forest Reserve boundary and into a light scattering of timber. Mohr pulls off the road and sets the hand brake. There you go, he says.

Above them, to the south, a pair of chain-chopped tire tracks weave away from the road and up to a sagebrush flat. They leave the car and start climbing, following the tracks. Virginia steadies herself on Charlie's arm. As they walk, the figure of a man in a black duster ladders into sight above them, standing next to an idling Arrow flatbed, shrouded in exhaust. A bandy-legged man, thin as a rake, with a mat of hair the color and consistency of sheep's wool. His name is Griffin, although she'll never know if it's his first name or last.

Charlie's hand tightens on hers as they walk. A contained excitement.

Griffin glances at Mohr still climbing behind them, then says to Charlie, You don't want a be bringin a pregnant woman up here. In all this snow? What the hell's wrong with you?

She can handle herself, Charlie says, releasing Virginia's hand.

I can handle myself, she says.

You ain't walkin out a here when that car of yours breaks down, and that means somebody else'll have to handle you.

I *beg* your pardon.

He shakes his head and turns. He raises his arm, pointing up the hill. Permit goes clear up to them fir trees up there, he says. It ain't so wide but it's long. When I first thought about sellin it I went up into the trees and drove down a corner post. You'll find it come spring when the snow melts.

Charlie?

He steps toward her, taking her hands with the ceremonial, rehearsed air of a stage actor. A reserve permit, Virginia, he says. I bought it myself. No help from anyone. Not my father, not your mother, not anyone.

Mohr stands behind them, ears buried in the collar of his frock coat, hands bunched in the pockets: a straight mark of charcoal on a white page. A ceremony about which he's already been made aware. Griffin leans an elbow on the fender of the truck, staring at them, picking at a tooth with his fingernail.

Charlie turns to him. Do you have the deed?

Griffin reaches inside his coat, his eyes going over Virginia — her face, her stomach — and pulls out a square of paper, folded and folded again. He hands it to Charlie.

Charlie turns back to Virginia, the paper pinched between his thumb and forefinger. I bought it for you, he says, handing it to her.

She holds the folded square of paper. I don't understand.

A wedding gift.

A gift?

He takes her by the shoulders and draws her to him, her arm and the piece of paper caught between them. He kisses her cheek, whispering, Or maybe it's an apology.

He steps back and says loudly, with a poorly contained humor, Now you can tell everyone you were out visiting your ranch in Wyoming.

My ranch. She glances past his shoulder, past the truck and its haze of exhaust. A rolling, dry shoulder of ground, dotted here and there with snow-covered mounds of sagebrush. The green wall of forest behind. Unremarkable ground, empty of fence or creek or road. On the upper edge of the grassland, a single volcanic pillar thrusts from the ground like a raised finger.

What . . . how, how much is there?

Forty acres, the man says. Give or take. Enough for a lodge. It ain't wide but it's long.

What's that rock up there? she asks. Does it have a name?

Griffin cranes his head around, staring at the formation as if seeing it for the first time. That there's what you call No Name Rock, he says.

You can name it, Virginia, Charlie says. After we build our lodge.

Our lodge?

He is suddenly bright, manic: stepping toward Mohr, then back toward Virginia. We'll build our lodge on this flat here, he says, waving his palms over the ground. Put up a little store out front. Sell soda pop and candy and tomahawks to tourists coming through on their way to Yellowstone. Maybe some gasoline, too.

You want to run a store here? In Wyoming?

But he doesn't see her, hear her. He is waving, painting with the strokes of his arms how this ground will look. Mohr stands apart, hands in his pockets, studying them.

I'll spend the winters lining up clients for Frank in New York, Charlie says. Make a trip or two to Philadelphia. Boston. We'll take a commission and in the summers we'll come west and run this place. Help Frank with his guests. They'll need somebody that speaks their language.

You want to run a store, Charlie?

Virginia, he says, rushing up and hugging her, rubbing vigorously at her stomach.

You want us to spend our summers here?

I thought you liked it here.

I don't know if I do, Charlie. I don't know.

He steps away from her. Well, he says, suddenly sullen. Well well.

I just . . . Every summer, Charlie? I can't imagine.

What?

No, she says. I don't want it. I can't imagine anything worse. She tries to pass the deed back to him, but he shoves his hands deep in his pockets.

His lips roll like pale strips of dough, and for a moment she's sure he's going to cry. Then all she sees is anger. What are you going to do? he asks, stepping close. Are you going to go back to your cowboy? I don't see him. Where is he? Is he here?

Charlie . . .

You know, he whispers, stepping close, the frozen cloud of his breath pluming around her cheeks. You know, I told your mother about that night. That night. Told her that I fucked you biting and slapping.

Oh Charlie.

And you know? She didn't seem to mind.

Listen, Virginia says. This is fine. It's fine. Really. Whatever you want.

I don't think you mean it.

The anger is gone, and in its place she sees a childish pout, a downturn at the corners of his mouth. She takes his arm, feeling it hang dead. Do you have a pen? she asks.

I have to have it notarized in town.

Then let's go have it notarized in town.

Today?

Or tomorrow, she says, shaking his arm.

We could go in tonight, I guess. Do it tomorrow morning. He smiles at her, finally.

That would be just fine, Charlie. Just fine.

You don't even need to go if you don't want to.

Well, that's fine.

All right then. I'll go tonight.

And for the next ten minutes, Charlie pivots foot to foot, blowing into his hands, telling Griffin what he's going to do with this ground, the man listening coolly. Shaking his head once. Charlie lights a cigarette. Mohr walks to the edge of the flat and stares back toward his ranch. Later, as they make their way down the hill — Virginia's hand tight on Charlie's arm and Charlie walking, for her benefit, in the deeper snow between the tracks — she tells herself, reminds herself, that life is only what *happens* to you, after all. And it will happen to her. It will happen indeed. Who would have thought that she would ever, *ever* own her own ranch. *Gin Price in Wyoming,* she thinks. Tries to think. Who would have thought it possible. Has she ever owned anything before that was entirely hers? Dolls. A few schoolbooks, maybe. Nothing else.

106

THE WORLD has no features. A warped indentation of valley crimped with dark branches, gray trunks, as if seen through a fogged lens. A spot of red crawling west along the river, slow as a drip of blood. The grind of the motor reaches him, faint and broken across the expanse. The road is closed not much farther along, and so the car must perforce travel east again. He is proud of this particular bit of reasoning. A car. He stumbles down the slope, staggering, lurching, his buffalo coat skirted in heavy, swinging tinsels of ice, the thongs of his snowshoes unraveling, crosspieces split and broken. Earlier in the day, he had found a fistful of uncooked beans deep in the corner of one pocket and has since been sucking on them, moistening them until they can be chewed. But as he walks he loses patience and starts swallowing them one by one, tossing them back like pills. He is still more than a half mile above the road when he sees the car going east again, shortly followed by George Griffin's flatbed. He watches them go, panting. When they are gone, he turns to take a leak.

107

KING ME, Adze says.

Stinker, Virginia says.

Yessir, nothing like a row a kings. Just look at all that royalty lined up back there.

You *are* a stinker, Adze.

Now, just let me move one of these monsignors over here . . . and now you've got a jump me.

Where's Dewey these days? I haven't seen him around.

And now I got a jump you back. Stompin broncs down by the lake. Are you gettin cold, Miss?

A bit.

Adze nods and pushes himself to his feet, grimacing, rubbing his hip. He squats in front of the fire and tosses in another piece of split wood. This cold weather, he says, sitting back down, all this snow, it sure ain't easy on us old horse trainers.

That little fire can put out a lot of heat, though.

Those rocks gettin heated up does it much as anything.

We might as well start over, I guess.

You want a play again?

Sure.

What I like to hear, Adze says, rubbing his palms.

The house has been mostly quiet around them. The creak of rafters pushed by periodic gusts of wind. Fingernails of snow tapping against the window. But as they're setting up the pieces again, the quiet is broken by a heavy, muted thump from deep inside the house. Wood against wood.

What in the world? Virginia says.

Nothin, Adze says, straightening his back row of checkers with the edge of his hand. Wasn't nothin.

It was *too* something.

They hear it again. Another thump, not quite so loud, followed by the light tinkle of breaking glass. Coming from down the hall, from the bedrooms.

Virginia heaves herself to her feet. What in the world?

We got us a checker game here, Miss.

She stares at Adze. At his studied nonreaction. He turns a checker in his fingers.

There is a long pause of no sound at all, then glass breaks again.

That ain't none a our business back there. Now you're the red ones, so you go ahead and move there.

What's wrong with you?

A shadow passes over Adze's face. He raps once on the table. Nothin, he says.

I've just got to go and see what that is.

Adze pushes away from the table and grabs her wrists with his hands. That's none a your business back there. Virginia. Please.

Please yourself, she says. Jerking away. And even as she dismisses him, she realizes that he has never called her by her given name before.

She walks down the hall, hearing glass break again. Then another, more familiar sound. She knows this sound. How could she ever forget? The smack of flesh against flesh. The pop of knuckles on bone.

The hall is dark save for a wedge of light under the door to the back bedroom. Tentatively, she pushes at the door, slowly revealing bed linens twisted and piled to one side. The flattened rows of framed snapshots on the bureau. Glass shattered in one corner. And Frank Mohr standing at the foot of the bed, his back to her, a dented tin milk jug open in his hand. Rose lies quiet at his feet, curled, face buried in her arms. In different circumstances, their poses would recall certain Greek statues: a classical arrangement of conquest and defeat. As Virginia watches, Frank upturns the jug and splashes the last clear remnants of booze up and down Rose's body, shaking a few drops out over her head.

Might as well tell me, Frank says. Might as well. He tosses the jug at the wall and grabs up a fistful of fabric at the back of Rose's dress. You'd be surprised what I know, he says. Virginia hears the rip of fabric, the pop of stitching. How long, he says, shaking her. How long's . . . he been . . . stealin from me? With his other hand, he punches her in the ribs. Then again. Then he lets go of her.

Hey, Virginia says. Hey there. Let her alone there! Hey!

Frank turns. And they are staring at each other. Motionless. Rose lifts her face. Blood trailing from her nose, one corner of her mouth. But she is shaking her head, shaking her head.

Frank nudges Rose with his toe, then reaches into the small of his back, under his vest, to pull out a pistol. He weighs it flat in his hand. A little black thing, small enough to fit into a handbag. He hefts it up and down, then points it at her.

Drama, Virginia thinks. The same instinct that leads him to open wine bottles around campfires. But it *is* a pistol, and it is pointed at her. They remain paired like this for a long moment, the man motionless, the girl feeling a slow terror. Oddly, this isn't fear for herself. There is nothing Frank can take away from her that she wasn't already prepared to give to Charlie. No. This is fear for her child. Wholly unexpected. A sense of maternal protection that screams through her, stomach to skin. At this moment, she would do anything, commit any atrocity, to see her baby live.

Rose moans, Don't. Don't.

Frank looks away from Virginia to the woman piled at his feet. He bends at the knees and hits her on the shoulder with the pistol grip. Then he stands and in one abrupt motion tosses the gun aside, flinging it away in a gesture of disdain, of dismissal. Don't tell me don't, he says, his voice flat, conversational.

Virginia says Rose's name, then begins to cry. The first tears in months.

Get back to your cabin, Frank says in the same tone, staring down at Rose. Stay there.

I'm going . . . I'm not going back to my cabin. I'll tell you that right now.

She turns and, in her hurry, stumbles against the jamb. Recovers. Rushes down the hall, hands over her mouth. There is no sound behind her. No sound until Frank yells after her, Get back to your cabin!

In the dining room, in the flickering candlelit dark, Adze sits hunched at the table, a cigarette forgotten in his fingers.

A sob from Virginia. A shrill intake of air.

You goin back to your cabin? Miss?

She rubs her cheeks with her palm. Adze, she says. How could you? Just . . . sit there.

She won't let nobody help her, he says sadly, clearing his throat. Never has.

You could, Adze. You could.

And after that? Adze notices his cigarette and scrapes the long ash off into his ashtray. Where's she goin a go, Miss?

There's always a place to go. Virginia jerks her jacket off its hook by the door and slides her feet into boots.

At the table, Adze draws on his cigarette. Not always, he says. Not always.

She opens the door and steps out onto the porch. Snow drops in determined sheets, spinning and shifting in the light from the window. The wind shrieks, mirroring the scream she feels building inside her chest. She holds a hand against her cheeks, one and then the other. And steps off the porch.

Behind her, she hears the door open. Adze calls her name.

Only a few feet away from the buildings, the wind and snow push at her, toss at her. She turns and runs, the pendulum motion of her stomach knocking her into each stride. She runs toward the car shed, feeling the wind abate in its lee. At her side, her own little red car, mounded now with fresh snow. She touches the hood, resting. Coming to a decision.

She pries open the door and slides into the front seat, feeling the cold leather slowly mold to her legs. The starter button is familiar under her thumb, and she pumps the gas a few quick times. The engine sputters. Catches. She ducks her hands into her sleeves and steps back outside to sweep the snow from the windshield.

There's always someplace to go, she thinks. Who else does she know in the valley? Who does Rose know? That woman who had wanted Rose to midwife? With that awful sister. What was her name? She has to run somewhere. There has to be somewhere she can go. Maybe Cody. Can she make it to Cody? Anywhere away from here. Away for Rose. Away for herself and her baby. She can't forget. Can't ever forget. She is running for two.

She pulls away from the house, tires spinning and sizzling over the snow. Frantic now, seeing only Rose's bloody mouth, she fishtails past her empty cabin, past Adze silhouetted in the lodge's front door, up the steepest section of the driveway and over the cattleguard, turning out onto the main road.

108

HENRY, she thinks. *Henry.*

The steering wheel rubs against the bulge of her stomach. Her eyes, tight as balloons, throb in time to a faint hitch in the transmission. The tires rise and fall over slopes of drifted snow.

Oh, Rose.

What could she have done differently? Could she have made a choice that would have led to some other end? That would have saved her from driving blind through a Wyoming snowstorm? She thinks of her first drink of gin. Her first knock on Henry's door.

A pine sapling shapes itself from the maelstrom glow of her headlights, a bent cone of snow precisely where she had been seeing the curve of the road. And although she is not going fast, her jerk of the wheel slews the front tires to one side, sliding her gently into the tree. The car settles slowly, tilting as if in a pool of water, accompanied by the faint crunch of breaking branches, bending metal.

She sits for a minute collecting herself, rubbing the wheel creases from her fingers. *Oh, Rose.* The engine rumbles through the floorboards, then quits. The headlights fade to a lower register and it is quiet. It's so quiet. She presses the starter button, kicks at the gas pedal. The engine churns, flooding the car with the smell of gasoline. Cold air seeps in from around the windows.

Nothing for it, she supposes, but to take a walk.

She opens the door. The car is at a steeper pitch than she had thought, and she drops out heavily onto her hands and knees, jolting her stomach into a nonspecific ache. Her fear, which had shriveled away since leaving the ranch, flares up again. A wound reopened. She stands outside the dimming circle of headlights, rubbing her hands. The whole world spins, stands still. Snow falls around her with a faint, continuous hiss and she finds herself panting.

She takes a step away from the car, then two. She's dressed warmly enough, she thinks. Her dress is thick with pleats. Nevertheless, her legs are much colder than the rest of her body. Wind washes at the snow around her feet. She takes another step, feeling the texture of her skin, the insides of her thighs sticking to each other. The moisture. *Of course,* she thinks. *Of course.* One more thing. There have been times in her pregnancy when she wasn't sure that she could make it to the bathroom, but she never thought that it would happen so suddenly. And it's this smallest complication, this most incidental breach of her earliest inhibitions — peeing her pants — that wants to push her screaming through the snow.

She forces herself to stop, to breathe. To study the tire tracks still visible in the diffuse glow of the storm. She climbs back up onto the road, slipping and catching herself, walking carefully until she feels gravel under her feet. She just can't believe she wet herself.

If she follows the road toward Cody she'll find a driveway. An open fence. Then she'll knock on a door. And after she knocks on the door, she'll send the man out in the storm to fetch Rose. She'll accept a fresh pair of drawers from the lady. These are kind people. Country people. They'll understand. She starts walking, the moisture between her legs warming with the exertion.

She stops briefly, hands on her hips. Except for the wind, it's so quiet. Nearly peaceful.

She feels her first contraction.

109

HENRY FOLLOWS her away from the ranch, stepping his horse in the ribbon of her tire tracks. Tracks that swerve drunkenly side to side, occasionally bouncing off to either side of the road. He rides until he finds the car angled against the tree, half buried in snow, and sees the drifting line of footprints trailing away. He dismounts and leads the horse for a few steps. But the tracks are more visible from a height, and he climbs back into the saddle, kicking the horse into a trot. The horse fights against the reins, trying to turn back toward the ranch, and he punches it on the neck with his fist. Then again with the flat of his hand. Piece of *shit,* he says.

110

BECOMING LOST is a process of accretion, a build and roll from the first vague sense of unease to a contained panic to growing desperation. In a snowstorm, the light that exists — and there is light, glowing from the ground as much as from the sky — is worse than no light at all, throwing every potential landmark, every stunted tree, into sizes out of all proportion with reality. Worse, there is the constant sense of a space just behind the storm, a window of visibility no more than a step or two away. If you can only walk far enough, you tell yourself, you'll be able to find your bearings.

She doesn't know that she has left the road until the ground starts falling away, until she stands looking down at the frozen curves of the river. She turns in a circle. She could have sworn she had been walking in a straight line. Slower now, she turns back, head down, hands under her arms. The snow deepens, dragging at her feet. When the ground rises, suddenly so steep that she is forced to use her hands, she knows that she has missed the road again. She turns back, frustrated, nearly crying. Why try to walk anywhere. She works her way along the slope of the mountain, reasoning that if she sidehills then she'll at least be traveling in a constant direction.

Has she ever felt so . . . abandoned? Where is her mother now? Where is Charlie now? Where is her father? Where is . . . is Henry?

Contractions roll through her every ten or fifteen minutes. Low, rumbling aches that force her to bend over her knees, her breath whistling in thin, reedy gasps. Long minutes of dull plodding broken by increasingly sharp, quick bursts of pain.

She is so early. She's not due for what, another month? Six weeks.

That . . . that *Frank,* she says out loud. That damn Frank. Some part of her revels in this sudden lack of inhibition. The middle of a snowstorm, who's going to hear her? She screams the words: Damn Frank! Then, Damn *Charlie!*

She walks until the featureless white monotony of the storm breaks into a rim of stone, a thick, crumbling spine that she thinks she might recognize. The same rock, maybe, that she rode up all those months ago — years ago, it seems — with Henry and Adze. On their way to Clara's. Could she have walked so far? How has she come so far? How far had she driven before putting the car in the ditch?

Clara's, she thinks, befuddled. Would Clara be home?

She slogs forward, hunched, trailing postholes in the snow: hair clogged with the spindrift of her breath, lungs seared black.

She scoops snow into her mouth with a dead hand and touches the stone formation at her side, reassuring herself of its solidity. Fresh moisture seeps down her thighs. She screams with a contraction, whimpering as it fades. She wants nothing so much as to lie down. To spread her legs away from her belly, the pain in her pelvis.

She has resigned herself to an eternal balancing of pain and exhaustion, to the endless cycling of one foot in front of the other. The rocks pass behind her and she enters the timber, cresting the hillside, staggering as the ground drops away. She falls and, after a long moment in the snow, pulls herself up, hands bleeding. In front of her, just there, the horizontal eaves of a cabin. An unnatural collection of timber, stacked just so. A ramshackle corral in the trees. The wind whistles and cheers and she has never been so tired, so cold.

Lacking strength, she leans against the cabin door. The boards give way with a slow, rusty squeal and throw her hard to the dirt floor. She kneels there, gasping, tasting a dry mulch of dusty, rotted wood. Then she collapses onto her side, nails scrabbling at the packed dirt. Barely aware of the motion, she twists her head to one side and vomits. Nothing more than a small puddle of snowmelt. Such a delicious lack of wind, of snow needling her face, her eyes.

She is so tired. The side of a nail or the fallen corner of a board presses painfully into her back, but she doesn't care to roll away.

She has drifted off, has nearly fallen asleep, when the electric pain of a contraction jolts her into clarity. The worst one yet. Sending the skin of her neck into a rictus of tensed muscle and vein. When it passes, tears have lined her temples, streaming from the corners of her eyes. The odor of blood fills the cabin.

111

SHE LIES on the floor, eyes closed. So warm, so tired. Aware only of her warmth, her tiredness, the deep spasms of pain twisting at her spine.

Her arm moves. She feels someone moving her arm. Then there is a hand on her face, on her forehead. Fingers on the pulse of her neck.

She slides deeper into her luxurious sense of warmth. A chill in the dim background that warms her even by its opposition to the heat: the way a cold room in the morning can make the quilts so hard to leave.

She hears the dry split of branches breaking. Even the pain isn't so bad anymore. A dimly burning bulb in her stomach and thighs.

Firelight flares through her eyelids. She tries to open her eyes but the muscles in her face are stiff, unresponsive.

There are hands beneath her arms, under her shoulders, sliding her across the floor.

Firelight flares stronger now, baking against her side, against her arm. Hands are rubbing at her legs. Brisk strokes twisting at her skin, as if rolling out chaff.

She blinks open her eyes, against the dim light. A narrow, ragged form hunches at her feet, rubbing along her calves. She thinks that the cabin must not have been abandoned after all.

The form straightens, stretching, and swings its face briefly into the light.

She gasps and tries to sit up. Pain flares through her. There is suddenly no distinction between the pain in her stomach and a new ache in her chest, in her ribs.

Stay quiet, Henry says.

She is astonished by his thinness. By the flesh pulled tight across his cheeks and forehead. She thinks he must be a ghost. His eyes are so empty, so dark. But a ghost would not tremble like that. Would not move along her legs, ankle to knee, with such a needful rush. Would not stare at her as he is staring at her now.

She tries to form words with her wooden tongue. She moistens her lips and whispers, Dead?

He mistakes her meaning. You'll be fine, he says. You'll be fine. You will. You will.

You're bleeding, she whispers. With the greatest effort, she lifts her arm, touches his shirt. The dark splash on his chest.

Blood's not mine, he says. Only some of it. Virginia. Virginia.

Who?

Pap's. Rest is Pap's.

He has lifted her shoulders from the ground and is hugging her to him. Rocking her. She gasps with a contraction. Cries. Grabs at his shoulder.

You're going to be fine, he says. Just fine.

She's cold again, so much colder.

"You spend your life struggling to see the world through a lover's eyes. Only to fail, reduced to words. Words. Describe the color blue to a blind man. He was beyond me, as I was beyond him. The tiny papercut rejections, the salt-smeared regrets. Always my own. His own. No one else's."

112

THE HEAT from her open legs warms his hands, and the line of his breathing rises in staccato punctuation, blending with the steady current of steam from the open cavity in front of him: an aether of smoke birthed from this hairy and bloody mouth. Even now, even in the face of this child's fighting its way into the world, this eternal desire.

She screams, and the narrow muscles inside her thighs quiver. A trickle of blood gathers at the lowest protrusion of skin in her vagina, gathers and spills out to pool on the floor: a quivering, shining comma that soaks immediately into the dirt. Henry breathes, and in the space of that breath fluid pulses from her in a wash. She grabs at the floor, kicking blindly at the loose soup cans scattered along the wall.

The baby's head crests within her — a small, hairless gray crown pushing out like a fist. He watches the lips of her vagina stretch, sees the skin pale. The paleness cracks into radiating lines of red, and then the crown pauses in the opening, bending in, hourglassing away from the pelvic wall. Should he pull it? Should he rotate it? Her vagina tears at its base, just above the rectum, and a line of darker blood adds itself to the mix of fluid soaking into his knees. Then the head is through and the shoulders are trying to follow the head, each joint no larger than Henry's thumbs. He lays his hands on her legs and pushes them to the floor. The baby's skin gray and covered with what looks like a thin gruel of cheese, its eyes closed and the lashes surprisingly long. Then the shoulders are through, and the rest of it follows in a wet rush. Connected still by the birth cord: a rope leading back to the world's only security, consolation.

It's a girl, he says.

113

He cradles Virginia's head in his chest and arm, her wet hair tangled around his elbow. She holds the baby to her bare breast. Touches the bloody crown with her lips. Wrapped in Henry's shirt, motionless but for the faint jerking in its chest, it waves one fist, then lies quiet again. Virginia touches its cheek with the back of her finger, smoothing the residue of moisture away from the eyelids.

He pulls a strand of hair away from Virginia's face, pressing it with his palm. He tells her about the life they'll have together, the ranch they'll build. He creates corrals for them, then rodeos within the corrals. Parties on the porch. A garden. Flowers in pots. The porch will wrap around the house, he says, and they will sit outside and watch the sun rise and set.

She looks so pale to him, her mouth flaccid and empty. But red, as if she has bled through the lips. We'll go fishing, he says. We'll hunt around the world on the money we'll make on horses and sheep. He says that he doesn't want anything to do with cows, those lousy shit-smeared beasts. He tells her that they will build a life insulated from greed and jealousy. Theirs will be the farthest house from the farthest city.

Where will Molly go to school?

Who?

The baby.

What was that name?

Her name's Molly.

Henry pauses. Says, You can teach her, can't you?

Virginia nods, so tired. She says, I'm hungry.

Wait until the afterbirth.

What?

Wait a time, he says.

And within a few minutes, she stiffens again in his arms, crying with the force of new contractions. Crying long, until the placenta and cord lay expelled, shimmering in the dirt. He returns the child to her and opens a can of soup, setting it in the coals until it's warm. He cradles her head in his lap, feeding her noodles and pieces of chicken with his curled fingers. The metal cools, and he tilts the can to her mouth. She sips, her hand going over his. He winces at her touch, drawing her attention to the fresh wounds on his knuckles. The skin stripped back and the pieces hanging in small, accordioned flaps. She kisses his fingers, then, more softly, the raw wounds. In the firelight, his face is stone.

Rose, she says, and he nods.

She brings the baby to her breast, watching it attach itself to her, feeling its warm mouth against her cold skin. It sucks briefly and then sleeps. Just before she falls asleep herself, the child cradled against her side, skin to skin, she asks him what happened.

Nothin much, he says.

You fought him. Her voice blurs, stumbles over itself.

Needed doin. You want any more a this soup?

She shakes her head, seeing how he has turned away from her, how he has busied himself with the fire. And it's with a vague, unexplainable regret that she rests her head on the ground, on the arm of his coat.

114

A PERIOD OF GRACE. A few hours. A day in which the blocks of her life drop precisely into place. The baby nursing hard at her breasts, working for milk that is just now starting to flow well. Such a sweet child, content even with the ragged sore left by the umbilical cord, the bend in her skull.

In the gray light of early morning, Henry stacks firewood by her side. He tells her that he needs to leave for a few hours, to find something to eat. She has in mind a freshly killed deer, a rabbit to spit over the fire — her man foraging in the wild — but he returns in the afternoon with cheese sandwiches brought from a homesteader's cabin down the creek. Dinner rolls wrapped in a napkin. Vegetable soup in a crock sealed with candle wax.

While he's gone, she spends the morning alone with her child, her back propped against the wall. Studying the baby's nose, the eyes, the wrinkled ears bunched like closed buds. This is what's been inside her for almost eight months. Little Molly. She says it out loud: Molly. The eyes so fully dark, so wise. A triangle of downy black hair sampled over her crown.

Midmorning, Virginia walks outside to pee, swaying against the unaccustomed lack of a belly, then runs back inside, feeling an urgent need to hold the child again. She talks to it, makes noises with her lips. Plays with its hands, its cheeks, trying to elicit a reaction from the little face. It stares at her, or closes its eyes to work its mouth around an absent nipple. A nipple that she is happy to provide. It coughs against the milk, mews weakly. Its face seems flushed. With health or heat, she can't decide. But its little fists are so strong!

In the afternoon, stomachs filled, she and Henry lay on the floor, the baby asleep on her stomach. He says that when he was out looking for something to eat, he ran into Gus. Out ridin, Henry says. Guess they got a whole search party goin.

A search party?

They found your car. I told him we'd be down tomorrow. Maybe the next day.

Where's Rose?

Nettie's.

Thank God.

Henry shakes his head. Probably back at the home place by now.

Even now? Even still?

It ain't so easy to break the habit of a person. He nudges her shoulder. How you feeling?

Good.

And it's true. Except for a cough, for pale spots of numbed frostbite on her hands, Virginia feels fine. Healthy, considering. She lies in Henry's arms, listening to his heart. The whisper of his blood.

They lie together through the afternoon, spreading out the days year to year until they are old. For the first time, it seems possible that she might find contentment. That she might age gracefully.

She falls asleep that night with Molly on her chest, the rhythms of their hearts matched beat to beat. The baby's light breath (*hsst, hsst, hsst*) pulls her into an unexpected dream. A dream of her father. They are walking on a beach. He says something and reaches out his hand. The surf rolls against the shore (*hsst, hsst, hsst*) and she reaches out her hand. What does he say?

She wakes to the baby's faint mewling — such a small sound to startle her like this — and then the blind kick of its heel into her side. She brings the baby to her nipple, enjoying the feel of its little mouth, discomfited by the unexpected sexual tug. Her milk has started to flow well, and Molly feeds for a long time. Afterward, Virginia shifts the baby down onto her stomach, both of them already falling asleep again. Molly cries a little, and coughs the tiniest cough, and Virginia feels her taken away. She looks up to see Henry walking with her in the light of the fire, cradling her. Bouncing in the awkward, mistimed dance of men with babies. She smiles at them and drifts into sleep, waking again only when he puts Molly back onto her stomach. Waking only long enough to touch the crown of the head, to cup the palm of her hand around the tiny, tiny feet.

When she wakes again, it's nearly dawn. The baby's face is shadowless, smoothed between the faint, competing lights of hearthfire and morning. Henry has rolled away from her, and when she holds her breath there is no other sound in the room.

No other.

Outside, Henry's horse shifts, rubs against the corner of the cabin, shaking the logs, sending down dust motes from the ceiling.

Dust falls on the soft curve of her baby's cheek. Virginia brushes it off. The baby moves under her hand, but by no intention of its own. It moves all in a piece, the arms tilting up in a wooden and carved mirror of Virginia's stomach.

She shakes it. Then shakes it harder. The baby does not wake, does not cry. The head does not roll loose on its tiny shoulders.

Virginia opens her shirt and places the baby to her breast, cradling the back of its head with her hand. She rocks, smoothing the downy hair. Exuded milk, pushed from her breast, drips into the open mouth to trickle unswallowed across its cheek. She wraps the tiny cold fist around her finger and leaves it there, waiting for it to grab hold. All the paints in a box mixed together are no color at all. Every thought she has ever had, every rage and fear and jealousy and hope that has ever pounded through her, has been squeezed under the fingers of this little limp fist. This lack of intention. She holds the child to her leaking breast and she is nothing inside.

That all of this could have been made only to be thrown away. Is this what it was all for? All this, aligned toward a final nothing? Everything alive that will be dead. She holds her child in her arms, the fat legs loose over her arm, the wrinkled wrists and the fingernails, so tiny, lost in her hand. She feels how the heat has left its body. Her baby had been warm but now it is cold. The skin gray, resilient; the lips half open; the mouth slack in a drooping *oh* of surprise. It stares out at her from the bottoms of its lids, eternally curious. Molly is her name and she is not dead. No, no, no. Her name is Molly and she is not dead.

115

THERE ARE no happy endings, only because there are no endings.

They do not speak. Only the word careful as he helps her mount. She moves awkwardly, using one hand to straighten the stirrup, the other to clutch her child, its set face exposed to the light of the sun. He avoids her eyes as he leads them along the volcanic dike of the Stovepipe, stopping often to let her rest. He winces as she winces, flinches as she flinches. For all the hardship, all the heartbreak he's seen in his young life, he's unable to look directly into this baby's face.

He leads the horse down the middle of the road, the woman behind him hunched and hooded. A girl no longer. A good observer would find something eternal in their postures — their hesitant movements, their brief, brief touches. Arbiters for every soul. Every man and woman faced with the next childless day, and the next. Until the end of their lives.

They ride through a valley shuddering awake under a deep cover of snow. An engine starts somewhere, lost in the seamless roll of frozen land. They smell cedarsmoke and hear a faint metallic sound of hammering. It seems like the greatest crime to them both — although neither is aware that the thought is shared — that this day should begin so unchanged. That the lives in this valley should persist so unaffected, should care so little for a child's coming and going. Should register this day just like all others: sunrise, sunset, darkness. The eye of the world rolls under them, unblinking. Dry at their passing.

In the field above the ranch, Dewey stands balanced on a haystack, sweeping off the snow with the side of his boot, forking hay down into the bed of the waiting sleigh. Adze is below him, holding the horses steady. Outside the hay fence, cows mill in a loose ring, bawling in one long, broken note. The steam from the animals' bodies and breath rises in a pale white balloon, an amnion that contains within it both man and beast. Dewey sees the two riders on the road and pauses, leaning on his pitchfork to watch them pass.

Inside the yard, Henry ties his horse to the porch rail and reaches to help Virginia off the saddle, arms encircling the woman and the baby in the woman's arms. She lets herself be pulled away from the horse, heel trailing limply over the saddle. The house seems quiet, although shadows move behind windowglass. A curtain drops. Then the front door opens and Frank is on the porch, Charlie behind him.

Henry takes Virginia by the hand and leads her up the steps. Frank stands in front of the door, one side of his jaw swollen up like a stob of wood, both eyes puffy and just beginning to turn green, yellow. An ear inflated away from his head. The overall impression is one of a garden squash, bruised into lopsided disfigurement. He leans against the doorjamb, eyes darting between Henry and Virginia.

They wait, the two of them: Virginia studying the child in her arms, touching its cheek with the back of her finger. Then she steps past Henry toward the open door. Stopping when he puts his hand on her shoulder. With the gentlest of movement, he unwraps the baby from her arms, pulling its legs up and out of the crack of her arm. He takes it up to his own chest. She stares at him, and the fear in her face — her pale and wide eyes — has nothing to do with him, with her. She moves to take her child back and he shakes his head. He places his hand on her back. After a moment, she hugs her empty arms and steps past him, past Frank. Past Charlie.

After she is gone, Henry approaches his father, standing inches away, eye to eye. The child a hard little pod of cold flesh, of blanket-wrapped stovewood, in his arms.

I want you to take a look at this, Henry says.

What? Frank says, wincing and touching the corner of his mouth.

Look at this.

Frank glances at the dead child in Henry's arms. That's nothin to do with me, he says,

Damn you, it's everythin to do with you. Now look at it. Henry holds out the body of the child, pushing it at Frank, backing him up against the wall, forcing him to stare down into the hard, gray countenance of the child. This wrinkled fist of a face.

After a long moment, the time it takes to draw a deep breath, Henry nods and steps back, holding the child close to him.

There, he says, covering its face. There now. He looks around him, at the yard. Takes an interest in the smoke trailing from the kitchen's stovepipe. Then glances at the little man standing behind his father. Charlie, he says, nodding.

He looks past them both. Virginia, he says, stepping into the house.

"I have grown toward those last days, aged toward them, trying to imagine his story as well as mine. But it is, in the end, only mine. Only mine." She leaned her cheek against her fingers, easing back into her story. Sinking like a knee in a bath.

An evening wind blows over the cliffs of Jim Mountain. A small bat untangles its wings to take erratic flight through the pines. Above the bare cliffs, a bighorn sheep stretches out of its bed to browse, scratching at its belly with a hind leg. On the top edge of the mountain, on the final clattering ridge, a red-tailed hawk lifts its wings into a rising thermal and flies. Flies without the least effort.

Epilogue

Above the stones of last year's river, the
foundation of our lives
must be laid.

Your children will grow into my
face, hands battered
by barbed wire

And our wrinkled breasts will finally sag alike,
two hearts locked in the skin of
the same chest.

— Virginia Mohr, from her journal
August 26, 1925

SHE WOULDN'T have been able to imagine, crowded inside the shroud of their little cabin only a month before, playing hand after endless hand of poker, that this country could change so quickly. All but the deepest drifts melting under warm breezes, the moisture drawing out skirts of pale green grass and pink blooms of locoweed, white phlox, wild iris. In the riverbottoms, the cottonwoods are budding into tiny, translucent leaf. The top has been twisted off the valley and green poured in.

Once every few days Henry makes a trip into town, returning in the Model T truck they had bought after trading in Virginia's car, its bed stacked with wooden boxes of nails, hinges, milled lumber spread out from ropes, a new crosscut saw tied to the roof and resonating with warped gongs. All supplies paid for out of the dwindling stack of Henry's booze money. The last hill is too steep for the truck's forward gears. If he's carrying any load at all, he has to take the hill in reverse, backing up with his head twisted out the window. Virginia waits for him, first on bare ground, then on the platform of their foundation, then inside the beginnings of a doorway.

In his absence, she has been working in the small garden he had tilled for her with their mule and splintering plow. She approaches the work with an eagerness that surprises her. The distraction of it, she supposes. Early on, she had made the transition from patting small mounds over each seed of corn to dropping them from her hip and burying them with her toe. She thinks of each yellow seed as a minuscule life, a slowly (slowly!) beating heart. With any luck, beating strong enough to push up through the warming, fertile soil. She has planted tomato seeds, but thinks now that she should have tried starting them inside. But none of this bothers her. She likes the idea of making mistakes. Nettie has been up to see her twice, although it's a long trip for her, and they have sat gossiping, looking out over the valley and drinking hot tea boiled on the campfire grill. But Virginia has refrained from asking her about the garden. She wants everything to be her own. Even her mistakes.

She takes her morning constitutional before the sun rises in the valley, walking from their half-finished cabin to the finger of stone that she will always think of as No Name Rock, sitting at its base and watching the empty road below her, listening to the trill of nameless mountain birds, the toy-drum rattle of flickers pounding against trees. She watches deer feed into the timber.

It's a good house site, according to Henry, although high. With the mountains just behind, they are sheltered from the worst weather. They have cut their logs from the timber on the top edge of the property, dragging them down to be peeled in the front yard. Peeling has been her principal job, and her arms have come to constantly ache inside her elbows, the seat of every pair of pants stiff with sap from scooting down the logs. She closes her eyes at night and sees the narrow strips of bark curling away from her drawknife, feels the jerk of the blade as it hits a knot. The heavy lever of her cant hook turning the logs.

A few times each day, Henry calls her away from the peeling to help hold a board, to steady a scaffolding. They glance at each other at these moments: from under their arms, from over their shoulders. Glances that stand between them like knives against skin.

She is most often confused. Aware of her loss, yes, but more aware of the necessity of motion, of momentum. Work is the opposite of despair. Resting in the shade with a jug of water, they touch hands, study each other's fingers. Henry's hand dark with grease and sawdust. Virginia's hand soft but thickening. Already, her blisters have popped and begun to grow hard crusts. In the first days of building, she had caught her thumb under a rolling log and split its nail to the bloody quick. The crude linen bandage they had fashioned had begun to catch and unroll immediately, and she had finally tossed it to the ground, preferring to leave her thumb bare, wiping it occasionally on the leg of her trousers. By what agency, she wonders, by what awareness is decided this working out of acquisition and loss?

But she likes the work. The rhythm of activity, of muscles moving and pausing. Of breath in and out of her chest. She likes being able to watch Henry while he works. He wears heavy denim pants, tight around the waist (they don't snag as easily, he says) and a cotton work shirt bunched above his wide leather belt. His waist is so narrow. She catches herself wanting to run the flat of her hands around his shoulders, down to the slight bulge of his hips. She loves the shape of him. Loves the fluid, athletic motion of him. Every move, as he makes it, seems premeditated. He drops his ax into an uncut log, standing and kneading the small of his back with his hands. Then he wrenches the ax away to raise it over his head with a resolve that shows in tightened shoulders, in the tilted, meditative set of his neck. That sure is a narrow waist.

He talks constantly as he works, the rhythm of his words matching the efforts of his labor. This man who has always said so little, who has conserved his words so carefully, spends them now with extravagance, dropping each syllable, each phrase, into the empty space between his gasping exertions.

He says that this is where. They'll spend the rest of their. Lives.

And he rolls a log into its chopped notch, climbing after it to push it flush. He says that he will never stop loving her.

He straddles the log, pulling a spike from his apron and hammering it through the notch, log to log, with great precise swings of his single jack. He says they can add a room on the north. When they have. Babies.

And he walks balanced down the length of the log to spike the other end, adjusting it first with the strength of his legs. The snow's deep this high, he says, tapping at the nail until it is well started, and then pounding at it with force. But what we've got, he says. Is enough. To melt. The snow.

He says that he will love her. Until they. Die.

Author's Note

Last Year's River owes its existence to the support of my parents, Burl and Eunice Jones. Jeff and Susie Wetmore, among a thousand other kindnesses, dropped the seed of an idea, then generously allowed it room to grow. Ralph Beer, in addition to his invaluable criticism, loaned me the use of his horse Tony. Ester Johannson Murray's book, *A History of the North Fork of the Shoshone,* was essential to my research, as was her early reading of the manuscript. Hayes Goosey and Michelle Stevens-Orton were also thoughtful, early readers.

I am further indebted to ICM agent Lisa Bankoff and Houghton Mifflin editor Anton Mueller. Without Lisa's extraordinary advice and enthusiasm, my manuscript would not have found such a comfortable home. And without Anton's tactful, delicate shapings, this book would certainly have been much *less* of a book. Two more talented and considerate individuals no project could hope to find. Larry Cooper and Walter Vatter at Houghton Mifflin were also of great help.

Finally, I would not have begun writing about Wyoming at all had I not tried to imagine — after a brief lunch and interview — what it would have been like to know a certain remarkable woman in the strength of her youth. This book goes out, with heartfelt gratitude, to Dorothy.

This is a work of fiction. The Mohr ranch and its characters are all products of my imagination. If the ranch did exist, it would be located west of Jim Creek, across the river from Jim Mountain. Virginia isn't real, either.